WHERE THE DEAD LIE

WHERE THE DEAD LIE

A Sebastian St. Cyr Mystery

C. S. HARRIS

BERKLEY
New York

BERKLEY
An imprint of Penguin Random House LLC
375 Hudson Street, New York, New York 10014

Copyright © 2017 by The Two Talers, LLC

Library of Congress Cataloging-in-Publication Data

Names: Harris, C. S., author.
Title: Where the dead lie / C.S. Harris.
Description: First Edition. | New York : Berkley, 2017. | Series: Sebastian St. Cyr mystery ; 12
Identifiers: LCCN 2016032075 (print) | LCCN 2016038630 (ebook) | ISBN 9780451471192 (hardback) | ISBN 9780698167902 (ebook)
Subjects: LCSH: Saint Cyr, Sebastian (Fictitious character)—Fiction. | Great Britain—History—George III, 1760–1820—Fiction. | BISAC: FICTION / Mystery & Detective / Historical. | FICTION / Historical. | GSAFD: Regency fiction. | Mystery fiction.
Classification: LCC PS3566.R5877 W4775 2017 (print) | LCC PS3566.R5877 (ebook) | DDC 813/.54—dc23
LC record available at https://lccn.loc.gov/2016032075

First Edition: April 2017

Printed in the United States of America
1 3 5 7 9 10 8 6 4 2

Cover art by Gene Mollica
Cover design by Adam Averbach

This is a work of fiction. Names, characters, places, and incidents either are the product of the author's imagination or are used fictitiously, and any resemblance to actual persons, living or dead, business establishments, events, or locales is entirely coincidental.

For Huckleberry,
who kept me company through the writing of nineteen books
and provided the inspiration for Sebastian and Hero's Mr. Darcy.
Farewell, my friend.

When you lie dead, no one will remember you.

Not for you the roses of the Muses.

Your fate is to roam aimlessly through the Halls of Hades,

An unlamented pale reflection lost amidst the shadowy dead.

—SAPPHO, "WHEN YOU ARE DEAD," TRANSLATED BY CANDICE PROCTOR

WHERE THE DEAD LIE

Chapter 1

Monday, 13 September 1813, the hours before dawn

*T*he boy hated this part. Hated the eerie way the pale, waxen faces of the dead seemed to glow in the faintest moonlight. Hated being left alone with a stiffening body while he dug its grave.

He kicked the shovel deep into the ground and felt his heart leap painfully in his chest when the scrape of dirt against metal sounded dangerously loud in the stillness of the night. He sucked in a quick breath, the musty smell of damp earth thick in his nostrils, his fingers tightening on the smooth wooden handle as he paused to cast a panicked glance over one shoulder.

A mist was drifted up from the Fleet to curl around the base of the nearby shot tower and creep along the crumbling brick walls of the abandoned warehouses beyond it. He heard a dog bark somewhere in the distance and, nearer, a soft *thump*.

What was that?

The boy waited, his mouth dry, his body tense and trembling. But the sound was not repeated. He swiped a ragged sleeve across his sweaty face, swallowed hard, and bent into his work. He was uncomfortably aware of the cloaked gentleman watching from the seat of the cart that waited at the edge of the field. The gentleman had helped drag Benji's body over to the looming shot tower. But he never helped dig. Gentlemen didn't dig graves, although they could and did kill with a vicious delight that made the boy shiver as he threw another shovelful of dirt onto the growing pile.

The hole was beginning to take shape. Another six inches or so and he'd—

"Hey!"

The boy's head snapped around, and he froze.

A ragged, skeletally thin figure lurched from the gaping doorway of one of the tumbledown warehouses. "Wot ye doin' there?"

The shovel hit the ground with a clatter as the boy bolted. He fell into the newly dug grave and went down, floundering in the loose dirt. Feet flailing, he reared up on splayed hands, found solid ground, and pushed off.

"Oye!" shouted the ghostly specter.

The boy tore across the uneven field, his breath soughing in and out, his feet pounding. He saw the gentleman in the cart jerk, saw him gather the reins and spank them hard against his horse's rump.

"Wait for me!" screamed the boy as the cart lurched forward, its iron-rimmed wheels rattling over the rutted lane. "Stop!"

The gentleman urged the horse into a wild canter. He did not look back.

The boy leapt a low, broken stretch of the stone wall that edged the field. "Come back!"

The cart careened around the corner and out of sight, but the boy tore after it anyway. Surely the gentleman would stop for him? He wouldn't simply leave him, would he?

Would he?

The boy was sobbing now, his nose running, his chest aching as he fought to draw air into his lungs. It wasn't until he reached the corner himself that he dared risk a frantic look back and realized the skeletal figure wasn't following him.

The man—for the boy saw now that it was a man and not some hideous apparition—had paused beside the raw, unfinished grave. And he was staring down at what was left of Benji Thatcher.

Chapter 2

*S*ebastian St. Cyr, Viscount Devlin, braced his hands against the bedroom windowsill, his gaze on the misty scene below. In the faint light of dawn, Brook Street lay empty except for a kitchen maid scrubbing the area steps of the house next door.

He could not explain what had driven him from his bed. His dreams were often disturbed by visions of the past, as if he were condemned to relive certain moments over and over in a never-ending spiral of repentance and atonement. But for the second morning in a row he'd awakened abruptly with no tortured memories, only a vague sense of disquiet as inexplicable as it was disturbing.

He heard a shifting of covers and turned as Hero came to stand beside him. "Did I wake you?" he asked, sliding an arm around his wife's warm body to draw her closer.

"I needed to get up anyway." She rested her head on his shoulder, her fine brown hair sliding softly across his bare flesh. She was a tall woman, nearly as tall as he, with strong features and eyes of such piercing intelligence that she frightened a good portion of their contemporaries. "I promised my mother I'd come meet a cousin she has visiting, but first I want to read through my article one more time before I turn it in to my editor."

"Ah. So what's your next project?"

"I haven't decided yet."

She was writing a series of articles on the poor of London, an endeavor that greatly irritated her powerful father, Charles, Lord Jarvis. But Hero was not the kind of woman to allow anyone's opinions to dissuade her from what she believed to be the right course of action.

Sebastian ran his hand up and down her back and nuzzled her neck. "Who's the cousin?"

"A Mrs. Victoria Hart-Davis. I believe she's the granddaughter of one of my mother's uncles, but I could have that wrong. She was raised in India, so I've never met her."

"And she's staying with your mother?"

"Mmm. For weeks."

"Jarvis must be thrilled."

Hero gave a soft chuckle. Jarvis's low opinion of most females was notorious. "Fortunately he's so busy plotting how to rearrange Europe after Napoléon's defeat that I doubt he'll be around enough to be overly annoyed by her."

"Bit premature, isn't it?" Napoléon was in retreat, but he was still far from defeated.

"You know Jarvis; he's always been confident of victory. After all, with both God and the irrepressible sweep of history on our side, how can England fail? Such a brazen upstart *must* be wiped from the face of the earth." Her smile faded as she searched Sebastian's face, and he wondered what she saw there. "So what woke you? Troublesome dreams?"

He shook his head, unwilling to put his thoughts into words. Yet the sense of restless foreboding remained. And when a patter of rapid footsteps broke the silence of the deserted street and a boy appeared out of the mist, he somehow knew the lad would turn to run up their front steps.

Hero glanced at the ormolu clock on the bedroom mantel. "A messenger arriving at this hour of the morning can't be bringing good news."

"No," agreed Sebastian, and turned from the window.

Chapter 3

$\mathcal{P}$aul Gibson dropped the wet cloth he'd been using into the basin of water and straightened, his arms wrapping across his chest, his gaze on the pallid face of the half-washed corpse laid out on the stone slab before him. The boy had been just fifteen years old, painfully underfed and small for his age, his features delicate, his flaxen hair curling softly away from his face as it dried. What had been done to the lad's emaciated body twisted at something deep inside Gibson, something the surgeon had thought deadened long ago.

He was a man in his mid-thirties, Irish by birth, his black hair already heavily intermixed with silver, the lines on his face dug deep by the twin ravages of pain and an opium addiction he knew was slowly killing him. There was a time not so long ago when he'd been a regimental surgeon. He'd seen soldiers blown into unidentifiable bloody shreds by cannon fire and hideously maimed by sword and shot. He'd helped bury more butchered, mutilated women and children than he could bear to remember. But he'd never been confronted with something quite like this.

Not here, in London.

Reaching out, he tried to close the boy's wide, staring blue eyes, but the rigor still held them fast. He turned, his peg leg tapping on the flagged floor as he limped over to stand in the open doorway and draw the clean, damp morning air deep into his lungs. He used this small, high-windowed outbuilding behind his Tower Hill surgery for both official autopsies and the surreptitious, covert dissections he performed on cadavers filched from London's teeming churchyards. From here he could look across the yard to the ancient stone house he shared with Alexi, the vaguely mysterious Frenchwoman who'd come into his life some months before and stayed for reasons he'd never quite understood. The sun had burned off the last of the mist, but the morning air was still pleasantly cool and tinged with the smell of the smoke rising from his kitchen chimney.

As he watched, the rickety gate that led to the narrow passage running along the side of the house opened, and the man Gibson had been waiting for entered the yard. Tall, lean, and dark haired, Devlin was younger than Gibson, but only by a few years. Together the two men had fought George III's wars from Italy and the Peninsula to the West Indies. The experiences they'd shared had forged an unusual but powerful bond between the Irish surgeon and the son and heir of one of the grandest noblemen in the land. Now they sometimes worked together on murders the authorities couldn't—or wouldn't—solve.

"I received your message," said Devlin, pausing some feet shy of the building's entrance. His fine-boned face was taut and unsmiling, his strange, amber-colored eyes already narrowed as if in preparation for what he was about to see. "How bad is it?"

"Bad." Turning, Gibson led the way back into the room.

Devlin hesitated a moment, then stepped into the cold, dank building. At the sight of the battered body laid out on Gibson's stone slab, he sucked in his breath with a hiss. *"My God."*

So far, Gibson had managed to wash the dirt and blood only from the front of the boy's body. But against the pale, waxy flesh, the welts and cuts that covered the cadaver's arms, legs, and torso stood out stark and purple.

"What the hell happened to him?" said Devlin after a moment.

"Someone took a whip to him. Repeatedly. And cut him. With a small, very sharp knife."

"He was found like this? Naked?"

"Yes."

A muscle jumped along Devlin's set jaw as his gaze focused on the wide purple ligature mark around the boy's neck. "I take it that's what killed him?"

Gibson nodded. "Probably strangled with a leather belt or strap of some sort."

"Any idea who he was?"

"Actually, yes. His name was Benji Thatcher. According to the constable who brought him here, his mother was transported to Botany Bay some three years ago. He's been living on the streets of Clerkenwell ever since—he and a younger sister."

Devlin let his gaze drift, again, over the boy's thin, tortured body. "This was all done before he died?"

"Most of it, yes."

"Bloody hell."

Devlin went to stand in the open doorway as Gibson had done, his hands on his hips, his nostrils flaring as he breathed in hard. "Who's the magistrate dealing with this?"

"It should be Sir Arthur Ellsworth, of the Hatton Garden Public Office. The problem is, he's already closed the investigation. Seems Sir Arthur has better things to do with his public office's time than worry about the death of some young pickpocket. They held a cursory inquest yesterday afternoon and then released the body to the parish authorities for burial in the local poor hole. He's only here because that didn't sit well with one of the constables—a man by the name of Mott Gowan. So he brought the lad's body to me instead."

It was a long way from Clerkenwell and Hatton Garden to Tower Hill, and Gibson heard the puzzlement in Devlin's voice when he said, "Why here?"

Gibson hesitated, then said, "I know Gowan through Alexi. He's married to a Frenchwoman."

Devlin's jaw hardened, but all he said was, "Ah." The enmity between Alexi and Devlin was both long-standing and intense. "You say the boy was a thief?"

"Sometimes, yes."

Devlin turned to stare again at the small, battered corpse. And there was something about the expression that flickered across his features that made Gibson suspect his friend was thinking about his own infant son, safe at home. He said, "Over how many days was this done to him?"

"Two, maybe three. Some of the wheals were already beginning to heal, although most of the slashes and shallow stab wounds were probably done either right before he was killed or as he was dying."

Devlin's gaze focused on the raw wounds circling the boy's wrists. He'd obviously struggled frantically against his bonds. "Rope, you think?"

"I found hemp fibers embedded in the flesh, although there are signs he was also shackled at some point. He was gagged too; you can see the chafing at the corners of his mouth."

"So no one would hear him scream," said Devlin softly, letting his gaze drift, again, over the boy's pitiful, tortured body. "Where was he found?"

"On the grounds of the old Rutherford Shot Factory, off Brook Lane, just outside Clerkenwell. Some ex-soldier sleeping in one of the abandoned warehouses awoke and heard what sounded like digging. He listened to it for a while, then finally got up to investigate."

"And what he'd heard was someone digging a grave?"

"Yes. The digger ran off when the soldier shouted at him."

"Was this soldier able to provide your Constable Gowan with a description of the killer?"

"Not much of one, I'm afraid. He claims there were actually two men—one doing the digging and another fellow who stayed with the horse and cart."

Devlin's gaze met Gibson's. The thought of even one person capable of committing such an abomination was troubling enough; the existence of *two* such men seemed incomprehensible.

Devlin said, "You say Benji has a younger sister?"

Gibson nodded. "Sybil. Constable Gowan says he's tried to find her, to tell her about her brother. But no one's seen her."

Something leapt in Devlin's eyes. "For how long? How long has she been missing?"

Gibson felt a cold dread wrap around his guts and squeeze as he realized the implications of what he was about to say. "Three days."

Chapter 4

$\mathcal{S}$ebastian left Gibson's surgery and walked toward the old stone watering trough where his young groom, or tiger, waited with his curricle and pair.

A slight, gap-toothed lad, Tom had been Sebastian's tiger for nearly three years now, ever since that cold, dark February when Sebastian had found himself accused of murder and on the run. In those days Tom had been a hungry pickpocket left behind to fend for himself when his mother was transported to Botany Bay—just like Benji Thatcher. And Sebastian found himself thinking about the difference in the ultimate fates of the two boys as he watched Tom bring the chestnuts around and draw up, his sharp-featured face alive with curiosity.

"Is it murder?" said Tom. "Are we gonna solve it?"

"We?"

Tom grinned. "So it is murder?"

"It's definitely murder," said Sebastian, hopping up to the high seat to take the reins. "And yes, I am going to try to find the killer. If I don't, no one will."

Tom scrambled back to his perch at the curricle's rear. "So who's dead?"

"A fifteen-year-old Clerkenwell thief named Benji Thatcher." Sebastian saw no reason to burden Tom with the horrors of what had been done to the boy before his death. "Ever hear of him?"

Tom shook his head. "Reckon 'e picked the wrong cove's pocket?"

"I suppose that's one possibility," said Sebastian, and turned his horses into the Minories.

The district known as Clerkenwell lay on the northern outskirts of London, just beyond the line of the old city walls. In medieval times it had been the site of three grand monasteries: the London Charterhouse, the nunnery of St. Mary's, and the English headquarters of the Knights Hospitaller of St. John of Jerusalem. After the Dissolution, ambitious courtiers and favored nobles had taken over the district, while the area's numerous natural springs spurred the development of such fashionable establishments as New Tunbridge Wells, Spa Fields, and Sadler's Wells. By the early seventeenth century the gentle hills overlooking the city were thick with pleasure gardens, tearooms, bowling greens, and skittle grounds.

But those days were in the past. Tradesmen and artisans had long since moved into the once grand houses left vacant when "persons of quality" shifted to the West End. The erection of a smallpox hospital and three different prisons further accelerated the area's decline. Now rubbish dumps, gravel pits, and livestock pens dotted the once scenic hills.

The abandoned buildings of the Rutherford Shot Factory lay in the open fields beyond Clerkenwell Green and the close, on the banks of the sluggish remnants of the River Fleet. During the American revolt, Rutherford had produced a significant portion of the lead fired by Britain's armies and navy. But the facility had closed around the turn of the century, and after more than a decade of standing idle, the factory was a ruin, the windows of its warehouses broken and draped with cobwebs. The lichen-covered slate roofs were beginning to collapse, and tangled vines ran rampant over the old brick buildings.

"Gor," said Tom as Sebastian drew up beside the remnants of an old stone wall that had once enclosed the property. "Goosey-lookin' place, this."

Sebastian handed Tom the reins. "That it is."

He dropped lightly to the ground, his head tipping back as he stared up at the old shot tower. Soaring a hundred and fifty feet in the air, it looked much like a tall brick smokestack, only considerably larger. Once, molten lead would have been poured through carefully sized sieves at the top of the tower, with the lead droplets becoming round as they cooled and plummeted down to splash into a deep basin of water kept below. Then, loaded on carts and hauled to the brick warehouses beyond the tower, the shot would be dried, sorted, polished, and packed into bags or kegs for shipment. But those days were in the past. Now the overgrown field around the factory was strewn with everything from old grinding wheels to rusting pulleys and broken cartwheels.

Sebastian found a low, broken section in the old wall and picked his way across the uneven ground. He came upon the unfinished grave a dozen or so feet before the shot tower itself.

The area around the shallow hole had been hopelessly trampled and muddled by the heavy feet of the various parish and public office authorities called in to deal with the newly discovered body. But a shovel still lay abandoned amidst the nearby pile of loose earth.

Crouching down beside the grave, Sebastian reached out to touch the shovel's handle and found the wood smooth against his fingertips. It wasn't a brand-new shovel, but neither was it weathered and rusted, and he was frankly surprised to find it still here. But then, the official inquiry into Benji Thatcher's death had been both slapdash and brief.

Curling his hand into a fist, he shifted his gaze to a battered hat that rested upside down at the base of the hole. Benji Thatcher had been found naked, which suggested the hat in all probability belonged not to the boy but to his killer.

"Ye don't look like no constable nor magistrate I ever seen," said a raspy voice.

Glancing up, Sebastian found himself being steadily regarded by a ragged, painfully thin man leaning on a crutch. He stood at the gaping entrance to one of the old warehouses, a scarecrow of a figure with long, stringy ginger hair and gaunt cheeks matted with several weeks' growth of beard.

"You were here late Sunday night—early Monday morning?" said Sebastian.

"I was." The man lurched forward, crutch swinging, and Sebastian saw that his right leg ended midthigh. "Name's Inchbald. Rory Inchbald."

Sebastian pushed to his feet. "What can you tell me about the man who was digging this grave?"

Inchbald drew up on the far side of the pile of loose earth. He was younger than he'd first appeared, Sebastian realized, probably still in his thirties. But he looked ominously underfed and unwell, his skin a clammy, dirty gray.

"Weren't no man. Weren't more'n a lad. Sixteen, meybe seventeen."

"A lad?"

"Aye. The man was waitin' for him in a cart pulled up just over there." The scarecrow raised one clawlike hand to point to where Tom walked Sebastian's horses up and down the lane.

"Can you describe him? The man with the cart, I mean."

Inchbald lifted his thin shoulders in a vague shrug. "Wot's to describe? Reckon he was jist yer typical gentleman."

The midmorning sun felt uncomfortably warm against Sebastian's back. "What makes you think he was a gentleman?"

"Oh, ain't no doubt about that."

"You heard him speak?"

"No."

"But he was well dressed?"

Inchbald pursed his lips. "Not flash, but more'n respectable."

"So he could have been a merchant or tradesman."

A ghastly cough racked the ex-soldier's body. At the end of it, he turned his head and spat. "Nah. He was a gentleman, all right. Served under enough of the bastards in India to know when I'm lookin' at one of the buggers. Can't miss 'em." His mouth pulled into a grin that showed the gaping black holes of missing teeth. "Just like I knows you was in the army. An officer, wasn't ye?"

Sebastian met the ex-soldier's glittering, hostile stare. "Would you say the same about this man you saw? That he was an officer?"

"Nah. Not him."

A crow swooped in to land on the brick sill of one of the deep, arch-topped windows that pierced the thick walls of the tall shot tower. Looking up, Sebastian watched the bird's beak open, its raucous *caw-caw* echoing across the deserted, windblown field. "So tell me more about him. Was he thin? Fat? Short? Tall?"

"How'm I to know, with him wearin' a cloak and sittin' up on that cart?"

"Could you tell if he was dark haired or fair?"

"Nope. He had on a hat. But I reckon he was on the young side. Leastways he sat up straight and moved like a young man."

Sebastian supposed that was better than nothing. "You say he was driving a cart?"

"Aye. A two-wheeled cart with one horse. And don't go asking me what color horse, because I couldn't tell ye. It was dark."

"The horse?"

"I meant the night. But yeah, I reckon the horse was dark."

Sebastian said, "Gentlemen don't usually drive carts."

Inchbald snorted. "Gentlemen don't usually haul around dead bodies, neither, now, do they? What ye expect him to be drivin'? The family carriage? With a crest on the door and two footmen standin' up behind and a body under the front bench?"

Sebastian studied the ex-soldier's gaunt, hostile features. "Did you see the gentleman and the lad take the body out of the cart?"

"Nah. Didn't see nothin' till I found the lad diggin' the grave."

"At approximately what time was this?"

"Half past one."

"So certain?"

"Mmm. The church bells was strikin' just as I was hollerin' for the watch." Inchbald's watery gray eyes narrowed. "Why ye here askin' all these questions? You bein' an officer 'n' a gentleman 'n' all?"

"I'm trying to discover who killed Benji Thatcher."

"Why?"

Rather than answer, Sebastian said, "Did you know him? Benji, I mean."

Inchbald shrugged. "There's a heap o' children on the streets here-abouts. All look the same t' me."

"What about the lad digging the grave? You were considerably nearer to him than to the man in the cart. Did you recognize him?"

"Nah. But like I keep tellin' ye, it was right dark. And the mist was comin' in."

Sebastian reached to pick up the battered hat. "This his? The dig-ger's, I mean."

"Could be. Fell in the hole he did, when I shouted at him. I s'pose he coulda lost it then. But can't say as I remember one way or the other."

"It's hardly a gentleman's hat."

"Didn't say the boy was a gentleman, now, did I?"

"You're saying he wasn't?"

Inchbald's eyes narrowed. "How'd ye be dressed, if'n you was gonna be diggin' a grave?"

Turning the hat in his hands, Sebastian glanced beyond the ex-soldier to the row of crumbling brick warehouses. "Are there others who sleep here at night?"

"Not so much."

"No? Why not?"

"Most folks think the place is haunted."

"You don't?"

Inchbald's bloodshot eyes danced with amusement. "I been sleepin' here since midsummer and ain't seen nothin' till last night. And that lot sure weren't no ghosts."

Sebastian handed the crippled soldier two shillings and his card. The man was probably illiterate, but he could always get someone to read it for him. "The name's Devlin. If you should think of anything else that might be relevant, you can contact me at Number Forty-one, Brook Street. I'll make it worth your while."

The coins disappeared into the soldier's rags. But he continued to hold the card awkwardly between his index and middle fingers, his lips twisting into a sneer when he glanced at it. "Ah. Not only an officer 'n' a gentleman, but a nobleman too. *Viscount* Devlin." He coughed and spat a stream of spittle that this time came perilously close to Sebastian's gleaming top boots. "I hear tell that dead boy was a pickpocket. So tell me, why ye care what happened to some worthless young thief?"

"I care," said Sebastian and watched the sneer on the other man's face slide into something less confident, more confused.

🍧

Sebastian spent the next fifteen to twenty minutes walking the rubble-strewn grounds of the factory and poking about the abandoned warehouses. He didn't expect to come across anything of interest, and he didn't.

He arrived back at the curricle to find Tom squinting up at three crows perched in a row along the crenelated parapet at the top of the shot tower, his freckled face pinched and strained. "Ye reckon that boy was killed here?" the tiger asked as Sebastian leapt up to the high seat.

"Probably not. Most likely this was simply a convenient, out-of-the-way place to dispose of the body." The nearest cluster of cottages lay a good quarter mile away, by the crossroads. There were tile kilns on the far side of the lane, but they would have been deserted at night, while the open land beyond the factory's stone boundary wall was controlled by the New River Company and empty except for a network of wooden pipes that carried water to the city.

"So where was he killed?" asked Tom.

"I've no idea." Sebastian paused, the reins in his hands, to let his gaze drift down the hill, beyond the sprawling, high-walled complex of the Middlesex House of Correction, to the City itself. The ground here was high enough that he could see where the winding lanes of old Clerkenwell blended seamlessly into the vast, crowded streets of London—see all the way to the dome of St. Paul's Cathedral rising massive and gleaming in the morning sunlight, and beyond.

He had no way of knowing how much credence to give to Rory Inchbald's words. But he suspected that the basics of what the ex-soldier had told him were true. Which meant that somewhere out there on the streets of London roamed not one but two vicious killers: a man and a youth who had snatched Benji Thatcher and brutally tortured him for days before casually snuffing out his life with a strap tightened around the homeless boy's thin neck.

And what of Benji's little sister? Sebastian wondered. Had the killers taken Sybil Thatcher too? Did they still have her? Were they even now doing to her what they had done to her brother? Or was she already dead?

He felt his hands clench around the reins as a rising tide of tense urgency swelled within him. Who were these people? *Where* were they? And how the hell was he to find them when he had absolutely nothing to go on?

Nothing except a shovel and a battered hat and the unreliable testimony of a dying ex-soldier with a powerful, burning hatred of officers and gentlemen.

Chapter 5

*H*ero Devlin sat beside her mother in the morning room of her parents' vast Berkeley Square town house. A tea tray rested on the table before them, but the woman Hero was here to meet had stepped out for a walk shortly before her arrival and had yet to return.

"So are you enjoying Cousin Victoria's visit?" Hero asked as Annabelle, Lady Jarvis, reached for the teapot. "And be truthful."

Lady Jarvis smiled as she poured the first cup. "I am. Truly." Unlike her daughter, Annabelle Jarvis was small and delicately built, with pretty blue eyes and pale blond hair now gently fading to white. "Victoria is a lovely woman." She handed the cup to Hero, then added, "I was hoping to show off my grandson to her this morning."

"I thought about bringing him, but he's teething—and screaming his indignation and fury to the world. I didn't think Cousin Victoria would appreciate such a visit."

"Simon does have very powerful lungs," agreed his doting grandmother.

"Very." Hero took a sip of her tea. "I take it Cousin Victoria has no children of her own?"

Lady Jarvis shook her head and poured a second cup. "Unfortunately, no, despite being married and widowed twice."

"Twice?"

"Yes, poor thing. Her first husband was aide-de-camp to Wellesley but died of fever shortly before the regiment was to leave India."

"How tragic. Did she always live in India?"

"From childhood, yes. Her father was with the East India Company."

"And her second husband was also in the army?"

"Mmm. John Hart-Davis, eldest son of Lord Hart-Davis. He was killed at the siege of San Sebastián last month. She's only just arrived in England."

"She was with her husband in Spain?"

"She was, yes—as well as in Ireland and South America."

"What a tragic and yet extraordinarily adventurous life she's lived," said Hero, who had always longed to travel the world.

Lady Jarvis's eyes crinkled in a smile of understanding. Mother and daughter might be opposites in many ways, but Annabelle still knew her daughter well. "I think you'll like her. She's quite brilliant. Speaks Hindi and Urdu as well as Spanish, French, and Portuguese—" She broke off at the sound of soft, quick footsteps on the stairs. "Ah, here she comes now."

Hero couldn't have said precisely what she was expecting—perhaps a sturdy, no-nonsense woman in bombazine with sun-browned skin and hair pulled into a tight bun like a bluestocking? It certainly wasn't the ethereal, extraordinarily attractive woman with a halo of golden curls who swept into the room wearing an exquisite gown of French black silk.

"Cousin Hero!" she exclaimed, advancing on Hero with hands outstretched. "Thank goodness I didn't miss you! The garden in the square is so lovely, I fear I tarried far longer than I should have. I am so sorry."

Hero rose to greet her. "Please don't apologize. I've only just arrived myself."

"Goodness, you're as tall as your father," said Victoria, standing on tiptoe to kiss her cheek.

"Nearly." Compared to this delicate, diminutive cousin, Hero found herself feeling uncharacteristically awkward and overgrown.

Cousin Victoria laughed, revealing pretty white teeth and a dimple that peeked in one damask cheek. "I've heard so much about you from your mother, I feel as if I know you already."

"Please accept my condolences on the death of your husband."

"Oh, thank you." Cousin Victoria cast a sad, trembling smile toward Hero's mother. "I was on my way north to spend some time with John's family in Norfolk when Cousin Annabelle so kindly invited me to break my journey with her for a few weeks."

Lady Jarvis reached out to press her young relative's hand. "The pleasure is all mine, my dear; believe me."

"My mother tells me you've just come from Spain," said Hero, resuming her seat. "Is it true what they're saying—that our armies will soon be over the Pyrenees?"

Cousin Victoria sank into a chair near the hearth. "Undoubtedly. Oh, there may be a few French strongholds left in the Peninsula. But I believe Wellington intends to simply bypass them and press forward into France, driving all the way to Paris."

"This is good news," said Lady Jarvis, pouring her young relative a cup of tea.

"Yes. But then, our cause is just, which means our victory has always been inevitable."

"You sound like my father," said Hero, smiling.

Cousin Victoria nodded and reached for her cup. "Lord Jarvis was telling me something of his plans for the restructuring of Europe just last night."

For one long, awkward moment, Hero could only stare at the woman before her. Jarvis? Jarvis had not only condescended to entertain his wife's female guest, but actually discussed his plans for a post-Napoleonic Europe with her?

Jarvis?

"I was relieved to hear the Prince is dedicated to seeing Europe's monarchs restored to the thrones God gave them," said Cousin Victoria, sipping her tea.

Hero cleared her throat. "So he is. Although there's no denying that what God gives he can also take away—as we have seen."

"True," agreed the widow. "But he is now guiding our forces to victory, is he not?"

"God and Wellington," said Hero.

Cousin Victoria tilted her head to one side and laughed again with delight. She was some two or three years older than Hero, in her late twenties, with finely molded features and a milky-white complexion untouched by a lifetime spent in hotter climes. And it occurred to Hero, watching her, that Jarvis's indulgence of the young widow shouldn't have surprised her as much as it had. Jarvis had always enjoyed beautiful women, and Victoria Hart-Davis possessed precisely the sort of looks Jarvis admired most: petite and fair, with the same sky blue eyes that had once attracted him to Hero's mother.

It was a thought that disturbed Hero more than she could have explained.

Chapter 6

$\mathcal{A}$ few inquiries on the streets of Clerkenwell led Sebastian to what was known as Coldbath Square, where he found Constable Mott Gowan eating an eel pie from a cart parked along one side of the square.

Developed as a grand, marble-lined medicinal bath late in the seventeenth century, the famous Cold Bath was nearly hidden by a tall brick wall above which only the bathhouse's steeply gabled roof and the autumn-tinged golds and reds of the garden's treetops were visible. The houses fronting three sides of the square had been built by speculators with grand hopes of seeing Clerkenwell turn into a fashionable resort. But the construction of the massive Middlesex House of Correction on the fourth side of the square had seriously undermined the prestige of the neighborhood.

"Aye, I'm the one took Benji's body to Gibson," said Mott Gowan in answer to Sebastian's question. The constable was a tall, lanky man in his late thirties or early forties, his hair straight and sandy colored, his face bony and dominated by a prominent square jaw. "That Hatton Garden magistrate, Sir Arthur, he was all for dumpin' the lad's remains in the poor hole of St. James's and forgettin' about him. I said I'd see him given a proper burial, and I will." The man's eyes narrowed. "Didn't say I wouldn't try to figure out what happened to him, first, though."

"Do you recognize this?" asked Sebastian, holding up the battered hat he had brought from the shot factory.

"Don't think so. Why?"

"I found it at the bottom of Benji's grave. Was it his?"

Gowan shook his head. "I don't rightly know."

"Could the watchman or one of the constables have dropped it?"

Gowan frowned. "It's a pretty sorry-lookin' hat."

"Do you remember seeing it there last night?"

"No. But then, it was awful dark and foggy. I didn't look around much. And after that, the constables from Hatton Garden Public Office took over." Gowan's scowl deepened. There was obviously considerable animosity between the parish constables and the public office constables.

"How well did you know Benji?" asked Sebastian.

"I've known him and his sister, Sybil, for years. Their da used t' be a watchmaker over in St. John's Place, afore he died back in 'aught-eight. Annie—that's their momma—she managed to keep 'em for a while, takin' in washin' and such. But then she took sick—real sick. Seemed like every week Benji was haulin' somethin' down to the secondhand stalls, sellin' this and that—anything to buy food and pay the rent. But in the end there weren't nothin' left to sell, and their landlord kicked 'em out."

"So they were already living on the street when their mother was arrested?"

The constable nodded glumly. "Even if Annie had got to feelin' better, she wouldn't have been able to take in washin' no more. How could she, without her kettles?" His massive jaw worked as he chewed a large mouthful of his pie and swallowed. "I ain't sayin' it's right, what Annie done—takin' that card o' lace from Miss Tilly's shop. But what else was she gonna do? Other than turn to whorin', and she said she couldn't bring herself to do that."

Sebastian glanced up as a cool breeze shifted the leaves of the trees on the far side of the wall. A woman turning to prostitution risked being sent to the Bridewell. But if she were caught stealing anything worth more than a pittance, she could hang. "She was sent to Botany Bay?"

Gowan took another big bite of his pie. "Aye. Scheduled to hang at first, she was. But the sentence was commuted to seven years' transportation at the end of the sessions. She begged 'em to let her take the children with her—didn't have no family hereabouts t' leave 'em with. But the magistrates wouldn't do it. Said Benji and Sybil was old enough to fend fer themselves." The constable shook his head. "Sybil was five at the time. How was she supposed to fend fer herself?"

Sebastian stared across Baynes Row at the gloomy gray walls of the prison, where a group of laughing, half-grown boys were playfully pushing and shoving one another. He'd heard of children as young as two being left screaming on the docks as their hysterical mothers were rowed out to the convict ships.

"Benji weren't much more'n a little nipper himself," Gowan said. "But he stepped up and took care of his sister, he did."

"Have you seen Sybil since Benji was killed?"

"No." Gowan swallowed the last of his eel pie and wiped his greasy fingers on the seat of his breeches. "Ain't nobody seen neither of 'em these past three or four days. I been askin' around, but it looks like whoever killed Benji musta got Sybil too. And if they're doin' to her what they done to that poor lad—" The man's voice cracked, and he simply shook his head.

"When were they last seen?"

"Well . . . I seen Benji meself with one of his friends down in Hockley-in-the-Hole Friday ev'ning. I don't think Sybil was with 'em, but she may've been."

"How old is she now?"

Gowan frowned in thought. "Must be seven or eight, I s'pose. But she's a fey little thing. Don't look near so big."

"Light blond hair, same as Benji?"

The constable blew out a long, troubled breath. "Aye. Got her momma's blue eyes too."

"Where did Benji and his sister used to sleep?"

"Anywhere they could. When he had a spare penny or two, Benji'd sometimes buy space for 'em on a bed in one of the flophouses. But that weren't often."

"I hear Benji was a thief. Is that true?"

Gowan rubbed the back of his neck. "I s'pose. Oh, he'd run errands and help muck out the stables at the Red Lion when he could. But he weren't real strong. Who's gonna hire a slight boy like him to do hard work—not when they can get some big, strappin' lad for the same wages?"

The bell of the nearby church of St. James began to toll the hour, its steady peal echoed by that of the old medieval chapel of the Hospitallers that lay beyond it in St. John's Close. Sebastian said, "Do you know what time it was when Rory Inchbald found the boy's body?"

"Well, let's see. . . . The watch come and got me just afore two, so I reckon it was maybe one or half past."

It fit with what the ex-soldier had told him. Sebastian said, "Did you get a good look at what had been done to Benji before he was killed?"

As Sebastian watched, the skin seemed to draw tight across the prominent bones of the constable's face and his voice dropped to a whisper as he nodded. "It's why I took the boy's body to Paul Gibson. It ain't normal, what was done to him."

"Gibson says Benji was tortured over a period of two or three days. Do you know anyone who might do something like that?"

"Good Lord. I hope not. You'd be able to tell, wouldn't you? If somebody you knew was that twisted? That sick in the head?"

Sebastian wasn't so sure about that, but all he said was, "Did Benji ever have anything to do with any of the gentlemen around here?"

"Gentlemen? Not that I know of. Why?"

"Rory Inchbald claims he saw another man that night in addition to the boy digging the grave. A gentleman."

The constable grunted. "Huh. I know he says he saw a second fellow in a cart. But he never said nothin' to me about it being a gentleman. I wouldn't put too much stock in anything Inchbald tells you." Gowan leaned forward to tap one forefinger against the side of his head. "Ain't right in here, I'm afraid."

"You think he made that part up?"

"Let's just say Inchbald hates gentlemen. When he was in the army, some lord's son had him flogged to within an inch of his life for somethin' Inchbald claims he didn't do." Gowan hesitated, then added, "Wouldn't turn my back on him if I was you. You know what I mean?"

Sebastian watched as a man leading a donkey loaded with lumpy sacks of coal turned the corner near the band of ragged boys. The coal man was aged and stooped, his clothes and face black with coal dust. "What if the killers don't have Sybil?" said Sebastian. "What if she's frightened and hiding? Where do you think she would go?"

Gowan shook his head, his gaze, like Sebastian's, on the gang of boys now moving to range themselves across Coppice Row. "Can't think of anyplace I ain't already searched. But you might try askin' Benji's friends. I know they been lookin' for her too—lookin' for both of 'em till we found what was left of Benji yesterday mornin'."

"Do you know his friends' names?"

"Well, let's see. . . . There's Toby Dancing. He's the one I was tellin' you I seen with Benji on Friday." Gowan nodded to the pack of ragged, dirty boys that had now formed a ring around the old coal man and his donkey. "And Jem Jones—the tall lad with the red kerchief knotted around his neck you see there—he's one of Benji's mates too." The constable raised his voice. "Hey, Jem! Aye, I'm talkin' to you, lad," he said when Jem's head jerked around, his eyes widening, his gangly body tensing.

For a moment, Sebastian thought the boy meant to run. Then Gowan said, "No; don't lope off. You ain't done nothin'—leastways, nothin' I know about. But there's a lord here wants t' ask you some questions about Benji."

Jem Jones hesitated, then came toward them with dragging steps.

"Are ye really a lord?" he asked Sebastian, awe chasing doubt and mistrust across his features as he drew up eight to ten feet away. An underfed, long-legged lad, he could have been anywhere between a big fourteen and a small eighteen. His face was thin and nondescript, his hair a dirty light brown, his eyes a washed-out gray.

"Of course he's a real lord," snapped Gowan. "Viscount Devlin to you, lad. So you mind your manners, you hear? And you lot," he shouted, flapping his arms at the circle of boys as they began to close in on the coal man. "Stop that!" He pushed away from the wall. "Excuse me, my lord," he said in a rush and trotted across the street just as the donkey let out a panicked bray.

Jem Jones stayed where he was, his narrowed gaze fixed on Sebastian. "Why ye want to know about Benji?"

"I'm trying to discover who killed him."

"You? But . . . why?"

"Because no one else seems likely to make the effort."

Jem sniffed. "Mick Swallow disappeared last year, and nobody ever tried to figure out who killed him."

"Was his body found?"

"No."

"So what makes you think he was killed?"

"'Cause one day he was here and the next day he wasn't. He'd've told me if he was gonna go off somewheres. He's my cousin."

It occurred to Sebastian that if the ex-soldier hadn't interrupted the digging of Benji Thatcher's grave, Benji would simply have disappeared too, just like Sybil. And he felt a whisper of dread, a sense of standing on the precipice of something ominous. "Do street children disappear around here very often?"

"Often enough."

"How often?"

Jem twitched. "I dunno. Every few months or so. Sometimes they come back. But mostly they just stay gone."

Sebastian kept his gaze on the boy's thin, grubby face. "What do you think happened to Sybil and Benji and your cousin?"

Jem played with the frayed cuff of his cut-down man's shirt.

"Tell me," said Sebastian.

The boy's chin jerked up, his chest lifting as he sucked in a quick, deep breath. "I reckon somebody snatched 'em; that's what. Snatched 'em all."

"Any idea who might be doing it?"

Jem set his jaw and stared back at Sebastian, his entire body stiff with hostility and distrust.

"You know, don't you?" said Sebastian.

"No." The boy gave a quick shake of his head. "Nobody knows."

"But you have some suspicions."

Jem kept shaking his head. "No. It's just—" He broke off to cast a quick, apprehensive glance around. Constable Gowan, the coal man and his donkey, and Jem Jones's friends had all disappeared.

"Just—?" prompted Sebastian.

"Well, there's talk about *what* he is."

"Oh? What do they say he is?"

Jem tensed again, and for a moment Sebastian thought this time he really would run off rather than answer. Then the boy gulped and said in a whispered rush, "Folks say it's a gentleman."

At some level, Sebastian realized, he hadn't actually believed Rory Inchbald's tale of seeing a "gentleman" that night. Now it seemed considerably more likely that the ex-soldier had been telling the truth. Sebastian kept his gaze on the boy's face. "What makes people think that?"

"I dunno. It's just what they say."

"Who says?"

Jem's gaze flicked, significantly, over Sebastian's neatly tailored coat and doeskin breeches. "Just . . . folks."

Sebastian was beginning to realize he'd made a mistake in driving directly to Clerkenwell after leaving Gibson's surgery. He should have gone back to Brook Street and changed into the kind of old-fashioned frock coat, greasy breeches, and broken-down boots that were sold by the secondhand clothing stalls of Rosemary Lane. Amongst the poorest, roughest elements of places like Clerkenwell, a gentleman was more than an outsider; he was an enemy.

Sebastian said, "I understand Benji has another friend, a lad named Toby Dancing. Do you know where I might find him?"

"Nah. He was always more Benji's friend than mine."

"Constable Gowan tells me you've been looking for Benji's sister, Sybil."

The question seemed to take Jem by surprise. He hesitated a moment, as if fearing some sort of trick. "Aye."

"You've found no trace of her?"

"No."

"If Benji's killers don't have her, do you have any idea where she could be?"

The lad's lip curled in a sneer. "If I knew, then I'd look there, now, wouldn't I?"

"So you would. And where have you looked?"

Something pinched the boy's dirty features, a hint of some emotion that was there and then gone. "Around."

"If you find any trace of her, or hear anything that might help us understand what happened to Benji, you'll tell Constable Gowan?"

Jem nodded, his eyes narrowed and flinty, and Sebastian knew it for a lie.

Sebastian gave up then and turned toward where he'd left Tom with the horses. He'd almost reached the curricle when he heard footsteps running after him and swung about.

Jem skidded to a halt, his chest jerking.

"Finally remember something?" asked Sebastian.

Jem shook his head. "It's just . . . Well, I reckon the vicar of St. James's might be able to answer some of yer questions."

"Oh?"

The boy's face was once more a watchful, blank mask. "Reverend Filby is his name."

"Why?"

Jem looked confused. "What ye mean, why?"

"Why do you think the reverend might be able to answer some of my questions?"

The boy shrugged. "He just might."

Sebastian searched the boy's crimped features, looking for some indication of subterfuge or guile. He could think of no reason why a lad so obviously hostile and uncooperative should suddenly decide to volunteer what he considered helpful information. But the boy's face remained angry and closed.

And frightened, Sebastian realized. Jem Jones was terrified.

Chapter 7

"*D*on't glower at us, Jarvis," said His Highness, George Augustus Frederick, Prince of Wales and Regent of the United Kingdom of Great Britain and Ireland, his attention all for the task of selecting another bonbon from the gold-rimmed plate of Belgian chocolates he held in his plump hand.

The Prince half sat, half lay on one of a set of pink silk-covered settees styled in the shape of gilded swans that he'd just had made for his favorite withdrawing room at Carlton House. In his youth he had been both handsome and beloved by his people. But his slim good looks were lost long ago to gluttony and debauchery, and he'd destroyed the goodwill of his people by the selfish, heedless extravagance of his spending and by the unfeeling brutality of his treatment of his wife and daughter. Now in his early fifties, he was fat, spoiled, and foolish. But he was still the Prince Regent.

When Charles, Lord Jarvis—the man to whom this comment was addressed—remained silent, the Prince pursed his lips into a pout. "I simply want to think about it a bit more; that's all," said George, popping the chosen chocolate into his mouth. "Decisions of such magnitude require thought. Don't you agree?"

Jarvis stood stiffly just inside the chamber door, his hands clasped behind his back. A tall, fleshy man well over six feet, he was second cousin to the Regent's mad father, the King, and the real power behind the Hanovers' wobbly throne. It was a position he had earned not by his relationship to the King but by the brilliance of his mind, his dedication to the dynasty, and the utter ruthlessness of the methods he was willing to use to advance what he considered in the best interests of King and country.

For one telling moment, Jarvis's gaze met that of the third person in the room, the Prince's Foreign Secretary, Robert Stewart, Lord Castlereagh.

"Of course, Your Highness," said Jarvis. But he made no attempt to alter the gravity of his expression, and his tone was similar to what one might employ when humoring a sulky child. "As you wish." He nodded to the Foreign Secretary, and the two men bowed low. "We will leave you to . . . think."

Jarvis waited until he and Castlereagh were outside the chamber with the door closed behind them before saying in a quiet, ominously tight voice, "What the devil brought that on? He's been boasting of his determination to restore the Bourbons to the throne of France for the last twenty years. And now with our armies practically on the French frontier, Prinny suddenly decides he needs to 'think' about it?"

Castlereagh blanched. He was younger than Jarvis by more than ten years as well as both slighter and shorter in stature. And even though he was Foreign Secretary while Jarvis held no formal government portfolio, there was no question which of the two men was the most powerful. Foreign ministers came and went; Jarvis remained.

"Well?" demanded Jarvis when Castlereagh stayed silent.

"It's because of Sinclair Pugh," said the Foreign Secretary in a rush, raking his flyaway, reddish fair hair back from his forehead with a trembling hand. "I fear he's had Prinny's ear."

"Sinclair Pugh?" Jarvis frowned. A longtime member of Parliament, Pugh had a vast fortune and an overrated reputation as an amateur philosopher and serious thinker. "When did this happen?"

"At last night's soiree. Lady Leeds brought him to the attention of His Highness. Somehow in the space of an hour he managed to convince Prinny that not only will the French people never accept a Bourbon restoration, but that if we insist upon imposing the Bourbons by force, the result will be a second French Revolution even more disastrous than the first—a vast cataclysm with the potential to sweep away the Hanovers as well as the Bourbons."

Jarvis let out a scornful huff of air. "Pugh is a fool. The restoration of Europe's hereditary monarchs to their rightful thrones is the one thing that can and will secure the peace and stability of the world—now and for generations to come. Civilization as we know it depends upon it."

"Yes. But unfortunately His Highness seems to find Pugh's arguments damnably persuasive. He's asked the man to come back next Monday and expand upon his theories."

Jarvis paused beside the entrance to his own chambers. "Monday? Why was I not informed of this before now?"

Castlereagh's eyes bulged as the last of the color drained from his face. "Never mind. I'll take care of it."

"Good God." Castlereagh's voice rose to an undignified squeak. "You're going to kill him."

Jarvis gave a tight smile. "Only if I must. Fortunately there are other ways to eliminate those foolish enough to interfere where they don't belong."

Jarvis saw the Foreign Secretary open his mouth to ask, *How?*

Then Castlereagh wisely changed his mind, closed his mouth, and said no more.

๛

Afterward, alone in the elegant chambers set aside for his exclusive use at Carlton House, Jarvis stood for a time at the window overlooking the forecourt below. Then he sent for Major Burnside.

A tall, dark-haired former hussar major, Edward Burnside was one of an extensive string of spies, informants, and assassins Jarvis maintained across the length and breadth of Britain. Little of any importance occurred in the Kingdom without Jarvis becoming aware of it—which made the current situation all the more infuriating.

"I want to know everything there is to know about an MP named Sinclair Pugh," Jarvis snapped when Burnside appeared. "His associates, his holdings, his interests and tastes, and his weaknesses. Especially his weaknesses. Report back to me in—" Jarvis paused to glance at the clock on the mantel. "Twelve hours. At Berkeley Square."

"Yes, my lord," said the major and bowed himself out.

Chapter 8

*P*aul Gibson pulled the door to the stone outbuilding at the base of the yard closed behind him, his hands not quite steady. As he turned to cross the yard toward his house, the phantom pains from his missing leg flared hot and bright in a pulsating crescendo of agony that he found himself oddly welcoming. It gave him something to focus on, something to think about besides the horror of what had been done to the boy whose remains lay cold and still on Gibson's stone table.

He was no philosopher or theologian. He seldom paused to give thought to what drove men to cruelty or why some men valued kindness and empathy as virtues while others scorned those same traits as weaknesses. Years of war had taught Gibson much of the darkness that can lurk in men's souls. But war carried its own explanations, its own justifications that he realized now he had clung to as a defense against an uncomfortable reality. An uncomfortable reality and a truth he hadn't wanted to acknowledge. Or admit.

He knew the explanations offered by his church. Yet he'd always seen religion's externalization and personification of evil as mankind's shirking of responsibility. It reminded him of a child's excuse to avoid both punishment and blame: *He made me do it. It's not my fault. Satan tempted me.*

Not, *Satan is a part of me.*

I am Satan.

Chapter 9

The parish church of St. James lay just to the north of Clerkenwell's old village green, in the sweeping curve of an ancient lane known as Clerkenwell Close. Once the chapel of the long-vanished convent of the nuns of St. Mary's, the church had been rebuilt in brick some twenty-five years before in a plain style reminiscent of a New World meetinghouse.

"I knew the children were missing," said the Reverend Leigh Filby when Sebastian introduced himself and explained the purpose of his visit. "But it was quite a shock to hear yesterday that Benji had been found murdered. How perfectly ghastly it all is."

The reverend was a plump man of medium height with fine, flaxen hair framing a pink, ageless face. He wore the long black cassock favored by many of his calling and had been supervising the installation of new iron railings atop the churchyard's brick retaining walls when Sebastian came upon him. The two men turned now to walk along the sunken path that cut across the old churchyard toward the green, the reverend with his hands clasped behind his back and his chin resting against his chest.

"How did you know they were missing?" Sebastian asked, gazing out over the churchyard's thick forest of weathered gray tombstones.

"One of Benji's friends came around several days ago looking for him."

"Oh? Why would he come here?"

The Reverend Filby was silent for a moment, his lips working back and forth over his long, slightly protuberant teeth as if he were choosing his words carefully. "When it's dreadfully cold or wet and they have no place else to go, some of the children will come here. I let them sleep in the church."

"You say that as if you were almost ashamed to admit it."

The smile lines beside the reverend's soft gray eyes creased. "Ashamed? No. But hesitant? Perhaps. I fear some of my more comfortably situated parishioners do not appreciate my generosity toward the area's street children. A few have even gone so far as to hold me responsible for their increasing numbers. Unfortunately, it's the presence in the neighborhood of three prisons that's to blame—that and the increasingly difficult economic situation of our times." He paused to expel his breath in a tight, pained sigh. "Odd, isn't it, how some parents will undergo every sort of unimaginable hardship and danger to feed their children, while others . . . others simply walk away, abandoning their offspring to fend for themselves?"

"Are many of the area's children abandoned by their parents?"

"Some, I'm afraid. But not Benji and Sybil. Their mother was transported. Although given how ill she was, I doubt she lived to see Botany Bay."

"They never heard from her?"

"No. I told her she could write to the children care of St. James's. But she never did."

"Could she write?"

"Oh, yes."

They walked in thoughtful silence for a moment, their footsteps crunching the gravel path. From this corner of the churchyard Sebastian could see Clerkenwell Green, which looked less like a village green and more like a brawling, busy marketplace. If there'd ever been any grass there, it was long gone.

"What was he like?" Sebastian asked. "Benji, I mean."

"Sensitive. Sad. But determined to keep his sister out of the poor-house." The reverend cast Sebastian a quick, worried glance. "You're saying no one has seen Sybil? Still?"

"I'm afraid not."

"Oh, dear. That's not good, is it?"

"No, it's not," said Sebastian. "A lad named Jem Jones tells me other children have disappeared from around here in the past. Is that true?"

The reverend frowned. "It's hard to say, actually. Sometimes a lad will seem to disappear, only to show up again a few months later. They drift into different parts of the city in search of work or other"—he paused as if fumbling for the appropriate word and finally settled on—"opportunities. Most return eventually. But some don't."

"I understand Benji had a friend named Toby Dancing. Do you know where I might find him?"

The reverend shook his head with a faint smile. "Now, there's a lad who comes and goes all the time. He's like quicksilver, that one. It's one of the reasons they call him the Dancer—although I suspect there's more to it than that."

Sebastian nodded. "Second-story dancer" was a slang term for a certain kind of housebreaker. But he saw no reason to explain that to the reverend.

"He's not missing as well, is he?"

The reverend's eyes widened. "Not to my knowledge, no. I believe he spends more time than he should down by Hockley-in-the-Hole. I've seen him there several times."

Constable Gowan had also mentioned Hockley-in-the-Hole, a noto-riously insalubrious quarter of Clerkenwell given over to cockpits and bearbaiting and prostitution. Sebastian found himself wondering what the good reverend had been doing in such a district. But he kept those thoughts to himself.

"Benji wasn't simply killed," said Sebastian. "Whoever murdered him first held him for days and tortured him. Have you ever heard of anything like that happening around here?"

Reverend Filby brought up tented hands to press them against his nose and mouth. "Merciful heavens, no. It's too horrible to even think about."

"Yet it happened."

The reverend remained silent, his gaze on the workmen fixing a section of iron spikes in place. The spikes were to discourage the resurrection men who made a comfortable living stealing the bodies of the recently interred and selling them to medical schools and anatomists such as Paul Gibson.

Sebastian said, "Have you ever noticed anyone paying unusual attention to the street children? Perhaps some of the 'more comfortably situated' gentlemen of the parish you mentioned?"

Filby shook his head and kept on shaking it long after it was necessary. "No. Oh, no."

"Can you think of anyone I could speak with who might know more?"

"I'm sorry; no," Filby said in an odd rush, dropping his hands to clench them in the cloth of his cassock. "And now you must excuse me, my lord. I've duties to attend to."

And with that he turned and hurried away through the ancient, overflowing churchyard, his head bowed, his gaze fixed determinedly on the scuffed toes of his shoes, as if to look either right or left would only invite more questions he obviously had no wish to answer.

≷

Sebastian considered visiting Hockley-in-the-Hole in what would doubtless be a futile search for Toby Dancing. But after some consideration, he changed his mind and turned his horses instead toward Covent Garden and the Bow Street Public Office.

Two and a half years before, when Sebastian was accused of murder and on the run, the official tasked with seeing him brought to justice was a dour, earnest little magistrate named Sir Henry Lovejoy. In the time since, Sebastian and Lovejoy had come to both know and respect each other, and there was no one whose integrity or devotion to justice Sebastian trusted more.

Lovejoy now served as one of Bow Street's three stipendiary magistrates. As both the first and the most powerful of the metropolis's public offices, Bow Street enjoyed a supervisory authority over all of London and beyond. It wasn't Bow Street's role to investigate the death of a fifteen-year-old in Clerkenwell, but if anyone had heard of other cases similar to Benji's, it would be Lovejoy.

"Tortured?" said the magistrate as he and Sebastian walked down Bow Street toward the entrance to Covent Garden Market. "Paul Gibson is certain?"

"I'm afraid so."

"Oh, dear, oh, dear." Lovejoy shook his head with a heavy sigh. He was an unusually small man, barely five feet tall, with a bald head and wire-framed glasses and pinched, unsmiling features. Once, Lovejoy had been a moderately successful merchant. But the death of his wife and daughter some twelve years before had led to a spiritual crisis that not only turned him toward the Reformist church but also inspired him to devote the remainder of his life to public service. "Yet the Hatton Garden Public Office chose to do nothing?"

"I suppose that as far as they're concerned, children like Benji and Sybil Thatcher are nothing more than a nuisance causing trouble. It's only thanks to one of the parish constables that the boy's body was sent to Gibson for autopsy rather than being dumped in the poor hole after what I gather was a rather hurried inquest."

Lovejoy frowned as the two men turned together into the narrow lane leading toward the arcaded market piazza. Covent Garden Market did its busiest trade in the early morning hours; by now, the crowds were beginning to thin and some of the stall keepers were already putting up their shutters. With the increasing heat of the day, a sweet, sickly stench had begun to rise from the layers of cabbage leaves, smashed fruit, and manure underfoot.

Sebastian said, "You haven't heard of any similar deaths in other parts of London?"

"Good heavens, no."

"But then you weren't told about Benji and his missing sister, either."

"True," admitted Lovejoy, his face troubled. "Yet surely this is an isolated case?"

"It could be." Sebastian watched as a ragged girl of nine or ten snatched an apple from a nearby stall and took off running across the piazza, her bare feet sliding in the muck, the stall keeper's shouts lost in the din of the market. "What worries me is that Benji was only found by accident, and there are rumors of other children disappearing from the streets of Clerkenwell. If what I'm hearing is right—if Benji's killers are gentlemen—then it's possible they've taken street children from other parts of the city as well. Why confine themselves to Clerkenwell?"

There were tens of thousands of ragged children on the streets of London. Some had at least one parent, but many were utterly alone. They eked out miserable existences, sweeping crossings, running errands, and selling watercress picked from the ditches outside the city. And when that failed, they frequently turned to begging, stealing, and prostituting themselves. Sleeping in doorways, under bridges, or beneath the stalls of markets like Covent Garden, they formed the most vulnerable segment of the city's motley population of poor. Someone could pull one child under in Clerkenwell, another in Tower Hamlets, another in St. Giles, and no one would ever notice. Or care.

Lovejoy reached for his handkerchief and pressed the clean white folds to his lips. "What you're suggesting is unbelievably monstrous."

"Yes, but unfortunately not without precedent. Have you ever heard of Gilles de Rais?"

The magistrate shook his head.

"He was a lord of Brittany and Anjou famous as a companion of Joan of Arc during the Hundred Years' War. He even rose to become a marshal of France. But in his spare time, he murdered young boys and girls—perhaps as many as several hundred."

"Surely we're not dealing with something of that nature here. In *London?*"

A man in one of the nearby rows of stalls dropped a shutter, the loud bang startling the pigeons on the ridge of the ancient church's Tuscan pediment. Sebastian watched as they rose against the clear September sky in a quick, gray-white whirling of wings. "I hope not. But . . . how would we know?"

Lovejoy tucked his handkerchief away, his lips pressing into a tight line. "I'll send inquiries to the various public offices—ask if they've had any similar deaths or inexplicable disappearances amongst their street children."

"That would help. Thank you."

Lovejoy nodded, but his expression remained troubled. "The problem is, what if it's been happening and no one has noticed?"

Chapter 10

By the time Sebastian returned to Tower Hill, the light was turning golden and the shadows lengthening with the approach of evening. He was hoping to find Gibson finishing the autopsy of Benji Thatcher's remains. But the stone outbuilding at the base of the yard was already shut up for the night, forcing Sebastian to knock at the house.

The door was opened by a slight young woman with fiery red hair and dark brown eyes that glittered with hostility. Alexi Sauvage was not Gibson's wife, although she had lived with him for months now as if she were. But Sebastian had first met the enigmatic French doctor years before, in the mountains of Portugal, when he had killed her lover and she had sworn to avenge him.

Sebastian was not entirely convinced that she had abandoned that intention.

She stared at him now, her nostrils flaring with the agitation of her breathing before she reluctantly stepped back to open the door wider. "My lord."

"Gibson's here?"

She closed the door behind him. "In a sense."

"Meaning?"

She turned away. "See for yourself."

He followed her down a flagged passageway to the room Gibson used as a parlor. Once it had been an untidy space with tattered drapes and a moth-eaten carpet and dusty piles of books and newspapers that spilled from the cracked leather sofa and chairs. Gibson's alcohol-filled jars of strange specimens were still lined up along the mantel, but in the last six or seven months Alexi had transformed the space with ruthless determination—and lots of soap and water.

Her campaign to save Gibson from his self-destructive downward spiral had been less successful. The Irishman sat sprawled in a chair near the hearth, his cravat loose, his eyes unfocused, his face slack. The opium he'd obviously consumed had reduced his pupils to pinpricks.

"How long has he been like this?" asked Sebastian.

"An hour or so."

"Bloody hell." He swung away to stand at the entrance to the kitchen, his hands braced against the doorframe. "You said you could help him stop doing this."

Alexi Sauvage watched him, her arms crossed at her chest. "It's unreasonable to expect him to give up the opium as long as he's in so much pain from his amputated leg."

"You said you could help him with that too."

"Only if he'll let me."

"I don't understand. Why the hell won't he?"

"Probably because he knows that once the pain is gone, he'll no longer have an excuse to keep taking the opium."

"It's going to kill him!"

"You think I don't know that?" she said, her jaw tightening.

She'd been trained as a doctor, this woman, in Italy. But because women could not be licensed as physicians in England, she was allowed to practice here only as a midwife. Gibson considered her brilliant, and Sebastian suspected he was right.

He pushed away from the doorframe and went to stare out the window overlooking the yard. Alexi's hand was visible here too, with the once weedy path neatly lined with stones and the old pink rosebush brought under control. "Did he finish the autopsy on Benji Thatcher?"

"He did, yes. I suspect it's part of what drove him to the opium. Normally he approaches an autopsy like a puzzle—a fascinating exploration of a body in death. But this . . . this troubled him more than he'll ever admit."

Sebastian glanced over at her. "Did he find something else?"

She nodded, the cords of her throat working as she swallowed, her face strained as her gaze shifted to the distant building where Benji Thatcher lay.

"The boy was raped, wasn't he?" said Sebastian, his voice hoarse and grating.

"He was, yes. Repeatedly and brutally."

Sebastian felt his breath ease out in a long, painful sigh. "My God."

Alexi said, "You knew he was strangled?"

"Yes."

"Gibson thinks he probably died not long before the body was found."

"And there was nothing to suggest where he was killed?"

"He had straw in his hair and stuck to the dried blood of the wounds on his back."

"That could be from the bed of the cart he was moved in."

"I hadn't thought of that, but, yes; it makes sense." She hesitated. "Have you discovered anything? Anything at all?"

"Only that Benji might not be the first child to have disappeared off the streets of Clerkenwell. The truth is, I hardly know where to begin with this. There used to be a brothel in Chalon Lane that was willing to accommodate some pretty ugly practices. But it was torn down a year or so ago by a mob that beat to death the man and woman who used to run it."

She tilted her head to one side. "Have you ever heard of Number Three, Pickering Place?"

He shook his head.

She said, "I've delivered babies to some of the girls who work there. Most are little more than children. And while Number Three isn't as bad as the Chalon Lane house, they do accommodate those with an interest in *le vice anglais.*"

Le vice anglais: the English vice. It was a nice, sanitized expression for the practice of gaining sexual pleasure by whipping others—or being whipped. Sebastian had always wondered if it was actually more common amongst the English, or if the French simply preferred to attribute it to them.

"I'll look into it," he said. "Thank you." He turned to start back down the passage but paused again at the entrance to the parlor, his gaze on his friend. "What are we going to do?"

"I don't know."

Her gaze met his, and for one unexpected moment he saw her self-control slip, giving him a glimpse of all the frustration and anger, fear, and intense, fierce love for the Irishman that she normally kept so well hidden. And he knew then that while he and this woman might be old enemies, they were united in this.

This desperate fight for the life and sanity of the man who was so dear to them both.

Some time later, Sebastian walked into his house on Brook Street to find a familiar silver-tipped walking stick and high-crowned beaver hat resting on a chair in the entry hall.

"The Earl of Hendon is here to see you, my lord," said Sebastian's majordomo, Morey, his face wooden. "His lordship is waiting in the drawing room."

Sebastian jerked off his gloves. "Is Lady Devlin at home?"

"No, my lord."

Sebastian handed his gloves, hat, and driving coat to Morey. Then he hesitated a moment before climbing the stairs toward the man he'd once called Father.

Chapter 11

*S*ebastian was the third son and fourth child born to the marriage of Alistair St. Cyr, Fifth Earl of Hendon, and his beautiful, vibrant Countess, Sophia. The Earl's first two sons, Richard and Cecil, had been much like him in looks, temperament, interests, and talents. But the third son, Sebastian, was the one who was always different: a strange child with a passion for poetry and music and a tendency to lose himself in the works of radical French and German philosophers. A child with inexplicably yellow-hued eyes in place of the famous St. Cyr blue.

Yet somehow, despite it all, despite even his father's cold, distant detachment, Sebastian had never imagined that he was not Hendon's son but the result of one of the Countess's many scandalous affairs. Unwilling to publicly declare himself a cuckold and secure in the possession of two older sons, Hendon had acknowledged Sebastian as his own. Then Richard drowned in a riptide off the coast of Cornwall and Cecil died of fever four years later, leaving Sebastian as Hendon's heir. And still Hendon claimed Sebastian as his son. Sebastian had discovered the truth only by chance some fourteen months ago.

It wasn't easy, but he was slowly coming to accept that he was not exactly who he'd always believed himself to be. But he wasn't sure he would ever be able to forgive Hendon for using the lie of his birth to drive Sebastian away from a woman he'd once loved and planned to marry.

Hendon was standing before the bay window overlooking the street when Sebastian entered the room. A broad-shouldered, barrel-chested man with heavy features and white hair, the Earl had once stood over six feet tall, taller even than Sebastian. He was creeping toward seventy now, and in the last few years he'd begun to shrink, his shoulders rounding in a way Sebastian found disconcerting. But there was nothing frail or pitiful about Hendon. As Chancellor of the Exchequer, he was one of the most powerful men in the government—and the only one willing to go head-to-head with Charles, Lord Jarvis.

"Ah, there you are," said Hendon, turning from the window, his voice gruff with irritation. He'd never been able to abide being kept waiting—especially by Sebastian.

"You should have left a note," said Sebastian, closing the door behind him.

"And if I had, would you have returned my call?"

Rather than answer, Sebastian walked over to pour two glasses of brandy and held one out to the Earl. The two men had barely spoken since that fateful day when Sebastian learned the truth about his parentage and understood just how damaging and self-serving Hendon's many lies had been. And so he knew that whatever had brought Hendon here today must be important.

Hendon took the drink and stood staring down at it, his heavy jaw set hard. Then he swallowed half the brandy in one long pull. "Stephanie is betrothed. The announcement will appear in the morning papers."

Sebastian knew a flare of surprise. Miss Stephanie Wilcox was one of Hendon's two grandchildren by his only legitimate daughter, Amanda, the Dowager Lady Wilcox. The girl was beautiful, vivacious, and well dowered. But she had recently finished her second season without accepting any of the dozens of offers that had come her way. Sebastian had long suspected that his high-spirited niece was enjoying herself far too much to settle down, for in temperament as well as looks Stephanie Wilcox greatly resembled her infamous grandmother.

Sebastian said, "Amanda must be relieved."

Hendon tossed back the rest of his brandy. "Amanda is more than relieved; she's ecstatic. The man in question is the only son and heir of the Marquis of Lindley."

Sebastian froze with his own glass raised halfway to his lips. "Ashworth?"

"Yes."

"Bloody hell." Sebastian walked over to stand beside the room's cold hearth. Anthony Ledger, Viscount Ashworth, was thirty-two years old, handsome, wellborn, and extraordinarily wealthy. He was also so debauched and dissolute that the patronesses of Almack's—normally more than ready to overlook the faults of any marriageable young man of wealth and breeding—had barred him from that august establishment. The thought of Stephanie marrying a man of Ashworth's ilk brought a sour taste to Sebastian's mouth. For however strained his relationship with his sister, Amanda, might be, Sebastian had always had a fondness for his vibrant, spirited young niece.

"Amanda agreed to this?" he said after a moment.

Hendon snorted. "Of course she agreed to it. Do you think she'd pass up the opportunity to see her daughter a marchioness?"

Sebastian took a slow swallow of his brandy and felt it burn all the way down. "Assuming, of course, that Ashworth lives long enough to succeed his father."

Hendon said, "If half the stories told of the man are true—"

"They are. I was at Eton with him, remember? He bullied one young, sensitive lad named Nathan Broadway so mercilessly the poor boy committed suicide. Forced him to drink a pint of Ashworth's piss."

Hendon frowned down at his empty glass.

"More brandy?" offered Sebastian.

Hendon shook his head.

"Does Amanda know what Ashworth is like?" asked Sebastian.

"Oh, she knows. I tried to reason with her, but she simply laughed in my face and called me old-fashioned."

"Perhaps in the end it will come to nothing. When is the wedding?"

"A week from this Thursday."

"Why so soon?"

"Presumably because she doesn't want to risk letting the future Marquis slip from her grasp."

Sebastian took another sip of his brandy. "I must confess, I never had Ashworth pegged as the marrying kind."

Hendon pursed his lips, his jaw working back and forth in that way he had.

"What?" asked Sebastian, watching him.

Hendon blew out a harsh breath. "I've heard the old Marquis is behind it. That Lindley's cut off Ashworth's allowance until he marries and begets an heir. Ashworth held out for a while, but now he's caved."

"That I can believe. And Stephanie? How does she feel about all this?"

"Amanda swears the chit is head over heels in love. There's no deny-ing Ashworth is a handsome devil. And he can be damnably charming when he wants to be."

"Yes. But how long will he want to be—particularly if he's only marrying to maintain his allowance?"

Hendon swiped one thick hand over his face. "You know Ashworth better than I do. I was thinking that if you were to speak to Amanda—tell her—"

He broke off as Sebastian threw back his head and laughed. "You can't be serious. You do know my dear sister's opinion of me, don't you? It hasn't been three years since she tried her best to see me hanged."

"That doesn't mean she won't listen to you."

Yes, it does, thought Sebastian, although he didn't say it. Amanda had hated him since the day he was born and probably before. When they were children, she'd hated him as a constant reminder of their mother's infidelity. And she hated him even more now that he stood to inherit all the titles and positions that would have been hers, had she been born male.

"What about Bayard?" suggested Sebastian. "Have you spoken to him?" Bayard Wilcox was Amanda's only surviving son and the current Lord Wilcox.

"Bayard?" Hendon gave a rude snort. "The boy's never been right in the head. Apart from which, Amanda despises him."

"Not as much as she despises me."

Hendon slammed his brandy glass down on a nearby table. *"God damn it.* Will you not at least try?"

Sebastian met his father's blazing eyes. *No,* Sebastian reminded himself; not his father's. Yet he could not deny the unwelcome tangle of disturbing emotions that surged through him. He knew what it must have cost Hendon to come here and ask this of him, despite the estrangement between them, despite everything. And the truth was, the thought of pretty, laughing young Stephanie married to a man like Ashworth was an abomination.

Sebastian set aside his own brandy. "I'll try."

Hendon nodded and tugged at the hem of his waistcoat, as if embarrassed by the emotional intensity of his outburst. "Amanda is engaged for dinner this evening with Countess Lieven, after which they plan to attend Lady Holbrook's soiree. But I believe she's at home tomorrow afternoon."

"I'll try then."

Hendon nodded again and turned toward the door, pausing only long enough to look back and say, "I suppose it's possible we're wrong about the man. I mean, surely he can't be as bad as they say?"

"On the contrary," said Sebastian, his gaze meeting the Earl's. "He's worse."

❧

Sebastian was standing at the drawing room's bay window and watching Hendon's familiar form descend the front steps, when Hero's yellow-bodied town carriage swept around the corner to draw up before the house.

Hendon paused on the footpath, the stern lines of his broad face softening as Hero descended from the carriage to grasp his hands and kiss his cheek.

Lately Hero had been making it a practice to take their infant son, Simon, to visit Hendon at least once or twice a week. The seven-month-old child was, in truth, no more than a distant cousin to the Earl. But Hendon publically acknowledged the babe as his grandson, and some-day Simon would in his turn be Viscount Devlin, before becoming the Earl of Hendon.

Sebastian turned away from the window.

❧

Hero came in a few moments later trailing a very fetching straw bonnet by its dusky pink velvet ribbons. She wore a deeply flounced muslin walking dress with a dusky pink velvet spencer fastened by a row of tiny mother-of-pearl buttons up the front. She was not smiling.

Sebastian said, "I gather Hendon told you about Stephanie?"

Hero tossed the hat on a nearby chair. "She can't be allowed to marry that man. He's shockingly bad ton."

"He's heir to a marquis. A very wealthy marquis."

"He's bad ton," she said again.

"He's worse than bad ton." Sebastian retrieved his brandy and took a long, slow drink. "Hendon is laboring under the illusion that Amanda might listen to me. But she won't." He drained the glass and went to pour another. "So tell me: Did you meet Cousin Victoria?"

"I did." Hero went to work on her spencer's row of buttons. "I must say, she's nothing like what I was expecting. She's only a few years older than I am and very pretty. She's so tiny she makes me feel like a hulking giant when I stand next to her, although—" She broke off.

"Although?" he prompted.

"Although I'm not convinced she's quite as sweet and innocent as she likes to appear."

Sebastian glanced over at her. "You didn't like her?"

"Honestly?" Hero shook her head. "Although I can't precisely say why. I have the most lowering suspicion that I'm simply jealous of the extent of her travels."

He found himself smiling. "I find that difficult to believe."

"Well, thank you. I'm flattered, even if I'm not entirely convinced." She jerked off her spencer. "So tell me about the murder."

Another man might have been inclined to hide such an ugly reality from his gently born wife, but Sebastian knew Hero well enough to suspect she'd be both furious and insulted if he were ever so presumptuous. He said, "The victim is a fifteen-year-old street urchin named Benji Thatcher. Someone raped and tortured him for days before finally strangling him, and the only reason his body was found is because an ex-soldier chanced to interrupt the killers before they could bury him at an abandoned shot factory outside of Clerkenwell."

"'Killers'? As in, more than one?"

"Evidently. A gentleman driving a cart and a youth digging the grave. And as if that weren't bad enough, the boy's little sister, Sybil, is missing too."

"Dear God. Do you have any leads?"

"Not exactly. According to Alexi Sauvage, there's a house in Pickering Place that caters to men who like their whores young and have an interest in whips. I suppose it's a place to start."

"You mean Number Three?"

He stared at her. "Good Lord. How do you know that?"

"I heard about it when I was researching the correlation between the current economic situation and the increasing number of women being pushed into prostitution."

"How much did you hear about it?"

"Not a great deal, fortunately. It's run by twin sisters named Grace and Hope Bligh. I'm told they're dwarfs, although I don't know if that's true."

"Dwarfs?"

"Mmm. I gather they're nasty characters. Quite nasty. Most of their girls are little more than children. Do you plan to go there?"

He nodded. "Tonight. Although I doubt I'll find them overly anxious to disclose the names of their customers."

"You will be careful," said Hero. Characteristically, it was not so much a request as an instruction. In some ways she was very much her father's daughter.

He reached out to cup her cheek with his palm, gazed deep into her beautiful, intelligent, worried eyes, and smiled. "I will."

She did not look convinced.

Chapter 12

*S*ebastian left Brook Street later that evening, riding in his town carriage with two footmen standing up behind. As usual he carried a knife sheathed in his right boot, and tonight he'd also slipped a small, double-barreled flintlock pistol into one pocket.

St. James's Street was the Upper Ten Thousand's male preserve, home of exclusive gentlemen's clubs such as White's and Brooks's, of fashionable shops that ranged from Lock & Co. hatters to the venerable old establishment of Berry Bros. & Rudd, where Beau Brummell and the Prince Regent could sometimes be found checking their weight on the firm's giant coffee scales. Single, well-heeled young men—and the mountebanks who preyed upon them—kept rooms both on the street itself and in the surrounding district. Pickering Place lay just to the northeast, practically within the shadow of the old brick palace built by Henry VIII.

Leaving his carriage outside Berry Bros. & Rudd, Sebastian passed through a narrow arched passage paneled in oak that ran beside the shop. The passage was long and tunnel-like and opened out into the tiny, completely enclosed square known as Pickering Place. The century-old, tall brick buildings surrounding the square housed an unsavory collection of gambling dens and brothels and, in one darkened corner, the discreet establishment known simply as Number Three.

He paused, lingering for a time in the shadows and watching as the light from the single oil lamp mounted high on the house's wall flickered over the plain facade. Two shallow, flagged steps led up to a shiny black door with a polished brass knocker and freshly painted white surround. The rest of the square rang with male laughter, high-pitched female squeals, and the tinkling of a badly tuned pianoforte played with more energy than skill. But Number Three remained oddly quiet, the curtains at its front windows tightly closed.

Sebastian mounted the steps to ply the knocker, then stood listening as the sound faded into silence.

He could feel someone watching him, evaluating him, through the peephole in the closed door. He knocked again, his head tipping back as he studied the windows of the first floor above—

And caught the cautious footfalls of a heavy man creeping through the passage behind him.

"Interesting way to answer the door," said Sebastian, one hand in his pocket as he shifted to stand sideways. He had no intention of turning his back to that door.

A massive, big-headed man drew up abruptly some feet away. A relatively new purple scar split his left eyebrow, and he had the swollen knuckles, broken nose, and cauliflower ear of someone who'd spent years in the ring. He was making no effort to conceal the three-foot section of iron bar he held clenched in one meaty fist.

"What ye want here?" he demanded, thrusting forward a jaw that reminded Sebastian of a coal barge.

"Presumably what every other man who knocks at this door wants."

The big, dark-haired man shook his head. "Miss Grace don't think so." He tightened his grip on the iron bar. "Why don't ye jist sod off? Huh? We don't need no trouble."

"What makes you think I'm trouble?"

"Miss Grace knows who ye are."

"Oh?"

A second man came through the passage to range alongside the first. This one was both larger and uglier, and carried a knife rather than a length of iron.

Sebastian said, "If Miss Grace knows who I am, then she should also realize that I'm wise enough not to have come here without informing others of my destination. Attempt violence against me, and this establishment will bring down upon itself precisely the sort of attention she is most interested in avoiding."

The door beside him opened, spilling light down the steps. He smelled beeswax and incense and flowers, their scents mingling in a way that reminded him, perversely, of a church. At first glance Sebastian took the figure standing in the doorway for a child—a pretty little girl of seven or eight with fair hair and eerie, light-colored eyes. Then he noticed the swell of white breasts above the plunging bodice of her blue silk gown, the fine delineation of her cheekbones and nose, and realized this was no child but a tiny woman somewhere in her late twenties or early thirties.

When Sebastian was a boy, in Cornwall, he'd known an incredibly nimble, good-humored dwarf named Matt Downey. Matt's arms and legs had been short, his head large, his thick torso the size of a normal man's. But unlike Matt, this woman was essentially a perfectly proportioned adult in miniature: slim and finely made, yet standing no more than four feet tall.

She studied him thoughtfully for a moment, her expression giving nothing away. Then she opened the door wider. "Come in."

For reasons he could not name, Sebastian found himself hesitating as an unpleasant chill tingled along the back of his neck.

Something of his reaction must have shown on his face, because a smile touched her bow-shaped lips. "Do we frighten you?"

"Is there a reason I should be frightened?"

"With a carriage and two footmen awaiting you in St. James's? I don't think so. But Joshua and Thomas can stay out here, if you prefer."

He followed her past an opulent, aggressively sensual reception room with red velvet curtains and a number of lurid paintings, to a smaller but considerably more tasteful chamber hung with hand-painted Chinese wallpaper and furnished with delicate chairs and exquisitely carved commodes in the style of Louis XV. A second golden-haired woman, identical to the first and wearing the same blue silk gown, sat perched like a child on an armchair near the fire, her hands folded in her lap. Neither woman moved nor spoke, but simply stared at Sebastian with those strange, light gray eyes.

He was not invited to sit.

"Would you like some wine?" asked the woman who had opened the door.

"No, thank you."

She turned to a marble-topped table that held a selection of decanters and glasses. "Even if I promise it's not poisoned?"

"No, thank you," he said again, his gaze flicking over the oil paintings in heavy, gilded frames that adorned the walls. He recognized a Watteau, a Boucher, and several Fragonards. Providing very young girls to the most debauched of London's wealthy men was obviously highly profitable. He felt his stomach heave, his blood surge with a raw fury he had to fight down.

She said, "I trust you don't mind if Hope and I do?"

He brought his gaze back to her face. So this was Grace. "If it were up to me, you'd be in Newgate by now."

She poured wine into two sparkling cut-crystal glasses. "Oh? Yet you seem very determined to speak with us."

"The body of a fifteen-year-old boy was discovered yesterday in Clerkenwell," Sebastian said bluntly. "He'd been raped as well as tortured with a whip and knife before being strangled. His younger sister is also missing. It's been suggested you might know something about that."

She set the wine carafe aside. "I hope you're not insinuating these incidents have anything to do with us."

"It struck me as a possibility, yes."

Something shimmered in the depths of this tiny woman's strangely pale eyes, something that reminded him of coiled snakes and glacial lakes in the dead of winter. Her voice took on a dangerous, silken edge. "We don't generally lose our workers."

"Not generally? So what about occasionally?"

"This isn't Chalon Lane. We are very careful in the selection of our clientele." She turned to hand one of the wineglasses to her sister, who still didn't say anything. "Those who refuse to abide by the house rules are no longer admitted."

"Simply because they abide by the rules here doesn't mean they behave the same elsewhere."

"We have no control over that." She reached for her own wineglass but did not bring it to her lips. "What do you want from us?"

"Names."

She laughed out loud. "Our customers expect confidentiality. If we were to give you what you seek, we would be out of business."

He let his gaze drift, significantly, around the room again. "You and your sister appear to have done quite well for yourselves."

"Thank you. Or was that meant as a threat rather than a compliment? Are you thinking of informing against us?" Again, that faint smile curled her perfectly molded lips. "Do you seriously believe the authorities don't know we're here?"

"Perhaps. Yet there are ways to make establishments of this nature . . ." He paused as if searching for the right word, then said, "Uncomfortable. And unprofitable."

He saw it again, that lethal glitter of raw malevolence. And he found himself wondering about her background, about how she and her sister came to be here. Her voice and manner were educated, although he knew that could be an act.

And why the hell didn't her twin speak?

She said, "What you ask is impossible."

"Then give me the names of those customers who played so rough that they're no longer welcome."

The twins exchanged glances. It was as if they were so in tune with each other's thoughts that words were unnecessary between them.

Grace Bligh set aside her wine untasted. "Very well. We will give you two names. The first is an actor: Hector Kneebone."

Sebastian knew a flicker of surprise. Kneebone was one of the stage's most promising young actors, gaining rapidly in popularity, particularly amongst the more influential members of the ton. "What did Kneebone do to violate your rules?"

"He became . . . unmanageable."

"Meaning?"

"Why don't you ask him?"

"And the second man?"

Grace Bligh hesitated, her gaze sliding again to her twin. He saw Hope Bligh's tiny hands clench, hard, around the arms of her chair. But to his surprise, Grace Bligh smiled.

"The second man was blackballed after whipping one of our girls half to death."

"That's against the rules? I thought that was part of what you offered here."

"It's not supposed to be taken to such extremes."

Sebastian felt it again—that urge to lay violent hands upon this diminutive, evil woman. He suppressed it with difficulty. "And his name?"

Her chin lifted, her strange, wintry eyes glittering with a raw, visceral hatred she made no attempt to disguise. "I assume you know him, seeing as he's approximately your age and a viscount, as well. His name is Ashworth. Lord Ashworth."

Chapter 13

 $\mathcal{G}$ race Bligh could be lying.

Sebastian acknowledged the possibility even as he prowled the gentlemen's clubs and fashionable coffeehouses of St. James's, looking for Viscount Ashworth. If the betrothal of Miss Stephanie Wilcox to the Marquis of Lindley's handsome, dissolute son had already been made public, then Sebastian would have been inclined to view the nasty little brothel keeper's words as nothing more than pure malice. But the betrothal was not known, and that made Grace Bligh's information considerably more intriguing. Not reliable, by any means, but definitely worth looking into.

When he drew a blank in the area that had once been known as St. James's Fields, Sebastian shifted his search farther east to Covent Garden. It was there, near Drury Lane Theater, that he came upon his niece's betrothed.

Anthony Ledger, Viscount Ashworth, was a tall man, nearly as tall as Sebastian, with the broad shoulders and trim, muscular frame of a Corinthian. They were sporting men, the Corinthians: gentlemen of rank and fortune known for their dedication to hunting and horses, who spent a sizeable chunk of their time boxing at Gentleman Jackson's and fencing at Angelo's. The Viscount's honey-colored hair was fashionably disheveled, his dark blue coat, doeskin breeches, and high-topped boots exquisitely fitted and very expensive. He was on the verge of entering a tavern in the company of a group of friends when Sebastian hopped down from his carriage and said airily, "Ah, there you are, Ashworth. If I might have a word with you?"

The Viscount paused, his lips curling into a pleasant if faintly puzzled smile.

"It won't take long," said Sebastian. "Walk with me a ways?"

"Of course," said Ashworth, excusing himself to his companions with a bow.

He and Sebastian turned to walk along Catherine Street. Both Drury Lane and Covent Garden theaters were scheduled to open for the season in a few days, which meant that dress rehearsals were now under way. Laughing crowds of excited young men thronged the footpaths and spilled out onto the pavement; the air was heavy with the smell of ale and tobacco smoke mingling with the occasional, elusive whiff of hashish.

Ashworth said, "I take it you've heard of the announcement that is to appear in tomorrow's papers?"

Sebastian stepped wide to avoid a reeling, red-faced young buck waving a bottle of brandy and shouting verses of Virgil to the night. "I have. Although that's not why I'm here."

"Oh?"

"I'm told you've been blackballed from Number Three, Pickering Place for half killing one of their girls."

Ashworth squinted up at the sky as if assessing the possibility that the gathering clouds might bring rain. "I really don't know what you're talking about."

"Yes, you do."

Ashworth drew up and swung to face him, that pleasant smile never slipping. "Do you imagine that knowledge of some of my more unorthodox sexual interests might complicate or even end my betrothal to Miss Wilcox? If so, then I'm afraid you don't know your niece very well. Or your sister. After all, what are the bleatings of some ignorant trollop when set against the lure of a coronet?"

Sebastian made no effort to keep his reaction off his face. "The Bligh sisters don't provide their clients with women. They supply very young girls—some of them essentially children. And boys, if one is discreet and willing to pay enough."

"I've no interest in children, if that's what you're suggesting. But I won't deny I prefer my Cyprians on the young side, given that they tend to be both cleaner and less jaded."

"How young?"

"You seriously think I ask?" Ashworth threw a telling glance toward his waiting companions, an edge of exasperation creeping into his tone. "Why are we having this conversation?"

"Because a young street urchin by the name of Benji Thatcher was recently raped and tortured before being strangled to death. And his little sister, Sybil, is missing."

"Street urchins?" Ashworth laughed out loud. "And you suspect me?" The smile vanished as if it had never been. "First of all, I like girls, not boys. Secondly, I don't *kill* them."

"But you do enjoy playing with whips. And you've been known to get carried away."

"Don't be ridiculous. The girl at Number Three was not seriously harmed. I blame the Bligh sisters for what happened; the ninny was not properly prepared."

"Prepared," said Sebastian. He had expected Ashworth to deny Grace Bligh's accusations. Instead, the man had confirmed everything without hesitation or remorse.

Ashworth's jaw hardened. "Yes; prepared. And now you really must excuse me."

"Where were you at half past one early Monday morning?" said Sebastian as the man started to turn away.

Ashworth swung to face him again. "Why do you ask?"

"Because that's when Benji's killers were interrupted in the process of burying the body at the old Rutherford Shot Factory."

Ashworth smiled wide, his teeth gleaming even and white in the lamplight. "As it happens, I dined Sunday evening with your own dear sister, Lady Wilcox, and my beautiful bride-to-be. We then attended Mrs. Hanson's soiree before putting in an appearance at Lady Littlefield's ball. I escorted the ladies home shortly after two." He tipped his head as if in thought. "You know, one might almost suspect you of not wanting this match."

"Of course I don't want this match. I haven't forgotten Nathan Broadway."

"Who?"

"The boy at Eton you bullied to death."

"Ah. That was a long time ago."

"I haven't heard anything to suggest you've changed."

That unpleasant smile still firmly in place, Ashworth executed a mocking bow and strolled away.

Sebastian called after him, "You wouldn't happen to know the actor Hector Kneebone, would you?"

There was a faint yet definite hesitation in the Viscount's stride. But he kept walking and did not look back.

⚜

Sebastian roamed the crowded, boisterous streets of Covent Garden, feeling oddly detached from the noisy gaiety that swirled around him.

The discovery that Stephanie was about to marry the kind of man who paid to abuse young girls—and who had carried that abuse to a degree that alarmed even the jaded abbesses of Pickering Place—filled him with deep disquiet. He had a nearly overwhelming urge to storm into Lady Holbook's soirée, grab Amanda by the shoulders, and ask what the bloody hell she could be thinking, encouraging such a match. But he forced himself to keep walking. If he were to have any hope of convincing his sister, he would need to approach her calmly and carefully.

And so he turned his thoughts instead to the second man named by Grace Bligh: the actor Hector Kneebone. The fact that Grace had told the truth about Ashworth didn't necessarily mean that she was being similarly honest about Kneebone, but it did make it more likely. Rory Inchbald had insisted the man he saw driving the cart the night of Benji's murder was a gentleman. And while it was doubtful that Knee-bone had been born a gentleman, he certainly played one quite successfully on the stage.

❧

Covent Garden Theater lay on Bow Street, not far from the famous Bow Street Public Office. It was a place Sebastian had once known quite well, for long ago when he was barely twenty-one and just down from Oxford, he had fallen blindly, passionately in love with a young, little-known actress named Kat Boleyn. In the years since then Kat had risen to become the most acclaimed actress of the London stage. And while fate—in the form of the Earl of Hendon—had driven Sebastian and Kat apart not once but twice, she would forever be an important part of Sebastian's life.

She had spent the past year away from the stage recovering from a personal tragedy. But she was back in London for the coming season and would be appearing as Viola in *Twelfth Night* when it opened at Covent Garden Theater in just two days.

He found her in her dressing room making last-minute adjustments to her costume. She looked around as he entered, the light from the candles on her dressing table flaring golden and warm over her famous high cheekbones; small, upturned nose; and wide mouth.

"Devlin!" she cried with a laugh, pushing up to come toward him with her hands outstretched and a sparkle of delight in her eyes—those vivid blue St. Cyr eyes she had inherited from her natural father, the Earl of Hendon.

He caught her hands in his and held them, his gaze searching her beautiful, familiar features. He hadn't seen her since the dark days following the death of her husband, Russell Yates, twelve months before. Her marriage to the colorful ex-privateer had been one of convenience, but Sebastian knew that a real affection had developed between them, and Yates's murder—especially the circumstances surrounding it—had affected her profoundly. "How are you, Kat? Truly?"

"Much better. Truly. I've spent a great deal of time walking along misty seashores and forcing myself to confront any number of things I should have dealt with long ago." She tipped her head to one side. "And you? I hear you've a fine young son."

He smiled. "Simon. Seven months old, handsome, brilliant, and vociferously teething."

She laughed again. "I can see you're happy."

"I am."

"You know that's what I've always wanted?"

He squeezed her hands and let her go. "I know."

There'd been a time not so long ago when Sebastian had believed he could never love anyone but this woman, when the thought that she could never be his had sent him into a downward vortex that almost killed him. But then Hero had come into his life, and Simon, and together they had helped him find a powerful new love, one that brought a peace and deep contentment such as he'd never believed possible.

He loved Kat still and always would. Yet seeing her now underscored for him the ways in which his affections for her had shifted. And he realized with a certain sense of bemusement that at some point in the past year he had come to love her essentially as if she were indeed the half sister he'd once to his horror believed her to be.

She bent to tuck her breeches into her boots. "I saw Paul Gibson this afternoon." She paused, and Sebastian waited for what he knew was coming, for even after Hendon had done his best to drive Sebastian and Kat apart, she and Gibson had remained good friends. "He tells me he's asked for your help in another murder." She made no attempt to hide the worry in her voice. Sebastian's involvement in murder investigations had always troubled Kat, for she knew how much each one cost him.

"It's one of the reasons why I'm here," he said. "What can you tell me about Hector Kneebone?"

She straightened slowly. "You think Kneebone is involved in this?"

"Possibly. How well do you know him?"

She turned to her looking glass and began coiling her thick auburn hair up beneath a jaunty feathered cap. "Not all that well. He only arrived here from Bath a few years ago and he's mainly been at Drury Lane. He's very popular with audiences."

Sebastian rested his shoulders against the nearest wall. "What about with his fellow players?"

She shrugged. "He's arrogant and he can be abrasive. But then, he's hardly unique in that."

"What do you know of his taste in women?"

"Well . . . he is very handsome, and the gentlemen of the town have never been the only ones who like to choose their lovers off the boards." Something of his reaction must have shown on his reflection in the mirror, because she paused to look at him over one shoulder. "That shocks you?"

He gave a soft laugh. "I suppose it shouldn't, but I must confess it does. So who are his lovers?"

"I've heard his conquests include at least one duchess, three countesses, and any number of lesser ladies. But is it true? I don't know." She finished fussing with her cap and turned away from the mirror. "What makes you suspect him?"

"His was one of two names given me by a decidedly unsavory abbess in Pickering Place." He hesitated, then said, "The other was Lord Ashworth."

"Dear Lord," she whispered. "Have you heard—"

"About Ashworth's betrothal to Stephanie?" Sebastian nodded. "Hendon has asked me to use my nonexistent influence with Amanda to try to put an end to it. As if I could somehow convince her that she really doesn't want to see her daughter a marchioness."

He watched as a succession of troubled emotions flickered across Kat's face. She wasn't normally so transparent. She said, "I wish you could find a way to forgive Hendon for what he did."

"I can't."

"He only had your best interests at heart."

"Did he? In my experience Hendon's interest is all for the St. Cyr name and the St. Cyr bloodline and the St. Cyr legacy. If one of my mother's grandparents hadn't been a St. Cyr herself, do you seriously think I'd still be acknowledged as his heir?"

"You wrong him. You really do."

When Sebastian remained silent, her mouth curled up into a crooked smile.

"What?" he demanded, watching her.

"Hendon may not have sired you, but you're still far more like him than you'd care to admit."

"What the devil is that supposed to mean?"

The warning bell sounded in the distance, and she turned toward the door. "Think about it."

"Huh." He pushed away from the wall. "Where does Kneebone lodge? Do you know?"

"I believe he keeps rooms in Bedford Street." She hesitated, then reached out to rest her hand on his arm. "Gibson told me some of what was done to that poor dead boy. Whoever you're looking for is beyond vile, Devlin; he's evil. Please be careful."

"Is Kneebone capable of such a thing, do you think?"

She considered this for a moment. "I wouldn't have said so, no. But, then, whoever did this must be very good at hiding his true nature, wouldn't you say? And who is better at playing a part than an actor?"

Chapter 14

Hector Kneebone kept rooms in a once grand seventeenth-century house that had been broken up into respectable lodgings.

Sebastian spent some time nursing a tankard of ale in a nearby tavern called the Blue Boar, then followed that up with a glass of wine at a neighborhood coffeehouse. His seemingly innocuous questions elicited the exact location of the handsome young actor's rooms, along with a wealth of lurid details about the string of well-dressed, veiled ladies who arrived at his door in hackney coaches both day and night.

If Kneebone indulged in any other activities, no one seemed to know about them.

Some half an hour before rehearsals at Drury Lane were likely to end, Sebastian slipped up the stairs and let himself into the actor's rooms with a simple device known as a picklock. He eased the door closed behind him, then paused a moment to allow his eyes to adjust to the darkness.

The combination parlor and dining room was small but expensively furnished with grand, gilt-framed mirrors, an inlaid cherrywood table, and elegant settees covered in a striped burgundy and navy blue silk.

Through an archway he could see a massive tester bed and walls hung with burgundy silk and more mirrors.

Hector Kneebone obviously enjoyed looking at himself.

Sebastian searched the rooms quickly and quietly, all the while listening for the sound of footsteps on the stairs. He found an astonishing number of expensive snuffboxes and other trinkets, some with their scented billets-doux from the actor's admirers still attached. But none of it suggested any link to what had been done to Benji Thatcher or his missing sister.

Then Sebastian's gaze settled on a carved wooden chest set atop a low bookcase to one side of the bed.

Covered with scenes of Adam and Eve in the Garden of Eden, the chest was some eighteen inches long and twelve inches high. It opened to reveal crimson silk cords of varying lengths and thicknesses, a hemmed length of black silk such as one might use for a blindfold, and a leather whip.

Sebastian closed the chest and stared down at the volumes on the shelves below. Some were risqué classical works by the likes of Epicurus and Petronius. But most were by French writers of the last two hundred years, including Charles de Saint-Évremond, Claude Prosper Jolyot de Crébillon, Choderlos de Laclos, Rétif de la Bretonne, and the Marquis de Sade. Sebastian had no need to open one to understand the significance of Kneebone's collection.

They were known as "licentious books" or "bawdy stuff." Like the popular gothic romances of the day, their themes were often dark. But here were no supernatural elements, only an aggressive anticlericalism and radical philosophy wrapped up in an ostentatiously uninhibited exploration of sexuality that ranged from naughty and playful to cruel and depraved.

One of the books, ornately bound in tooled black cordovan leather, was particularly striking. Purporting to be by the Marquis de Sade, it bore the title of a manuscript lost long ago in the turmoil of the French Revolution. Slipping the volume from the shelf, Sebastian opened the book and found himself staring at an engraved depiction of a naked woman, her hands bound over her head, flinching away from a lash.

He was flipping through the pages, growing more and more disturbed, when he heard the outside door open below and a man's footsteps cross the entry hall toward the stairs. Sebastian thrust the book back into place. He paused long enough to select a length of silken cord from the carved chest, then went to flatten himself against the wall beside the hall door.

Holding one end of the cord in each hand, he listened as the footsteps reached the landing and continued up to the first floor. The man was whistling now, a soft, sweet rendition of an obscure piano concerto. The music broke off as he stopped outside the door, fumbled for his key, and tried to turn the lock. He grunted when he realized the door was unlocked. But he was obviously unconcerned, for the whistling started up again as he pushed the door open.

The lamp from the stairwell threw Hector Kneebone's shadow across the floor as he walked inside and half turned to close the door. Stepping away from the wall, Sebastian looped the silken cord over the actor's head and kicked the door closed behind them.

"Wha—" Arms flailing uselessly, Kneebone let out a frightened yelp as Sebastian cinched the cord up beneath the actor's chin.

"Relax," said Sebastian softly, his mouth close to the man's ear. "I'm here neither to murder you nor rob you. We're simply going to have a nice little conversation. Understand?"

As if he didn't trust his voice, Kneebone nodded, the whites of his eyes gleaming a ghostly blue as he tried desperately to see who was behind him. He was a well-made man with the curly black hair and light brown eyes so often seen in Cornwall and Wales. He was also at least four inches shorter than Sebastian.

"Good," said Sebastian, cinching both ends of the cord in his right fist. By rolling his hand inward, he could easily shrink the diameter of the loop while carefully controlling the pressure he was exerting. "Now tell me about Benji and Sybil Thatcher."

Kneebone suddenly found his voice. "Who? What? What are you talking about? Who are you?"

"Never mind who I am. I want to hear what you know about a missing little girl and her fifteen-year-old brother who was raped, whipped, and murdered."

"Murdered? I don't know anything about any murder! What boy?"

"Benji Thatcher."

"Never heard of him."

"He had a little sister named Sybil who is now missing. Ever hear of her?"

"Good Lord, no."

Sebastian rolled his fist ever so subtly. "I had a look at your bookcase. You've been reading the Marquis de Sade. Like that sort of thing, do you?"

"It's fascinating. Don't you think?"

"Actually, no."

Kneebone swallowed hard, his Adam's apple moving up and down against the cord. "Just because I read about that sort of thing doesn't mean I actually do it."

"No? Then why the silken bonds and whip in the chest?"

When Kneebone remained silent, Sebastian tightened his grip on the cord, pulling the actor back and off balance. "I know about Pickering Place. About how you're no longer welcome there since a certain incident they didn't care to particularize."

"That . . . that was a mistake. We were smoking hashish, you see— the girl and I. We were so focused on the moment I got carried away."

"Perhaps you 'got carried away' with Benji and Sybil Thatcher."

"Good God. Ask anyone; they'll tell you I like playing with women, not boys."

"And young girls," Sebastian reminded him. "Number Three is known for the youth of its 'merchandise.'"

"All right, yes; I like young girls. I'll admit it. But not too young."

"That makes it all right, does it?"

"Lots of girls are married at fourteen or fifteen." Kneebone tried again, uselessly, to twist around so that he could see Sebastian's face. "You don't know what it's like, having to tumble all the grand ladies who come here; being forced to smile and somehow pretend to like it while they grope me. Some of them are *old*."

"You say that as if you're expecting my sympathy. You could always turn them away."

"You think so? Have you any idea what it would do to my career, if I were to turn them down? How long do you think I'd last if the Duchess of X and my Lady Y flounced out of here in a pet to tell all their friends that, 'Oh'"—Kneebone's voice rose in a mocking imitation of a Mayfair matron's cut-crystal vowels—'I really didn't think that new young man at Drury Lane is so divine after all'?"

Sebastian kept the pressure on the cord. "Where were you early Monday morning? At, say, half past one?"

"I was here. In bed asleep."

"Alone?"

"Yes, for once. Why?"

"Because that's when Benji Thatcher's killers were interrupted trying to bury the boy's body in a field outside Clerkenwell."

Kneebone clawed uselessly at the silken bond around his neck. "I tell you, I don't know anything about some boy or girl named Thatcher, and I don't kill children. I've never killed anyone!"

"So who would?"

"What?"

"You heard me. Who do you know who might do something like that?"

"I don't know!"

"No? You must know others who share your interests."

"No one who would kill."

"No?"

"No!"

Sebastian released his grip on the silken cord and took a step back.

Kneebone whirled to face him. "Why, you—" The actor broke off, his eyes widening at the sight of the double-barreled pistol that had appeared in Sebastian's hand. "Good God. You're Devlin."

"Yes. And I should probably have warned you that I can become very cranky when I've discovered people lied to me. Particularly when the subject is murder."

"I haven't lied about anything!"

"Let's hope so. Because if I discover you have, I'll be back."

A restless wind was tossing the clouds overhead when Sebastian left Kneebone's rooms and turned toward where he'd left his carriage on Bridges Street, near Drury Lane.

The crowds in the district had started to thin, but there were still enough people on the streets that he might not have paid attention to the man in the bottle green coat and round hat if Sebastian hadn't noticed him before.

The man was quite ordinary, in his twenties, small and slim, with light brown hair and a thin face. But he looked enough like a long-dead corporal Sebastian had once known that he'd been struck by the resemblance when he'd passed the man earlier reading a playbill outside Covent Garden Theater.

Now walking at a moderate pace, Sebastian turned off Bedford Street into the lane that housed the bank of Miss Jane Austen's brother, Henry.

The green-coated man fell in behind him.

Chapter 15

*S*ebastian continued up the lane, his footfalls echoing in the narrow space, the wind cool against his face. A gentleman's carriage flashed past, its swaying lanterns throwing arcs of light across the looming facades of the surrounding buildings.

He was aware of the green-coated man staying some paces behind him. A young woman lingering in a nearby darkened doorway sidled up to pluck at Sebastian's sleeve. She was flaxen haired and winsome and looked as if she had only recently arrived in London from the countryside. In her eyes lurked a shadow of desperation that was painful to see.

"Lookin' fer fun, gov'nor?" she whined. "I'm willin'. Anythin' ye wants. Anythin'."

Sebastian shook his head and kept walking. He noticed she took one step toward the man who followed him and then backed away.

The lane emptied out into the southwestern corner of the vast open square that was home to Covent Garden Market. At this hour, the market stalls were shuttered and deserted except for the homeless children who sheltered here at night, their faces pale in the dim lamplight, eyes wide beneath matted hair as they watched Sebastian stride past. He picked up his pace.

His shadow did the same.

Sebastian slipped one hand into his pocket and found the smooth wooden grip of the flintlock. He'd almost reached the arched entrance to Tavistock Court when he swung about abruptly. "Who the devil are you and why have you been following me?" he demanded.

Startled, the green-coated man drew up so fast his feet slipped in the muck left from that morning's market. For one moment his light brown eyes met Sebastian's. Then he turned and ran.

Sebastian pelted after him.

They raced down Tavistock Row and skidded around the corner into Southampton Street. The man was nimble and fleet-footed, leaping over a stack of bricks and dodging a donkey cart as he darted across the street. A girl of no more than twelve dressed in a tawdry cut-down gown melted from a darkened doorway to croon, "Gov'nor . . ."

Green Coat grasped her by the shoulders and spun her around to fling her into Sebastian.

"Oye, what ye doin' to me?" she wailed, then let out a frightened cry as she smacked into Sebastian. He lost precious seconds, first in steadying her, then in retrieving his purse from her quick, opportunistic fingers. He disentangled himself barely in time to see Green Coat disappear down Maiden Lane.

Bloody hell.

Sebastian tore around the corner after him and then drew up at the sight of the street stretching empty before him. He could see a dog nosing a pile of offal near the corner and a pig doing the same farther down the block. The rising wind banged a loose shutter overhead and flapped the tattered laundry left hanging on a line stretched from one window to the next. Sebastian stood very still, listening for the sound of running feet, his gaze drifting over the rows of dilapidated old houses rising from the footpaths on either side.

Nothing.

Once long ago, Maiden Lane had been a simple path running along the southern edge of the ancient convent garden that once stood here. In their prime, the houses built here after the Dissolution had been respectable. But now they were falling down, their once graceful gardens vanished beneath a warren of ramshackle hovels infilled behind them a century or more ago.

Pistol in hand, Sebastian's gaze shifted to the black mouth of a noisome, rubbish-strewn passage that opened up to his left. Beyond it stretched a labyrinth of foul courts and wretched alleys that twisted between here and the Strand. A rat-infested refuge for whores and beggars, pickpockets and cutthroats, it had been known to simply swallow constables unwise enough to venture in after fleeing suspects.

A year ago Sebastian would have charged in there without hesitation. He even took one step, two, toward the beckoning shadows before drawing up short.

Then he sucked in a deep, shuddering breath, turned, and went home to his wife and infant son.

🌿

"Who would set someone to follow you?" asked Hero.

Sebastian had arrived at Brook Street to find her walking back and forth across the nursery floor, a fussy, drooling, miserable Simon in her arms. The babe's nursemaid, a Frenchwoman named Claire, was grabbing a few hours' rest in anticipation of what was expected to be a long night.

Sebastian stood with his shoulders pressed against one wall, his gaze on his son's chapped, tearstained face. "If I had to guess, I'd say the lovely Bligh sisters from Number Three."

Hero glanced over at him. "Why would they want to follow you? To kill you?"

"It seems a somewhat radical response, but it's certainly possible."

He watched Simon scrunch up his face and howl. "Are you certain there's not something else wrong with him? Surely babies don't always fret like this when they get their first teeth?"

"My mother tells me her two did. And Claire says the same." Hero caught the rubber teething ring as it tumbled from Simon's grasp and tried to interest him in it again. "You think Benji was lured to Number Three and murdered there?"

"Frankly, I wouldn't put anything past that lot. Then again, the 'gentleman' in the cart could easily have been Kneebone. He claims he was home alone in his bed that night, but from the sounds of things that's unusual for him."

"And Ashworth?"

"Ashworth says he was with Amanda and Stephanie until two o'clock that morning, which is about as solid an alibi as he could have."

"If it's true."

"If it's true. I can find out easily enough tomorrow when I see Amanda." He walked over to stand at the nursery window and stare out over the darkened rooftops and chimneys of the city. After a moment, he said, "I feel as if I'm floundering—flailing blindly. Normally I look for clues to a murder in the events of the victim's life and in the lives of the people he knew. But what if Benji was simply snatched off the street at random? The killers could be anyone out there—anyone at all. And when I think about what is in all likelihood being done to Benji's little sister right now, I want to put my fist through this window. I feel as if I ought to be out there doing something to find her—to *save* her. But I don't even know where to begin."

Hero came to stand beside him, Simon clasped in her arms. "You think these killers could have taken other street children in the past?"

"Jem Jones seems to think so." He reached out to lift Simon from her and hold the fussing child close. "But how would we ever know?"

"What a troublesome thought." She straightened the drooling bib around Simon's neck and then shifted her gaze to stare as Sebastian had done at the wind-tossed streets below. "I'm considering writing my next article on the children who are left to fend for themselves when their mothers are transported to Botany Bay. I wonder if this Reverend Filby you mentioned would be willing to speak to me."

"I should think so. You could also talk to Tom. Given the nature of this murder, I'm half-tempted to use Giles for the next few days, rather than the boy."

"Tom wouldn't like that."

"No, he wouldn't."

Simon started crying again, and Sebastian bounced the babe up and down in his arms. "Poor little man," he said softly. Then without looking up he said, "I went to see Kat tonight, to ask her about Kneebone."

"You say that as if you fear it might upset me."

He met her gaze then, and she smiled. "It doesn't, you know. She's Hendon's natural daughter. Even if he can't acknowledge her, she'll always be a part of our family and a part of our lives. And I have no doubts about the depth of your love for me."

He shifted Simon's weight so he could reach out one hand and cup her cheek. "I can't imagine my life without you and Simon in it."

"I know," she said—

Just as Simon spit up down the front of Sebastian's white silk waistcoat, and they both laughed.

*

Some hours later, Hero came to stand at the entrance to the darkened library. The faint reddish glow of the dying fire showed her the sleeping cat curled up on the sofa and the man who stood nearby staring thoughtfully at something he held in his hands.

She said, "Is there a reason you're lurking here in the dark? With a hat?"

Devlin balanced the hat on one finger and sent it into a spin. "Tell me: What do you see?"

Hero wrinkled her nose. "A very dirty and doubtless lice-ridden piece of headgear."

"Not something a gentleman would wear, is it?"

"Not unless he has a habit of buying disguises at the secondhand clothing stalls of Rosemary Lane."

"Huh. That's one possibility I hadn't considered. But given that the man Rory Inchbald saw driving the cart made no similar attempts at disguise, I'm willing to bet the youth digging Benji's grave was simply wearing his own clothes."

"In other words, he was no gentleman." She came to sit beside the black cat, who looked at her through slitted green eyes and then pretended to go back to sleep. "Of course, just because Rory thought the man in the cart was a gentleman doesn't mean he actually is one."

"True. Except that according to Jem Jones, Benji and Sybil aren't the first children to disappear in Clerkenwell, and word on the streets says 'a gentleman' is responsible."

"Word on the streets is often wrong."

"Yes. Although given that it reinforces Rory's claim, I'm inclined to believe it's true."

The cat began to quietly purr, and she reached out to pet him. "So exactly what are you saying?"

Devlin tossed the hat aside. "Ever since this morning, I've been working on the disturbing assumption I'm looking for two killers: the man driving the cart plus his more youthful companion. But I think that's wrong. I think there's only one killer—the 'gentleman' Rory saw waiting in the cart. I think the boy digging the grave is simply his servant."

"A servant? But . . . who trusts a servant enough to involve him in murder? And then drives off and abandons him? If the boy had been caught—"

"If the boy had been caught and then named someone such as Hector Kneebone or Lord Ashworth, who do you think would have believed him?"

"No one," she conceded. The cat lifted his head, and she obliged by shifting to scratch beneath his chin. "It's certainly less unsettling to think you're looking for only one killer rather than two. And yet what sort of servant agrees to help bury his master's murder victims?"

"Either one who is as depraved as his employer or . . ."

She looked up. "Or?"

"One who is very afraid."

Chapter 16

"You obviously made too much noise," said the gentleman, his eyes narrowed and dark beneath the brim of his fashionable top hat. "This is all your fault. You realize that, don't you?"

The boy felt a spasm of panic that came dangerously close to loosening his bowels. "I didn't know that one-legged cove was there!"

"You should have."

When the boy remained silent, the gentleman said, "You're certain nothing incriminating was left behind?"

"Incra—what?"

The gentleman expelled a harsh breath of exasperation. "Anything that might tell the authorities who you are."

"Oh; no, sir. Nothing!" the boy said quickly. Too quickly. He had actually dropped both the shovel and his hat, but he had no intention of telling the gentleman that. Besides, it was just an ordinary shovel. And an old hat.

The gentleman said, "You're certain?"

"Yes, sir."

"You went back to check?"

The boy hung his head.

"My God. I'm dealing with a fool."

"I can go back tomorrow."

"Tomorrow? And what would be the use of that? If you did leave any evidence, it's been discovered already."

The boy was crying now, sniveling like a small child. He scrubbed at his wet cheeks with a balled-up fist. "I didn't leave nothing!"

His aristocratic features pinched with revulsion, the gentleman turned away. "Let us hope."

Chapter 17

Shortly before midnight, with the house in Berkeley Square quiet around him, Jarvis received Major Edward Burnside's report on Sinclair Pugh.

After the major had gone, Jarvis remained seated at his desk in the library, the fingers of one hand tapping on the intricately enameled cover of his snuffbox, his thoughts turning over all he had been told.

He was still faintly smiling when the door opened and his wife's young cousin, Mrs. Victoria Hart-Davis, entered the room. She carried a small volume bound in blue leather in one hand and drew up in surprise at the sight of him.

"Oh, my lord; I do beg your pardon. I didn't mean to disturb you. I only came to exchange my book for another."

She would have turned away, but he pushed up to come around from behind his desk, saying, "Please; don't go. I'm delighted to know you've been making use of my library. What have you been reading?"

"The first volume of Euripides's plays. I thought I might begin the second."

Jarvis was aware of a flicker of interest. The edition she had selected was not a translation. He said, "You read ancient Greek?"

She had a way of smiling with her eyes that made a man think of clear blue skies and bluebells blooming beside a mountain stream. "Not as well as I'd like, but I can stumble through it. My father taught me." She hesitated, then said, "Have you received new dispatches from Spain?"

"What? Oh, no. Merely a report on a very foolish man who thinks he can stand in the way of history."

"Sounds like someone who needs to be removed."

"I'm working on it," said Jarvis, and was delighted to see a leap of understanding mingled with amusement in the depths of those deceptively soft blue eyes.

Chapter 18

*T*he following morning, Sebastian sent word to the stables to have Giles bring around his curricle. But when he walked out of the house some minutes later, it was to find Tom waiting with the curricle and pair at the kerb.

"I was under the impression I had asked that Giles be the one to bring the curricle around today," said Sebastian, leaping up into the high seat.

"Did ye? I reckon we didn't know that." Tom swallowed hard and stared straight ahead. "Is yer lordship peeved at me fer somethin'?"

"No. It's just—" Sebastian broke off as he thought about trying to explain his reasons to the boy. "Never mind."

He was gathering the reins when a gentlewoman's barouche and team of blood bays swept around the corner and drew up facing them.

"That looks like Lady Wilcox's rig," said Tom, eying the crest emblazoned on the barouche's panel.

"And so it is." Sebastian handed the reins to Tom and hopped down again. "I suspect I shan't be long."

Her ladyship's liveried footman was still scrambling to let down the steps when Sebastian walked up to the carriage. "Dear Amanda," he said as his tall, golden-haired sister appeared in the open doorway.

Amanda, Lady Wilcox, was Hendon's firstborn child, twelve years Sebastian's senior and a widow now for two and a half years. She had inherited their errant mother's slim build and graceful carriage, along with Hendon's somewhat heavy facial features. Her nasty disposition was all her own.

"To what do we owe this pleasure?" Sebastian asked, extending his hand to help her alight.

She acknowledged neither his hand nor his greeting, but simply swept past him and up the short flight of steps to where Morey was already opening the front door with a bow.

She managed to contain her fury while Sebastian followed her into the library, but he was still closing the paneled door when she exploded. "Are you doing this out of spite? Or have you finally gone absolutely stark raving mad?"

The big, long-haired black cat that had been sleeping on the hearth sat up with a startled yowl.

"You've frightened Mr. Darcy," said Sebastian.

"Whom?"

"The cat."

Amanda frowned at the hearth. "I hate cats."

"Of course you do." He finished closing the door and turned to face her. "As to your question, I've recently come to the conclusion all of us are at least slightly mad, each in our own way. But why do you ask?"

"Don't play the fool with me. As if it weren't embarrassing enough, the way you've been skulking about London for the better part of three years now, investigating murders like some common, grubby little Bow Street Runner. But this time! This time, you've gone too far."

He studied her tight, angry face. "May I offer you some tea? Or would you prefer something stronger? It is a little early for brandy, but perhaps a glass of—"

"I am not here to drink tea." She yanked off first one glove, then the other. "What could you possibly be thinking? For the love of God! To accuse Viscount Ashworth of all people—*the son and heir of the Marquis of Lindley*—of murder? Murder!"

"Don't forget I also accused him of torture and sodomy. Or did he leave that part out?"

Two ugly white lines appeared to bracket her thinned lips. "No, he did not."

Sebastian went to lean his hips against his desk, his arms crossed at his chest. "How can you be so certain Ashworth isn't guilty?"

"Don't be ridiculous. He was with Stephanie and me last Sunday night until well past two—as he told you."

"So he did." Sebastian let his hands fall to his sides again. "Ashworth may be innocent of this, Amanda, but he will not make Stephanie a good husband. I've seen him drop ten thousand pounds in one night at the gaming tables and beat a man who looked at him wrong half to death with his walking stick. But what disturbs me more than anything is the discovery that he likes to frequent a nasty little establishment in Pickering Place where wealthy, dissolute men can pay to whip and otherwise abuse young girls and boys—some no more than children."

Amanda stood with her gloves clenched in one fist, her spine painfully straight and her head thrown back. "I don't believe you."

He pushed away from the desk. "Believe it, Amanda. You can't let Stephanie marry him."

"Why are you doing this? Are you driven by envy? Is that it? Does the thought that my grandson will someday outrank you fester your soul and curdle your blood?"

He couldn't quite stop himself from laughing out loud. "Oh, Amanda; not everyone is like you."

Her face had turned blotchy now, cold white patches mixing with splotches of purple rage. "I could destroy you," she said, her jaw held so tight she was practically spitting out the words. "I may not be able to prevent you from becoming the Earl of Hendon, but I could make certain the entire world knows that exalted position will not be yours by right."

Sebastian found he'd lost all desire to laugh. "Tread carefully, Sister; truth is a dangerous weapon that more than one can wield. Or have you forgotten why Bayard and Stephanie's father died?"

She drew in her breath with a hiss. "You would do that?"

"No. But Hendon would. And we both know it."

For one glacial moment, half brother and sister stared at each other.

Then Sebastian said, "Speaking of Bayard, where was my decidedly troubled nephew last Monday morning at, say, half past one? Do you know?"

She strode past him to the library door. "I will not stay and listen to this nonsense."

"Where was he, Amanda?"

She jerked open the door, then paused to look back at him, her chest heaving with the agitation of her breathing. "As it happens, Bayard is visiting the Highlands with friends—and has been these past two weeks and more. You may ask Hendon if you don't believe me."

"That must be a relief for you. Now you need only worry about your future son-in-law."

"I hope you burn in hell for all eternity."

And with that she whisked herself from the room and slammed the door behind her.

Sebastian glanced over at the black cat that now sat regarding him with unblinking green eyes. "Somehow, I suspect that's not precisely the effect Hendon had in mind when he asked me to speak to Amanda," he told the cat. "Perhaps I should have tried a different approach. What do you think?"

But the cat simply yawned, arched into a stretch, and lay down again.

❧

"What we doin' back 'ere?" asked Tom as Sebastian reined in beside the broken wall that surrounded the shot factory.

Sebastian handed the boy the reins. "I want to take another look around—and perhaps talk to that one-legged soldier again while I'm at it."

Tom sniffed. "Oh."

Hiding a smile, Sebastian dropped lightly to the ground.

The smile faded as his gaze drifted over the ruined, ivy-draped buildings and nettle-choked wasteland that had come close to being Benji Thatcher's final resting place. And he found himself thinking, *Why here?* Why out of all the shadowy copses and deserted fields on the outskirts of London had Benji's killer chosen to bury him here?

Conscious of a trio of silent crows watching him from atop the shot tower, Sebastian picked his way across the uneven ground. The day was becoming increasingly overcast, with a brisk wind out of the northeast that swayed the high weeds and flapped a loose shutter somewhere in the distance.

He found the place where the young servant of Benji's killer had dug his grave, but in the last twenty-four hours someone had filled it in again and carried away the shovel. All that remained was a suggestive rectangle of mounded bare earth that would soon flatten and disappear beneath a tangle of knotweed and thistle.

Sebastian kept walking, toward the tumbledown brick warehouse where he'd first seen Rory Inchbald. He'd almost reached the gaping doorway when a skinny, ragged boy who looked maybe thirteen or fourteen appeared in the opening. At the sight of Sebastian, the lad faltered for an instant, face slack with surprise. Then he took off running.

Chapter 19

$\mathcal{S}$ebastian snagged the boy's elbow as he passed, spinning him around to grasp him by both arms.

"Let me go!" The boy twisted this way and that, yanking against Sebastian's hold and kicking out with badly shod feet.

"Ouch. Bloody hell," said Sebastian when one kick caught his shin. "Stop that. I have no intention of letting you go even if it means I must sit on you. But I warn you, Calhoun will not be happy if you force me to get grass stains on my breeches."

That startled the boy enough that he quit struggling, a lock of hair falling into his eyes as he stared blankly at Sebastian. "Calhoun? Who's Calhoun?"

"My valet."

The boy shook his head, not understanding. "Who are you? And what do you want with me?"

"My name is Devlin, and I simply want to ask you some questions. Why were you running from me?"

"How'm I to know you just want to talk? Maybe you want to do to me what was done to Benji."

"Rest assured, I do not. What's your name?"

"Toby." The boy drew in a quick gasp of air. "Toby Dancing."

"The one they call the Dancer?"

Toby the Dancer nodded, eyes wide with apprehension.

On closer inspection, the boy appeared older, probably more like fifteen or sixteen. He was a good-looking lad, with rich, tawny hair, well-formed features, and large, luminous green eyes alight with a wily kind of intelligence. Sebastian said, "If I let you go, do you promise not to run?"

The boy nodded again. Sebastian let him go, although he was ready to catch the lad again if he tried to bolt. He did not.

"What are you doing here?" Sebastian asked.

Toby swiped the sleeve of one arm across his sweaty forehead. "I heard this is where they found Benji. So I've been looking around, thinking maybe I might come across something to tell me what happened to Sybil."

"And did you find anything?"

The boy shook his head.

Sebastian said, "I understand you were with Benji last Friday evening, down in Hockley-in-the-Hole."

"Wh—who told you that?"

"I don't recall precisely," lied Sebastian. "Is it true?"

Toby started to shake his head again, then changed his mind and gave a quick, frightened nod.

Sebastian said, "What time was this?"

The boy tugged at the kerchief knotted around his neck as if it suddenly felt too tight. "Musta been about five, maybe? We were gonna go out to Sadler's Wells, to try and sneak in and watch the show. You ever seen it?"

"Unfortunately, no."

"You should. It's ever so grand, with boats and horses and whatnot. But the thing is, you see, Benji, he says he's got this job he's gotta do first, so he lopes off, saying he's gonna meet me out there. Only, he never shows up."

"What time was he supposed to meet you?" asked Sebastian, his voice so sharp the boy took a step back in alarm.

"When it got dark."

"What did he tell you about this 'job' he had to do?"

"He didn't tell me nothing."

Sebastian studied the boy's even features. "When you saw Benji in Hockley-in-the-Hole, was his sister with him?"

"Sybil? No, sir. Why?"

"She's still missing, isn't she?"

"Why else you think I'm looking for her?"

"Would she have gone with Benji to this job?"

"Maybe. I dunno."

"And what sort of 'job' is it likely we're talking about?"

"Could've been most anything, I guess."

"Did he tell you anything about the person who was hiring him?"

"No, sir." A new spasm of panic flared in the boy's eyes. "You won't say nothing to anybody about what I told you, will you?"

"Why? What are you afraid of?"

"What if whoever killed Benji thinks I know who he is and comes after me?"

"Do you know who he is?"

"No!"

Sebastian wasn't convinced the boy was being entirely truthful, but he let it go. "Who do you think killed Benji?"

The boy started to sidle away. "I don't know! How would I know?"

Sebastian put a hand on his arm, stopping him. "Do you know any other street children who have disappeared from around here in the past?"

Toby stared at him. "Lads come and go hereabouts all the time. But I ain't never heard of nothing like what happened to Benji."

"What about a boy named Mick Swallow? I'm told he disappeared last year."

"I didn't know Mick real good."

Sebastian glanced at the silent warehouse beside them. "There's a one-legged soldier who typically sleeps here. Have you seen him?"

"Today? No, sir. He's probably out begging."

"Do you know if Benji was acquainted with a gentleman?"

The shift in topic appeared to take the boy by surprise. "A gentleman?"

"That's right."

"Well . . . he did hang 'round the Reverend Filby more'n most, and he's a gentleman, ain't he?"

"He is indeed. Anyone else?"

The Dancer screwed up his face in thought. "I suppose the Professor was a gentleman, once. But he ain't no more."

"The Professor?"

"His real handle's Icarus Cantrell, but everybody calls him the Professor, on account of the shop he keeps over by St. John's Gate."

"What sort of shop are we talking about?"

"It's called the Professor's Attic. He sells all sorts of stuff in there. You know—pocket watches and handkerchiefs and such."

"In other words, he was Benji's fence."

Toby sucked in another of those quick, frightened breaths. "I didn't say that."

"No, you didn't. What about Mick Swallow? Was Icarus Cantrell his fence too?

Rather than answer, the Dancer yanked his arm from Sebastian's grasp and took off running across the rubbish-strewn field.

This time, Sebastian let him go.

❦

The secondhand shop known as the Professor's Attic occupied the ground floor of an old, two-story sandstone house built up against an ancient stone gateway. Once the gateway had led to the vanished community of the Knights Hospitaller of St. John of Jerusalem, but most of that vast, sprawling monastery had disappeared long ago.

An aged, bandy-legged fellow sat perched on a stool just inside the shop's open front door, knitting what looked like a woolen scarf by the fitful sunlight streaming in. He wore a suit of maroon velvet that must have been the height of fashion when it was made sometime in the previous century. A cascade of Brussels lace of the same vintage tumbled down the front of his shirt, more lace frothed at his cuffs, and he had a powdered wig perched like a nightcap atop his head.

He looked up when Sebastian stepped into the crowded, low-ceilinged shop, but his clicking needles never missed a beat. "Lost your way, have you?"

Sebastian let his gaze drift over the shop's strange medley of merchandise, everything from massive pieces of dark Tudor furniture to delicate Sevres plates and a clutch of dusty old peacock feathers. "I don't believe so. Are you Icarus Cantrell?"

The old man peered at him over the tops of gold-rimmed spectacles he wore perched on the end of his nose. "And what would the likes of you be wanting with the likes of me?" In age, he could have been anywhere between fifty-five and seventy-five. His face was weathered dark by obviously prolonged exposure to a hot sun, but his diction was as clear and precise as that of any Oxford don.

Sebastian said, "I understand you were Benji Thatcher's fence."

"His fence?" The old man gave a pained sigh. "I fear it's one of the hazards of running an establishment of this nature: People always assume you come by your merchandise illegally. As it happens, I do not."

Sebastian removed a card from his pocket and laid it atop the beautifully carved Renaissance chest at the man's elbow. "To be clear, I'm not concerned with the legality of your merchandise. I'm here because I intend to find whoever killed Benji Thatcher and probably his sister, too. I give you my word as a gentleman that anything you tell me will go no farther."

Cantrell glanced at the card and kept knitting. "Huh. Didn't think you had much the look of a Bow Street Runner."

"Thank you."

The man's lips quirked into a smile that quickly faded. "Unfortunately, I don't know what happened to Benji, so I'm afraid you're wasting your time with me."

Sebastian wandered the overstuffed shop, taking in the piles of rusting firedogs, the glass case jammed with snuffboxes, watches, delicate bracelets, and old-fashioned brooches. Through a low door at the rear he could see another room that looked like a small kitchen, with a narrow, steep staircase that led up to the floor above. "But you did know him."

"It would be folly for me to claim I did not, given that he has no doubt been seen coming in and out the premises on more than one occasion."

"Selling things he stole?"

"Selling things he *found*."

"Or so he claimed."

The old man shrugged and kept knitting. "I always ask. And I keep meticulous records and pay a fair price for what I buy. That's all the law requires."

Sebastian said, "When was the last time you saw Benji?"

The Professor looked thoughtful. "Couldn't say precisely. Must have been last week sometime—Wednesday or Thursday, perhaps? He brought me a lovely silk handkerchief he chanced to find lying in St. James's churchyard."

Sebastian paused beside a display of neatly laundered silk handkerchiefs in a variety of sizes and colors, each with any identifying marks carefully removed. "You have quite a collection for sale."

"Yes; we do a brisk trade in them. Seems people are always dropping their pocket handkerchiefs."

Sebastian continued his perambulations of the shop. "Who do you think killed Benji?"

"I've not the slightest idea."

"No? Did you know that whoever killed the boy held him for more than two days before strangling him? And that during that time, Benji was tortured with a whip and small knife as well as repeatedly raped?"

Sebastian turned to look back at the old man. "Who do you think would do something like that?"

The Professor's needles had stilled. "You don't want to know who I suspect did it."

"Why wouldn't I want to know?"

He folded his knitting with hands that were no longer steady and set it aside. "What if I told you the man you seek is a cousin of the King? Would you still want to know his name?"

Sebastian met the old man's dark, intense gaze. "Yes."

"You think so? And if I told you he's likewise cousin to Lord Jarvis— and by extension to your lady wife? Still interested?"

Sebastian kept his gaze on the old man's face. "Whom are we talking about?"

"Sir Francis Rowe."

Sebastian was acutely aware of the shop's collection of case and mantel clocks, all ticking at once. The Royal House of Hanover had a number of bastard branches. Most were unacknowledged, but some were. Sir Francis Rowe was one of the privileged few who were not only acknowledged but—thanks in no small part to his extreme personal wealth—actively courted.

Sir Francis's wealth came from his father, a once minor Highland baronet who had remained loyal to the House of Hanover and thus benefited handsomely from the confiscations and grand-scale thefts that followed the Jacobite defeat at Culloden. He had also benefited from his marriage to Maria Cumberland, the illegitimate daughter of the Butcher of Culloden himself: Prince William Augustus, Duke of Cumberland and third son of King George II. Sebastian did some quick calculations and figured Sir Francis's mother and the current King were first cousins. He was a bit hazier on Rowe's exact relationship to Jarvis and Hero, but there was no doubt it existed.

"I take it you know him?" said Cantrell, watching Sebastian with unblinking dark eyes.

"Not well."

"In that, you are fortunate." The Professor slid off his stool. "Did you hear about the boy Rowe caught trying to steal his pocket handkerchief on the Strand last month? Broke the child's neck the way you or I might snap a length of kindling. The lad was barely six years old. And in case you might be thinking it an accident, let me hasten to assure you that it was not. Rowe deliberately killed him, then simply tossed the child's body aside like so much rubbish."

Sebastian said, "There's a world of difference between killing a young thief in a fit of rage—as reprehensible as that may be—and what was done to Benji Thatcher."

"One was undoubtedly quicker. But then, it only involved a pocket handkerchief."

Sebastian studied the old man's hooded eyes. "What is it you're not telling me?"

"Someone recently relieved Sir Francis Rowe of his favorite snuffbox— a pretty little gold trinket with a miniature by Fragonard set beneath a domed crystal lid. Word is he vowed to catch the young thief responsible and make him rue the day he was born."

"You're suggesting that thief was Benji?"

The Professor blinked. "How would I know?"

Sebastian suspected the old man knew exactly who had stolen the royal cousin's painted snuffbox. He said, "I've never heard Rowe accused of an interest in boys."

"You think that's significant?" The weary lines on the Professor's face crumpled in a way that made him look much closer to seventy than fifty. "You and I both know that for a certain kind of man, rape is just another way to punish and control those they hate. And men like Sir Francis Rowe hate the world."

Chapter 20

$\mathcal{B}$efore Sebastian left Clerkenwell, he tracked down Mott Gowan again and asked the constable to make inquiries around Hockley-in-the-Hole on the off chance someone else had seen the boy there on Friday evening.

"For all we know he could have been snatched not long after you saw him," said Sebastian. "And I suspect you'll get more cooperation out of the locals than I would."

The constable nodded. "I'll look into it right away, my lord."

"You might also ask if they noticed anyone unfamiliar hanging around at the same time. Presumably someone dressed as a gentleman."

"Aye, my lord." Gowan scrubbed a hand across his lower face. His eyes were bloodshot. "Still no sign of what's happened to Sybil, my lord?"

"Nothing. I'm sorry."

The constable shook his big, rawboned head. "The poor wee lass. It's troublesome, it is, thinking about what she might be going through."

"Perhaps we'll get lucky and someone will remember having seen something," said Sebastian, although he doubted it.

He returned then to Clerkenwell Green, where he'd left Tom waiting with the curricle. "Go ahead and take the chestnuts home," said Sebastian. "I need to walk."

The tiger's features went slack with horror. *"Walk?"*

"Walk," said Sebastian, slapping the near gelding's rump. "Off you go, then."

He wandered the streets of the city, gradually winding his way westward, his troubled thoughts on the past. Any man who has ever gone to war understands only too well the worst of what his fellow men are capable. Rape, sodomy, murder, torture, mutilation, senseless destruction—Sebastian had seen it all. He'd watched men—comrades he thought he knew and respected—laughingly slice the ears off their dead enemies to make bloody necklaces. He'd ridden through villages where passing soldiers—he'd learned quickly it made little difference whether they were British, French, or Spanish—had slaughtered every living thing, from the sheep and cattle in the fields to aged grandmothers and the tiniest babes in arms. It had come to him eventually that such things were not aberrations; nor were they, as most would like to believe, "inhuman." He'd reached the conclusion that this capacity for barbarity actually forms a fundamental and inescapable part of whatever it means to be human, however much we might want to deny it—and however much we might want to deny those instincts within ourselves. Nor was he so delusional as to except himself: Hadn't he once, somewhere in the mountains of Portugal, beaten a French major to death with his own bare hands in a bloody blur of vengeful rage?

Yet Sebastian knew too that war has a way of bringing out the worst in some men, just as it could bring out the best in others. Normally, in the course of their daily lives, most kept such savage impulses so deeply buried as to remain unrecognized and unacknowledged. So what had driven the monster who brutalized Benji Thatcher? Anger over the loss of a favorite snuffbox? Was that really all it could take?

Looking up, Sebastian realized he'd reached St. James's Street. But he still had no answer to his troubling questions.

He found Sir Francis Rowe perusing the daily papers in the reading room of White's.

"Good afternoon," said Sebastian, pausing beside him. "Mind if I join you?"

Sir Francis looked up, eyebrows arching with the merest hint of the surprise he was too well-bred to otherwise betray. "Of course not."

He was perhaps thirty-four or thirty-five years of age, although he looked older thanks to the straight, light brown hair that was already receding rapidly from his high forehead. He was known as a natty dresser, without carrying the tendency far enough to be considered a dandy. His kinship to the Prince Regent could be easily traced in the long nose, protuberant lips, and thick Hanoverian build he had inherited from his infamous royal grandfather. He also shared with his princely cousin a similar faintly contemptuous and smirking smile.

"I was just hearing an interesting story about you," said Sebastian, settling into a nearby chair.

"Oh?" Rowe lowered his paper but did not fold it or set it aside.

"About how you summarily dispatched a young thief caught trying to pick your pocket last month. 'Snapped his neck like a stick of kindling' is the way it was described to me."

One of the Baronet's eyebrows arched even higher. "You say that as if you find my actions disturbing."

"I'm told the child was six years old."

"Something like that."

"It is generally considered customary to summon the constables in such situations."

"So I saved the Crown the cost of a hanging." Rowe gave a dismissive shrug. "Both the coroner and the jury at the decidedly tiresome inquest I was required to attend commended my actions. Perhaps if more gentlemen responded thus we'd be plagued with less theft. Certainly with fewer thieves, hmmm?"

"I also heard you've recently lost a favorite snuffbox."

The Baronet's vague smile tightened. "Not precisely. 'Lost' implies a certain negligence on my part. In point of fact, the snuffbox was stolen."

"In Clerkenwell?"

"Mmm. I had reason to attend the Sessions House, which is how I came to be on the green. Believe me, I sincerely regret not simply dispatching my secretary in my place. Why do you ask?"

"A young pickpocket was recently found murdered in Clerkenwell."

"And you're suggesting what, precisely? I haven't made it my personal mission to clear the streets of thieves, if that's what you're implying. Most of us have better things to do with our time than concern ourselves with activities best left to those officials we pay to deal with such unpleasantness." He hesitated a moment, then added, "Don't tell me you've now sunk to investigating random murders amongst the city's unwashed rabble? That will keep you busy. I fear the death houses are overflowing with the noisome wretches."

Sebastian said, "Where were you last Friday evening between five and seven?"

Sir Francis gave a halfhearted huff of amusement. "You can't be serious."

"I am, actually. Very."

"Good God. Are you accusing me of killing this nasty urchin you've become obsessed with?" At that, Rowe threw back his head and laughed out loud.

Sebastian waited until the Baronet's mirth had subsided. Then he said, "So where were you?"

A muscle jumped along Rowe's jowl. He was obviously no longer amused. "I see no reason to indulge this ridiculous conversation any further." The Baronet gave his newspaper an ostentatious shake and raised it to cover his face. "Now, if you will excuse me?"

"What about early Monday morning at half past one? Where were you then?"

The Baronet's fingers spasmed, once, at the edges of his paper. But he didn't lower it and he made no response.

For one long moment, Sebastian stayed where he was, his gaze on the arrogant, complacent man before him.

After the last Scottish uprising, the proud citizens of London had erected a grand equestrian statue of this man's infamous grandfather in Cavendish Square. Serenely untroubled by the methods Cumberland had used to suppress their rebellious northern neighbors, they even nicknamed him "Sweet William." It was the Scots who dubbed the Duke "the Butcher of Culloden." After Culloden, Cumberland ordered his soldiers to give no quarter to the Highlanders lying wounded on the battlefield or attempting to surrender, while what was done to the people of the area would forever remain a dark stain on England's soul. Untold numbers of women and children were herded into churches and crofts to be burned alive, with the survivors sent by the tens of thousands to the Colonies as slaves. So thorough was Cumberland's desecration of the region that he afterward bragged that a man riding through the Highlands could now go for days without seeing an unburned village or a living soul.

Sebastian pushed to his feet. There was no denying that war brought out the worst in some men, and Sebastian had never believed in attributing the sins of the fathers to their sons. But it was also true that a raging temper and a capacity for violence and cruelty could be inherited as easily as blue eyes or a tendency toward corpulence.

Which was a disturbing thought for a man to whom the identity of his own father remained a dark and troubling mystery.

Chapter 21

Shortly after midday, Hero ordered her carriage brought round and set out for the church of St. James's, Clerkenwell.

She had sent a message earlier that morning to Reverend Filby, requesting his assistance in arranging interviews with some of the street children of the area. His reply had been both courteous and encouraging, and when he met her at the church's porch he was practically quivering with enthusiasm.

"My dear Lady Devlin," he said, bowing low. "I can't tell you what an honor this is. A great honor! I have followed your series of articles on the city's poor with tremendous interest. It's a fine thing you're proposing to do, drawing attention to the plight of the children left behind when their mothers are transported. A very fine thing."

"Thank you," said Hero. "Are the two children who agreed to speak with me this afternoon here?"

"Yes, yes; they're waiting in the churchyard. And if your ladyship should wish it, I can arrange for others to come tomorrow or later in the week."

"That would be excellent, thank you." They turned to walk toward the churchyard. "Have you many such children in the area?"

Reverend Filby nodded sadly. "Dozens, I'm afraid. In addition to our own three prisons, we are so very close to Newgate. The mothers are generally allowed to keep their children with them in prison, you know. But when the women are sent to the ships, the little ones are simply turned into the streets. How the governors of the prisons can live with themselves, I do not know."

"It might be interesting to ask them that question."

The reverend gave a nervous laugh and looked away, toward the base of the churchyard where the two children waited. One, a ragged, incredibly grubby boy, was chasing a butterfly through the weathered tombstones. But the girl simply sat with her hands clasped in her lap, her gaze fixed on something in the distance that only she could see.

❦

The boy was introduced to Hero as Israel Barnes, although he confided after the reverend left that everyone called him Izzy. He was a short but sturdy lad with a plain, snub-nosed face, a surprisingly ready laugh, and hair so dirty and matted it looked like the hide of a dog that'd been dead a year.

He said he thought he was probably thirteen years old and had been on the streets alone since, as he put it, "the year the ole King went daft as a daisy and 'is son took o'er."

Hero was impressed that the lad even knew such an event had occurred.

Izzy laughed. "That's 'cuz me mum took me to see the grand spread 'e put on."

"You mean the fete at Carlton House to celebrate the Prince's elevation to the regency?" The common people had lined up for days afterward for the privilege of traipsing through the palace and gazing in wonder at the remains of their betters' magnificent feast.

"Aye; that were it. Me mum thought it was right peculiar, a son throwing such a bash to celebrate his da being nicked in the nob. I remember it weery well, ye see, because it were the weery next day that she kilt me da."

Hero almost dropped the pencil she was using to take notes. "Your mother was transported for murdering your father?"

"Aye."

Hero was envisioning some poor, abused woman defending herself against a drunken, brutish husband when Izzy said, "'It 'im in the 'ead with a fryin' pan, she did. Come 'ome from the grog shops more'n half-sprung, and there 'e was layin' in bed like 'e 'ad been ever since 'e broke 'is leg and couldn't work, and she said she was tired of 'im eatin' up all the food she brung, so she give 'im a good wallop. Claimed she didn't mean to 'it 'im 'ard enough to kill 'im, but I never believed it. She was always ornery as all get-out when she 'ad the drink in 'er. Reckon the magistrates didn't believe her neither, 'cause they sentenced 'er fer Botany Bay."

Hero studied the ragged boy before her. His shoes were so old that most of his dirty toes poked through the broken leather; his breeches were greasy and ripped; his shirt hung in tatters. From the looks of things, he hadn't bathed in years—if ever. She cleared her throat and consulted the list of questions she'd prepared. "Before your father was hurt, what did he do?"

"'E was a bricklayer, ma'am, till 'e fell off a scaffold. That's what did 'im in." Izzy watched with interest as Hero recorded his answer, then volunteered, "Me mum, now, she was a charwoman."

"And what do you do?"

"Well, when me mum and da was alive, I used t' mainly go out beggin'. I was pretty little then, ye see, and I'd sit on the corner by St. John's Gate and go"—the boy held up cupped hands and pitched his voice into a plaintive whine—"*Kind sir, pity the poor orphan.*" He laughed, then continued in his normal tone. "Only, I lost me corner when we was in Newgate, and the take never was weery good. So now I'm on me own hook fer real, I mainly sticks to fiddlin'."

"Fiddling?"

"Aye. Ye know: 'oldin' 'orses fer the swells and doin' odd jobs. I'm gettin' big enough now I can even tote trunks and such, if they ain't too 'eavy."

"Did you ever go to school?"

"Nah. Never."

"Would you like to go?"

"What fer?"

"To learn to read and write."

The boy laughed. "What'd be the use in that?"

Hero smiled. The boy might be dirty, ignorant, and growing up wild with no care or moral guidance, but there was nothing wrong with his spirit. "So what do you envision yourself doing in ten years?"

"What ye mean?"

"What sort of work would you like to do when you're a man grown?"

The boy rolled his shoulders in a shrug. "I dunno. I get a bit bigger, I reckon I could get on as a navvy, or maybe a bricklayer like me da."

"Would you like that?"

He rolled his shoulders again. "It's more regular than fiddlin'. There's ever so much buildin' goin' on, so I reckon I'd be set—as long as I don't fall and hurt meself like me da."

Or marry a woman with a taste for gin, thought Hero.

Gin, and frying pans.

❧

Hero next interviewed the little girl, whose name was Thisbe Cart-wright. A fey, fragile-looking thing the size of a six-year-old, she said she was ten. She was a painfully serious child, with brown hair and a pale, surprisingly clean face. Her dress was ragged but also clean enough that Hero wondered how she managed it. She said her mother had been transported eighteen months before, for stealing sawney.

"What is 'sawney'?" asked Hero.

The little girl looked surprised. "Don't you know, m'lady? It's bacon."

"Ah. And what happened to your father?"

"I don't know as I ever had one," said the little girl matter-of-factly.

The child's lack of any display of emotion clutched oddly at Hero's throat, and she had to pause a moment before she could go on. "Before your mother was transported, what did she do for a living?"

"She used to sell oranges and such, m'lady. But she was never very good at it. It's why she stole the sawney—to give to the mot of the ken."

Hero recognized that expression from her previous research. "The mot of the ken" was the mistress of a lodging house. Many also served as casual fences, usually for purloined food items. Lodgers who hadn't earned enough from their regular employment to pay for their beds could pay with stolen food.

Hero studied the little girl's thin, solemn face. Her diction was considerably better than that of Izzy Barnes. "Did you ever go to school?"

"No, m'lady. My mama had no way to pay for it. But she taught me to read and write herself, and I still remember it. I practice all the time on playbills and pages of newspapers I find in the streets." She paused, and then in a shy burst of confidence added, "I had a doll once."

"Did you now?" said Hero, forcing a smile even though the little girl's simple pride broke her heart. "What happened to it?"

"Somebody stole it while we were in Newgate."

It was hard to think about this gentle child locked up with her mother in the horrors of Newgate, but before Hero could investigate the topic further, Thisbe added, "The old woman I used to work for gave it to me."

"You were in service?"

"Oh, no, m'lady. It weren't nothing like that. I used to go to her house every Friday night and stay till Saturday night." The little girl gave a wistful half smile. "She used to let me have all the food I could eat and she'd pay me tuppence too. All I had to do was snuff the candles and poke the fire and such. She wouldn't do anything the whole time—even the most ordinary of things. So I did them for her. She called it 'Keeping the Sa-bath.'"

Enlightenment dawned. Hero said, "She was Jewish?"

"Yes, m'lady."

"But you don't go to her anymore?"

"No, m'lady. She died. Now I only sell flowers."

"Oh? Where do you sell them?"

"Usually on Clerkenwell Green."

"And do you make a good living?"

"Some days are better than others. I do best at Christmastime, when I can sell Christmasing. You know—ivy and mistletoe and such. And it's good when the primroses come in too, 'cause it makes people happy to see 'em. They'll say, 'Ah, primroses! Spring must finally be coming.' And then they'll buy a bunch."

"Who taught you to sell flowers?"

That wistful look was back in the child's eyes. "I learnt it from Mary. She was always better at selling than Mama. Mary said it was because Mama didn't grow up selling."

Hero was beginning to suspect that Thisbe's mother had been gently born, before being caught in a disastrous downward slide. "Who is Mary?"

"My big sister." The little girl's lower lip quivered. "I keep hoping she'll come back someday. The reverend, he tells me to pray to the good Lord about it, so I do. But I can tell he don't think she ever will."

"Where did she go?"

"I don't know. She went off one day last spring, saying she was gonna try selling her flowers out by Islington. And then she just . . . disappeared."

"How old is Mary?"

"Fifteen, m'lady."

Hero suspected that in all probability Mary had met and run off with some man, or perhaps realized she could make a better living selling her body than she was making selling primroses. But Hero kept those thoughts to herself.

She became aware of Thisbe watching her with sad, wise eyes. "I know what you're thinking—that Mary went off and left me. But she wouldn't do that. Not Mary. She wouldn't."

The certainty in the little girl's voice was oddly convincing. Hero said, "What do you think happened to your sister?"

"I reckon somebody took her. It happens, you know. Nobody likes to talk about it, but it does. Happens to both girls and boys. They go off one day just like they always do, only nobody ever sees them again. It's like . . ." Thisbe hesitated.

"Like . . . what?" prompted Hero.

Thisbe's chest jerked on a quickly indrawn breath. "It's like the ground just opens up and swallows them." And then she stared off across the churchyard again, a lonely little girl surrounded by the crowded memorials to Clerkenwell's known dead.

Chapter 22

"*I*s Calhoun in?" Sebastian asked when he walked into his Brook Street house some minutes later.

"He is, my lord," said Morey, taking Sebastian's hat and gloves. "Shall I send him to you?"

Sebastian turned toward the library. "Please."

He was reading the entry for Hero's unpleasant cousin in *Debrett's Peerage* when his valet appeared in the doorway with a bow. "You wished to see me, my lord?"

Sebastian set aside the heavy tome and came from behind his desk. "Have you ever heard of a Clerkenwell fence named Icarus Cantrell?"

Most gentlemen's gentlemen would be insulted by such a question. Not Jules Calhoun. The pursuit of murderers could be hard on a gentleman's wardrobe—and on the nerves of his valet. But while Calhoun did at times lament the loss of a favorite hat or coat, he nevertheless managed to take such things as blood, mud, and powder burns in stride. A slim, lithe man in his thirties with a boyish shock of straight, fair hair, the valet was as unfailingly cheerful as he was unflappable. He also knew virtually every cracksman, dollyman, and blacklegs in town, thanks to having been born and raised in one of London's most notorious flash houses.

"You mean the one they call the Professor?" he said.

"So you do know him."

"More by reputation than personally, my lord."

"Tell me about him."

"Well . . . they say he was born the younger son of a Northumbrian squire—even studied up at Cambridge for a time. But whether that is true or not, I couldn't say for certain."

"He does sound the part. How did he come to be running a secondhand shop in Clerkenwell?"

"Word on the streets is he was transported to the Colonies for seven years. I believe he acquired the shop when he returned after the expiration of his sentence."

"He was in Botany Bay?"

Calhoun shook his head. "Georgia, I believe, my lord. It was before the American revolt."

"What was his crime?"

"I've heard it was murder, my lord."

"Good God. Whom did he kill?"

"That I couldn't say, my lord."

"Do you think you could find out?"

Calhoun smiled and executed another of his inimitably graceful bows. "Certainly, my lord."

He was turning away when Sebastian said, "If a man were interested in purchasing licentious books, where would he go?" The collection of books on Hector Kneebone's shelf had given Sebastian an idea. It might be a long shot, but it wasn't as if he had much else to go on at the moment.

Calhoun paused. "There are a number of bookstalls and shops near the Strand that are known to those with such interests, my lord."

"And if said gentleman insisted on nothing but the highest-quality materials, is there one bookseller in particular he would be most likely to frequent?"

"That would be the shop kept by Clarence Rutledge in Holywell Street." Calhoun hesitated, then said, "Is it true what they're saying about the way that boy in Clerkenwell died?"

"I'm afraid it is," said Sebastian. He didn't bother asking how the valet had learned the details of Benji's death, since one of his mother's flash houses was in Clerkenwell. "If you should hear anything that might be helpful, I would be interested to know it."

"I could pay a visit to my mother. She and the Professor go back a ways."

"Given what I saw in his shop, I've no doubt they do," said Sebastian. Calhoun laughed. But he didn't deny it.

Named after a long-vanished sacred well of clean, sweet water, Holywell was a narrow, ancient street that forked off from the Strand before turning to run parallel to it. Most of the day the street lay deep in shadow, thanks to the overhanging upper stories of the decrepit old wooden houses that still lined much of its length. Once this had been an area occupied by silk merchants, Jewish tailors, and shops that supplied costumes and fancy attire to theaters and masquerade-goers. Their establishments still dominated the south side of the street. But in recent years Holywell had become more and more given over to booksellers and the kind of radical publishers who—inspired by the French Revolution—operated secret presses in hidden cellars. And because political tracts didn't sell particularly well, they financed their more serious endeavors with the production and sale of dirty books and prints.

In addition to the bookstalls lining the pavement barrow to barrow, there were also a number of shops. Sebastian found the one he sought in a crumbling old gabled house next to a low tavern called the Dead Dog. The original Elizabethan windows on the house's ground floor had been enlarged at some point, and the dusty glass panes now displayed a selection of bawdy prints—mainly fat naked men who looked suspiciously like the Regent and his brothers chasing nubile young women.

"Looking for anything in particular?" asked the solidly built, middle-aged proprietor when Sebastian stepped into the shop's musty, dusty interior. With his roughly cut, graying brown hair, broad face, and plain clothes, the man looked the part of a simple tradesman. But his fingers were stained with ink, and the fires of iconoclasm and revolution burned in his intelligent brown eyes.

"Actually, yes," said Sebastian, his gaze roving tables and shelves crammed with a jumbled collection of rare old books mixed in with dog-eared, largely worthless volumes. Much of Clarence Rutledge's business appeared to be devoted to vast collections of sermons indexed by subject and available for either sale or hire, so that Sebastian found himself wondering if Calhoun had sent him to the wrong shop. "I'm interested in a particular volume bound in tooled black Moroccan leather with the title in blood red. About this size—" Sebastian spread his hands in the approximate dimensions of the volume he'd found on Hector Knee-bone's shelves of erotic literature. "It purports to be a lost work by de Sade."

"I'm not certain I know what you seek."

Sebastian held the man's gaze steadily. "I think you do."

The bookseller blinked. "It's very rare."

"But you do have it."

Clarence Rutledge slipped behind the wooden counter that ran across the back of his shop. "Only fifty were produced, and of those, only three made it to our shores."

"How many have you sold?"

"Two."

"Let me see it."

Wordlessly, the bookseller turned to what looked like a solid paneled wall behind him. Pressing a style, he released a hidden catch and a section of the paneling slid back to reveal a secret cupboard filled with forbidden volumes. He selected one, then carefully slid the section back into place.

Unlike Napoléon's France, England had no clearly defined prepublication censorship laws. English plays could not be performed until licensed and approved by an officially appointed Examiner of the Stage. But one could technically publish whatever one wished. The sticky part was that authors, publishers, and booksellers could all be charged with "obscene libel" and disturbing the King's peace if the material they produced was deemed offensive. Blasphemy, improper language, and sexually explicit passages could all lead to imprisonment and the confiscation of any offending stock.

"How do you know I'm not with the Society for the Suppression of Vice?" asked Sebastian as the bookseller laid the book on the counter between them. One of the main objectives of the zealous members of the society was to destroy the trade in "bawdy stuff."

"I know who you are, my lord," said the bookseller, and turned the book to face him.

Like the book he'd seen on Kneebone's shelves, this volume was exquisitely produced, with a fine leather cover and gold leaf on the page ends. Sebastian opened the book to its title page and stared at what was printed there.

LES 120 JOURNÉES DE SODOME, OU L'ÉCOLE DU LIBERTINAGE
Marquis de Sade

"You've heard of it, my lord?"

Sebastian nodded silently. Oh, he'd heard of it, all right. Considered by de Sade as his magnum opus, *The 120 Days of Sodom* had been written in 1785, while de Sade was confined to the Bastille. Since he wasn't allowed paper, he'd composed the work on tiny scraps smuggled into the prison and then glued together to form one continuous, forty-foot roll he kept hidden in the walls of his cell. When the manuscript was destroyed in the demolition of the Bastille in 1789, the Marquis claimed to have wept tears of blood at its loss.

Sebastian looked up to find the bookseller watching him intently. "I assume it's a forgery? Someone's imaginative attempt to re-create the Marquis's lost work?"

"Oh, no. I can assure you, it is quite genuine. The Marquis's original manuscript was believed to have been lost, but it was actually discovered and rescued at the time of the Bastille's destruction. It was only recently smuggled out to Amsterdam and set in print."

"You've read it?"

"I have. Although I must warn you, it's not for the faint of heart."

Sebastian slowly turned the pages.

"Only the first part of the manuscript was complete," said Rutledge. "The rest is more in the form of an outline."

"So tell me about it."

The bookseller cleared his throat. "Well . . . Basically, it's the tale of four wealthy men who join together in search of the ultimate in sexual fulfillment. To this end, they kidnap a number of young boys and girls and shut themselves up for four months in an isolated mountain castle."

"And?"

Clarence Rutledge spread his hands wide. "It's de Sade at his most imaginative and depraved—a disturbing exploration of the darkest promptings of humanity's potential for evil. Incest, rape, sacrilege, flagellation, torture . . ."

"And murder?"

"Of course."

Sebastian closed the book. "How much?"

"Six guineas."

The price was outrageous. A nicely bound three-volume novel typically sold for a guinea, although bawdy books could go for three times that. Sebastian dropped the coins on the counter without comment and waited while the bookseller wrapped his purchase in plain brown paper.

Then he said, "Who bought the other two books?"

Clarence Rutledge froze. "I can't tell you that."

Calmly slipping his knife from the sheath in his boot, Sebastian came around the counter to back the bookseller up against the paneled wall. "I think you can."

The man swallowed hard, his eyes rolling inward toward his nose as he stared at the blade held inches from his face.

"Let me explain something to you," said Sebastian. "Earlier this week, the body of a young boy was discovered in Clerkenwell. He'd been whipped, tortured, raped, and strangled; his little sister is missing and has probably suffered the same fate. I am in no mood to humor anyone who is protecting the monster who did that. Tell me who bought the other two books."

The bookseller licked his dry lips. "The—the first was acquired by a veiled gentlewoman. I've no idea who she was. She said it was a gift for a friend."

Sebastian suspected Clarence Rutledge knew the veiled woman's identity very well. But since she was in all likelihood the source of the volume on Hector Kneebone's shelves, he let it go for now. "And the other?"

The bookseller's eyes slid away toward the street, then focused back on Sebastian's face. "The other volume was purchased by a French émigré. De Brienne."

Sebastian took a step back, the hand with the knife dropping to his side.

Amadeus Colbert, the comte de Brienne, was a well-known figure in fashionable circles. Slim, vivacious, and unmarried, he was both an entertaining dinner guest and an elegant dancer, always more than willing to please his hostesses by partnering shy young girls over-whelmed by their first Season.

"Is he a frequent customer?" asked Sebastian.

Clarence Rutledge carefully straightened his modest neckcloth. "Frequent enough."

"Then I wonder why you surrendered his name so readily."

An angry muscle jumped along the bookseller's hard jaw. "I don't like knives."

"Perhaps. But that's not the only reason, is it?"

"Let's just say that I had already heard about the boy they found in Clerkenwell."

"Do I take it the comte is particularly fond of de Sade?"

"Yes."

"Yet you must have other customers with similar inclinations."

The bookseller hesitated a shade too long. "None like de Brienne."

Sebastian slid his knife into its sheath and tucked the brown-paper-wrapped book under one arm. "If I find you've been less than honest with me, I will be back."

Clarence Rutledge's nostrils flared with a deeply indrawn breath. But he didn't say anything. And in the silence that followed, Sebastian's acute hearing caught the rhythmic *thump-thump* of a printing press hidden someplace deep below.

Chapter 23

$\mathcal{S}$ebastian found the comte de Brienne engaged in a fencing match on the terrace at the rear of his house on Half Moon Street.

Stripped down to shirt, waistcoat, and breeches, his épée held in a light, sure grip, the Frenchman parried and thrust with a skill virtually equal to that of his instructor. Sebastian stood for a moment and watched as, swords flashing, their stockinged feet dancing back and forth, the men surged across the stone flagging. Most gentlemen of their circle practiced the art of fencing at Angelo's salon on Bond Street. But de Brienne's fencing master obviously came to him.

"Impressive," said Sebastian when the fencing master had finished the exercise and bowed himself out.

De Brienne accepted the towel presented by a waiting manservant and wiped his sweaty face. He was a boyishly slim man in his late thirties, of medium height, with delicate, aristocratic features and thick dark hair he wore just a shade too long. His intricately tied cravat, figured waistcoat, and high shirt points suggested a tendency toward dandyism without veering into the ridiculous. "I hear you yourself are no mean swordsman. We must test each other's mettle sometime."

"Perhaps," said Sebastian.

The Frenchman looped the towel around his neck and nodded a curt dismissal to the manservant. "I take it you're here because of that boy they found in Clerkenwell? You've heard I like to play with whips, and you naturally leapt to the conclusion I might have had something to do with his death."

"And did you?" said Sebastian. He had been expecting the Frenchman to indignantly deny any such inclinations. But de Brienne was obviously too clever for that.

"No, I did not." The Frenchman sat on a white iron bench and reached for his boots.

"But you do like to play with whips?"

He thrust a foot into the first boot and stomped, hard. "I play with like-minded adults, not children. And I don't make a habit of littering London with discarded corpses."

"Do you know anyone who does?"

De Brienne gave a startled laugh. "Seriously? Do you?"

"No. But then, I don't like to play with whips."

De Brienne's lips curled into a tight, mocking smile. "How do you know? Have you tried it?"

"No."

"You should. You might find you enjoy it."

Sebastian studied the Frenchman's thin, bony face. His English was barely accented, for he had fled France more than twenty years before. In those days he had been a wellborn but impoverished youth, with an uncle and two cousins standing between him and the family title. All were now dead.

Sebastian said, "How did you know I was investigating Benji Thatcher's death?"

Still vaguely smiling, de Brienne reached for the second boot. "You haven't exactly been secretive about it, have you?"

"Benji's little sister, Sybil, is still missing," said Sebastian as de Brienne shoved his last foot home, then stood to reach for his coat. "Do you know anything about that?"

The Frenchman's attention was all for the task of drawing on his coat and adjusting the cuffs. "I did mention that I like to play with adults, did I not?"

"So you did."

De Brienne looked up. "Who told you of my tastes, anyway?"

"Why? Do you think someone dislikes you enough to suggest that you might be guilty of murder?"

The Frenchman shrugged. "I have many enemies. It's the inevitable result of revolution and war, is it not? Passions are aroused, grudges are held, and resentments build. One accumulates enemies."

It was an unexpectedly revealing comment. Sebastian said, "Where were you early Monday morning at half past one?"

De Brienne dabbed at his damp face again with the towel. "Playing with a friend. And no, I will not give you her name."

"What about Friday evening between, say, five and seven?"

De Brienne looked thoughtful for a moment, as if he could not immediately recall. Then he shook his head. "Same answer, I'm afraid. I am very fond of . . . play." He threw a significant glance toward the row of long French doors that led back into the house. "And now you really must excuse me. I'm promised to Lady Aldrich's for dinner this evening before her rout. She has a young cousin from Yorkshire staying with her, and the poor girl is sadly in need of social experience. I've offered to sit beside the girl and draw her out."

"You're very accommodating."

"I try to be."

It was not uncommon for gentlemen in their thirties or even forties to be partnered with seventeen- and eighteen-year-old girls. But given what Sebastian now knew about the Frenchman's sexual tastes, the thought of de Brienne with an innocent young girl barely out of the schoolroom now struck him as more than distasteful. He said, "I thought you didn't like to play with children."

Something flared in the Frenchman's eyes, something dark and dangerous. But rather than reply, he simply sketched an elegant bow, his lips curling into that practiced smile as he turned toward the house. "I'll send James to show you out. Good day, *monsieur le vicomte.*"

❧

"We've heard back from two or three of the area's public offices," said Sir Henry Lovejoy when Sebastian met with him later at a coffeehouse just off Bow Street. "So far all the responses have been negative. I'd like to think that's encouraging, but after my conversation with Hatton Garden I'm not convinced it signifies anything."

Sebastian looked up from his own glass of wine. "Met with them, did you?"

Lovejoy took a sip of his hot coffee and grimaced. "Sir Arthur Ellsworth. He insists that Benji Thatcher's injuries were most likely sustained in whatever accidental fall killed him."

Sebastian rested his shoulders against his bench's high, old-fashioned back. "And the ligature marks around his neck?"

"Sir Arthur doesn't seem to recall those."

"They're there."

Lovejoy cleared his throat. "I know. I went to Tower Hill to see for myself." He fell silent for a moment, as if lost in the horror of what he had found in the stone-walled outbuilding at the base of Gibson's yard. "Have you made any progress at all?"

Sebastian shook his head. "I've a few suspects. But their links to the boy vary from tenuous to nonexistent."

"And you still think there could be other such victims?"

Sebastian blew out a harsh breath. "I wish I knew."

Lovejoy nodded. "I've assigned two of my constables to make inquiries around Clerkenwell. They haven't turned up anything useful, but I've told them to keep looking." He hesitated, then wrapped both hands around his coffee mug. "I've also been reading up on that Frenchman you were talking about—Gilles de Rais. It's difficult to believe such evil exists."

"Yet it does."

Lovejoy raised his gaze to meet Sebastian's, and his eyes were bleak and haunted. "Let us pray to God it doesn't exist here."

Hero was standing at the entrance to the nursery, the evening sun streaming in through the high windows, when Sebastian came upon her. She was still wearing her carriage dress of French blue kerseymere, made high at the neck with a stomacher front and long, full sleeves tied up with primrose ribbons. She was leaning against the doorframe and quietly watching Simon maneuver his way around and around a footstool with outthrust arms and woefully unsteady legs.

Sebastian walked up behind her, slipped his arms around her waist, and drew her close. "What happened to his howling tears?"

"The tooth came through this morning."

"Thank God."

They watched together as Simon lurched from the footstool to a nearby armchair, hands reaching, his fat, bowed legs wobbling precariously. Hero said, "Your son is getting ready to walk."

"He's too young to walk."

She leaned her head back against his. "He doesn't think so."

Sebastian studied her tired, tightly held profile. "Something's wrong. What is it?"

She gave a soft huff of amusement. "How do you know something's wrong?"

"I'm a very perceptive man."

At that she laughed out loud, her hands coming up to rest atop his at her waist. "I was simply thinking how fortunate I am. How comfortable and safe my life is. How I'll never need to worry that Simon might someday end up spending the night under a bridge or market stall, so cold he can't sleep and so hungry it hurts. I don't often pause to appreciate that, and it shames me."

Sebastian was silent for a moment, his gaze on her strong, aquiline profile. "Started your interviews with the street children of Clerkenwell today, did you?"

She nodded. "A girl and a boy. The boy is growing up as wild, amoral, and ignorant as a puppy—although to tell the truth, I suspect his life isn't too terribly different from what it would have been had his mother not been sent to Botany Bay for dispatching his father with an iron skillet."

"Sounds like a charming fellow. And the girl?"

"Her story is far more haunting, and I suspect I don't know the half of it. She tells me she had an older sister named Mary who recently disappeared."

"How recently?"

"Last spring. I suppose it's possible the older girl decided her life would be easier without a little sister in tow and simply moved on, perhaps to the Haymarket. But Thisbe is convinced something dreadful happened to her, and I can't help but think about Benji Thatcher and his sister. You've still found no trace of the little girl, Sybil?"

"None. I've accumulated a few new suspects, including a decidedly unsavory French count and a Clerkenwell fence who was once transported for murder. But at this point, it's all just conjecture and supposition." He hesitated, then said, "How well do you know Sir Francis Rowe? He is your cousin, isn't he?"

"He is, yes. Although fortunately the relationship is distant enough that I can generally avoid him."

"You don't like him?"

"I'm afraid he's far too much like his grandfather for my taste." She shifted around so that she could see his face. "Why do you ask?"

"His name came up," said Sebastian, and left it at that.

❧

That evening, Charles, Lord Jarvis, put in an appearance at a fashionable rout given by Sir Basil and Lady Aldrich. He frequently attended such functions, for it was important that a man in his position be seen. But on this occasion he had a secondary purpose, a purpose that brought a suggestion of a smile to his lips as he entered Lady Aldrich's flower-bedecked, overcrowded ballroom.

He found his quarry at the edge of the dance floor, the man's full-cheeked, pug-nosed face suffused with paternal hope as he watched his rather plain daughter circle the room on the arm of some eligible young suitor.

Sinclair Pugh, the bloviating and decidedly imprudent member of Parliament for Gough, was a short, middle-aged man slowly growing stout despite his determined efforts to stave off the creeping pounds with regular sessions at Angelo's and Gentleman Jackson's Salon. His self-opinion and arrogance were legendary, although his background was more genteel than aristocratic and his wealth the product not so much of his estates—which were modest—as of a series of astute investments. He had grown very, very rich off King George III's wars.

His expression nothing but pleasant, Jarvis walked up to stand beside him, his gaze, like Pugh's, on the dance floor. "Your daughter, I take it?" said Jarvis, nodding toward the plump, pudding-faced Miss Pugh.

Pugh stiffened. "What do you want with me?"

"How shockingly uncivil," said Jarvis, his own voice unfailingly cordial. "Particularly when my purpose is simply to give you a word or two of advice." He watched as the laughing dancers arranged themselves into two facing lines. "Your opinion of His Highness's plans for the reorganization of Europe after Napoléon's coming defeat are best kept to yourself. I trust I make myself clear?"

"Very," snapped Pugh. "However, if your intent is to intimidate me into silence, then I fear you have failed."

"I suspected that might be the case," said Jarvis, his voice still even and pleasant. "Nevertheless, I did feel you deserved to be warned. The responsibility for anything that happens to you from here on out will now be on your own head."

"Is that a threat?"

Jarvis possessed an unexpectedly winning smile that he could use to cajole, placate, deceive, or confuse. He used it now with particularly chilling effect. "I suppose you could take it that way."

"I'm not afraid of you," said Pugh with an ostentatious show of foolish bravado.

"No? You should be."

And with that Jarvis walked away, still faintly smiling and leaving Pugh staring after him.

Chapter 24

*T*he gentleman paced up and down the dimly lit courtyard, his silk evening cloak swirling about his hard-muscled thighs, the heels of his dress shoes going *click-click* on the paving stones.

Painfully aware of the silence of the night around them and the smell of his own rank fear, the boy watched him.

"I hear you've been talking to Devlin," said the man. "What did he want with you?"

The boy sucked in a quick, frightened gasp of air. "How did you know that?"

The gentleman tightened his face in a way that made his nostrils appear pinched. "Answer the question."

"He—he wanted to know when was the last time I seen Benji."

"What did you tell him?"

"I lied."

The gentleman nodded. "What else?"

The boy frantically cast his mind back over that frightening conversation. "He asked about Sybil."

"Sybil? Who is Sybil?"

The boy felt as if his heart had plunged down into his gut. "Benji's sister."

"Why would Devlin be interested in Benji's sister?"

"'Cause nobody's seen her. It's like she just . . . disappeared."

The gentleman was silent for a moment. Thoughtful. Then he said, "It's possible she knows something."

"Sybil? How could she?"

"Then what has happened to her?"

"I don't know!"

"Is she hiding?"

"Why would she hide?"

"Because she may have seen something, you fool. You'd best find her. Quickly."

The boy sucked in a breath that hitched in a way that made it sound like a sob. He knew only too well what the gentleman would do to Sybil if he found her. "But I've tried!"

The gentleman's face had taken on that cold, flinty look that always made the boy's throat seize up and his bowels loosen. "Try harder."

The boy nodded, his throat so tight now he could barely force the words out. "Y-yes, sir."

Chapter 25

Thursday, 16 September

*T*he next morning dawned cold and blustery, with bunching gray clouds that promised rain.

Shortly before eight, Sebastian reined in beneath the shelter of one of the twin rows of plane trees that stretched along the southern boundary of Hyde Park. His neat black Arab shifted beneath him, wanting to stretch her legs. But he held the mare in check until the slim, golden-haired young rider he was waiting for appeared, followed at a proper distance by her groom.

He'd known she would come. Her restlessness was one of the things Miss Stephanie Wilcox shared with Sophia, the errant Countess of Hendon who had run off and left them all so many years ago. Her restlessness and a deep, elemental connection with horses. Sebastian could remember watching her as a girl of eight and ten gallop wildly along the cliff tops of Cornwall, the wind streaming her hair out behind her. He found himself thinking of that child now as he nudged his mare forward to bring the Arab in alongside Stephanie's big bay gelding.

"Uncle!" she said with a smile that flashed even white teeth but didn't quite reach her eyes. "If I didn't know better, I'd say you were lurking here with the intention of intercepting me."

"Well, I'm glad you know better."

She laughed out loud. She was nineteen and beautiful, and she knew it. She had her grandmother's elegant, graceful build and even, aristocratic features combined with the intensely blue eyes that were the hallmark of the St. Cyr family. He could see nothing in her to remind him of Martin, Lord Wilcox, the brutal, disturbed man who had fathered her. And it occurred to Sebastian to wonder what her child-hood had been like, growing up with an angry, sour mother and such a father.

Sebastian said, "Hendon told me of your betrothal."

"Oh? And are you here to congratulate me, Uncle?"

"No."

She turned her head to look directly at him. "Mother warned me that you disapprove. I suppose I should thank you for your honesty if nothing else."

"Did she tell you why I disapprove?"

Stephanie shifted her gaze to something in the misty distance, her body moving easily with the motion of her horse. "You think I don't know what Ashworth is like?"

"I'm quite certain you don't."

"In that, Uncle, you are wrong. I even know why he was blackballed from Almack's. Do you?"

"No."

"It was over something that happened years ago, when he was quite young. He fell in love with a girl down in Devonshire whose family had a long-standing quarrel with his. They refused even to consider the match, so the young couple eloped. They were intercepted before they reached Gretna Green, but the girl never got over it and eventually died of a broken heart. The family blamed Ashworth and have hounded him with lies ever since. It was the great tragedy of his life and the cause of much of the wildness for which he is condemned."

Sebastian said, "I'm not talking about the wildness of youth."

"So what are you talking about, Uncle? Debauched, brandy-soaked nights of vingt-et-un and faro? Decadent interludes with naked actresses and opera dancers? Pistols at dawn? And would you have me believe you were a saint before you married Hero? Is there anything I mentioned that you have not done?"

Sebastian shook his head. He'd done it all and more. But he'd never dabbled in the kind of evil offered by Number Three, although he knew there was no way he could ever make her understand just how vile that place was.

And so he said instead, his voice as calm and gentle as he could make it, "There will be no going back from this, Stephanie. If you find you've made a mistake, it can't be undone."

He saw her lips part, saw her throat work as she swallowed. She turned her face away. "I've made many mistakes in my life, Uncle. But marrying Ashworth isn't one of them."

He studied her beautiful, tense profile and knew an ache of sadness and useless foreboding. "Believe me in this, child: Even if I can't bring myself to congratulate you on your betrothal, I do wish you all the happiness in the world." He hesitated, thinking he probably should leave it at that and yet not quite able to stop himself from adding, "But you don't look very happy to me."

She gave a sharp, brittle laugh. "Is any of us ever really happy, Uncle? Truly, blessedly happy?"

"Always? No; of course not. But I am happy in my marriage, Stephanie; profoundly, passionately, and yet also peacefully happy—more than I could ever say and far more than I ever dreamt possible. There's no reason you can't have that too. But you won't find it with a man of Ashworth's ilk. That way lies heartache and a world of grief."

Her chin came up, her blue St. Cyr eyes flashing. "I'm glad you're happy, Uncle. But you're not me." And with that she touched her heel to the bay's side and brought her crop down on its withers sharply enough to send the big gelding in a wild gallop down the Row. Her groom scrambled to follow her.

Sebastian watched her go. Proper ladies did not gallop in Hyde Park. But then, Stephanie had never been one to trot sedately, to follow conventions or play by the rules. And as troubled as Sebastian had been before, he was even more disturbed now.

❧

Wheeling his horse, Sebastian rode across Hyde Park to the grand Park Lane residence of the Dowager Duchess of Claiborne.

She'd been born Lady Henrietta St. Cyr, elder sister of the current Earl of Hendon. For more than fifty years she'd reigned as one of the grandes dames of Society. She was proud, opinionated, bossy, judgmental, nosy, and ferociously intelligent. She was also one of Sebastian's favorite people. And even though she was, in truth, only a distant relative of his, he still called her Aunt Henrietta. The affection between them ran deep and had little to do with things like bloodlines and tangled family trees and the expectations of their world.

It was the Duchess's well-known practice never to leave her dressing room before one. The bells of the city's churches were just striking the half hour when Humphrey, her oh-so-proper butler, opened the door to Sebastian's knock.

"My lord," said the butler, so far forgetting himself as to groan out loud. "Please. No."

"Sorry, Humphrey," said Sebastian, heading for the stairs. "I won't be long. Make certain that urchin I've left holding my mare doesn't steal her, would you?"

He ran up the grand, curving staircase to the second floor and entered his aunt's bedchamber after the briefest of knocks. He could hear her snoring gently from the depths of her grand, velvet-hung bed, and crossed quickly to pull back the heavy window drapes with a cheerful, "Good morning, Aunt."

"What?" She sat up, one hand groping for the quizzing glass she kept beside her bed. "Good God. Devlin. It's you. What in heaven's name are you doing here? Go away and come back at a decent hour."

"I'm sorry, Aunt, but this is important."

She glared at him, the lens of the quizzing glass hideously distorting her eye. "What is important?"

"I need to know why Ashworth was blackballed from Almack's."

The Duchess let her quizzing glass fall. She was a large woman, built much like her brother but with more flesh. She also shared Hendon's heavy, blunt features and his gruff way of talking. "What time is it?" she demanded.

"Half past eight."

She lay back with a groan. "You wake me up at the crack of dawn to ask me about something that happened ten years ago?"

"Was it ten years ago?"

"Nearly."

"So what happened?"

Henrietta gave a heavy sigh and sat up again. "It's quite a sordid tale. Ashworth persuaded the younger sister of one of his friends to run off with him. The foolish chit thought they were headed for Gretna Green. Instead he took her to a hunting lodge in Melton Mowbray. By the time her father and brothers tracked them down some weeks later, the girl was already with child."

"I'm surprised they didn't kill him."

"They tried. Unfortunately, it was one of her brothers—Ashworth's friend—who was killed. And since the brother had fired first, the death was ruled justifiable homicide."

"What happened to the girl?"

"She died in childbirth. She was so very young."

"How young?"

"Thirteen."

"Good Lord. You say this was ten years ago?"

"Thereabouts."

"Ashworth was—what? Twenty-two? Twenty-three?"

"Yes."

"Why did the tale never get out?"

"The family confided the truth to the patronesses of Almack's in the hopes of protecting other gently reared young girls. But they asked that the details be kept quiet out of respect for their dead daughter. Even Sally Jersey can keep her mouth shut when she needs to."

"Have you told Stephanie?"

"Of course I told her. But the girl is nineteen. She refused to listen. She'd already heard Ashworth's version of the story and accused me of simply trying to discourage her."

"Which you were."

"Well, of course I was."

"What about Amanda?"

Henrietta gave a derisive snort. "You think Amanda would let a little thing like rape and kidnapping stand in the way of seeing her daughter become a marchioness? She knew the truth long ago."

"Yet you haven't told Hendon."

"Seriously, Devlin; do you want to give him an apoplectic fit?"

Sebastian went to stand at the window overlooking the park. After a moment, he said, "What can we do?"

"I'm afraid there is nothing we can do."

"Ashworth will make her life a living hell."

"Yes. But it's her choice, isn't it?"

He pushed away from the window. "What does she know of men? She's nineteen—and she grew up with a man like Wilcox as a father. Not to mention Bayard as a brother."

Henrietta sat up a little straighter and cleared her throat.

"What?" said Sebastian, watching her.

"You do know Wilcox wasn't actually her father."

Sebastian stared at her. "He wasn't? So who was?"

"I've no idea. All I know is that once Amanda provided Wilcox with Bayard and that other little boy—what was his name?"

"William."

"That's right; William. Who names a child William Wilcox? At any rate, once she'd provided Wilcox with two heirs, she shut him out of her bedroom. Refused to relent even after the younger boy died."

"Does Stephanie know?"

"She may suspect, but I doubt Amanda ever told her the truth. It's rather ironic, isn't it? Amanda always hated your mother for playing Hendon false. Yet she turned out to be far more like Sophia than she'd ever care to admit."

"Amanda is nothing like my mother."

Henrietta sniffed. "Well, you can hardly say the same about Stephanie. She even looks like Sophia, which is more than Amanda ever did. Perhaps she'll prove us all wrong and somehow manage to reform Ashworth. It does happen."

"Ashworth isn't wild. He's evil."

"Now you're starting to sound like some sort of Papist." She wrinkled her nose. "What is that dreadful smell?"

"Probably me. I've just come from riding in the park."

"Oh, lovely. It wanted only that." She hesitated a moment, then said, "Hendon tells me Hero has been bringing the baby to see him. It's very kind of her. He quite dotes on the boy, you know."

Sebastian knew what she was trying to do, and simply remained silent.

She said, "One of these days, Devlin, you really must find your way to putting the past behind you. Not simply for Hendon's sake but for your own."

"I can't forgive him for what he's done."

"Are you so certain that's what's driving this, Sebastian?"

"What the devil is that supposed to mean?"

"Think about it." She flopped back down and put a pillow over her eyes. "Now go away. You're making my bedroom smell like a stable."

🙖

It was a short time later, when Sebastian was changing into clean clothes, that Calhoun said, "I've discovered the answer to your question about Icarus Cantrell, my lord."

Sebastian made a final adjustment to his neckcloth. "And?"

Calhoun held up Sebastian's coat of Bath superfine. "Seems he murdered a fellow student while up at Cambridge. He claimed it was self-defense, but the jury convicted him of murder."

Sebastian shrugged into his coat. "So he was at Cambridge."

"He was, my lord."

"How did he kill this fellow?"

Calhoun assembled Sebastian's hat and gloves, his features grave. "He strangled him, my lord."

Chapter 26

*S*ebastian arrived at the Professor's Attic just as the first drops of rain were beginning to fall. As he watched, a ragged, dark-haired young girl of twelve or thirteen darted from the shop's door. She threw Sebastian a frightened glance, then scurried away through the ancient central arch of the nearby St. John's Gate, her head bowed and her shawl drawn up in a way that hid her face.

"Thought you'd be back," said Icarus Cantrell when Sebastian pushed open the battered door and walked inside. The old man was standing at a table with a tub of water near the back of the room and was using salt and a cut lemon to polish a badly tarnished brass tray.

Sebastian carefully closed the door behind him. "Oh? Why?"

The Professor gave a curiously tight smile and returned his attention to his tray.

Sebastian said, "Do I take it the young girl I just saw leaving is one of your"—he paused, searching for the right word—"suppliers?"

Cantrell kept his gaze on his work. "Most of the district's street children find their way to my door at one time or another."

"Oh? Did you know a young girl named Mary Cartwright?"

"Can't say I did. Why?"

"She disappeared last spring."

"Benji wasn't the first street child to disappear around here, you know."

"So I'm beginning to realize. Although I don't recall you mentioning that when I was here before. Why?"

"I wasn't convinced you were ready to listen."

Sebastian let his gaze drift over the jumbled pile of tarnished brass waiting to be polished. "I hear you were once at Cambridge."

Cantrell dipped the now gleaming tray into the water, washing away the salt and lemon juice. He did not look up. "Do I take it you've also heard what happened there?"

"I have. Although not in detail."

"The details are not important."

"They might be. Why did you kill him?"

Cantrell lifted the tray from the water and reached for a drying cloth. "The lord's son I killed was six feet tall and weighed close to eighteen stone. Sound anything like Benji Thatcher to you?"

"Why did you kill him?" Sebastian asked again.

"He left me no choice."

Sebastian shook his head. "I might believe that if you'd shot him or bashed in his head. But you strangled him. It takes a long time to strangle someone to death. And it's not something you do accidentally."

"I did strangle him, yes. And the world is a much better place with him out of it. I don't regret what I did, even taking into consideration the seven years of hell I endured in the sugarcane fields of Georgia because of it."

"How old were you?"

"When I killed him? I was fifteen." The Professor hesitated, then added, "Benji's age."

Fifteen was young for a lad to head off to Cambridge, but it wasn't unheard of.

"My father disowned me, of course," said the old man, carefully drying his tray.

"And your mother?"

"She cried. I don't know what she'd have done once I made it back from Georgia. But by the time I'd served my sentence and managed to return, she was dead. If I regret anything, it's the impact my actions had on her." He set the tray aside and selected a badly tarnished chocolate pot from the pile. "So tell me: Did you look into Sir Francis Rowe?"

"I did."

"And?"

"He made no attempt to deny killing the six-year-old pickpocket in August. In fact, if anything I'd say he is rather proud of it."

"And Benji?"

"That he does deny. And while I might have reason to suspect him of killing Benji, he has no reason I know of to harm Sybil—or any of the other children who seem to be missing from around here."

"True." The Professor sprinkled salt on the pot, reached for another sliced lemon, and scrubbed for a moment in silence. Then he said, "I knew a young girl once who went into service as a parlormaid in a gentleman's household. She was a pretty, winsome thing. But her master abused her terribly. He used to tie her up and take a whip to her."

"Oh?" said Sebastian, wondering where the old man was going with this. "Why did she endure it?"

"He threatened to accuse her of theft if she complained or left."

"And?"

"The girl usually came home to visit her mother on her half days off. Except, one week she didn't come. The mother feared the girl must be sick, so she went to the gentleman's house to see her daughter. They told her the girl had been dismissed three days before. The mother didn't believe it; she was convinced something had happened to her— that the gentleman must have killed her. But no one would listen to her." Cantrell paused. "She never saw her daughter again."

Sebastian watched the old man rub the lemon over the dull surface of the chocolate pot, leaving it gleaming. He couldn't shake the conviction that Cantrell was toying with him—had been toying with him. That the man knew far more than he was actually saying. "What was the girl's name?"

"Bridget Leary. It's been—oh, two or three years now."

"I'd like to speak to Bridget's mother."

Cantrell shook his head. "Unfortunately, she's dead. Died less than a year later of a broken heart."

"And the gentleman's name?"

"Ashworth. Viscount Ashworth."

Sebastian crossed his arms at his chest. "You do know Ashworth is betrothed to my niece?"

"I didn't know yesterday, but I do today." Cantrell plunged the chocolate pot deep into his tub of water. "Even if Ashworth had nothing to do with what happened to Benji, you don't want him marrying your niece. Believe me."

"Unfortunately I have no say in the matter."

"That is indeed unfortunate."

"As it happens, Ashworth was with my sister and niece Sunday night."

"And you think that eliminates him as a suspect, do you?"

Sebastian studied the Professor's aged, sun-creased face. "What aren't you telling me?"

He lifted the chocolate pot from the water and reached again for his towel. "A stint as a slave in the sugar fields of America teaches a man much about the human capacity for evil. About the depraved things some men—and women—will do when they think they can get away with it."

"Whoever did this won't get away with it. And they won't do it again."

"You're very confident, my lord." Cantrell set the gleaming brass pot aside. "Only I'm not convinced you know what you're up against."

"And you do?"

Something flickered in the depths of the old man's eyes, something he hid as he turned to survey the waiting collection of tarnished brass. "Enough to tell you to be careful, my lord. Very, very careful."

From another man, the words might have been taken as a threat. But they weren't a threat. They were a warning.

❧

Lindley House, the grand London residence of the Marquis of Lindley, lay on Park Lane, not far from the home of the Duchess of Claiborne. But the Marquis's heir, Viscount Ashworth, kept his own establishment in Curzon Street.

The address was fashionable enough, although the house itself was modest and not particularly well kept. As he climbed the front steps, Sebastian found himself remembering what Hendon had said about the Marquis cutting his son off financially in order to force him to wed. The red paint on the front door was dull and beginning to peel, the area steps were in want of sweeping, and the aged butler who answered Sebastian's knock looked as if he should have been pensioned off years before.

"Is his lordship expecting you?" asked the wizened old butler, peering at Sebastian with watery, myopic eyes.

"He should be."

"It is very early."

"Shockingly so," agreed Sebastian. It was half past twelve. "But I've no doubt you'll find his lordship agreeable."

The butler looked unconvinced, but he showed Sebastian to a dusty library and then tottered off to ascertain if his lordship was receiving yet. He returned some minutes later, ashen faced and breathless from his climb up and down the stairs. "His lordship is still in his dressing room, but he will see you now."

Ashworth's plump little valet scooted himself out of the Viscount's dressing room when Sebastian walked in. His lordship was seated at his dressing table, his fingertips soaking in a crystal bowl of warm water. He was clad in exquisite doeskin breeches and a fine linen shirt still open at the neck. The man's house might be suffering neglect, but Ashworth's losses at table and turf were obviously not allowed to impact the glory of his wardrobe.

"You're lucky to find me up," said Ashworth, shaking a wayward lock of honey-colored hair from his eyes. "What in the name of all that's holy are you doing abroad at this hour?"

"Trying to catch a killer."

"Still?"

"Still." Sebastian went to stand beside the window overlooking the street. But he kept his gaze on the other man's face. "Tell me about Bridget Leary."

Ashworth calmly lifted his fingers from the water and began pushing back his cuticles with a soft cloth. "Who?"

"Bridget Leary. She was one of your housemaids."

"Do you seriously think I know the names of my current housemaids, let alone those who've left my employ?"

"I'd think you'd remember this one. She was quite pretty, and you used to tie her up and abuse her with a whip."

Ashworth laughed. "Abuse? I think not."

"What would you call it?"

Ashworth tossed the towel aside and swiveled on the bench to face him. "You must have been talking to that ridiculous mother of hers."

"So you do recall the girl."

"Vaguely."

"And you don't deny whipping her?"

"No. But I don't think you quite understand. She enjoyed our sessions—or at least she was perfectly willing to pretend she did in exchange for a few extra guineas."

"So where is she now?"

"I've no idea. I'm afraid she thought she was far too clever for her own good. The silly chit tried to blackmail me, although she backed down quickly enough when I threatened to have her prosecuted. I always assumed she went home."

"She didn't."

"No? Then she must have left London for fear I meant to carry through on my threat."

"Her mother thinks you killed her."

"Really? I should have the old harridan taken up for slander."

"You can't. She's dead."

"Contacted you from the grave, did she?"

When Sebastian remained silent, Ashworth rose from his dressing table and reached for one of the cravats his valet had laid out for him. "I wonder, has anyone in the course of this decidedly plebeian investigation of yours pointed you toward the comte de Brienne?"

"As a matter of fact, they have. He claims he only plays with consenting adults."

"And you believe him?"

"As much as I believe you."

Ashworth froze in the act of looping the cravat around his neck, then continued, his face a serene mask. "Did you never wonder how a man who fled his home as a penniless young refugee twenty years ago manages to finance such a comfortable lifestyle today?"

Sebastian pushed away from the window. "What are you suggesting now?"

Ashworth positioned himself before one of the room's full-length mirrors. "I should think that rather obvious. How else would a French émigré without land or investments accumulate such impressive wealth?"

"I can think of several possibilities."

"Can you?" Ashworth glanced over at him. "You obviously possess a more active imagination than I."

"I doubt it," said Sebastian.

But the Viscount only smiled.

Sebastian turned toward the door, then paused to look back at him and say, "Tell me: What do you think of the Marquis de Sade?"

"De Sade?" Ashworth kept his attention on the intricacies of tying his cravat. "Have you read him?"

"Not a great deal."

Ashworth adjusted a fold. "Some find his works titillating, some find him boring, while others consider him revolting."

"And you?"

"The truth is, there's nothing he writes about that can't be found in any collection of old Popish paintings. Did you never wonder why our religious forebears took delight in such vivid, detailed portrayals of lovely young virgins being sexually mutilated or broken naked on the wheel?"

"Actually, no; I never did."

"'Ferocity is always either a supplement or a means to lust.'"

"I take it that's a quote from de Sade?"

"Is it?"

Sebastian said, "Have you read *Les 120 journées de Sodome?*"

For one telling moment, Ashworth's gaze met his in the mirror. "Unfortunately that work was lost in the destruction of the Bastille."

"Was it?"

Ashworth smoothed the folds of his neckcloth and swung away from the mirror, his brows drawn together in a frown, his hands resting on his hips. "What has any of this to do with the death of some Clerkenwell pickpocket?"

"I don't know yet," said Sebastian, opening the door. "But I'll figure it out."

Chapter 27

The boy walked the rolling hills above Clerkenwell, his head bowed, his collar turned up against the cold wind. He was tired and his feet hurt, but he'd already looked everywhere there was to look for Sybil in Clerkenwell, and so he'd taken to searching the fields beyond.

"Sybil?" he called, pausing to cup his hands around his mouth. "Sybil! Where are you?"

He stood still, listening. But he heard only the wind shifting the branches of a nearby hawthorn and bending the tall grass around him.

He didn't want to find the girl. He'd always liked Sybil and he knew only too well what the gentleman would do to her if he got his hands on her. At the thought of it, the boy shivered and wiped his sleeve across his runny nose.

He didn't want to find her, but not as much as he was afraid he might not find her. Because if he didn't find her, he knew what the gentleman would do to him. The gentleman was already getting impatient with him. The boy could tell. He was afraid it was only a matter of time before the man found another boy to replace him. And then he would end up like Benji.

And all the others.

He stumbled on a tuft of grass and went down, hitting the ground hard and cutting the palm of one hand on a sharp stone. He lay there for a moment, winded and trying not to cry. He told himself he needed to get up, needed to keep looking for Sybil.

Instead, he simply squeezed his eyes shut and buried his face in the sweet-smelling earth.

❧

"I was disappointed not to find you at Lady Aldrich's ball last night," Lady Jarvis told Hero as mother and daughter walked companionably side by side along the wind-ruffled Serpentine in Hyde Park. "I thought you might attend."

"Devlin is investigating the murder of a child in Clerkenwell—in fact, two, in all likelihood."

"Children? How perfectly dreadful."

The distress on her mother's face made Hero regret mentioning it. She added quickly, "Plus I've begun the research for a new article."

"Have you?" Her mother smiled. "Won't Jarvis be pleased?"

Hero laughed out loud. "So how was Lady Aldrich's party?"

"A terrible squeeze, which is surprising, given how thin of company London is at the moment. It's a pity Cousin Victoria couldn't go with us; she would have enjoyed it immensely. Unfortunately, such entertainments are out of the question for a year. Although I do think it's wrong to ask a young woman her age to mourn a husband for *two* years, as some suggest."

"Oh, definitely." Hero studied her mother's relaxed, smiling face. "You like her a great deal, don't you?"

"I do, yes; more and more. And I am particularly grateful to have her with me now that Emma has had to leave."

Hero drew up in surprise. "She what?"

Emma Knight was the impoverished relative who'd served as Lady

Jarvis's companion since Hero's marriage the previous year. Although once vivacious and energetic, Lady Jarvis had seen her health seriously undermined by a long string of tragic miscarriages and stillbirths. Her last, disastrous pregnancy had brought on an apoplectic fit that left her so weakened in mind and body that Hero had taken over running the various Jarvis households from an early age. And when she married Devlin, she'd found the young, widowed Emma to take her place. "When did this happen?"

"She left this morning," said Lady Jarvis, turning to watch a pair of ducks take flight from the water's surface. "She received an urgent message from her family last night. Seems her father is gravely ill and is asking to see her before he dies."

"It was my understanding Emma's father had disowned her."

"He had. Which makes his decision to reach out to her now so heartwarming, don't you think? Sometimes the approach of death leads us to reevaluate what we consider important. She asked me to apologize to you for her hasty departure, but I told her she need have no qualms about leaving me in Cousin Victoria's care."

"I'll start looking for someone to replace her right away."

"No need to be in a rush, my dear. Victoria has assured me she's quite happy to stay until we find someone suitable."

Hero started to say something, then swallowed it. Cousin Victoria's presence in Berkeley Square should have made Hero feel better. She tried to tell herself that her instinctive dislike of the woman was irrational and baseless.

But the sense of uneasiness remained.

Chapter 28

They buried Benji Thatcher that afternoon, in a light, misty rain that fell out of a low gray sky.

Sebastian stood beside the gaping hole of the dead boy's new grave, his heart heavy with sadness and frustration as he listened to the reverend's voice drone on. "'In sure and certain hope of the resurrection to eternal life . . .'"

The assembly of mourners was small. Constable Mott Gowan and Icarus Cantrell were there, along with Jem Jones, while Toby the Dancer watched from the far edge of the churchyard as if afraid to draw any closer to—what? Sebastian wondered. That silent, shrouded form? Constable Gowan? Or Sebastian himself?

Paul Gibson appeared halfway through the short graveside service, looking disheveled and shaky. He had his coat collar turned up and kept his head bowed, although Sebastian suspected that was less because of the rain and more out of a desire to hide his gray, unshaven face and sunken eyes.

"'We commit his body to the ground; earth to earth, ashes to ashes, dust to dust. The Lord bless him and keep him. . . . Amen.'"

The rain was falling harder now. The sexton set to work, quickly shoveling dirt back into the grave while the Reverend Filby tucked his Bible up under the shelter of his arm and drew Sebastian beneath the cover of the nearby church porch. "No sign yet of what's become of Benji's sister?" asked the clergyman, his jowly pink face slack with concern.

Sebastian shook his head. "I'm sorry, no."

The reverend let out his breath in a pained sigh, his gaze narrowing as he stared off across the wet, crowded mass of gray tombstones. Toby the Dancer had disappeared. "I worry about them—the street children, I mean," said Filby. "They are so dreadfully vulnerable."

"I suspect that's why the killer preys on them," said Sebastian. "They make easy targets."

"'Suffer the little children,'" quoted the reverend, sadly shaking his head. "'*Suffer the little children . . .*'"

Afterward, Sebastian hauled Gibson off to a pub on Clerkenwell Green.

"You look like hell," said Sebastian, setting two tankards of ale on a table in the dark corner where Gibson was hiding.

Gibson hunched his shoulders. "Don't start on me. I've already heard it all from Alexi."

"She's worried about you." *I'm worried about you,* Sebastian thought, but he didn't say it.

The Irishman rasped one hand across his beard-stubbled face. "It doesn't often get to me, what I do. But this time . . . this time it has. I keep trying to imagine what manner of man could do such a thing, but I simply can't. I mean, even though I believe it's wrong, at some fundamental level I can still understand someone who kills in a fit of rage or jealousy or fear. Those are emotions every one of us has felt at some time or another, haven't we? The only reason we don't all go around murdering people isn't because we don't feel those emotions; it's because something stops us. Whether you call it conscience or empathy for our fellow beings or obedience to the dictates of God, the fact remains that *something* stops us. So even though we don't kill, we can still understand the compulsions that drive your typical killer. But this? I can't begin to understand what was in the mind of the man who did that to Benji Thatcher. That wasn't the unbridled manifestation of some emotion we've all experienced. It's something else. And I'm not sure I want to understand what it is."

Sebastian took a long, slow drink of his ale. "I think what drove Benji Thatcher's killer was a desire for pleasure."

Gibson looked up at him with haggard, bloodshot eyes. "How can anyone derive pleasure from causing an innocent such unimaginable fear and pain?"

"That I can't answer."

Gibson dropped his gaze to his ale again. He started to take a drink, then changed his mind and pushed the tankard aside. "You have to find this killer. Anyone who kills for pleasure will do it again and again, until he's stopped."

"I know," said Sebastian. "That's what worries me."

Sebastian was leaving the tavern when he heard his name called and turned to find Constable Mott Gowan trotting after him.

"My lord," panted the constable, skidding to a halt on the wet paving. "I meant to tell you before, but it went clean out of my head after we buried the boy."

"Tell me what?" said Sebastian, guiding the man out of the path of a heavily laden brewer's wagon.

"I asked around Hockley-in-the-Hole, the way you suggested. But I couldn't find anybody who remembered seeing either Benji or Sybil last Friday."

"I'm not surprised. I suspect most people would be hard-pressed to tell one ragged child from the next."

Gowan nodded sadly. "Is there anything else you can suggest I do, my lord? Because the truth is, I'm plumb out of ideas."

"I can't think of anything right now. But I'll be certain to let you know if I do."

The constable nodded again. "There is one thing I heard you might be interested in," he said hesitantly.

"Oh?"

"An ostler at the Red Lion mentioned seeing a gentleman in a bang-up rig—not that evening, mind you, but a couple days before."

"What did he look like?"

"The gentleman? The ostler couldn't remember nothing about the man himself. But he had a clear recollection of the rig: a yellow phaeton drawn by a real showy dapple gray." Gowan paused, his eyes narrowing. "That means somethin' to you?"

"Yes," said Sebastian. "It does."

Gentlemen of the ton were frequently known for their favorite horses and carriages. Lord Petersham owned only brown carriages and brown horses; Mr. Markham favored a shiny black curricle pulled by a perfectly matched snowy white pair. And Sir Francis Rowe was famous for his dashing little yellow-bodied phaeton drawn by a lovely dapple gray mare.

It took some time, but Sebastian finally tracked the Butcher of Culloden's grandson to an exclusive shop on Bond Street, where he found the Baronet inspecting an array of diamond-encrusted fobs presented on a velvet-lined tray by an obsequious jeweler.

Sir Francis lifted his head as Sebastian came to stand beside him. "Not you again."

Sebastian showed his teeth in a smile. "Yes."

The Baronet signaled the jeweler to leave them and turned his back to the counter. "Do I take it you're still obsessed with the death of that Clerkenwell pickpocket?"

"Yes."

"Whatever for?"

"Because the boy's little sister is still missing. And because I object to sharing my city with anyone capable of that kind of barbaric cruelty."

"Oh? And what has any of this to do with me, precisely?"

"You were seen in Hockley-in-the-Hole several days before the boy disappeared."

"And this strikes you as nefarious, does it?"

"Is there a reason why it should not?"

"As a matter of fact, there is. My family has long owned property in the area. It's the same reason I was in Clerkenwell the day my snuffbox was stolen."

"Manage your property yourself, do you?"

"Not on a day-to-day basis, no. But I do sometimes take a hand in matters when necessary." Rowe rested his elbows on the counter behind him. "I do hope you don't intend to continue hounding me over this ridiculous affair."

"Actually, given that you refuse to say where you were either Friday evening or Sunday night, I suspect I shall."

Sir Francis let out a long, ostentatious sigh. "Very well; although I warn you, you'll feel the fool for pressing the matter. As it happens, I was with my dear cousin the Prince Regent from mid–Friday afternoon till the wee hours of the morning. And if you are inclined to doubt my word, you may verify it with your own wife's father, for Jarvis was there, as well."

"And late Sunday night?"

The Baronet's eyes gleamed with amusement that bordered on derision. "Sorry; I think I've indulged your vulgar curiosity more than enough." He pushed away from the counter. "I wonder; have you thought to check the area's numerous houses of correction for this missing brat? If I were you, that's where I would start, given that she's no doubt a thief—just like her brother."

And with that he nodded to the jeweler and walked out of the shop.

Chapter 29

*I*t seemed unlikely, but on the off chance Rowe might be right, Sebastian spent what was left of the afternoon visiting every metropolitan prison from Newgate and the Bridewell to the Marshalsea and the Clerkenwell House of Correction.

He undertook the task himself rather than sending an inquiry or delegating the chore to someone like Constable Gowan because he wanted to be certain the negative responses he received were reliable. At each somber, noisome, high-walled slice of judicially sanctioned hell, he asked after not only Sybil Thatcher but also Mary Cartwright and Mick Swallow, the missing boy Jem Jones had mentioned. All were unknown to London's prison authorities.

As the shadows lengthened toward dusk, Sebastian sent Tom home with the tired horses and turned his steps toward Covent Garden Market.

At this hour the market was given over almost entirely to the flower sellers, their stalls of chrysanthemums, lavenders, Michaelmas daisies, and viburnum forming gay splashes of gold, purple, blue, and red against the shadowy, timeworn sandstone columns of Inigo Jones's Italianate arcades. He was here looking for Kat, and he smiled fondly when he spotted her wandering the rows of flower stalls, the handle of a wicker basket looped over one arm, a vague smile on her lips. She often came here before her performances, both because she loved flowers for their own sake and, he suspected, because they formed an elusive link to her lost mother.

"Devlin," she said when she saw him. "How did you know to find me here?"

"I know you," he said simply, and she smiled.

They turned to walk along the piazza's arcade, the scents of the flowers mingling with the stronger odors of brewing coffee, roasting meats, and spilled ale. He said, "Someone recently suggested that the comte de Brienne supports his lavish lifestyle in ways he'd rather not have advertised. Do you know anything about that?"

She hesitated just a shade too long before answering, and Sebastian said, "He works for the French, doesn't he?" It was a time-honored technique: Paris provided a cash-strapped émigré with the financial resources required to live comfortably in exile, in return for which the émigré provided Paris with a steady stream of information.

She glanced over at him. "You know I can't answer that."

"I know."

Kat herself had once passed information to the French, not because she had any love for Napoléon but because she longed to free her mother's people, the Irish, from the onerous yoke of their English conquerors. Given what the English had done to her mother, Sebastian had never been able to blame her for that. And while she had severed her ties with the French months ago, she still knew more about their operatives in London than almost anyone—except, perhaps, Jarvis.

He said, "So what does the comte do? Coax secrets from his lovers? Tempt those with useful knowledge into playing his erotic games and then use the threat of embarrassing exposure to extract secrets from them?"

"Something like that." Kat stared off across the crowded marketplace. She was no longer smiling. "But surely you don't think de Brienne killed that boy they found in Clerkenwell?"

"I don't know what to think. How well do you know him?"

"Not well. He's a self-absorbed, vain, and selfish man. But I can't say I've ever felt there was any real evil in him, despite the somewhat unorthodox nature of his sexual interests."

"Those he blackmails into betraying their country might disagree with you."

"True," she said.

"He arrived here—when? 'Eighty-nine? 'Ninety?"

"Later, I believe; perhaps as late as 1793. From what I've heard, his early life was difficult. His parents died when he was a young child, and the uncle who raised him was quite brutal. There are even rumors . . ."

"Yes?" he prompted when she hesitated.

"I've heard it said he killed his uncle and two cousins with his own hands—that he fled France not so much because of the Revolution but to escape the consequences of what he'd done."

"Do you think it's true?"

"Honestly?" She swung to face him, the setting sun shining fleetingly through the shifting clouds to light her face. "I think it could be."

"Yet you say you think there's no malice in him."

"He's a very complicated man."

"Most killers are."

Sebastian found Amadeus Colbert, the comte de Brienne, eating a large beefsteak in solitary splendor at an exclusive little inn on Mill Street known for the quality of its dinners.

"Mind if I join you?" asked Sebastian.

De Brienne paused with a slice of rare beef on his fork. "And if I said yes, I mind? Would you go away?"

"No." Sebastian slid into the seat opposite with a smile. "In the course of a murder investigation, it's inevitable that the names of innocent people will come up. But when someone is suggested by two very different sources, I do tend to take notice."

De Brienne chewed his slice of meat and swallowed. "People have been talking about me, have they?"

"You did say you have a number of enemies." Sebastian leaned forward and kept his voice low. "But then, those who engage in blackmail generally do. Especially when they force their victims to betray their country's secrets."

De Brienne's lips relaxed into a smile. "Actually, in my experience, people resent being blackmailed into revealing state secrets far less than they resent being bled of their own money."

"I suppose I must bow to your superior knowledge of the subject. Although I'm surprised to hear you admit it so readily."

"Oh? Why?"

"The sort of activities we're discussing do tend to be hazardous to one's health."

De Brienne looked puzzled for a moment, then laughed, although Sebastian noticed that his eyes had narrowed. "Precisely who told you about me?"

"Does it matter?"

The Frenchman threw a quick glance around, but they were quite alone in this corner of the restaurant. "I had assumed it must be your father-in-law. But obviously in that I was mistaken."

"If Jarvis knew you were passing information to Paris, you'd be dead."

"And so I would be—if he hadn't maneuvered long ago to control the contents of the information Paris receives from me."

Sebastian studied the comte's strongly boned, aristocratic face. "You would have me believe you are Jarvis's tool?"

"The phraseology is somewhat indelicate, but you could say that, yes."

"And Paris suspects nothing?"

De Brienne's lips curled into a smile as he spread his arms wide. "I'm still here, am I not? Like Jarvis, Napoléon does have a tendency to eliminate those he knows have betrayed him."

"Napoléon is somewhat distracted these days."

"Not that distracted."

Sebastian watched the Frenchman carefully rest knife and fork on the edge of his plate. "Will your family's ancestral estates be returned to you, do you think? In the event of a restoration?"

"Oh, there will be a restoration. Make no mistake of that."

"And does the soi-disant King Louis XVIII know you killed your noble uncle and cousins?"

The skin pulled oddly across de Brienne's bony cheeks, as if his entire face had tightened up. He was no longer smiling. "My uncle and his sons were such fervent adherents of the Revolution that not even the excesses of Robespierre and the massacres in the Vendée could cool their ardor. They died the week Robespierre fell, and there is no one in France or here in England amongst the émigrés who mourns their passing."

"That doesn't exactly answer my question," said Sebastian, watching him push back his chair and rise to his feet.

"No? I rather thought it did." The French count executed an elegant bow. "And now you must excuse me, my lord." He started to turn away, then paused to say, "I fail to understand what you imagine my ties to Paris—or to Jarvis—could possibly have to do with the death of that boy in Clerkenwell."

"You did read *Les 120 journées de Sodome*, did you not?"

Something passed over the Frenchman's tight features, something that looked oddly like a quiver of revulsion. "De Sade was a very sick man when he wrote that book. It is the ravings of a madman. A dangerous madman with a dark and twisted soul."

"Whoever killed Benji Thatcher is a madman. His friends and family simply haven't realized it yet."

"I'm not convinced you could hide that level of depravity—not from those who actually knew you." De Brienne bowed again. *"Monsieur."*

❦

Sebastian contemplated the Frenchman's words as he left the inn and turned toward Brook Street. He had the sense that he was missing something—something important that kept hovering just beyond his thoughts, taunting and yet maddeningly elusive.

He walked on, turning his collar against a biting cold wind that had driven most people indoors and left the narrow street largely deserted in the misty lamplight. He could see only a stout man with a muffler wrapped about his lower face studying the wares displayed in the window of a nearby haberdasher and a second man who leaned against a spiked iron fence mounted atop the low stone knee wall that separated the footpath from the dark apse of St. George's, Hanover, at the corner.

As he neared the looming bulk of the church, Sebastian studied the slim young man who stood there, seemingly absorbed in the task of loading tobacco into his clay pipe. He wore a buff-colored coat rather than a green one, but there was no mistaking that thin, ordinary face: It was the same man who had followed Sebastian through Covent Garden.

Sebastian felt himself tense in anticipation. Without his flintlock or a walking stick, he was left with only the dagger sheathed in his boot. And his wits.

"I take it you're waiting for me?" said Sebastian, his voice ringing out loud and clear in the damp air as he approached the church.

He thought the man might deny it, or maybe even run away as he had before. Instead, the man stayed where he was, his head coming up as he tucked away his pipe. "Didn't expect you to recognize me," he said, his French accent faint but unmistakable.

Sebastian drew up some feet away. "Why? Because you changed the color of your coat?" He was aware of the sound of running footsteps coming up the street behind him, fast.

Then the slim man pushed away from the fence and threw himself at Sebastian.

Chapter 30

$\mathcal{S}$ebastian grabbed the younger man's coat front and swung him around, putting this assailant's body between Sebastian and the second, unknown assassin now running toward him with a knife clenched in one hand: the stout man in the muffler.

"You sons of bitches," swore Sebastian, driving his knee toward the buff-coated man's groin. "Who sent you?"

Buff Coat twisted his hips at the last instant, grunting as Sebastian's knee slammed into his thigh, hard. The impact sent the thin man stumbling off the kerb and bought Sebastian just enough time to yank the dagger from his boot.

The stout man came at him with a guttural snarl, his knife driving straight at Sebastian's stomach. Sebastian swung his left forearm in a blocking sweep that deflected the man's blade as Sebastian stepped in to bury his own dagger in the assailant's chest.

The stout man's eyes widened, blood spilling from his mouth. But such was the momentum of his attack that he kept coming, bowling Sebastian over to knock him off his feet. Sebastian slammed his right shoulder and the side of his face against the knee wall. The dying man landed on top of him.

"Hell," swore Sebastian. Hands sticky and wet with blood, he shoved the heavy body aside and fought to free his dagger as the buff-coated man came up out of the gutter to lunge at him again—this time with a blade in his hand.

Sluing around, Sebastian kicked up to smash both feet into his would-be killer's chest with enough force to send the man staggering back. Then Sebastian jerked his dagger from the stout man's chest and threw it.

The blade whistled through the air to sink deep into the base of the slim man's throat. He gurgled, dark red blood spraying in all directions as he crumpled.

"*Hell*," said Sebastian again, swiping the blood from his face with a crooked elbow as a distant shout went up, followed by the familiar whirl of the watch's rattle.

Charles, Lord Jarvis, was in his chambers at Carlton House, penning detailed instructions to the Regent's representative in Vienna, when Devlin strode in the door. Jarvis's clerk followed, ineffectually sputtering and fluttering at the Viscount's heels.

"We need to talk. Now," said Devlin. His hat was gone, his cravat askew and soaked with blood, his coat ripped and smeared with more gore. It looked as if he'd made an attempt to wipe the dried blood from his face, but a fresh line trickled down the side of his cheek from a cut above his eye.

Jarvis nodded the clerk's dismissal. "Leave us."

Devlin said, "First of all, tell me this: Was Sir Francis Rowe with you and the Prince last Friday evening?"

"As a matter of fact, he was. Why do you ask?"

"For how long?"

Jarvis set aside his pen and leaned back in his chair. "From midafternoon to early Saturday morning. Please tell me you're not so foolish as to suspect Rowe of killing this wretched little thief you're so obsessed with."

"He strikes me as someone you might have an interest in protecting."

"And so I would, if there were any need." Jarvis let his gaze travel over the man before him. "You're looking decidedly more disheveled than usual."

"Two men just tried to kill me."

"And they failed? How . . . disappointing."

Devlin bared his teeth in a hard smile. "Did you send them?"

Jarvis reached for his snuffbox. "Did they say I did? Is that why you're here?"

"Unfortunately, they neglected to name their employer before they died."

"In that case I suppose I should be thankful you didn't drag their corpses here with you." Once, Devlin had dumped a dead would-be assassin on Jarvis's drawing room carpet. The bloodstains were still there.

Devlin came to flatten his palms on the top of Jarvis's desk and leaned into them. "Did you send them?"

Jarvis opened his snuffbox with a flick of one thumbnail. "Why— apart from my natural desire to rid the world of annoyances—do you imagine I sent men to kill you tonight?"

Devlin pushed away and went to stand at the window overlooking the lamplit palace forecourt. "I'm told the comte de Brienne is a double agent. That you discovered he was blackmailing sensitively placed government officials and, rather than eliminate him, you decided to use your inimitable persuasive skills to convince him to funnel tainted information to Paris. Is that true?"

"And if it is?" Jarvis raised a pinch of snuff to one nostril. "Do you intend to inform Paris of this discovery? Because otherwise I fail to conceive why I should be interested in eliminating you."

Devlin held himself very still. "So it is true? De Brienne is your creature?"

"Of course he is."

"How much do you know about the unusual nature of his sexual interests?"

Jarvis closed his snuffbox with a snap. "Frankly? Far more than I'd like."

"Then perhaps you won't be surprised to learn there is a very real possibility he was involved in the recent torture and murder of the boy found in Clerkenwell."

Jarvis slipped the snuffbox back into his pocket. "Oh? And you think this information should alarm me? Because let me hasten to assure you, it does not."

Something flared in the Viscount's unpleasant yellow eyes. "It's possible Benji Thatcher is not the only child de Brienne has killed in this way. The boy's sister is also missing, and there may have been others."

Jarvis laced his fingers together and rested his hands on his stomach. "If you're right—if de Brienne is a killer—then after Napoléon is defeated, you may have him. But not before. I trust I make myself clear?"

"You can't be serious."

"Oh, but I am. The information de Brienne feeds Paris is too valuable for me to allow you to harm him in any way—particularly at this critical moment. As far as I'm concerned, defeating Bonaparte is worth the life of each and every ragged urchin ever to infest the streets of London. Most of them only grow up to hang anyway." Jarvis reached for his pen again, then paused with the nib suspended above his ink. "If you do anything to interfere with what I have so painstakingly set up— *anything*—then believe me, I will send men to kill you. And this time, you won't see them coming."

"You'd best hope I don't," said the Viscount.

For one lethal moment, the two men stared at each other.

Then Devlin turned on his heel and left.

Chapter 31

"So who of the many people you have angered over the past three days would want to kill you?"

Hero asked the question as Sebastian leaned back in his tub, the steam from the hot water rising around him. He swiped a hand across his dripping face and looked over to where she stood with her hands cupping her elbows to hold her arms close to her chest. Both the flippancy of the words and the tone were belied by the tension of her posture.

"If I had to make any bets," he said, "I'd probably put my money on the Bligh sisters." He stood up, water streaming from his naked body as he reached for a towel. "But I could be wrong."

"Were they following you, do you think?" she asked, watching him.

"If they were, they must have had a merry time chasing me all over London. Which makes me wonder if I shouldn't rather suspect the last two men I spoke with."

"Who were?"

"The comte de Brienne and Sir Francis Rowe."

"Ah; my dear cousin. You said his name had come up, but you didn't say you suspected him."

Sebastian ran the towel over his wet arms and chest. "Benji may have lifted the Baronet's snuffbox."

"And that's a reason to suspect him?"

"It is when you know that last August he broke the neck of a six-year-old who tried to pick his pocket on the Strand."

"Dear Lord."

"However, your father verified that Rowe spent last Friday with the Prince, so I don't see any reason for the man to want to set someone to kill me."

"Which leaves de Brienne and the Bligh sisters."

He roughed up his wet hair with the towel, then tossed it aside. "Yes."

"You need to be more careful."

He reached for her, pulling her into his arms. "I'll try."

"Huh." She slipped her hands around his waist and nipped at his ear. "Try harder."

He kissed her nose. "Yes, ma'am."

She let her hands slide lower on his hips.

He said, "The cut over my eye is still open. I don't want to drip blood on your gown."

"Mmm." Her hands slid lower. "What can we do about that?"

He gave her a crooked smile and tugged at the tapes of her gown. "Take it off?"

❧

It was some time later, after dinner, that Sir Henry Lovejoy stopped by Brook Street to drink a cup of tea beside the library fire and tell Sebastian the results of the inquiries he'd sent to the metropolitan area's various public offices.

"I wish I could say their responses surprise me, but they don't," said Lovejoy, his gaze on the black cat assiduously washing itself on the hearth. "Most expressed frank incredulity that we would even ask. I fear the only time your typical magistrate or constable pays attention to the comings and goings of his district's orphaned and abandoned children is when they cause trouble."

"You said, 'most.' So not all?"

Lovejoy set aside his teacup and reached into his coat for a folded paper. "Sir Alexander Robbins—he's the chief magistrate at Bethnal Green—reports that they had a rash of such disappearances in the past, but they've since ceased."

Sebastian sat forward. "When was this?"

"He believes the first child went missing sometime in 1807 or 1808, although he can't recall precisely. The disappearances continued over a three- or four-year period and then stopped."

"Does he provide the names of the children who disappeared?"

"He does, yes." Lovejoy passed him the paper. "They are listed in the order in which they went missing, although he says most of the ages are only approximate. He admits there may have been others, but these are the ones who had a close friend or a sibling—someone who was able to convince him the youngsters were unlikely to have gone off without telling them."

There were four names on the paper, two boys and two girls.

> *Jack Lawson,* 14
> *Emma Smith,* 15
> *Jenny Hopkins,* 14
> *Brady Barker,* 16

Sebastian looked up from the list. "May I keep this?"

"Of course." Lovejoy reached again for his tea. "I've also set one of my men to looking into the ownership of that shot factory."

"And?

"I gather it's rather complicated. He's still making inquiries." Lovejoy took a sip of his tea and looked up. "Have you discovered anything at all?"

"I wouldn't have said so, except that my questions must be making someone uncomfortable: Two men tried to kill me this evening near Hanover Square."

The teacup rattled in Lovejoy's hands. "Tonight? Who were they?"

"Hirelings. But I've no idea who sent them."

"We'll make them talk," said Lovejoy grimly.

Sebastian took a deep swallow of his own brandy and felt it burn all the way down. "Unfortunately they're both dead."

"Ah. Well, that does make it more difficult. But I'll set some of the lads on it first thing in the morning. They'll soon sort it out."

Sebastian suspected that whoever they were dealing with was too clever to betray himself to hirelings. But he kept the thought to himself.

After the magistrate had gone, Hero came to stand in the entrance to the library.

"You heard?" Sebastian said.

She walked over to scoop the sleepy black cat up from the hearth and cradle him in her arms. "I was discussing tomorrow's menu with Cook, but yes, I did hear most of it." He had told her of that day's conversations with Ashworth and the comte de Brienne, along with some of what he'd learned from Jarvis. But he had stopped short of telling his wife that her father had threatened to kill him. "I wonder where else in London street children have disappeared without anyone noticing?"

"It's a disturbing thought, isn't it?" He went to pour himself another drink, then came to stand beside her, his gaze on the flames.

"What?" she asked, watching him.

He glanced over at her. "I think I'll pay another visit to the Rutherford Shot Factory in the morning."

"Why? What are you looking for?"

He downed his brandy in one long pull and reached for the Bethnal Green magistrate's list of missing children. "More graves."

☙

Friday, 17 September

Sebastian reached Clerkenwell just as the rising sun was spilling its
golden light across the gentle hills beyond the city.

Leaving Tom with the horses, he walked across the weed-choked,
rubble-strewn field to the factory's cluster of ruined buildings. "Inchbald?" he called and heard his voice echo in the stillness.

It was too early, surely, for the ex-soldier to be out begging. Yet
when Sebastian reached the gaping doorway of the brick warehouse
that Inchbald had made his home, he found it empty except for some
rusting machinery, piles of broken crates, and a mound of what looked
like ragged blankets and old clothes.

"Rory Inchbald?" he called again, breathing in the unpleasantly
dank, moldering air.

Sebastian turned, hands on his hips, to look out over the uneven
wasteland. He had walked the factory grounds before and found nothing, although at the time he hadn't exactly been looking for more graves.
The problem was, in this muddle of weeds, tumbled old bricks, and
abandoned, rusting machinery, how obvious would an older, overgrown
burial be?

The cawing of a crow drew his gaze to the nearby shot tower. He
stared thoughtfully at the medieval-style parapet at the structure's top.
Then he crossed to the door at the tower's base. The door was locked,
but the weathered, ancient wood splintered easily with his first kick.
Two more hard kicks and the old panels tore away from the lock. The
door swung inward to bang against the brick wall behind it.

The interior was dusty and dim, lit only by small, arched windows
that pierced the thick walls at infrequent intervals. Here at its base the
tower stretched perhaps thirty feet across, although it narrowed per-
ceptibly toward the top far above. A rickety wooden staircase wound

around the inside of the curving brick walls, and Sebastian climbed it carefully, testing each step before trusting it with his weight.

Once, coal and lead would have been hoisted up through the tower's open central core to the rough wooden platform above. There the coal would stoke a furnace that melted the lead. The melted lead would then be poured through a screen to form neat round balls as it fell toward the water kept far below. Decades of thick coal dust and splattered lead now grimed the walls, and as he neared the top, Sebastian found everything covered with a thickening greenish crust thanks to the arsenic once used to help the molten lead pour smoothly.

The staircase ended at an upper chamber some twenty feet across. A broken iron tripod and rusting cauldron still stood beside the trap door in the center of the plank floor; the remnants of an old pulley system hung suspended from the ceiling above. Even with the cold morning breeze blowing in through the open doorway that led to the parapet, the air here was foul.

He crossed quickly to the crenelated outer walk. The golden light of the early sun threw long shadows across the uneven ground far below, highlighting each mound and depression. Some of the irregularity, he now realized, came from the abandoned, overgrown channels that had once carried water from the Fleet, for water was an important part of the shot-manufacturing process. He picked out old blast mounds and abandoned sluice gates. And then, as he continued to study the rugged field's patterns of shadow and light, he noticed several inexplicable rectangles the size and shape he was looking for.

One, near the wall of the closest warehouse, was thick with crabgrass, knotweed, and ragweed, annuals that typically germinated in spring and then grew through summer. But while the surrounding field also showed the tall flowering stalks of biennials such as Queen Anne's lace and mullein, both were conspicuously absent from that six-by-two-foot depression.

And he knew then that he was looking at a recent grave.

Chapter 32

$\mathcal{S}$ebastian stood with his arms crossed at his chest, one shoulder propped against the warehouse's rough brick wall as he watched Paul Gibson carefully scrape dirt from the bones slowly emerging from the soft earth of the grave.

"How long do you think it's been here?" Sebastian asked.

"Hard to say." Gibson grimaced as he shifted his position in a way that threw his peg leg out to one side. "You bury a body four feet deep, and it can take two or three years to reduce to a skeleton. But at twelve inches like this? There can be nothing left except bones after six months."

"So he could have been killed in early spring?"

"Probably. Although I don't think this was a 'he.'"

"You can tell?"

"Not with absolute certainty. But the indications are we're looking at what's left of a young girl. Somewhere between fourteen and sixteen."

"It's probably Mary Cartwright," said Sebastian, and felt something tear deep inside him.

Gibson gently lifted the skull free from the earth and turned it in his hands. "She was buried facedown."

"I guess whoever buried her didn't want to look at her face." He gazed off across the rubbish-strewn field to where Mott Gowan, the parish constable, was supervising a party of volunteers clearing weeds from every suspicious-looking mound and hollow. And he knew a rising tide of frustration and helplessness laced with raw, potent fury. "How the blazes will we ever identify any of them when all that's left is bones?"

Gibson set the skull aside and reached again for his trowel. "We can't."

❧

They found the grave of Rory Inchbald next, buried just six inches beneath the earthen floor of the warehouse.

"Bloody hell," said Sebastian, staring down at the one-legged soldier's pale, dirt-covered face. "He didn't know anything. Why kill him?"

Mott Gowan swiped one forearm across his face. "Maybe somebody thought he saw more'n he did that night. Or maybe he wasn't tellin' us everything he knew."

"Bloody hell," said Sebastian again and turned away.

❧

By the time Sir Henry Lovejoy arrived at the shot factory after his morning court sessions, they had uncovered three more skeletons.

The day was clear but blustery and unseasonably cold, and the little magistrate huddled deep into his greatcoat as he stared down at one of the half-uncovered skeletons. "*Five* graves?"

"So far," said Sebastian. "One body, four skeletons. Gibson says all were probably buried sometime in the last two or three years."

Lovejoy swung his head to stare at Sebastian. "How can he know that?"

Gibson knew these things because he buried cadaver parts in his own yard and then studied the effects of the passage of time on flesh and bone. But Sebastian could hardly tell the magistrate that. He chewed on the inside of his cheek. "From his experiences in the war, I suppose."

Lovejoy gave him a hard, steady look. "Yes; I suppose."

Together they watched Constable Gowan supervise the loading of a box of bones onto a waiting cart. Sebastian said, "Any luck yet discovering who owns this place?"

"We're making progress. Seems the factory used to belong to a woman named Margery Deighton, who inherited it from an uncle. But she went mad somewhere around the turn of the century."

"That's when it was shuttered?"

Lovejoy nodded. "She died without a will four years ago, and her heirs are still fighting over it."

"Over who owns it?"

"No; over what to do with it. Some want to start the factory up again, some want to lease it, while the more affluent simply want to sell the land."

"How many heirs are there?"

"A dozen or more."

"Do you have their names?"

"No. But my lad is still on it." Lovejoy stared out over the windswept field, his face held in tight lines. "Even after we received the report from Bethnal Green, I still kept hoping that what happened to Benji Thatcher was an isolated incident. But this . . . this tells us otherwise."

"Gibson says all were probably under eighteen when they died—with most considerably younger."

Lovejoy took off his spectacles and rubbed his eyes with a splayed thumb and forefinger. "Merciful heavens. I can't understand what manner of man could do this."

"Someone who values his own fleeting pleasure above the lives of his fellow beings."

Lovejoy looked over at him. "Who could possibly derive pleasure from doing this?"

"A very twisted soul."

A shout went up from one of the excavations near the boundary wall, drawing their attention. As they watched, Constable Gowan reached into the shallow grave to pick up something. He studied the object in his hand for a moment before spitting on it and rubbing it between his fingertips. Then his hand closed in a tight fist and he turned to come loping toward them, one elbow cocked skyward as he held his hat clamped down against the wind.

"What did you find?" Sebastian asked.

"This." Gowan opened his fist as he held out his hand.

An old Spanish piece of eight lay on his dirty palm. At some point, someone had punched a crude hole through the center of the coin and threaded a rawhide cord through it. Now the cord was frayed and stained dark from the body fluids of the dead boy or girl it had rested against.

"There was a lad name of Mick disappeared last winter. Used to wear this tied around his neck, he did. Said it was his good-luck piece."

Sebastian reached to take the coin. "You mean Mick Swallow? Jem Jones's cousin?"

"Aye. That's the one."

🌹

Jem Jones sat beneath the lone plane tree on Clerkenwell Green, his head bowed, his gaze on the dirty Spanish coin he held cradled in one palm.

"Is it your cousin's?" Sebastian asked.

Jem nodded and swiped the back of his other hand across his nose.

Sebastian handed the boy his own handkerchief. "Tell me about Mick."

The boy sniffed. "Wot's there t' tell?"

"How old was he?"

"Fourteen or fifteen, I reckon."

"When was the last time you saw him?"

Jem sniffed again. "Guy Fawkes Day, last year. He was supposed t' meet me at the bonfires, only he never showed up."

Sebastian found himself remembering the Dancer's story of Benji Thatcher's disappearance. He said, "You told me the other day you thought someone grabbed him. What makes you think that?"

Jem ducked his head, his fingers rubbing the old coin's surface over and over. "I hear they found a bunch o' graves out by that old shot tower where somebody tried to bury Benji. Is that where ye got this?"

"Yes."

"Yer sayin' Mick was in one o' them graves?"

"Probably."

Jem's lower lip began to tremble, and he bit it.

Sebastian said, "Why did Mick wear this?"

"He'd found it the last time he went toggin' with his da."

"His father worked the sewers?" It was a nasty and dangerous way to earn a living, combing London's ancient network of underground sewers for items of value that had been swept underground by the rains.

Jem nodded. "One day they was down in the sewers when Mick, he spots this coin layin' out there on a mud flat. So he goes to pick it up. Only just as he's reachin' for it all excited, he hears this rumblin' and a big stretch of that old tunnel just caves in and swallows his da. If it hadn't been fer this coin, Mick woulda been standin' by his da and he'd've been swallowed too. Mick figured the coin saved his life. Didn't matter how hungry he got, he wouldn't never sell it. Punched that hole through it and wore it around his neck, he did. Always. Said it was his good-luck piece."

Jem fell silent, as if struck by the realization that the lucky piece of eight had failed spectacularly to keep Mick safe from the hideous fate that had befallen him.

Sebastian said, "When did this happen?"

"I dunno. Three, maybe four years ago."

"And after his father died, did Mick continue togging?"

"Oh, no, yer honor. He never went down in them sewers again. Just the thought of it was enough to make him turn all pale-like and start to shake."

"So how did he live?"

Jem looked away toward the Middlesex Sessions House at the far end of the green. "This 'n' that, I s'pose. Same as anybody else."

"Did he ever pick pockets?"

Jeb stared at Sebastian with wide, studiously guileless eyes. "Oh, no, yer honor."

"Of course not," said Sebastian dryly. "But if he found, say, a pocket handkerchief on Clerkenwell Green, where would he take it?"

Jem screwed his mouth into a scowl, as if weighing the benefits of telling the truth against the risks of lying.

"Tell me," said Sebastian in the stern voice that had once commanded men in battle.

The boy's grimy fist tightened around Sebastian's sorely abused handkerchief. "The Professor. Mick was a big favorite with the Professor."

Icarus Cantrell was putting a kettle on the fire in the back room of his shop when Sebastian walked in.

"You keep coming here," said the old man, straightening with the slowness of aged joints aching in cold weather.

"Your name keeps coming up. Why is that, do you think?"

"In many ways, Clerkenwell is still a small village."

Sebastian laid Mick Swallow's piece of eight on the well-scrubbed kitchen table that stood between them.

Cantrell went very still. "Where did you find that?"

"In a shallow grave on the grounds of the old shot factory. I take it you know who it belonged to?"

The Professor picked up the old coin with gentle fingers. "He was a sweet boy, Mick. His mother died when he was just three. Jack Swallow had nothing else to do with the lad, so he used to take him down in the sewers with him from the time Mick was a little tyke. Mick practically grew up down there." He shook his head sadly. "The boy was never quite the same after Jack was killed right in front of him."

"You knew Mick had disappeared?"

"Of course I knew."

"So why didn't you tell me about him?"

Icarus Cantrell set the coin back on the table. "What do you think? That I'm the one killing these children?"

"You do seem to be acquainted with all of them."

The Professor turned away to fuss with the preparation of his teapot. "There's a lad you might want to talk to," he said without looking around. "Last winter, he was over by the Charterhouse one evening when a gentleman pulled him into a coach and forced him to drink what I suspect was a powerful dose of laudanum. What happened to him after that sounds a great deal like what you say was done to Benji. The difference is, Hamish managed to escape."

Sebastian felt a quickening of interest reined in by the suspicion that Icarus Cantrell was in some way he couldn't define toying with him. "Once again, I can't help but wonder why you kept this to yourself until now."

The old man poured the boiling water into a simple brown teapot. "Because I respect what's told to me in confidence and I didn't have the lad's permission to tell you what happened to him. Now I do."

"Where is he?"

"He left Clerkenwell shortly after it happened. He was afraid the man might find him again and kill him."

"Does he know the man's identity?"

"No."

"Yet he must know something—what the man looks like, surely, and where he was taken."

Cantrell set the heavy kettle aside. "I asked if he'd be willing to talk to you. He's frightened, but he has agreed."

"When? Where?"

The Professor glanced out the window at the cold blue sky. "Come back in two hours. He'll be here."

Chapter 33

*T*he skinny, ragged boy sat huddled on a low, rush-bottomed stool beside the fire in the back room of Icarus Cantrell's shop. He was a wiry lad with a head of thick dark hair, a tense, closed face, and haunted hazel eyes. He said his name was Hamish McCormick and he'd be fifteen years old on All Souls' Day.

"I don't like talkin' about this," he said when Sebastian settled on a nearby bench.

"I understand."

The boy gave him a long, hard look. "Do ye?"

Sebastian met Hamish's gaze and knew that he could never begin to understand either what this boy had been through or the nightmares that must haunt him still. "Thank you for agreeing to speak with me."

The boy blinked and looked away.

Sebastian said, "The Professor tells me a man in a carriage grabbed you a year or so ago. Do you remember the date?"

"No. Not sure I ever knew it. It weren't long after Christmas, though."

"What did the man look like?"

The boy scrubbed his hands down over his face. "I dunno. Whenever I think about it, all I can see is his hands 'n' his eyes. The rest o' him . . . it's just a blur."

Sebastian had to work to keep the disappointment out of his voice. "Tell me about his hands."

A faint trembling shivered the boy's thin frame. "They was white. Soft."

"A gentleman's hands?"

Hamish nodded, his throat working as he swallowed. "He was a swell, all right. Talked real fine, he did. Liked t' hear himself talk, I reckon."

"How old was he?"

"I dunno." He studied Sebastian thoughtfully. "Older'n you. How old're you?"

"I'm thirty. You say you remember his eyes?"

"They was like nothin' I ever seen. Ye look at him, 'n' it's like yer peerin' into the heart o' hell."

"What color were they?"

Hamish began to rock back and forth on his stool, hugging himself. "When I think about 'em, they're red. But that can't be, can it?"

Sebastian suspected the boy's memories of that night were colored by the opium he'd been forced to drink as well as by the horror of the experience. And he began to wonder how much Hamish would actually be able to help him. "Tell me about when the man grabbed you."

Hamish went very still. It was as if he were drawing into himself, bracing himself against the horror of remembrance. "I was with Paddy Gantry. We was walkin' down by Charterhouse Square."

"Who's Paddy Gantry?"

"He's jist a boy."

"Did the gentleman take him too?"

Hamish shook his head. "Paddy ran."

"Do you think Paddy would be willing to talk to me?"

"Ain't nobody seen him since that winter."

Sebastian thought about the shot factory's silent, overgrown graves and nameless skeletons. "You think the gentleman might have grabbed him too? Perhaps later?"

"I dunno. Sometimes I wonder if maybe—" Hamish broke off and shook his head.

"Wonder what?" Sebastian prompted.

Hamish rolled one shoulder and stared out the window at the gathering darkness.

Sebastian tried a different tack. "You say the man pulled you into a carriage. Do you remember what the carriage looked like?"

"Only that it was old. Fusty smellin'. Like one o' them hackney coaches ye see that used t' belong t' some grand lord a hundred years ago 'n' more."

"There was a driver?"

"I suppose there musta been. But I don't remember him."

"Where did the gentleman take you?"

Hamish started rocking again. "A house."

"Tell me about it."

"It was an old farmhouse or somethin'."

"What was it made of? Brick? Stone?"

Hamish shook his head. "It was a white and black."

"It was half-timbered?"

"Aye. Reminded me o' that old tavern near the corner o' Liquorpond Street and Grays Inn Lane. Ye know the one I mean? Where the top story sticks out over the ground floor at each end but not in the middle?"

"You mean the Cat's Tail?"

"That's it."

Although long used as a tavern, the old Cat's Tail in Liquorpond Street had actually been built centuries before as a farmhouse. A distinctive type of construction that dated back to the fourteenth and fifteenth centuries, such houses were once the homes of yeomen farmers, with a medieval-style central hall open to the rafters and flanked by two-story, jettied bays. Surely there couldn't be many such houses left on the outskirts of London?

Sebastian said, "What happened at the house, Hamish?"

The boy squeezed his eyes shut, his voice dropping to a scratchy whisper. "Ye cain't tell nobody. Promise me ye won't tell nobody."

"My word as a gentleman," said Sebastian, then decided his use of the expression was unfortunate, given what a gentleman had done to this wretched, impoverished child. "What happened, Hamish?"

Hamish sucked in a jerky breath that flared his nostrils. "He . . . he took me t' this big room. Upstairs, it was."

"What did the room look like?"

"It didn't have much in it—jist an old wooden bed 'n' a table, 'n' chains sunk into the wall like some old dungeon." The boy bowed his head, his chin to his chest, his gaze on his bare feet, his voice dropping to little more than a whisper. "I didn't know people did the sort o' stuff he done t' me there. I never done him nothin'; so why'd he want t' hurt me?"

"You've heard what happened to Benji Thatcher?"

Hamish nodded. He did not look up.

"Is that what happened to you?"

Hamish nodded again.

Sebastian said, "How did you manage to escape?"

The boy fiddled with the frayed hem of his coat. "All the while he was hurtin' me, he kept shoutin' at me. He was mad 'cause I was so woozy—I reckon on account o' that stuff he made me drink. It was like a part o' me was there, but the important bits o' me wasn't. Like I could just go away inside me head 'n' forget what he was doin' t' me for long stretches at a time. He kept tellin' me t' wake up, sayin' it weren't no fun for him if I weren't enjoyin' it." A look of horror mingled with helpless confusion convulsed the boy's features. "As if anybody could enjoy what he was doin' t' me. In the end he got so mad he left, tellin' me he'd be back in the mornin'."

"He locked you in that room?"

Hamish nodded. "Left me tied up to one of the bedposts."

"So how did you get away?"

The boy rubbed his thumbs over his wrists, which Sebastian now saw were thick with purple scars. "You know how a fox'll gnaw off its own foot t' get out a trap? Well, I decided even if I had t' chew off me own hands, that cove wasn't gonna find me there in the mornin'. Not alive. Took me the better part o' the night, but I finally got them ropes off me. Then I shimmied out the window as quick and quiet as I could. I was too scared t' take the time even t' grab me clothes."

"Did you look back at the house when you were running away?"

"Maybe once. I dunno. Why?"

"Can you remember anything more about it? Were there any out-buildings?"

"Aye, a whole jumble of 'em—corn barn 'n' poultry house 'n' dove-cot 'n' such."

"Whitewashed?"

The boy thought for a moment. "I don't think so. Gray stone, meybe. They was mostly fallin' down."

"Do you know where it was?"

Hamish shook his head. "I jist ran across the fields. I didn't know where I was goin'. All I could think about was gettin' away from there. When the sun started comin' up, I hid under a haystack 'n' fell asleep. It was afternoon by the time I woke up."

"Where were you?"

"Not far outside Islington. At first I was so confused, I thought meybe it'd all been a bad dream. But I knew it wasn't 'cause I hurt so bad."

"What did you do then?"

Hamish cast a quick glance toward the front of the shop, where Icarus Cantrell was busy winding the dozen or so clocks he kept clus-tered on a shelf near the door. "I waited till it got dark again, 'n' then I come here to the Professor. He helped me get better. And then he told me it'd be better if I stayed away from Clerkenwell and anybody I knew."

"Because of the gentleman?"

Hamish nodded.

"Did you ever see Paddy Gantry again?"

"Nah. I went lookin' fer him. I wanted t' ask why the blazes he didn't try t' help me when that cove grabbed me, or at least run 'n' tell somebody what'd happened. But I couldn't find him."

"That's when he disappeared?"

Hamish nodded.

Sebastian said, "What do you think happened to him?"

The boy twitched one shoulder. "I reckon that cove got him next."

Sebastian said, "Can you remember anything else—anything at all—about the gentleman or his carriage or the house that might be useful?"

The boy shook his head.

"Did the man by chance have a faint French accent?"

Hamish looked at him blankly. "Don't know as I can say. Ain't never heard that many grand swells, French or otherwise."

"Do you remember anything else he said?"

"I dunno. He talked real queer."

"What do you mean?"

"Some of the things he said; they made no sense."

"Such as?"

"Well, he kept tellin' me the only way t' get to pleasure is through pain. What kind of nonsense is that? And then another time, he sticks his face up against mine 'n' says, 'Did you ever imagine what it would be like to snatch the sun from the sky? Now, that would be a crime.'" The boy's face convulsed again in silent horror. "Who talks like that?"

"Sounds like the Marquis de Sade," said Sebastian, half to himself.

"You think that's the cove's name?"

"De Sade? No; last I heard, de Sade was in an asylum somewhere in France."

"So meybe he got loose somehow 'n' come over here."

"He's quite aged—probably in his seventies by now."

"Then it ain't him," said Hamish, obviously disappointed. He studied Sebastian through narrowed eyes. "The Professor, he said if'n I was t' tell ye everythin' then meybe you'd be able t' get the swell what's been doin' this."

"I intend to try."

"You'll kill him?"

Sebastian met the boy's gaze and saw the tumult of fear, shame, and fierce determination that roiled within him. "If I have to."

"You need to kill him," said the boy with sudden vehemence. "They'll never hang a grand swell like him."

"Even peers of the realm can be hanged for murder," said Sebastian. Yet even as he said it, it occurred to him that Jarvis would never allow someone as useful as the comte de Brienne to be arrested. And no jury would convict a man as well connected as Ashworth without an impossible level of proof.

Hamish thrust up from his stool, his face held tight, his breath coming hard and fast. "They don't hang fer hurtin' boys like me," he said and ran from the cottage into the gloaming of the day.

Chapter 34

"So, do you still consider me a suspect?"

Icarus Cantrell asked the question as he and Sebastian sat facing each other across the worn, scrubbed surface of the Professor's kitchen table. Two tankards of ale rested on the boards between them; a small fire glowed on the nearby hearth, chasing away the chill of the coming night.

Sebastian took a long, slow swallow of ale. "You've definitely slipped toward the bottom of my list."

Cantrell looked startled for a moment. Then his eyes tightened with a smile he hid by raising his own tankard to drink deeply.

Sebastian said, "Why did Hamish come to you when he escaped that farmhouse?"

"Where else was he to go?" The Professor shifted his weight on the hard bench. "He was grievously hurt. Not only had he been flogged, brutalized, and cut, but his wrists and hands were a wretched mess from chewing his way out of his bonds. It's amazing he survived. I've always suspected the man who abused him assumed the boy had died in a ditch somewhere after running away. It was a very cold December night."

"You didn't contact the authorities?"

Cantrell snorted. "In case you hadn't noticed, Hatton Garden Public Office isn't exactly interested in the welfare of the area's street children. Constable Gowan might have been more sympathetic, but Hamish begged me not to tell anyone. When a boy lives on the street, he can't afford to have word of something like that getting out about him."

"It wasn't his fault."

"Doesn't matter. You know what people are like."

Sebastian shook his head, but not in disagreement. "He's an amazingly resourceful lad."

Cantrell's breath eased out in a heavy sigh. "He's never been the same since, I'm afraid. You don't get over an experience like that. It would change anyone, let alone a homeless orphan of fourteen."

The two men sat in silence for a moment. Then Sebastian said, "Hamish makes seven that we know for certain: Seven boys and girls this twisted bastard has snatched off the streets."

Cantrell looked puzzled. "Seven?"

"Hamish, Mick Swallow, Benji and Sybil Thatcher, and the three unknowns we found buried at the shot factory."

"We don't know that he's killed Sybil."

"No. But if he hasn't, then where is she?"

"She is younger than the others."

"True. But I'm not convinced that's significant."

Cantrell was silent, his gaze on his ale, as if he might find the answer in its depths. His breath eased out in a long, painful gust. "They don't stop," he said quietly. "Once they get a taste for it, they don't stop. They get some twisted, erotic pleasure out of causing other people pain and watching it. Only, it's not just about sexual pleasure. It's also about power. It's as if his kind feed off the helplessness and fear of others—it makes them feel bigger than they know deep down inside they are. And it's a sickness with no cure except death."

Sebastian studied the Professor's weathered, craggy face. There was a raw, personal edge to the old man's anger, and for some reason Sebastian couldn't have named he found himself thinking about the lord's son Cantrell had killed so long ago.

You don't get over an experience like that.

Cantrell sipped his ale. "Was Hamish able to tell you anything useful?"

"Not as much as I'd hoped, although he did reinforce my belief that it's a gentleman we're looking for. And his description of the old farmhouse where he was held should be useful—assuming of course that I can find it." Sebastian reached for his hat as he rose to his feet. "I just hope to God it's not some jumbled creation of the boy's opium-fogged memories."

"It could well be. Opium plays strange tricks on the mind."

Sebastian met the old man's worried gaze. "I know."

Night had long since fallen by the time Sebastian collected his curricle and turned the horses toward home.

"Folks around Clerkenwell, they cain't talk about nothin' else but whoever's been snatchin' them children," said Tom as they drove through cold, dark streets lit only by flaring torches and the occasional smoking oil lamp.

"Hear any theories as to who's doing this?"

"Oh, aye; they're blamin' everythin' from the Hammersmith ghost to Black Annis and a grindylow. Right scared, they are."

"With good reason." The chestnuts were restless and playful, having spent the better part of the last twelve hours eating their heads off in a stable near Coldbath Square. And as Sebastian brought them under control, it occurred to him that the events of the day had left his young tiger loitering about the dangerous streets of Clerkenwell, alone, for far too long.

"What we gonna do next?" asked Tom as they turned onto Holborn.

"There's no 'we,' Tom," said Sebastian, coming to a decision. "Not this time. We're dealing with a killer who preys on boys your age, and that means I want you safely away from it all. Starting tomorrow I'll be using Giles until I catch whoever's doing this."

"*Gov'nor.* No!"

Sebastian put a hard edge to his voice. "Let me make this clear: I'll brook no arguments and humor no disobedience. If you bring the horses around again tomorrow morning, I'll send you right back to the stables. Is that understood?"

The tiger sniffed.

"Understood?"

There was a long silence. Then the boy said in a small, tight voice. "Yes, my lord."

After that, Tom subsided into a tense, wounded silence that endured the rest of the way home.

Sebastian ignored him. The tiger would survive his hurt feelings. But it was doubtful he'd be as lucky if he were to encounter the Clerkenwell killer.

⁂

"An old half-timbered farmhouse built like the Cat's Tail?" said Jules Calhoun when Sebastian asked the valet if he knew of such a farmstead somewhere to the north of London.

"You're familiar with the style?"

"I am, my lord. I remember there being a few such places near Islington when I was a lad. But they're gone now."

"This one is far enough outside London that it's surrounded by fields, and it still retains some of its outbuildings—or at least it did as of last December. The boy thinks the barns are of gray stone, but he could be wrong."

"I'll ask around and see what I can find, my lord."

"But watch yourself, Calhoun," said Sebastian as the valet started to turn away. "This killer . . . He's like nothing I've dealt with before. He doesn't kill out of anger or greed or fear. He kills because he enjoys it."

Calhoun nodded, his lips pressed into an unusually serious line. "I'll be careful, my lord."

Late that night, long after the lamplighter had passed on his rounds, Paul Gibson stood with his hands dangling at his sides, his gaze on the stacks of wooden boxes filled with what was left of the unknown, pitifully young victims from Clerkenwell. He'd lit the lantern and hung it from the chain above the stone slab in the center of the room. But he couldn't seem to bring himself to move. He could feel the dank cold of the outbuilding seeping deep into the marrow of his being, and it was as if he were absorbing the horror of it, breathing it all in along with the scents of dirt and bones and death.

A whisper of sound brought his head around. Alexi stood in the doorway, a tiny, impossibly brilliant slip of a woman with a cloud of fiery red hair and a mysterious essence that somehow continued to elude him—even after eight months of going through the pattern of his days with her. Eight months of joining his body to hers at night.

She said, "Are you all right?"

"Sure, then. Simply feeling a touch overwhelmed, I suppose."

"You're certain that's all there is to it?"

He met her gaze, and the moment stretched out to become one that required brutal honesty. He pressed his lips together in a tight line and shook his head. "After all those years of war, I thought I'd seen every horror mankind's Manichean nature can produce. But I never expected to see something like this here. Not here, in London. I don't know why, but to find this kind of savage cruelty in the midst of normal, everyday life makes it somehow worse."

She came to lay her hand against his cheek and look at him with her wise brown eyes. And he found himself wondering not for the first time what she saw in him. Why she stayed. Why she loved him.

She said, "How's the leg?"

He could lie. He could tell her it hurt like the bejesus. He could use it as an excuse to take refuge in the sweet, soothing bliss of opium. But the truth was the leg troubled him little at the moment, despite a day spent cramped in awkward positions in the cold. Because it wasn't actually his leg that hurt; when the agony came, it emanated inexplicably from the foot and part of his leg that were no longer there.

He gave her a crooked smile. "Not so bad."

She didn't smile back, just drew a deep breath that parted her lips. "One of these days you're going to need to find your way to letting me help you with that."

"One of these days."

"Soon," she said. And he felt his old fear grip him—the fear that eventually she would leave him whether he managed to free himself from the opium's death grip or not.

And then he wondered what she had seen in his eyes, because she said, her voice husky with its evocatively lilting French accent, "It's late. Late and cold. I'll help you wash these bones tomorrow. But now—" She smiled and took his hand to lay it on her breast and hold it there. "Come inside."

And so he did.

Chapter 35

$\mathcal{T}$hat evening after dinner, Sebastian paid a rare visit to Hendon House in Grosvenor Square.

He found the man he'd once called Father seated alone at his dining table, a glass of port at his elbow and his white head bowed over the well-worn collection of Cicero's orations lying open before him.

"I should think you'd be able recite those by now, as much as you read them," said Sebastian, pausing in the doorway.

Hendon looked up, the leap of joy in his eyes painful to see. But all he said was, "I find a never-ending delight in the man's incomparable use of language." He closed the volume and pushed it aside. "Pour yourself a glass and sit."

Sebastian brought a glass from the sideboard and came to pull out a nearby chair. "I spoke to Amanda. She wouldn't listen."

"I know; she told me. At least you tried. Thank you."

Sebastian poured himself a measure of port and settled back in his chair. It felt unexpectedly comfortable and right, to be sitting in this familiar, candlelit dining room, drinking port with this man and listening to the fire crackle on the hearth. He pushed the thought away and said, "Unfortunately, I've discovered Ashworth is even worse than I knew. Have you ever heard of Number Three, Pickering Place?"

Hendon shook his head.

"It's an exclusive but nasty little establishment that caters to two main types of customers: those who like their prostitutes very, very young and those with a taste for flagellation. Or both."

Hendon reached for his port and took a long, slow swallow. "You're telling me Ashworth frequents this place?"

"He did until he hurt one of their girls so badly they black-balled him."

"My God."

"I tried talking to Stephanie, but she refuses to hear anything to Ashworth's discredit."

Hendon fingered the stem of his glass, his lower jaw working back and forth in that way he had when he was thinking or troubled.

Sebastian said, "There's more."

Hendon looked up, tensing.

"He's also been known to take a whip to at least one of his house-maids. He says the girl was willing, but I'm not convinced. And the most worrisome part is that the girl has now disappeared."

"Stephanie can't marry him."

"Unfortunately I don't see how we can stop her," said Sebastian, unconsciously bringing up a hand to touch the cut on his forehead.

Hendon said, "What happened to your face?"

Sebastian let his hand fall. "Someone tried to kill me last night."

"Good God. Who?"

"Hirelings. I don't know who they worked for."

"They? How many were there?"

"Two."

"*Two?* And you still managed to fight them off?"

"Yes."

Hendon's eyes narrowed. "You killed them, didn't you?"

"Yes."

"Amanda told me you've involved yourself in another murder inquiry."

"Yes."

Hendon's nostrils flared with a predictable combination of anger and concern. "I'd hoped you were done with that nonsense."

Sebastian felt his own irritation rising, for this was an old, familiar, and aggravating source of contention between the two men. Rather than answer, he reached for his port and drained the glass.

Hendon said, "When's the inquest for these men you killed?"

Sebastian pushed to his feet. "First thing tomorrow morning at the King's Head in Swallow Street."

"Do you expect trouble?"

"Not really." He reached for his hat and turned to leave.

Hendon said, "What murder are you investigating?"

Sebastian paused to look back at him. "Amanda didn't say?"

"No."

"Someone's been killing poor children. Out at Clerkenwell."

"Children? God help us. Do you know who's responsible?"

We all are, Sebastian wanted to say. *You. Me. This city. This nation. Everyone who ever saw a cold, hungry child alone on the streets and simply looked away.*

But all he said was, "Not yet," and left it at that.

❧

An hour later Sebastian poured himself a brandy, settled beside his own library fire, and opened the Marquis de Sade's *Les 120 journées de Sodome.* He'd been avoiding reading it. But he was beginning to realize that if he were to have any hope of bringing this killer to justice he needed to understand what was driving him. Only, how could he ever understand such a twisted mind?

He was vaguely familiar with some of de Sade's other works. But this one was far different in degree if not exactly in kind. It was as if the infamous Marquis had taken a lifetime's frustration and rage and poured it forth in a vile torrent of horror, blasphemy, debauchery, sickening imagery, and unimaginably fiendish cruelties. At several points Sebastian was tempted to set the book aside. He kept going only with difficulty. And with each page, it got worse. He hadn't realized it was possible for a book to be both repulsive and achingly boring at the same time.

He was perhaps three-quarters of the way through when Hero came to lean over the back of his chair. "I'm not sure it's wise to read that before trying to sleep."

He looked up at her. "You read it?"

"I did."

"The entire thing?"

"Yes."

Sebastian closed the book and set it aside. "I don't think I can."

She came around to settle on the rug at his feet, her back resting against his chair. "Frankly, I wish I had not."

They sat for a time in a troubled, companionable silence, listening to the hiss of the fire on the hearth and the quiet whispers of the night around them.

Sebastian said, "Is he mad, do you think?"

"De Sade? He is certainly troubled. But I think he had a definite purpose in writing that book."

"What? To amass a catalogue of every horror ever imagined by mankind—and then some? If so, he succeeded."

"Perhaps. But I don't think it's a coincidence that the four perpetrators of all that fiendishly debauched cruelty are wealthy, powerful men: a banker, a bishop, a judge, and a duke. Or that the victims of their unbridled excesses are all poor."

Sebastian played with a dark curl that lay against the nape of her neck. "You think he was making a political statement?"

"Political and philosophical." She shifted to face him. "After all, there's a reason he was in the Bastille. And I doubt it's because the

French King was troubled by the Marquis's unorthodox antics with his valet and some servant girl."

"Well, he was an admirer of the Revolution—until their excesses disgusted even him." Sebastian paused. "Which is rather horrifying to think about."

She took his hands in hers. "Frankly, I think it's a pity the manuscript wasn't lost in the destruction of the Bastille, the way de Sade thought it was. The world would have been better off without it."

"Yes."

She ran the pads of her thumbs across the backs of his hands. "You think this book could be inspiring the Clerkenwell killer?"

Sebastian shook his head. "I doubt our killer needs de Sade for inspiration. But I can see how someone who enjoys inflicting pain would enjoy reading it." He nodded to the ornate black leather volume on the table beside him. "There's a line in there that echoes something Hamish told me his captor kept repeating to him, about true pleasure coming only through pain."

"It's possible that line can be found in some of de Sade's other works."

"Perhaps. But I suspect anyone who admires de Sade enough to quote him would want to own this book. Which means I probably need to take another look at the comte de Brienne and Hector Kneebone."

She was silent for a moment.

"What?" he asked, watching her.

"You've eliminated Ashworth as a suspect?"

"Not entirely. But that's mainly because I don't like him. The fact that he was with Amanda when Benji was killed really should rule him out."

"And my dear cousin Sir Francis Rowe?"

"He also has an alibi—courtesy of no less a personage than the Prince Regent. And your father."

She rested her head against his knee. After a moment she said, "Benji's little sister, Sybil, is dead, isn't she?"

"I don't want to think so, but she must be. She's so young. If she weren't dead, someone would have found her by now."

"Yet she wasn't buried at the shot factory."

"No. But we have more missing children than we have graves. I'm afraid the killer has probably been burying his victims someplace else too."

She watched the fire in silence for a moment. Then she said, "All those poor, abandoned, unloved children. Their lives were already so wretched, with no one to take care of them. No one to love them. No one to hug them and hold them. And then to meet such an unimaginably frightening end . . . You'd think that whoever is doing this must be so evil, you could feel it radiating off him if you were ever near him. Yet obviously you can't."

"I suspect he doesn't see himself as evil."

She lifted her head. "How could he not?"

"He knows what he's doing isn't considered acceptable, which is why he's careful not to get caught. But I think he feels entitled to take his own pleasure at the expense of others—especially those he considers his inferiors."

"Like the banker, the bishop, the lord, and the judge," she said softly.

Sebastian took her hand to lace his fingers with hers, and held her tight. "I'm afraid de Sade knew what he was talking about. Which is as depressing as it is unsettling."

❧

Saturday, 18 September

Sebastian came out of the house the next morning to find his middle-aged groom, Giles, waiting with the curricle. "Huh," said Sebastian, gathering the reins. "I must confess, I half expected another go-around with Tom. He's not normally this easy to bring to heel."

"Oh, he's in a high dudgeon, no mistake about that, my lord. Nothing flicks the lad on the raw more than being reminded of how young he still is." Giles grinned. "Know what he told me he wants to be when he's a man grown?"

"A groom? A mail coach driver? A postilion?"

Giles shook his head. "A Bow Street Runner."

"Oh, dear Lord," said Sebastian, and turned his horses toward Swallow Street and the King's Head.

Shortly after Devlin's departure for the coroner's inquest, Hero walked down to the stables to find Tom perched on an upended barrel and muttering to himself as he worked at rubbing soap lather into a saddle. She could have sent to have him come up to the drawing room, but she suspected he'd be more at ease if she came to him and let him talk while he worked. Tom was slowly becoming more reconciled to Devlin's marriage than he had been at first. But the truce between Hero and the young tiger was still an uneasy one.

"Ye want t' interview *me*?" he said, staring at her when she explained her reason for venturing down to the stables. "Fer yer article?"

"Devlin suggested it."

Tom's brows drew together in a frown, and it occurred to Hero that under the circumstances, perhaps mentioning Devlin hadn't been such a good idea.

"What ye want t' know?"

"How old were you when your mother was transported?"

Tom bent his head over the saddle again. "Reckon I was maybe nine," he said vaguely, although Hero had long suspected the boy remembered far more of those early days than he was willing to let on. After a moment, he added, "Huey was older; 'e was twelve."

Huey, Hero knew, was Tom's brother. He'd been hanged as a thief at the age of thirteen.

"What did you and Huey do after your mother was taken out to the transport ship?" Hero asked. "How did you survive?"

Tom twitched one shoulder. "It weren't easy, at first. But after a while we got taken on by this old cull kept a livery stable on Long Acre. 'E used t' let us sleep in the 'ay loft in exchange for muckin' out the stalls and such."

"That's when you learned to like horses?"

"Oh, I always liked 'orses, milady," said Tom, looking up with a smile. The smile faded. "The problem was, that old cove, 'e didn't give us enough t' eat and 'e didn't pay us nothin' either. But we 'ad t' work so long doin' everythin 'e wanted that there weren't time to find the ready we needed fer more food. That's when Huey got took up fer stealin'."

"What did you do then?" Hero asked quietly.

Tom shrugged again. "Without Huey, that old man, 'e wouldn't let me stay there no more. Said I was too little to do everythin' needed t' be done. So 'e brought in some bigger lads and I had t' find a new rig."

"And what was that?"

"Whatever I could." The boy had given up all pretense of cleaning the saddle now and simply sat with the sponge clenched in his fist. "It's a terrible place t' be, all alone like that, not knowing where yer next meal is gonna come from or where yer gonna sleep. I was always comin' upon dead boys and girls, curled up under the bridges and by the bog houses. I reckon most of 'em jist give up 'n' died. I guess they figured, why keep fightin' it? Yer crawlin' with critters and yer belly's so empty it's like ye got somethin' live inside ye, clawin' at yer backbone. And yer 'ands, they're so covered with chilblains from the cold that they aches like they's on fire. But you know what's the worst of it? The worst part is, *nobody cares.* Nobody cares that yer hurtin'. Nobody cares that yer hungry and cold and scared. And nobody cares when ye die." Tom looked up, his sharp-featured face held so tight and bleak, it broke her heart. "I don't like rememberin' them days. Do we need t' keep talkin' about this, milady?"

Hero closed her notebook. "I think I have enough. Thank you, Tom." And then she walked back up to her grand, comfortable house, feeling intensely ashamed of her city and her world.

Feeling ashamed of herself.

Chapter 36

$\mathcal{T}$he formal inquest into the deaths of the two men Sebastian had killed was held in a tidy eighteenth-century brick inn on Swallow Street, not far from where the men had died.

Inquests were held in taverns and inns simply because they were amongst the few spaces large enough to contain them. The bodies of the dead were always put on public display, and when they were particularly mangled and bloody they tended to attract huge crowds.

The dead men had been identified as Samuel Cash and Pierre Le-Blanc, both with unsavory reputations as petty criminals and worse. But not even Bow Street's finest had been able to discover who had hired them to kill Sebastian.

The verdict of justifiable homicide was never in much doubt.

Afterward, Sebastian stood in the taproom staring down at the still, pale forms of the men he had killed. He was only dimly aware of the raucous, shouting, boisterous, malodorous crowd surging around him. *Who sent you?* he wanted to ask the silent dead men. *Was it the Clerkenwell killer? Or someone else?* And he found himself studying the pallid features of the young, thin-faced man identified as Pierre LeBlanc. The fact that one of his would-be killers was French could, of course, be entirely coincidental. Then again it might not be.

Which meant that the comte de Brienne had some explaining to do.

❧

Amadeus Colbert, the comte de Brienne, was coming down his front steps just as Sebastian turned into Half Moon Street. The Frenchman cast Sebastian a long, thoughtful look, then turned to stroll toward St. James's.

"You're abroad unusually early," said Sebastian, handing the reins to Giles and hopping down.

De Brienne glanced over at him. He wore an exquisitely tailored greatcoat of fine gray wool, with supple leather breeches and gleaming top boots ornamented with silver tassels. Tucked beneath one arm he carried a walking stick with a silver handle that no doubt concealed a sword. "So are you."

"I had an inquest to attend," said Sebastian, falling into step beside him. "Someone tried to have me killed Thursday night."

"Oh?"

"Was it you, by any chance?"

De Brienne kept walking. "No; sorry."

"It's the oddest thing, but I find myself straining to believe you."

"Then why bother to ask?"

"One of my assailants was French."

"And you think that implicates me? London is full of Frenchmen. Unfortunately, it's inevitable that a certain number of undesirable characters will slip in along with the more deserving refugees."

"True," said Sebastian. "But then, what is one to do? Turn all away and let them die by the tens of thousands?"

"There are those who would advocate for it—and still call themselves good Christian men."

"True. But then, most people do tend to have a rather limitless capacity for self-deception."

De Brienne threw him a swift, sideways glance. "Meaning?"

"The man who tried to kill me was named Pierre LeBlanc. You wouldn't happen to know him, would you?"

"Not to my knowledge."

"Ever hear of him?"

"Isn't that the same thing?"

"Not exactly."

De Brienne drew up and turned to face him. "If I wanted you dead, monsieur, I would do it myself. I have something of a reputation for doing my own killing, remember?"

"Perhaps you're adaptable. You've certainly proven yourself to be in other respects."

"You say that as if adaptability were a bad thing."

"It can be." Sebastian studied the Frenchman's tightly held face. "We've found the bodies of more murdered children; did you know?"

"And do you expect me to care? Perhaps counterfeit compassion?"

Sebastian shook his head. "No. That would be out of character for you. And you're always very careful to stay in character, aren't you?"

The Frenchman's eyes narrowed. "I did not try to have you killed." Then his lips curled into a nasty smile. "Have you by chance thought to ask this question of your father-in-law?"

"As a matter of fact, I did."

"Then I'm afraid I can't help you. And now you must excuse me; I've an appointment with my tailor."

"I wonder," said Sebastian as the Frenchman started to turn away. "How did you come to know three volumes of *Les 120 journées de Sodome* had been smuggled into England?"

De Brienne turned slowly to face him again. "Rutledge told me, of course."

"He knows of your interest in de Sade?"

"All good merchants are attuned to their clients' tastes, are they not? But I fear you have been misinformed, my lord; Rutledge received five copies of de Sade's lost book, not three."

"Is that what he told you?"

"He had no need to tell me; I saw them myself. I was in his shop the evening they arrived. All but two had been reserved—or at least so he claimed."

"Did he say by whom?"

"Do you seriously think he would? I'm afraid that's a question you'll have to ask Rutledge." And with that he executed a neat bow and continued up the street as if entirely preoccupied with the important task of selecting the cloth for his new coat.

❧

Despite the brightness of the day, the narrow, ancient street of Holywell still lay in cold shadow, its ragged booksellers shivering and stomping their feet beside their barrows. Sebastian had come here determined to discover exactly how many copies of de Sade's nasty little book had been imported to England and who besides the comte de Brienne and Hector Kneebone's aristocratic female admirer had bought them. He was in a foul enough mood to do whatever was needed to shake the truth out of Clarence Rutledge. Except that when he drew up before the bawdy bookseller's it was to find the shop closed.

"Well, hell," he swore under his breath.

He handed the reins to Giles and jumped down, his gaze traveling over the ancient house's silent, shuttered facade. Even though he knew it was useless, he banged his fist on the door panels hard enough to rattle the ancient door in its frame. "Rutledge?" he called. "Rutledge!"

"'E ain't there," said a voice behind him.

Sebastian turned to find himself being addressed by a ragged but startlingly pretty girl of perhaps fifteen. She had a heart-shaped face with a small, straight nose and enormous brown eyes, and she looked both very young and very wise to the ways of the streets. "'E ain't opened up fer days."

"Does he do that often—go away for days at a time and shutter his shop?"

"'E does when the authorities nabs 'im."

"And have the authorities 'nabbed' him this time?"

The girl twitched one shoulder. "Not so's I 'eard. But meybe."

"Where does Rutledge live?"

She glanced toward the closed casement windows of the old house's jutting upper story. "Up there."

"When was the last time you saw him?"

The girl stared at Sebastian in expectant silence, her pretty face a study in quiet extortion.

Sebastian swallowed an oath of impatience and handed her a shilling.

"Thursday mornin'," said the girl, the coin disappearing into her rags.

Sebastian knew a faint whisper of concern. There was no reason to suspect that Rutledge had fallen victim to anything more sinister than their age's harsh laws against selling lewd literature or printing seditious tracts advocating democracy.

Yet even as Sebastian told himself these things, the sense of uneasiness remained.

Chapter 37

Balked of his first objective, Sebastian drove next to Covent Garden.

He found Hector Kneebone still abed, surrounded by a frothy cocoon of lace-trimmed fine linen and gleaming burgundy silk. His handsome mouth hung half-open, emitting a crescendo of snores heavily perfumed by last night's wine. The morning might be gone, but the actor's bedroom was still dark thanks to the heavy, tightly closed drapes at the windows. Sebastian plucked Kneebone's copy of *Les 120 journées de Sodome* from its shelf and tossed the book onto the actor's stomach.

Kneebone half strangled on his last snore and sat up with a jerk, his nightcap flopping down over his forehead. "What? What?" His gaze settled on the double-barreled flintlock pistol in Sebastian's hand, and he froze.

"Relax," said Sebastian with a smile as he eased back the first of the pistol's two hammers with a menacing click.

"Relax?" Kneebone scooted back until he was pressed against the bed's ornately carved headboard. "You sneak into my bedroom, throw things at me, point a pistol at me, and tell me to relax? What the bloody hell?" He cast a frantic glance toward the darkened parlor. "Where's Dugger?"

"If Dugger is your manservant, he's been called away on an errand. He should return in an hour or two."

Kneebone's gaze shifted back to Sebastian's pistol. "What do you want from me?"

"The book," said Sebastian, wiggling the flintlock's muzzle toward the black leather volume that had flopped to the counterpane beside Kneebone's hip. "I want to know where you got it."

The actor brushed the volume away with a swipe that sent the expensively bound tome sliding to the floor with a loud thump. "It was given to me."

"By whom?"

"I can't tell you that!"

"Why not?"

"Because that's not the way these things are done and you know it. The ladies can brag about their conquests all they want. But let a man dare breathe one word—*one bloody word!*—and he's instantly labeled a vile cad."

"Which obviously isn't good for an actor's career."

Kneebone's brows drew together in a scowl. "No, it's not."

Sebastian shifted the pistol's muzzle to a lower part of Kneebone's anatomy. "Neither is a bullet. Tell me where you got the bloody book."

The actor's eyes widened, his tongue darting out to wet his lips. "Lady Sutton," he said on a gusty exhalation of breath. "Lady Sutton gave it to me. She said she bought it from some shop on Holywell Street, but I don't know which one. I swear!"

Sebastian blinked. He was vaguely acquainted with Lady Sutton, a baronet's wife somewhere in her late forties with a reputation for drinking too much, laughing too loudly, and wearing her gowns cut too low.

Her husband was in his late eighties.

Sebastian nodded toward the book again. "Have you read it?"

"It's in French. How the blazes am I supposed to read it? My father was a costermonger. Where do you imagine I learned French?"

"You don't sound like a costermonger's son."

Kneebone put up a hand to straighten his nightcap and hold it in place as he executed a short, mocking bow. "Thank you."

Sebastian pulled back the second hammer. "If you can master Mayfair's version of the King's English, why not French?"

"That's different."

"Is it?"

"I do not speak French," said Kneebone again, enunciating each word carefully. "And I wouldn't want to read that book even if I did."

"Oh? Why's that?"

"Because I looked at it; that's why. The first few engravings are titillating enough, but by the end—" The actor's famous features convulsed in a grimace of horrified revulsion that may or may not have been genuine. "That thing would give the devil himself nightmares. It's sick."

"It's meant to be."

Kneebone shook his head. "I don't understand it. I've performed in some of de Sade's plays over the years, and they're nothing like that."

"True. But then, they weren't written in the Bastille." Sebastian shifted his weight. "Tell me about the woman who gave you the book—Lady Sutton. Does she like that sort of thing?"

Kneebone's eyes widened. "What? Young boys being skinned alive and beautiful young women rent limb from limb? I hope not. I think she likes to shock, to test the bounds of—of everything, actually. She prides herself on being different, on not being afraid of anything. For her, I suspect much of the book's appeal lies in its history—that, and the fact that only five copies were smuggled into England."

"Who told you there were five copies?"

"She did. Why?"

The way Sebastian figured it, Kneebone had one copy, Sebastian himself had one, and de Brienne had one—which left two still unaccounted for. "Did Lady Sutton buy one for herself?"

"I don't know."

"When did she give it to you?"

"Must have been a year ago, at least. It was right before she retired to the country with her lord."

"Are they still there?"

"In the country? Last I heard, yes; the old bugger's been quite ill. Why?"

"Does her lord share her tastes?"

"I gather he did, once. But he's quite old now—essentially an invalid." Kneebone sat up straighter, his fists clutching the bedclothes to the front of his nightshirt the way a woman might do. "I wonder: Have you . . . have you looked into Number Three, Pickering Place?"

"Obviously," said Sebastian. "They're the ones who gave me your name, remember?"

Kneebone's tongue crept out to wet his dry lips. "Yes, of course. I'd forgotten. But did you know there was a young girl killed there a few weeks ago? They gave it out as a suicide, but it wasn't. The only reason they weren't able to cover it up completely is because a customer saw the dead girl's body before they could get rid of it. I gather he set up quite a ruckus."

"And how do you happen to know this?"

"A friend of mine was there that night."

"A friend. And why should I believe him—or you?"

Kneebone's strong jaw hardened. "Ask the Bligh sisters about it yourself. The girl's name was Jane. Jane Peters. My friend, he says that establishment must be protected by someone to get away with something like that. Someone with a great deal of power."

Sebastian pushed away from the wall. "Why didn't you tell me this before?"

"Because I only just heard about it myself."

"Oh? So what's your friend's name?"

"I can't tell you that!"

"Yet you expect me to believe you?"

"I'm telling the truth," said Kneebone with great dignity.

Sebastian gave the actor a hard smile. "How was she killed?"

Kneebone swallowed and looked away. "He said she was strangled."

Sebastian had no reason to believe the actor's tale. But Kneebone's willingness to provide him with the dead girl's name lent a certain amount of credibility to his story.

Before heading to Pickering Place, he drove first to the Tower Hill surgery of Paul Gibson, where he found the Irishman in the high-windowed outbuilding at the base of the yard, surrounded by boxes of freshly washed bones and the draped body of Rory Inchbald. A tub of water had been set up on the stone table in the middle of the room, and Gibson was scrubbing the contents of the last box and laying the bones out to dry. A second tub stood nearby, suggesting that someone— probably Alexi—had been helping him at his task. The room smelled of wet stone, dank earth, and death.

"I hope you're not here looking for answers," said Gibson, glancing up from his task, "because I don't have any."

"Nothing?"

He jerked his head toward the one-legged soldier's silent form. "Well, I can tell you Rory Inchbald there was stabbed in the back. But beyond that, I have the bones of five dead youngsters—"

"Five?"

"We found another grave after you left. Two boys, two girls, and one who could be either. One of the girls' bones are small enough she could have been as young as twelve, and the oldest is likely this fellow." Gibson shook water from a femur stained dark for reasons Sebastian didn't want to think about and laid it to dry with the others on the stone slab. "He was perhaps as much as seventeen, although he wasn't very big, either."

Sebastian studied the unknown boy's collection of bones. Some of the graves they'd found were shallow enough to have been disturbed by stray dogs and pigs. But this skeleton looked fairly complete. "How much do you know about Number Three, Pickering Place?"

"Not a great deal. And most of what I do know comes from Alexi— she's delivered babies to several of the girls there. I never have. Why?"

"She told me the other day she thinks it's not as bad as Chalon Lane."

"It isn't. Nowhere near as bad."

"So you don't think there's a chance these children could have been killed there?" It didn't seem likely, given what Hamish had told him. And yet . . .

Gibson shook his head. "Every brothel occasionally loses workers to customers who turn violent. But five or six? I think I'd have heard about it. I mean, I heard about the Chalon Lane house. You can't keep that sort of thing secret for long." He paused. "Can you?"

"Where does Number Three get their boys and girls?"

"Off the streets, mainly. Some are runaway apprentices, but most are orphans or abandoned children. There are some places in London that snatch them off the street, but it's not that difficult simply to lure them in. When you're starving and unbearably cold and alone, what the Bligh sisters are offering probably doesn't look so bad—a roof over your head, a bed to sleep in, lots of food, and warm clothing. Beats dying of starvation in a ditch someplace."

"Perhaps. Perhaps not." Sebastian stared down at the hideously grinning skull Gibson had set at the edge of the stone slab. Stripped of flesh and sinew, one skull looked much like any other. And it occurred to him just how lucky they'd been, to identify Mick Swallow by the coin he'd worn around his neck. The rest of these dead youngsters were utterly anonymous and would doubtless remain so. "We'll never know who any of them were, will we?" he said after a moment.

"Probably not. If they'd been buried in their clothes, we might have been able to identify them that way. But they weren't."

Sebastian went to stand in the doorway, his hands braced against the frame as he stared out at the windblown sky. And he felt it again, that welling of frustration and anger that was as potent as it was pointless. "Whoever is doing this doesn't simply rob these poor children of their lives," he said, watching the wind ruffle a nearby patch of pretty blue Michaelmas daisies. "He dumps them in shallow, unmarked holes like they're garbage. If we can't identify them, no one is ever going know what happened to them." Sebastian pushed away from the door and swung to face the room full of bones again. "There must be some way to figure out who they were."

Gibson fished the last of the skeleton's ribs from the tub, then shook his hands and reached for a rag to dry them. "A bone is just a bone. I don't see how we'll ever be able to tell one person's bones from the next. Maybe it's better this way—that at some point we all lose our individual identities and simply become part of the earth."

Sebastian stared at the boxes filled with the remains of unidentified children and felt his heart break for the unnamed, forgotten lives so cruelly cut short by untold hours of unimaginable pain and fear. "At some point, perhaps," he said. "But not yet. And not like this."

Chapter 38

$\mathcal{S}$ebastian arrived at Pickering Place to find the small square nearly deserted in the flat light of a cloudy afternoon. He rapped on the shiny black door of Number Three and listened to the approach of a man's footsteps. But the door remained closed.

"I know you're there," said Sebastian. "Tell your mistress we need to talk about Jane Peters."

The footsteps went away. His acute hearing picked up a distant, hushed argument in which the unseen doorman hissed, *"Ye shoulda let me kill the bugger the first time he come round."* His female employer answered calmly—and ominously, *"Don't be a fool; there's a time and place for everything."* Then the heavy footsteps returned and the squinty-eyed prizefighter with the scarred eyebrow and jutting jaw yanked open the door.

"Ye were told ye ain't welcome hereabouts," he growled.

"So remind me: Are you Thomas? Or Joshua?"

The pugilist's scowl deepened. "Joshua." He stepped back and jerked his head toward the end of the corridor. "Ye know where t' find her."

Grace Bligh sat drinking a cup of tea in the chair previously occupied by her strangely silent sister. Her long, golden hair hung loose about her shoulders, and she wore nothing except a thin silk wrapper that clung to every swell and hollow of her body. And even though she was a woman grown, there was something about her diminutive size that caused Sebastian to feel vaguely uncomfortable, seeing her like this.

As if she knew exactly what he was thinking, a gleam of amusement lit up her pale gray eyes. But all she said was, "Who told you about Jane?"

"Does it matter?"

She raised the delicate, rose-sprinkled teacup to her lips. "Our customers usually know better than to be telling tales out of school."

"In my experience, most people find the sight of murder disturbing. As a result, they tend to feel the need to talk about it."

Grace Bligh shook her head. "I fear you've been misinformed; Jane Peters committed suicide."

"By strangling herself?"

"It can be done."

"Benji Thatcher—the Clerkenwell boy who was raped and tortured—was strangled."

She lifted her silk-clad shoulders in a dismissive shrug. "It's a common enough means of murder."

"I thought we were talking about suicide?"

She took another sip of her tea. "So we are."

"And in point of fact, strangling deaths are not as easy to accomplish as you might think."

"Oh? Well, you would know more about that than I."

"Would I?" Since she hadn't invited him to sit, Sebastian wandered the room, taking in the expensive marble-topped commodes and massive Sevres vases bracketing the fireplace. "Where's your sister?"

"Hope rarely leaves her room before three."

"Why doesn't she speak?"

Grace Bligh shook back her loose hair in a mockingly seductive gesture. "Perhaps you can ask her, next time you see her."

"You're from—where?" He paused beside a glass-fronted bookcase ornamented with engraved brass brackets. "Sussex?"

"Kent."

He scanned the titles in the bookcase, looking for de Sade, but found only the likes of Shakespeare and Donne and Chaucer. "You have an interesting taste in literature."

Something flashed in her eyes. "Why? Did you imagine us illiterate? Our mother was a vicar's daughter and our father the village schoolmaster."

He wanted to ask how she and her sister had ended up in Pickering Place, running a London brothel that catered to some of the male sex's most depraved tastes. Except that he suspected he already knew the answer. Village schoolmasters lived a desperate, hand-to-mouth existence. If the unfortunate Mr. Bligh and his wife had died while their daughters were still young, the sisters would have been left dangerously vulnerable. Someone had obviously exploited that vulnerability. The girls must have learned very quickly that certain men like their females young—or at least to look young. And the Bligh sisters were astute enough—and ruthless enough—to have capitalized on that knowledge.

He said, "Who killed Jane Peters?"

Two tight white lines appeared to bracket Grace Bligh's lips. "I told you: She killed herself."

"And the authorities believed this tale?"

She gave an exaggerated sigh. "Why bother asking questions if you don't listen to or remember the answers? I told you when you were here before: The authorities do not bother us."

"So you did." He let his gaze drift, significantly, over the rows of exquisite paintings in heavy gilt frames, over the tables crowded with fine porcelain pieces and impressive bronzes. He found it difficult to believe that even a house as exclusive as this one was profitable enough to enable its owners to pay off the local authorities and still have enough left to fund the acquisition of such treasures. West End magistrates could most certainly be bribed, but they did not come cheap.

He said, "It occurs to me that a business such as this would lend itself handsomely to blackmail."

She watched him with those strange, silver-gray eyes. "Blackmail is a dangerous game best left to experts."

"Actually, I think you'd be rather good at it."

Her lips curled up into what looked like a smile of genuine amusement. "I'll take that as a compliment."

He said, "Of course, there is another possibility. An establishment of this nature would also be quite useful to the French."

She laughed out loud. "An interesting theory. But you're still wrong."

And then he knew. He looked into her cold, still smiling face, and he knew why she was so untroubled by the threat of exposure. The sisters weren't beholden to some corrupt, petty local magistrate for protection. They didn't need to be. Their nasty little establishment was shielded by the most powerful man in the Kingdom—a man who no doubt made very good use of whatever information they passed him.

"I see," said Sebastian, and he knew by the utterly controlled way she held herself still that he was right.

He started to turn toward the door, then paused. "Someone tried to kill me Thursday night. You wouldn't happen to know anything about that, would you?"

She stared back at him, her eyes glittering but her face a mask. And he found himself thinking, *They're all actors, not just Hector Kneebone, but also de Brienne and Grace Bligh.* All three presented a carefully constructed and utterly false facade to the world.

And then she lowered her lashes, hiding her eyes. "I imagine you have many enemies. My lord."

"True. But you're the only one I've overheard disputing the proper time and place for my killing with her henchman."

For the first time he saw her confident smile slip, just as someone rapped an impatient tattoo at the front entrance.

"Bit early for customers, isn't it?" he said.

Grace Bligh sat stiffly in her chair, her tea going cold in her hands. "Some men have commitments that make it difficult for them to visit us in the evening."

"You mean, commitments such as wives and children of their own."

The smile was back in her eyes. "That troubles you, does it, my lord? Why? Are you tempted?"

"I think the word you're looking for is 'disgusted,'" he said, and turned away.

He could feel the lethal animosity of her gaze boring into his back as he walked toward the front door. The new arrival had already been ushered into the front room with its gaudy red brocade settees and rich velvet hangings and enormous canvases of naked, nubile women frolicking in vaguely oriental seraglios. As Sebastian passed the room's wide entrance, he could see the establishment's latest customer standing in the center of the carpet, his fashionable top hat in his hands, his stocky legs braced wide, his stout torso held ramrod straight as he considered the two painfully young girls being offered for his selection. Even from the back, there was something about the short, middle-aged figure that seemed vaguely familiar. Then the man half turned, and Sebastian recognized one of the more outspoken members of Parliament. Pugh was his name.

Sinclair Pugh.

Chapter 39

"We've never been explicitly told that Lord Jarvis controls Number Three, Pickering Place," said Sir Henry Lovejoy, his elbows propped on his office desk and his cupped hands tapping against his chin. "But we have been warned by the Home Office to leave the place alone. I can assure you it goes sorely against the grain with me. Some of the tales we hear of that establishment are beyond troubling."

Sebastian leaned back in his chair and—out of respect for the magistrate's austere religious sensibilities—somehow managed to swallow the oath that rose to his lips. "I gather you heard about the 'suicide' a few weeks ago of a girl there named Jane Peters?"

Lovejoy nodded. "The findings of the inquest were preposterous, of course. But I'm afraid in such cases the coroner does what he is told."

"And was she buried at the crossroads with a stake through her heart?" It was the common fate of those found guilty of having committed the crime of self-murder, considered by the church the greatest sin of all.

The magistrate rose abruptly and went to stand looking out the window at the crowded, raucous street below. His silence told Sebastian all he needed to know. After a moment Lovejoy said, his voice hoarse, "You think Number Three is behind the bodies discovered in Clerkenwell?"

"I honestly don't know. I spoke to a boy who was abducted from near the Charterhouse last year, and the story he told doesn't suggest any involvement by the Bligh sisters. Yet simply because I don't see a connection doesn't mean there isn't one."

"Let us hope there is not."

"And if there is?"

The two men's gazes met, and Lovejoy's features took on the pinched, troubled look of a conscientious man whose hands are tied by the ominous power of the authorities above him.

Pushing to his feet, Sebastian turned toward the door, then paused as another thought occurred to him. "There's a bookseller in Holywell Street named Clarence Rutledge who hasn't been seen for several days. He could simply have been arrested or he could have decided to lay low for a while. But it's also possible something has happened to him."

"Holywell, you say?" The disapproving frown on Lovejoy's face told Sebastian the magistrate was well aware of the sort of literature to be found in the street's bookstalls and shops. "I'll set one of the lads to look into it. You think this bookseller could be connected to the murders?"

"Not connected, precisely. But he may know more about this killer than is healthy. For him."

※

Sebastian was crossing Bow Street toward where Giles waited with the chestnuts when he heard a familiar cockney voice hollering, "*Gov'nor. Gov'nor!*"

Sebastian turned to find his tiger pelting down Bow Street, dodging barrows piled high with turnips and cabbages, and nearly tripping over an Italian musician's dancing monkey.

"Tom? What the blazes are you doing here?"

The boy skidded to a halt, his chest jerking, his face red and damp from his run. "I found it!"

"Found what?"

"That old black 'n' white 'ouse yer lookin' for."

Sebastian rested his hands on the boy's heaving shoulders and somehow resisted the urge to give him a good shake. "How the devil do you know about that?"

"I 'eard Calhoun askin' the scullery maid about it. She's from Pentonville, ye know."

"No, I didn't know." Pentonville was a small village to the west of Islington. "And was the scullery maid familiar with such a house in the area?"

"No. But once I knew why Calhoun was askin'—"

"He told you?"

Tom grinned. "I reckon ye didn't warn 'im not to."

Sebastian studied the boy's sharp-featured, freckled face. He was right; Sebastian hadn't thought to issue such a caution. "How did you find it?"

"I asked the drovers at Smithfield. This cove name o' Striker Bolton told me 'bout a place sounded just like what yer lookin' for. So I went and took a gander—"

Sebastian felt his stomach give an unpleasant lurch. "You went out there by yourself? My God. Have you any idea what kind of monster we're dealing with here? I ought to thrash you within an inch of your life."

Tom's jaw jutted out mulishly. "'Ow else was I t' know it was the right place? Besides, Striker went with me, to show me where it was."

"How old is this Striker?"

"Thirteen."

Sebastian made a strangled noise.

"I reckon it's the right place," said Tom, eying him warily. "The 'ouse has them bits that sticks out at each end on the top floor, jist like the Cat's Tail. And there's a slew of old stone barns and such."

"Where is it?"

"It's sorta 'ard to describe," Tom said airily. "I reckon I need to show it to ye."

Sebastian studied the boy's wily, stubborn face. "I ought to beat you; you know that, don't you?"

But Tom simply flashed him a cocky grin and scrambled up into the curricle's high seat.

The farmstead lay on a narrow, shady lane that curled through the gentle hills north of Pentonville. Nestled in a kind of hollow and half-hidden by an overgrown copse of frost-nipped beech and chestnuts, it would be easily missed if one didn't know it was there.

By the time Sebastian drew up beside the farm's low, tumbledown stone wall, the trees in the copse were thrashing back and forth in the wind and the sky had turned dark and menacing. His gaze narrowing, he studied the house's exposed timber framework and steep, hipped roof. Like most surviving relics of its kind, the traditional fourteenth-century structure had been modified over the years. Someone back in the days of Queen Elizabeth had replaced the original wooden slatted windows with diamond-paned casements. The roof was now tiled rather than thatched, and at some point three chimneys had been added to make the old house more comfortable. But the basic layout was still the same, with a medieval-style hall in the center bracketed at both ends by two-story bays, each with an upper room that jutted out beyond the ground floor's facade. A jumble of gray-stone outbuildings including a ruined dovecot lay off to one side.

He handed the reins to Tom. "You stay here." Sebastian swung around to address Giles. "And if he even thinks about getting down, throttle him."

"Yes, m'lord," said Giles.

"But—" began Tom.

"No buts."

Sebastian hopped down, thankful for the small, double-barreled flintlock he'd slipped into his pocket that morning. He approached the house cautiously, although the place looked deserted. No smoke curled from the three silent chimneys, weeds choked the front walk, and the surrounding fields were thickly overgrown with thistle and nettle. The farm obviously hadn't been worked in years.

He banged on the ancient, arched-top door, not really expecting an answer. Somewhere in the distance a dog barked, but it was far away, probably from one of the cottages he'd passed on the other side of the hill. He listened to the wind whistle through the eaves and lift a loose tile. Except for the dog and the wind, the place was eerily silent. No birds sang in the nearby copse; no lizards darted across the cracked, weedy paving stones.

Reaching out, he tried the latch. It was locked.

He turned and walked toward the huddle of gray-stone farm buildings. They clustered around a muddy yard strewn with broken cartwheels and moldering hay and piles of abandoned rubbish. Most of the structures around the quadrangle were in various stages of ruin, their roofs collapsing, their shutters hanging broken or missing entirely. But the manure pile in the center of the quadrangle was fresh, and a cart shed and attached stable showed signs of repair. Sebastian was about to open the shed's wide double doors when a guttural voice behind him shouted, "Wot ye think yer doin' there?"

Sebastian turned to find a roughly dressed man striding toward him across the rubbish-strewn yard. He was a big man, as tall as Sebastian and considerably bulkier, with powerful shoulders and a neck like a tree stump. His face was large too, with beady little eyes and a small nose and mouth that were all scrunched together in the midst of great, slablike masses of jowls and jaw.

"You live here?" asked Sebastian.

The man drew up a few feet away, his big, work-roughened hands dangling at his sides. "Who wants t' know?"

Sebastian drew a card from his pocket and held it out between two fingers in a deliberately condescending gesture. "Viscount Devlin. Who is your master?" He didn't often use his title, but it could at times be effective.

This didn't appear to be one of those times. The man poked at the wad of tobacco distorting his lower lip and made no move to take the card. "Wot makes ye think this ain't my place?"

Sebastian tucked the card away and nodded toward the untilled fields. "Because this farm hasn't been worked in at least two years. Your master: What's his name?"

The caretaker's nasty little eyes shifted this way and that as he struggled with the effort of deciding what name to give.

Sebastian said, "And don't even think of giving me a false name. If I find you've provided false information, the consequences will be severe."

The man's nostrils flared. "Herbert. It's Richard Herbert." *And damn you all the way to hell and back,* said the glare that accompanied his response.

"How long have you been in his employ?"

"Two years or thereabouts. Why? Wot's it to you?"

"Where is Mr. Herbert now?"

"I dunno. He don't live here."

"Oh? So what does he do here?"

Something flickered across the man's scrunched features, something that looked like the first faint whiff of apprehension. "I ain't gotta answer yer questions."

"Would you rather speak to Bow Street?"

The caretaker's face hardened. This was obviously not a man who frightened easily. A natural-born bully, he plowed his way through life using his height and his weight and an ugly demeanor to intimidate and to cow. "I don't know nothin', ye hear? All I does is take care o' the horses and such."

"So where would I find this Mr. Richard Herbert?"

"I told ye, I dunno. He comes when he comes."

Sebastian nodded to the loft of the stable behind him. "You sleep up there?"

The caretaker obviously found this new line of questioning confusing. "Aye. Why?"

It meant, of course, that Sebastian could safely come back later, after dark, to quietly break into that oddly silent, half-timbered old farmhouse. It also made it unlikely the mysterious Mr. Richard Herbert and his unknown young helper could come and go without the caretaker knowing it. But Sebastian wasn't about to tell the big, aggressive countryman that.

Even with a pistol in his pocket.

Chapter 40

O̶ver Tom's indignant objections, Sebastian drove the young tiger back to Brook Street and left him there with strict instructions to obey orders or die.

He sent word to Bow Street, asking them to look into the mysterious Richard Herbert. Then he spent the rest of the afternoon talking to the various inhabitants of Penniwinch Lane. He discovered the farmstead in the hollow was known as "the Morton House," after a family that had lived there for generations but died out sometime in the late eighteenth century. Like much of the land in the area, the farm belonged to Lord Cobham. The current tenant had taken up the lease on the property several years before, but no one Sebastian spoke with seemed to know much about him.

"Keeps hisself to hisself," said a gangly, middle-aged farmer Sebastian found cutting back hazel in a coppice a quarter of a mile down the lane.

"But you've seen him, haven't you?" said Sebastian.

The farmer kept his focus on his task. He had a slow way of talking and a habit of thinking long and hard before answering any but the simplest of questions. "Reckon I seen him once or twice."

"What does he look like?"

The farmer took another whack at the hazel. "Nothin' you could say stands out."

"Would you call him a gentleman?"

Whack, whack. "'S'pose you could. Looks like one. But then, I ain't never spoke to him meself."

"How does he come here? In a carriage?"

"Nah. Always riding a horse, he is."

"What color horse?"

Again that long, thoughtful silence. "Couldn't rightly say."

"Can you tell me anything at all about him?"

Whack. The farmer stood back, squinted at his handiwork, and said, "Nope."

Sebastian gave up and moved on.

A woman he found pegging out wash on a line stretched between her small stone cottage and a mulberry bush was more pleasant, but she wasn't really any more informative.

"To tell the truth," she said, smoothing the sleeves of a wet blue smock hanging on the line, "most folks give Morton House a wide berth these days. My boy, Jonathan, he went pokin' around there one evenin'—even though we've told him time and time again not to—and that nasty brute of a caretaker fired a blunderbuss at him."

"What's the caretaker's name? Do you know?"

"Lyle, maybe?" The woman frowned as she selected a nightshirt from her basket and gave it a shake. She was somewhere in her thirties, with big, strong hands and a powerfully boned face colored a rich tawny gold by a life lived in sun and wind. "No, that ain't right. It's Les. Les Jenkins . . . or something like that. He ain't from around here. Heard he spent a stretch in Newgate, but that could just be people talkin'."

Sebastian said, "Have you ever seen anyone else around the place? Perhaps a young boy of fifteen or sixteen?"

"Can't say that I have. Sorry."

"Did you ever meet the tenant? I'm told his name is Richard Herbert."

"Aye, that's what they say. But I've only seen him once or twice, and that from a distance. Comes mainly at night, he does."

"Do you know what he does there?"

"No." Her basket was empty, and she reached to pick it up. "I'm sorry I can't tell you more about him, but the fact is, the place spooks me. I ain't never considered myself a fanciful person, but that house— it's like it throbs with evil. Even the birds and hedgehogs avoid it. Why would they do that?"

Sebastian had felt it himself—the unnatural stillness that hung over the ancient farmstead like a darkness that had nothing to do with the thick clouds bunching overhead to shut out the sun. He said, "Thank you for your help," and turned to leave. Then he paused. "How old is your boy, Jonathan?"

Something convulsed the woman's face, something that looked very much like fear. "Twelve. He's twelve."

"You're wise to keep him away from that place."

She swallowed hard and nodded.

It wasn't until he was walking away that it occurred to Sebastian that she hadn't asked him why.

※

Sebastian returned to Brook Street feeling hot and tired and discouraged.

He climbed the stairs to the nursery, where he found Claire down on the floor with Simon, trying to interest the boy in a set of tin nesting cups and looking more than a bit frazzled.

"Leave him with me for a while," he told the Frenchwoman when she glanced up, a lock of lank hair falling into her eyes. "Get yourself a cup of tea or go for a walk in the garden."

"You're certain, my lord?"

"Yes, of course."

After she had gone, he went to hunker down beside his son and assemble the scattered cups. "What have you been doing to your poor nurse, hmmm?"

"Da-da-da-da," said Simon, crawling determinedly away toward the door.

Sebastian let him reach the corridor before catching him and hauling him back.

Simon wiggled, anxious to be free. But Sebastian closed his eyes, held his child close, and tried for one stolen moment to block out the horror of the world they lived in.

"Da!" Simon squirmed, waved his arms, and hollered a string of indignant gibberish.

Sebastian laughed and let him go. "All right. You're free."

Simon plopped on his rump and babbled enthusiastic nonsense.

Rather than settle beside him again, Sebastian simply stood where he was, his gaze on the now happily chattering baby. He felt his love for this child swell within him, so sweet and fierce it took his breath and brought a rare and wholly unexpected sting of tears to his eyes. And it came to him in a kind of wonder that if he were to find out tomorrow that this funny, determined, stubborn, unbelievably precious little boy was no true child of his, it would make no difference at all to his love for Simon. Oh, he'd be angry. He'd be furious at Hero for having deceived him and rage at the fates for depriving him of the joy of having fathered one he loved so intensely. He'd be hurt and devastated and bereft more than he could imagine. But his love for the child himself would be undiminished.

Sebastian watched, humbled and troubled, as Simon seized two of the cups, one in each hand, and banged them together with a wide grin that revealed his new tooth.

And he fell in love with his own child all over again.

❧

That afternoon, Hero returned to Clerkenwell for interviews with two more of the area's abandoned children.

The first child was a wan-faced girl of ten named Judith Simmons, whose widowed mother had been transported for passing forged documents, or uttering. The second was a lean, bright-eyed, attractive boy of about fifteen who said he was Toby Dancing.

"You're the one they call the Dancer?" said Hero, looking at him with interest.

He laughed. "Aye. That's what they call me."

"Care to tell me why?"

He laughed again. "No, ma'am."

He was better dressed than the other street children she had interviewed. When she remarked upon it, he said it was because he knew how to sweet talk the old clothes sellers of Rosemary Lane.

"Are you certain it's not simply because you're better at certain other things you do, as well?"

She said it with a smile, and the lad's eyes sparkled with answering amusement, but he simply ducked his head and kept silent.

"The reverend tells me your mother was transported," Hero said, starting a new page in her notebook.

The quiet laughter drained from his face as he shook his head. "It was my father. When I was twelve." His accent and diction were good, Hero noticed; surprisingly so.

"What was he charged with?"

"Embezzlement, my lady. He used to be a bookkeeper at the Exchange. Always claimed he weren't guilty, of course. But I reckon he was."

"Have you heard from him since he left?"

"No, ma'am. But he was transported for life, so he won't be back."

"Did your mother die before or after he was convicted?"

The boy stared at her a long moment, then gave another little shake of his head. "I told the reverend she's dead. But the truth is, after my father was sentenced at the assizes, my mother took off and left us. Can't tell you where she went, but wherever it was, I reckon she figured she had a better chance of making a new life for herself without a couple of children."

It was said casually enough. But nothing could disguise the boy's hurt and soul-deep devastation. Hero herself could not begin to imagine it. How could any mother abandon her own children? But she knew it happened. It happened more than she could bear to think about.

She forced herself to focus on his words. "So you have a sibling?"

"I had a little sister; Gabby was her name. But she died of the flux just a couple weeks after my mother left. I always figured it was something I gave her to eat that made her sick. I wasn't real good at finding food in those days."

"I'm sorry," Hero said quietly.

The Dancer nodded and looked away, his throat working as he swallowed.

Hero consulted her notes. "Did you ever go to school?"

"Yes, ma'am. Before Father was arrested, I was hoping someday I could set up as a shopkeeper. Maybe sell tea or tobacco. Tobacco would be grand."

"You don't still want to do that?"

"To tell the truth, ma'am, I don't often let myself think too much about that sort of thing."

"But when you do?"

"I dunno. Sometimes I think I'd like to sign on with a merchant ship and just sail away. I hear those merchant ships, they don't treat you anywhere near as bad as the navy." A glow of enthusiasm lit up the boy's smooth young face. "Then maybe I could go to America. They say a fellow can start over in America, make himself whatever he wants to be." That brief flare of hope died. "But the truth is, ma'am, I'll probably always be what I am now."

"And what's that?"

He swung his head to look directly at her, his soft green eyes now painfully bleak in a solemn face. "Just alive. I reckon I'll be happy if I grow up to be alive."

Devlin was sitting cross-legged on the nursery floor and building a tower for Simon out of upside-down tin nesting cups when Hero came to stand in the doorway.

"That's not exactly the idea," she said with a smile.

"I know." Sebastian looked up just as Simon squealed with delight and swiped out one chubby arm to send the latest creation crashing to the floor. "But they're so much fun to knock down."

"Seems there should be a warning in there somewhere."

She went to hunker down beside them, the hem of her sprigged muslin gown trailing over the nursery's scrubbed floorboards.

He said, "I take it your interviews today were troubling?"

"How did you know?"

He reached out to touch a fingertip, gently, between her eyebrows, where a line always formed whenever she was concentrating or disturbed by something. "This."

"Ah." She took Simon's hands and held him steady as he pulled himself up to a stand. "I thought I'd take a break from it all tomorrow. Maybe go with Simon to see my mother. She's been wanting to show him off to Cousin Victoria." The babe babbled and reached out to close his fist over the lace trim of her dress, and she laughed. Then she looked up, her smile fading when she noticed Devlin's expression. "You don't appear to have had a particularly pleasant day yourself."

He told her then about the half-timbered medieval farmhouse on Penniwinch Lane. "I plan to go out there again late tonight and take a better look about the place."

"You will try not to get yourself killed, won't you?"

He gave a sharp laugh. "I will try."

"And have you ever heard of this man before? Richard Herbert?"

"No. I've spent the past week harrying everyone from the comte de Brienne and Hector Kneebone to the King's cousin and my own niece's betrothed. And while I've no doubt they're all varying degrees of nasty, it now appears possible that none of them has anything to do with these killings at all."

"Unless 'Richard Herbert' is an assumed name."

"That's always a possibility," he said, reaching for Simon as the boy staggered from her to his father. Devlin was silent for a moment as he held the child. Then he looked up at his wife, and the strain of these last days on him was plain to see. "If that's true—if it is a pseudonym—then I'll be right back where I started with nothing to go on. Nothing at all."

It was sometime later, when they were dressing for dinner, that a message arrived from Bow Street.

Lovejoy reported they were still pursuing the mysterious Mr. Richard Herbert. But the bookseller Clarence Rutledge had been found in the back room of his Holywell shop with a dagger sticking out of his back.

Chapter 41

"Y ou told someone about the house, didn't you?" hissed the gentleman, his big hand spanning the boy's face to pin him against the stone wall behind him. *"Didn't you?"*

"No, sir," sobbed the boy. "I swear I didn't. I never!"

The gentleman squeezed his thumb and fingers together, painfully pinching and distorting the boy's face. "So how did Devlin discover it?"

"I don't know! Honest."

"Honest?" The gentleman's lips curled away from his teeth. "This has caused me considerable aggravation. You realize that, don't you?"

The boy tried to say something, but the only sound that came was a whimper. His heart was thumping so hard he could feel it throbbing in his hands and feet.

The gentleman said, "Have you found that last boy's sister yet?"

"Sybil?" It was becoming increasingly difficult for the boy to breathe. "No, sir."

"Why the bloody hell not?" The gentleman's voice was as sharp and cutting as a lash.

"I don't know where else to look."

"She can't simply have vanished."

"I'm trying!"

The gentleman ground the back of the boy's head against the wall, then stood back and let him go. "Try harder."

The boy's legs buckled. He slid down the wall to huddle at its base, his hands splayed out at his sides, his breath coming in painful, frightened gasps. He watched as the gentleman's shiny Hessians turned and strode away, leaving him there alone.

But the boy was shaking too hard to get up. And he knew now without a shadow of doubt that once he found Sybil, the gentleman would kill him.

Kill them both.

Chapter 42

The night sky was white with a drifting mist that deepened as Sebastian left the deserted cobblestoned streets of the city and spurred his neat black Arabian into the low hills beyond Pentonville. He rode through stubbly fields of harvested grain, the earthy odors of ripe elderberries and quince and plums hanging heavy in the moist autumn air. Already the cold-nipped maples and hazels were turning a deep scarlet and gold, with the paler yellow of the birch seeming to glow out of the damp gloom.

He rode past the cottage where the woman with a son named Jonathan had been pegging out her wash. The cottage was dark, its inhabitants no doubt long since lost in the deep sleep of those whose days were spent laboring hard with their bodies. The dog he'd heard before bayed once in the distance and then fell silent.

The fog was thicker in the hollow. He turned his horse into the overgrown copse that nearly hid the ancient, half-timbered farmstead from the road and slipped from the mare's back. She nickered as he tied the reins to a stout sapling, and he touched his hand to her soft muzzle, shushing her. Then he crept toward the house, treading warily, conscious of each snapping twig, every rustle of underbrush.

At the far edge of the copse he paused to study the house standing silent before him. There was still no smoke showing from the three chimneys. He listened carefully, heard the restless movement of horses in the distant stable but nothing more. A flicker of swift black shadows caught his eye. Bats.

Slipping the picklock from his pocket, he crossed to the door, grateful for the mist that swirled damply around him. The lock opened easily, the door swinging inward with only a slight nudge. Les Jenkins obviously had orders to keep it well oiled.

Slipping his pistol from his pocket, Sebastian stepped cautiously inside and quietly closed the door behind him. After a brief moment to allow his eyes to adjust, he moved easily, for he'd always possessed an extraordinary ability to see well in the dark. He found himself in a narrow cross passage, its air faintly stale with disuse. Another outside door lay at the passage's far end. To his right two round-topped doors led to what in days gone by would have been the buttery and pantry; at the far end of the passage a narrow set of stairs climbed up toward what would have served as quarters for servants and retainers.

But while the farmstead's end bays consisted of two floors, the central block of the structure was one soaring space that opened all the way to the smoke-darkened rafters high above, forming an old-fashioned, medieval-style hall smaller than and yet similar to what would have been found in the homes of noblemen of the day. On the far side of the hall a second, more imposing staircase rose to what hundreds of years ago would have been the family's solar.

He took me t' this big room, Hamish had said. *Upstairs, it was.*

Sebastian crossed the ancient hall cautiously, noting the comfortable armchairs drawn up before the cold, eighteenth-century hearth, the marble-topped table with its array of brandy decanters and crystal glasses that ordinarily would have no place in such a simple farmhouse. He took the dusty, worn stairs in a rush, then paused at the half-open door to the upper room, his breath coming hard and fast in expectation of what he might find there.

Tightening his grip on the pistol, he nudged the door open wider and breathed in the thick, pungent odor of raw blood.

His horrified gaze took in the shackles sunk high into an old oak support post in the far wall. He saw the dried blood splattered over the whitewashed walls, the stomach-churning assortment of whips and knives that lay jumbled on a nearby table. The only other piece of furniture in the room was a massive old-fashioned oaken bedstead, its mattress stained with more dried blood. At its base, his back propped against the heavy, dark footboard, sat Les Jenkins, his legs sprawled out before him, his chin sunk to his massive chest, his hands curling limply at his sides. The hilt of the dagger that had killed him still protruded from his blood-soaked chest, holding in place what looked like—what *was* a sheet of fine parchment paper.

Sebastian went to crouch down before the dead man. He was still quite warm, probably dead no more than an hour or two. The front of his worn blue smock gleamed with the dark sheen of his blood. More blood had soaked the edges of the note his killer had left for Sebastian to find, the words printed in bold block letters.

YOU LIKE FINDING BODIES, DON'T YOU, DEVLIN?

Chapter 43

*D*riven by a powerful sense of urgency, Sebastian searched the silent, ancient farmhouse looking for Sybil Thatcher.

Kicking open the doors to the old pantry and buttery, he found the first room completely empty and the second nearly so, with only a washstand and a bare wardrobe. The old servants' quarters above were likewise empty. And so, pistol in hand, he expanded his search to the ramshackle farm buildings.

Going first to the cart shed, he threw open the wide double doors and found himself staring at an antiquated carriage. Once it had been a grand affair, the town coach of some eighteenth-century nobleman or prosperous merchant, with a carved garland of gilded acanthus leaves running along the top like a crown and seats of elegant cream leather. Now the leather was stained and cracked, the paint of the body dull and worn, the gilt tarnished. And yet, he noticed, the braces and limbers were relatively new, as were the wheels and undergear. The carriage had not simply been moldering here for decades; someone was taking good care of it.

He looked over at the pair of curious bay carriage horses hanging their heads over their stall doors to watch him. "If only you two could talk."

They nickered at him softly. Then his gaze fell on the rough market cart that stood nearby, its bed filled with straw, and for a long moment Sebastian could only stare at it, a chill running down his spine.

He swallowed and turned away.

He searched the haystacks and Les Jenkins's crude quarters over the stables. Then he moved on to the ruined buildings surrounding the quadrangle. He'd thought he might at least find some indication that Sybil had once been here, or perhaps something to tell them more about the mysterious Richard Herbert. But in the end he had to admit defeat.

Whoever had killed Les Jenkins had made certain of that.

🌹

On his way back to Brook Street, Sebastian stopped by Sir Henry Lovejoy's house in Russell Square. He told the nightcapped, blinking magistrate what he'd found and arranged to meet Lovejoy and his constables out at the farmstead first thing in the morning. Then he went home and tried to grab a few hours' sleep.

He was not successful.

He was standing with one hand braced against the bedroom mantel and his gaze on the glowing coals on the hearth when Hero came to touch his shoulder. "You need to rest," she said.

He shook his head. "Every time I close my eyes, I see that room." He set his jaw. "Death is too good for whoever is doing this."

"Yes," she said simply.

He turned his head to look at her. "I'll never understand how some people can be so full of selfless love and compassion, while others . . . others are the vilest creatures ever to walk the face of the earth."

"With humanity's capacity for great good comes the capacity for unfathomable evil."

"You think that explains it?"

"No," she admitted.

He turned to take her in his arms and hold her close. "What if I can't find him? What if I can't stop him?"

"You'll find him. That note he left—everything he does—shows him to be both arrogant and contemptuous. Men like that are too confident of their own superiority to be cautious or wary, and that means he'll make mistakes—he has made them. You're getting closer."

"It doesn't feel that way. I've been grasping at associations, suggestions, and shadows. What if everyone I've been looking at is wrong?"

"Then discovering that will be progress." She pressed a kiss to his throat. "You know what would help?"

He shook his head.

"Sleep."

He threaded his fingers through her hair and smiled as the sweet, clear notes of a lark broke the silence. "It's already morning."

࿓

Sunday, 19 September

A cold wind whipped through the hollow, banging the loose tile on the farmstead's roof and thrashing the limbs of the ancient oaks in the overgrown copse. A light rain had fallen earlier, but now the clouds simply bunched overhead, dark and ominous.

Sebastian stood with Lovejoy on the cracked pavement before the old, half-timbered farmhouse. It was considerably warmer inside the house than out, but neither man was inclined to linger within those horror-drenched walls. Sebastian had searched the house once again in the dreary morning light, as had several of Lovejoy's constables. But they'd found nothing to tell them the true identity of its tenant or suggest what had happened to Sybil Thatcher.

"The note was addressed to you by name," said Lovejoy, hunching his shoulders against the wind. "The killer knows you're after him."

"I did identify myself to the caretaker."

"True."

They watched in silence as two constables labored to maneuver the death house shell with Les Jenkins's heavy body though the old narrow door and down the overgrown path toward a waiting cart. "Watch it," said one of the constables as the murdered man's hand slid off his chest to drag through the mud.

Lovejoy cleared his throat. "I'll organize some men to begin searching the fields for graves first thing tomorrow morning."

Sebastian wasn't happy with the delay. But there were church strictures against conducting such work on Sundays, and Lovejoy would never violate them. And the truth was, another twenty-four hours would make no difference to any forgotten, homeless child already buried here.

He said, "Were you able to learn anything yet about the farm's tenant?"

"Only that it appears his name is, indeed, Richard Herbert."

Sebastian turned up the collar of his driving coat. The cold was starting to get to him too. "So who the devil is he?"

Lovejoy eased out a heavy breath. "We've no idea. Lord Cobham's estate agent communicated with Mr. Herbert's solicitor, while the solicitor claims he never actually met his client."

"The solicitor must have had an original address for the man."

"He did. A house in Bethnal Green."

Sebastian met the dour little magistrate's gaze. "I don't like the sound of that."

Lovejoy nodded grimly. "We haven't had a chance to check into it more thoroughly, but it seems the house in Bethnal Green was also leased. Richard Herbert was there four years, from 1807 to 1811."

"In other words, at precisely the time when the street children of Bethnal Green were disappearing."

Lovejoy shivered again. "I'm afraid so."

☙

Leery of what he might find next, Sebastian left Lovejoy at Penniwinch
Lane and drove east, to Bethnal Green.

The house once occupied by the mysterious Mr. Richard Herbert
was a surprisingly ordinary-looking brick cottage. It stood on the eastern
edge of the parish in an area of market gardens and orchards and open
fields occupied by a rope walk and a tenting ground. There were no near
neighbors, no one to watch and wonder at any odd comings and goings.

No one to hear a terrified youngster's desperate pleadings and screams.

Built sometime in the last century, the cottage had sashed windows
and a front door painted a cheerful red. Yet even with rows of soft blue
Michaelmas daisies lining the front walk, there was something vaguely
grim and forbidding about the place that Sebastian couldn't define—
and that he fully acknowledged could be nothing more than a product
of the horror he'd found in that upstairs chamber in Penniwinch Lane.

"I wish I could help you," said the plump, flaxen-haired woman who
answered Sebastian's knock. "But I really don't know anything about
the people who used to live here." She was young, probably no more
than twenty-five, with a chubby baby on one hip and a big-eyed, tow-
headed toddler clutching her skirts. She said she was originally from
Bermondsey; her husband, John, had been supervisor at the tenting
ground for eighteen months now.

"You never met Mr. Herbert?"

She shook her head. "No, never. From what we hear, nobody did.
And he was gone a good six months before we come." The baby on her
hip began to whimper, and she jiggled him up and down. "If it was up to
me, I'd be out this house tomorrow. But my John, he tells me I'm too
fanciful, that it's a nice place and we're lucky to have it."

"Is something wrong with it?"

A faint flush touched her cheeks, and her gaze slid awkwardly away from his. "It's just . . . there's a reason it sat empty forever before we come. Nobody wanted to live here."

"Why?"

"They'll tell you it's because of the body, but that can't be true because they didn't find the body till the house had already been empty for months."

"Body? What body?"

She jerked her head toward the rear of the house. "The neighbor's dogs dug it up. In the back garden."

Sebastian felt a hollowness open up within. "A boy's body?"

She shook her head. "Oh, no; from what I hear, it was some big, strappin' fellow. Most folk reckon it was a man by the name of Jim Kimball who used to look after the place most the time. But the body was too far gone to tell for certain."

"This Kimball was a caretaker? So Mr. Herbert was away often?"

"So they say. Nobody liked this fellow Kimball, so they weren't sorry to see him go when he disappeared. Can't say they were sorry to find him dead, neither."

"Did anyone ever ask Mr. Herbert about it?"

"How could they? He was long gone by then, wasn't he?" She reached down to ruffle the hair of the little girl at her side. "I can tell you this: I don't let our Sarah dig none in the back garden. I mean, if somebody buried one body back there, how do we know there ain't another?"

Sebastian thought the woman was probably wise. But all he said was, "Do the authorities know how the man they found was killed?"

The baby started fussing again, and the woman shifted him to her opposite hip. "Weren't hard to figure out, I guess. They say the knife was still there, stickin' out his back."

"He was buried facedown?" It came out sharper than Sebastian had intended.

"He was, yes." The woman was no fool; her eyes narrowed. "That's important; why?"

Sebastian looked into her pretty, open face and didn't have the heart to tell her.

❧

He sent a message to Lovejoy, suggesting Bow Street and the local magistrates might want to consider also searching the back garden of the Bethnal Green cottage. Sebastian then spent the next several hours speaking to a range of people up and down the country road.

It didn't take him long to learn that the plump young mother was right: The little brick cottage had a decidedly unsavory reputation. But how much of that was due to the discovery of the moldering dead man with a dagger in his back was hard to say. Once again, no one could tell him much about the house's previous tenant, whom they'd rarely seen.

Sebastian was about to give up when he found a gnarled, white-haired old man named Corky Baldoon. Corky was sitting on the front stoop of his tumbledown cottage and nimbly weaving a basket from a pile of supple hazel branches when Sebastian reined in the curricle beside him.

"The fellow what used t' live in that brick cottage? Aye, I seen him a few times," said the old man in answer to Sebastian's query.

"What did he look like?" asked Sebastian, watching the basket take shape beneath the old man's liver-spotted hands.

"Well, he was young," said Baldoon, his bony, surprisingly spry fingers flashing in and out with impressive skill.

"How young?"

The old man cackled, showing gums long since denuded of teeth. "What ye thinkin'? That when yer my age, even a man in his fifties looks young?"

"This man was in his fifties?"

Corky laughed again. "Didn't say that."

Sebastian smiled. "So how old was he?"

"'Bout yer age, I reckon." The old man squinted up at Sebastian, his pale blue eyes watery and nearly lashless. "Meybe a mite older."

"Can you describe him?"

"Aye. Me legs might be worthless these days, but there ain't nothin' wrong with me eyes. Not yet, anyways."

Sebastian waited, but the old man simply kept weaving his basket. Finally, Sebastian said, "So what did he look like?"

"Hmm. Fine-lookin' cove, he was. Tall and handsome in a way reminded me of a nasty bugger I used t' know long ago. Course, it couldn't have been him, seein' as how it's been fifty years or more since I knew the bloody bastard. But there's no denying he looked like him."

Tall and handsome. Sebastian wondered how many tens of thousands of tall, handsome young men lived in London. To an age-shriveled old man like Corky Baldoon, even the average-sized Hector Kneebone would probably appear tall. And some might call a slim, well-dressed man such as the comte de Brienne "handsome."

"Wasn't jist his looks, though," Corky was saying. "There was somethin' about the way he sat up on that horse—like he was the bloody king of the world and he knew it. Reminded me of his lordship, it did."

"His lordship?" prompted Sebastian, more out of politeness than in expectation of learning anything useful.

"Aye. Viscount Ashworth he was in them days." The old man turned his head and spat. "Course, now he's the high and mighty Marquis of Lindley, God rot his soul in the hottest part of Hades for evermore."

Sebastian held himself very still. "How do you know the Marquis of Lindley?"

"Hail from Devon, I do," said Corky Baldoon, pausing to survey his handiwork. "Or I did, till he and his da, the old Marquis, stole me land with their bloody Act of Enclosure back in 'sixty-five." The old man's eyes narrowed as he whipped a cane in and out of the basket's top edge. "M'wife died in the poorhouse that winter, along with our two young lads. After that I spent a lot of time thinking about killin' them slimy bastards— Lindley and Ashworth both. But I still had me little Jenny then. Just five years old, she was. And what would've become of her, if her da got hisself hanged for murder? So I didn't do it. But I wanted to. Ain't no denyin' I wanted to. And I ain't never forgot what that bastard looked like."

Corky Baldoon set his basket aside unfinished, his hands falling idle in his lap. And Sebastian realized the old man had stopped because tears had welled up in his eyes so that he could no longer see. "I'll remember that till the day I die."

Chapter 44

$\mathcal{T}$he Duchess of Claiborne was coming down her front steps when Sebastian drew up before her Park Lane home.

She wore an impressive carriage gown of fine, soft mauve wool trimmed with turquois satin piping and paired with a truly awe-inspiring mauve and turquoise turban. At the sight of Sebastian, she paused, one hand groping for the quizzing glass that hung from a darker mauve riband around her neck.

"Aunt," he said cheerily, handing the reins to Giles and jumping down.

"Not now, Devlin. I'm on my way to—"

"It won't take but a moment." He cupped her elbow to steer her back into the house. "You knew the Marquis of Lindley fifty years ago, did you not? When he was still Viscount Ashworth?"

The Duchess let her quizzing glass fall. "I did, yes. Why do you ask?"

"What did he look like when he was young?"

She frowned with thought. "Well, let me see . . . Tall. Broad shoul-dered. Extraordinarily handsome. All in all, a fine figure of a man—much like his son, actually. Same dark blond hair and strong jaw. Charming in that same smooth, not entirely sincere way. Not to say that there was ever anything mean or dissolute about Lindley, then or now. Not like Ashworth."

Sebastian suspected Corky Baldoon might disagree about the mean part, but he kept that thought to himself.

Aunt Henrietta pursed her lips. "You haven't said why you're asking."

"Would it be possible for someone who knew the Marquis all those years ago to recognize the resemblance of the father to the son if they saw Ashworth today?"

"I suppose it's possible. But—"

"Do Amanda and Stephanie go to Lady Jersey's ball tonight?"

"Oh, no; Amanda has quarreled with Sally. I believe Ashworth is escorting them to Lady Farningham's musical evening instead. She has an Italian harpist or some such frightful person." The Duchess was not fond of harps.

Sebastian planted a loud kiss on her powdered and rouged cheek. "Thank you, Aunt."

"But what has all this to do with Stephanie?" she called after him as he turned to run down the steps. "Devlin? *Devlin.*"

⚜

Leaving Park Lane, Sebastian went next to Tower Hill, where he found Paul Gibson standing in the center of the outbuilding, his thoughtful gaze on the big, naked body of Les Jenkins.

"Ah; I was hoping you'd come," said Gibson. "Look at this."

Pale and waxy and already shrinking in death, the caretaker lay on the stone table in the middle of the room. Two purple slits, one large, the other quite small, showed clearly against the white flesh of the dead man's hairy chest.

"That doesn't make sense," said Sebastian, staring at him.

Gibson leaned back against a shelf piled with the boxes of washed bones from the shot factory. The room was getting uncomfortably crowded. "It does when you realize he was stabbed twice—once in the back with a blade long enough for the tip to go all the way through his body, and again in the chest. The one in the back killed him. The other was just to leave you a message."

Sebastian looked up. "Heard about that, did you?"

Gibson nodded. "Nasty. Not to mention more than a touch disturbing."

Sebastian looked at the dead man's chest again. "Same dagger both times?"

"Nope. The knife holding your note wasn't long enough to go all the way through and come out the other side like that."

"So—what? A sword stick?"

"Probably."

"Lovely." Sebastian shifted his gaze to the boxes of bones. "And the burials from Clerkenwell? Did you find anything that might identify any of them besides Mick Swallow?"

"One, the twelve-year-old girl, had an old break in her forearm that had healed well. That's it."

Sebastian let his breath ease out in a sigh and went to stand in the doorway.

Gibson said, "Lovejoy has asked me to take part in a search for more graves out at the farmstead where you found this fellow."

Sebastian nodded. "There's another house needs to be searched, as well. A cottage in Bethnal Green."

"You think that's where the children were tortured and killed? At those two houses?"

"Judging by what I saw out at Penniwinch Lane, I don't think there's much doubt about it. The houses were both leased by the same man, although he doesn't seem to have actually lived at either one."

"My God," said Gibson. "What sort of man keeps a house simply to have someplace to kill children?"

Sebastian pushed away from the doorframe. "A very wealthy one."

☙

Sebastian arrived back at Brook Street to find that Hero had yet to return from visiting her mother in Berkeley Square.

"This came not long ago from Lady Devlin," said Morey, looking grim as he held out a silver tray with a sealed missive. "Her ladyship also sent Claire home with Master Simon, along with a message for Cook saying not to expect her for dinner."

Puzzled, Sebastian broke the seal. *I'll be late,* Hero had written in her strong, rather masculine hand. *My mother's not well, but don't worry.*

Sebastian fingered the note as he turned toward the stairs. She had explicitly told him not to worry. But he also knew Hero well enough to suspect that she would downplay her concerns about her mother's health in order to avoid distracting him from such an important investigation.

And for that reason, he couldn't help but be troubled.

☙

Lady Farningham's musical evenings had quickly become a fixture of London Society. Featuring everything from French opera singers to Austrian pianists and Spanish cellists, the gatherings were popular amongst those members of the Upper Ten Thousand with musical inclinations—or at least with pretentions to pose as such. Amanda fell into neither category and typically avoided them. But alternate entertainments were scarce on a night chosen by one of Almack's powerful patronesses for her ball.

Sebastian arrived at Mount Street to find music already floating through the Countess's spacious reception rooms. As usual the ladies in attendance occupied rows of chairs set in a horseshoe around the harpist, the famous Italian virtuoso Valentino Vescovi, while the gentlemen tended to prop up the walls on the periphery. He spotted Amanda and pretty, golden-haired Stephanie in one of the last rows, with Ashworth lounging against a nearby pilaster. For one moment, his gaze met Sebastian's across the elegant room. Then he pushed away from the wall to stroll casually toward a nearby salon where a refreshment table had been set up.

Sebastian followed.

"We need to talk," said Sebastian, coming to stand on the far side of the heavily laden table.

The Viscount reached for a plate. "Oh? Why?"

"Where were you last night?"

Ashworth hesitated, as if considering the rival merits of asparagus versus haricots verts. "As it happens, I was with your lovely niece and her mother. Why?"

"For how long?"

"Really, Devlin; if you—"

"For how long, damn you?"

Ashworth glanced up, a muscle jumping along his tight jaw. "From eight until approximately half past one this morning. Why? Has there been another death no one seems to care about besides you?"

Sebastian figured Les Jenkins had been dead at most an hour or two by the time he found the man's body at around two that morning. Which meant that it was impossible, again, for Ashworth to be the killer.

When Sebastian remained silent, the Viscount gave a short, sharp laugh. "Good God; I've nailed it, haven't I?" The amusement faded abruptly. "Are you really so desperate to keep me from marrying into your family as to try to pin a murder on me?"

Sebastian said, "I wonder, have you ever spent much time in Bethnal Green?"

"Bethnal Green?" Ashworth gave all his attention to the task of spooning buttered crab onto his plate. "You must be joking. What would I be doing in Bethnal Green of all places?"

"Torturing and killing desperately poor, starving children."

"In Bethnal Green? And here I thought you were hanging around Clerkenwell these days." The Viscount pulled a face. "You really ought to pick more fashionable neighborhoods, you know."

"Why? You obviously don't."

Ashworth's lips curled up into what might have been a smile. "Are you calling your sister and niece liars?"

"Not exactly."

"Then what? *Exactly?*"

Sebastian studied the other man's smooth, handsome face. What could he say? That an eighty-year-old man with a grudge against Ashworth's family was convinced he saw a younger version of the Marquis of Lindley riding away from a house that may or may not have something to do with a long string of missing street children?

"At a loss, are you?" said Ashworth.

Sebastian shook his head. "I might not have figured it all out yet. But I will."

Ashworth set aside his filled plate. "Well, be certain to let me know when you do," he said, and walked away.

"You're still at it, aren't you?" said a familiar tight, angry voice behind him.

Sebastian turned. "Dear Amanda."

She stood tall and elegant, a formidable presence in silver silk trimmed with exquisitely fine lace. "Why must you persist? Why can't you simply accept defeat and move on to some other amusement?"

"Amusement? You think that's what this is? "

"You must be enjoying it. Otherwise why are you doing it?"

"Because people are dying. *Children* are dying."

She raised one delicately arched eyebrow. "Oh? Has another of your grubby street urchins been killed?"

Sebastian looked into her cold, fiercely blue St. Cyr eyes and wondered how he and this woman could possibly have come from the same loving, laughing mother. "Thankfully not a child this time, Amanda. A man. Actually, two of them. Two men who presumably could have identified the killer."

"And when did this happen?"

"The most recent murder was last night at around midnight—give or take an hour or so."

"Well, there, you see? Ashworth was with us last night—along with some of the most distinguished men in the Kingdom including Castlereagh, Pugh, and Liverpool. Feel free to speak with them as well if you care to embarrass yourself. They'll all tell you the same thing. But I hope you'll have the decency—not to mention the intelligence—to stop this nonsense."

She made as if to brush past him, but he caught her arm and swung her around to face him again. "Even if by some chance I'm wrong and Ashworth isn't responsible for this string of vile murders, he's still not a good man, Amanda. And you know it."

Oozing with contempt and condescension as only Amanda could, she let her gaze sweep over him. "Lord Ashworth is a gentleman born and bred. How dare you of all people presume to judge him?" Her gaze fixed on his hand gripping her arm, and he let her go.

Then he stood and watched her walk away, the plumes of her dowager's turban nodding in the candle-heated air.

Chapter 45

Sebastian lay awake in the darkness, his gaze on the tucked blue satin of the tester overhead. Outside, the wind had come up again, keening like a live thing through the eaves. In his tormented, exhausted state, he imagined for one moment he could almost hear it whispering of the things he should know—the things he could know if he only listened hard enough.

He felt Hero shift beside him, her warm hand coming to rest on his chest. She'd arrived home not long after Sebastian, looking tired and frightened. Her mother, never particularly strong, had collapsed midway through what had until then been a pleasant afternoon playing with her grandson.

He slipped his arm beneath her shoulders to draw her close as she nestled her head in the crook of his shoulder. "Worried about your mother?" he asked softly.

She nodded. "It's all so sudden. I don't understand it." She was silent a moment, then said, "You're thinking about all those dead children, aren't you?"

He buried his face in her hair. "I keep coming back to what the old man out at Bethnal Green told me. What are the odds that this mysterious Mr. Herbert should remind Corky Baldoon of Ashworth's father?"

"It is rather bizarre. But that doesn't mean Ashworth actually is Richard Herbert."

"No."

He felt her smile against him. "But you believe he is, don't you?

"Yes."

She said, "Ashworth was with your sister when Benji Thatcher was being buried and again when Les Jenkins was killed. He simply can't be the man you're looking for."

"I know."

"No, you don't. If anything, you're more convinced it's him than ever."

He put his chin on the top of her head and ran his hand up and down her side. "I like to think it's all reason and deduction, what I do. That I carefully weigh evidence and uncover information and secrets until I finally see my way to a solution. But that's only part of it. The truth is, a lot of it is simply intuition . . . a hunch . . . whatever you want to call it. And my gut tells me the killer is Ashworth even though I know it's impossible."

"It's not exactly impossible," she said. "The boy who was seen trying to bury Benji could have killed the caretaker out at the farmstead."

"He could have. But the swordstick and note argue against it. And even if he did, then who was the gentleman in the cart when the boy was digging Benji's grave?"

"Les Jenkins?"

"I don't think anyone could have mistaken Les Jenkins for a gentleman."

For a time, only the crackle of the fire on the hearth filled the silence. Then she said, "What do you think happened to Benji's little sister, Sybil?"

"She must be dead. They'll probably find her buried in one of the fields around the farm when they start searching in the morning." Just saying it out loud caused something painful to pull across his chest. "I don't want to think about how many graves they're going to find between Penniwinch Lane and the cottage in Bethnal Green."

"How long could this have been going on?"

"Who knows? Gilles de Rais got away with it for years. I've heard some put the number of his victims as high as five hundred."

"Good God. How is that possible?"

"Money and power. De Sade knew what he was talking about. Whoever we're dealing with here is wealthy enough not only to lease those houses, but to hire servants and keep a carriage and horses he uses for nothing except brutalizing the impoverished, wretched children he snatches off the streets of London."

"The young servant who was digging Benji's grave," said Hero. "He's still out there."

"Perhaps. Or perhaps we simply haven't found his body yet. This killer seems to make a habit of periodically changing his houses. And killing his servants."

Monday, 20 September

It rained again during the night, a hard rain this time that soaked the ground and left the trees dripping and the air filled with the scent of sodden vegetation and wet earth.

Sebastian arrived in Bethnal Green to find Lovejoy standing on the brick cottage's back stoop, an umbrella in one hand and his features set in grim lines.

"They've found one so far," said Lovejoy. "And I'm afraid it's only the beginning."

Sebastian stared out over the soggy, bedraggled garden and hoped the pleasant young mother and her two babies had taken refuge far away from this horror. "Have you heard anything yet from the crew out at Penniwinch Lane?"

"Only that one of my constables spoke to a woman who says Les Jenkins used to pay her to come out to the farmhouse every few weeks to clean. Interestingly, she says the doors to two of the rooms were always kept locked: the upstairs solar and the old buttery. She was never allowed to enter either one."

Sebastian frowned. "I can understand the solar. But why the buttery? There was nothing there except an empty wardrobe and a washstand."

The two men watched as one of the workers at the base of the garden called to a nearby companion.

Lovejoy sighed. "All indications are that Richard Herbert is an assumed name."

"I'm not surprised."

"So we're essentially back where we were before."

Sebastian squinted up at the dreary skies. "Not entirely. We now know we're looking for someone with considerable resources at his disposal. Someone who hires servants to help dispose of his victims. Someone who is clever and plans very carefully."

Lovejoy pursed his lips in a frown. "Which is particularly worrisome, given he knows you're after him and is openly taunting you."

"Yes," agreed Sebastian, just as a shout went up from the two men working near the garden's far wall. "Ah, Christ; they've found another one."

❧

It was midday by the time Sebastian drove out to the ancient farmstead in Penniwinch Lane. As he drew up his curricle beneath the stand of dripping oaks, he could see a dozen or more volunteers spreading out across the wet, overgrown fields. Paul Gibson stood before the old house with his hands on his hips, watching them.

"No sign of any graves?" asked Sebastian, handing the reins to Giles and landing with a *squish* on the muddy ground.

"Not yet," said Gibson. "Thank God."

"You should have gone to the Bethnal Green house instead. They were just uncovering a third skeleton as I left."

"Agh. Mother Mary." Gibson dropped his hands so that they hung limply at his sides. There was a drawn, haggard look to the surgeon's face that Sebastian suspected mirrored his own. "Please tell me you're close to figuring out who's doing this."

Sebastian shook his head, his gaze on the men walking the distant fields, throwing their circle ever wider. He supposed there was a chance that the searchers might still come upon something, but he doubted it. If Sybil Thatcher were buried here, her raw new grave would surely have been found by now.

So where the hell was she?

"You know what's one of the most frightening aspects of all this?" said Gibson. "It's the realization that this monster is somewhere out there right now, a normal-seeming man moving amongst his family and friends, all of whom have no idea—no idea whatsoever—that he is in truth a creature from their worst visions of hell. How is that possible?"

Sebastian watched one of the lines of men come up against a far hedgerow and then turn to walk back. "Some people are very, very good at hiding who they really are."

⚘

Sometime later, as if drawn by an irresistible compulsion, Sebastian pushed open the front door of the ancient farmhouse and walked inside. He had already searched the place twice—once after finding Les Jenkins's body, and again the following morning. Lovejoy's men had likewise gone over each room carefully. They'd found nothing. Yet even as the house repulsed him, it also beckoned to him. He kept thinking there must be something here. Something he'd missed.

In the dull light of the overcast day the house looked somber and unlived in. The drawers from the chests in the hall lay scattered across the floor where they'd been thrown by various searchers; rugs were rolled up, cushions overturned. Crossing the lofty, now chaotic space, Sebastian climbed the stairs to what had once, no doubt, been a pleasant room—before it was turned by the mysterious Richard Herbert into a chamber of horrors.

He had to force himself to enter the room. There he turned in a slow circle, taking in the blood-splattered walls, the dusty old bed, the now empty table. The Bow Street men had taken away the killer's nasty collection of whips and knives. But Sebastian doubted they would learn anything from them. This killer was too clever to leave anything that could be linked to him in any way.

Outside, the wind gusted up, rattling the panes in the windows. And Sebastian found himself wondering why he had come here again; why he'd forced himself to endure once more the waves of fear and agony and despair that seemed to emanate from this place. What had he imagined the cold, calm light of a new day might show him that he'd missed before? There was nothing.

Returning downstairs, he went next to the old buttery that opened off the entrance passage. Although Sebastian had found the door ajar, the charwoman had insisted that it was always kept locked. Why had she been kept out? Why lock a room that's empty except for a couple of simple pieces of furniture?

There was no rug on the scarred wooden floor, only the wardrobe he remembered from before and the plain washstand bearing a simple white pitcher and bowl. He went to open the doors to the wardrobe and stared again at the empty shelves. In a room that was never cleaned, the shelves were tellingly free of dust. Which suggested the wardrobe had, until quite recently, held clothes. Clothes that were no longer there.

Sebastian ran his hand thoughtfully across the top shelf. Whoever had tortured and killed Benji would have ended up splattered with blood. But no wealthy gentleman could go home to his valet in such a condition without arousing dangerous suspicions. So that meant either the killer's valet was as complicit as Les Jenkins and the unknown, grave-digging boy, or the killer had regularly come to this room to wash and change his clothes before going home.

Sebastian closed the wardrobe's doors with a click that seemed to echo in the nearly empty room. It was telling that the killer had taken his blood-splattered clothing away with him when he cleared the house of everything incriminating. A good tailor would be able to recognize his own work and identify its purchaser. The killer had anticipated that the same way he had anticipated so much else.

"Who are you?" Sebastian said aloud to the empty room. Then he shouted it, his voice raw and torn with the reality of this horror he seemed incapable of stopping. *"Who are you!"*

His voice echoed back to him, mocking and futile.

He was suddenly seized with an intense need to get out of this house. He felt himself rendered unclean simply by standing in a place once occupied by such a monster, by touching objects the killer had touched before him. So great was that welling of revulsion that it drove him out of the house to stand on the cracked, weed-choked front walk with his arms outspread and his face lifted to the softly falling rain.

As if the heavens could somehow cleanse him of the horrors this unknown killer had wrought.

Chapter 46

Hat in hand, Sebastian stood beside Benji Thatcher's grave in St. James's churchyard. The rain had eased up again, leaving a dismal, flat white sky against which the blazing leaves of a nearby row of maples and horse chestnuts stood out in brilliant flushes of scarlet and yellow.

He couldn't have said why he'd felt the need to come here. But as he stared down at that muddy patch of earth, he was aware of a heavy sense of sadness settling over him. He was failing this child and all the others like him in death, just as their society had failed them in life. And because of those failures a vicious killer was still out there waiting to prey on another frightened, homeless child, and then another and another.

He sucked in a deep breath of damp air. And it came to him that his emotional reaction to both the ages of these victims and the horror of their deaths was undermining his ability to reason and analyze. He needed to find a way to assess what he knew with a calm detachment that kept eluding him.

He stared out over the thickly clustered, lichen-covered gray tombstones, his eyes narrowing. What was he missing? Was there some sort of telling pattern?

Something?

He forced himself to run through everything they'd learned. Six years ago a mysterious, wealthy gentleman calling himself Richard Herbert had leased a house in Bethnal Green, hired a servant named Jim Kimball, and spent the next several years murdering the neighborhood's street children. He then leased a new house, the one in the hills above Pentonville. He killed Kimball, buried the servant beside Bethnal Green's murdered children, hired Les Jenkins as caretaker, and transferred his nasty hobby to a new location.

Except that this time the killer didn't bury his young victims in his garden. He buried them several miles away on the grounds of an abandoned shot factory with the help of a young boy who was in all likelihood as poor as his master's victims. Why the change? The farmhouse on Penniwinch Lane was even more isolated than the Bethnal Green cottage, which meant the killer could easily have buried his victims in its untilled fields. Yet for some reason he had chosen not to.

Why?

Perhaps it had something to do with the reason Jim Kimball had ended up in an unmarked grave with a knife in his back. So why had "Richard Herbert" killed his Bethnal Green caretaker? Because Kimball knew where the bodies were buried and had in some way become a threat?

It was a thought that brought Sebastian back again to the unknown boy who'd left his hat at the bottom of what was to have been Benji Thatcher's grave. Where was that boy now? Was he dead too, like Les Jenkins?

The darting shadows of swifts drew Sebastian's gaze to the white sky hanging heavy above. And he knew again the growing fear that this monster was slipping through his fingers; that he had chased the killer away from both his burying ground and his latest torture chamber only to leave him free to set up again someplace else.

How do you identify a killer who has no real connection to his victims? How?

Part of the problem, Sebastian acknowledged, was that he had allowed not only his emotions but also his prejudices to influence his thinking. He kept circling back to Viscount Ashworth, both because of a long-standing dislike of the man and because of his concerns for Stephanie's future. But Ashworth, like Sir Francis Rowe, had a good, solid alibi—in Ashworth's case for the nights both Benji and Les Jenkins were killed. And while it was true that Corky Baldoon was convinced he'd seen someone who looked like a younger version of Ashworth's father riding away from the cottage in Bethnal Green, just how reliable was the old man? It was possible, even likely, that any arrogant young gentleman on a horse would remind Baldoon of the lord who had destroyed his life.

Sebastian liked to say he didn't believe in coincidences, but the truth was, he'd seen many a strange and wondrous coincidence in his life. Perhaps it would be more accurate to say he was highly suspicious of coincidences when it came to murder. Yet they could and did happen. The only thing he knew for certain was that unless his own sister and niece were lying, he was wasting precious time and energy focusing on someone who simply could not be the killer.

So that left him with—what? A nasty brothel in Pickering Place that in no way he could fathom seemed to fit with what he'd discovered about this killer? A royal cousin who also possessed a solid alibi? A French émigré financed by both Napoléon and Sebastian's own father-in-law?

An actor with a taste for young whores and *le vice anglais*?

Could someone like Hector Kneebone afford to lease houses and keep horses and a carriage he used only for killing? Sebastian found it doubtful, but nevertheless possible. And what about de Brienne? Sebastian allowed his thoughts to linger on the French comte. De Brienne had the wealth to indulge his various tastes and interests. And Sebastian had no doubt the émigré was capable of killing—had in all likelihood killed his own uncle and cousins before fleeing France.

The wind kicked up, scattering a shower of scarlet maple leaves across the churchyard, where they lay against the rain-sodden head-stones and nestled in the rank grass like splotches of old blood. He'd been aware for some time of a ragged boy hovering near the church wall. Sebastian now realized the boy was Toby the Dancer. Their gazes met and Toby stiffened, his face tight with fear. For a moment Sebastian thought the boy would run. Instead Toby came toward him, not stopping until he stood on the far side of Benji Thatcher's grave.

"Hullo," said Sebastian.

Toby stared at him, his eyes wide, his body so tense he was quivering. He said, "I hear they found a bunch more graves out at the shot factory."

"They did, yes."

"Was Sybil one of 'em?"

"No."

The boy sucked in a jerking breath, his gaze shifting to stare off across the churchyard. "I've looked everywhere I can think of and I can't find her. How can that be?"

Sebastian shook his head. "I don't know."

It was a lie, of course. Sebastian had no doubt that Sybil remained missing simply because they hadn't found her grave yet. He saw no reason to burden this poor, orphaned boy with such a painful truth. But Toby slanted a look at him that told Sebastian the boy wasn't fooled. He knew Sybil was probably dead, and Sebastian had basically confirmed that suspicion.

Sebastian said, "Whoever killed Benji has been taking children from around here for years. He must select them somehow. He probably even watches them for a time before he actually abducts them. You've never noticed anyone paying special attention to the street children?"

The boy shook his head, his eyes wide with raw, naked fear. "The shopkeepers all watch us real close. But most ev'rybody else acts like we ain't there—like they don't even see us when they pass us on the street. Only body knows any of us is Constable Gowan. And I s'pose the vicar."

"Reverend Filby?"

"Aye."

Sebastian felt an unpleasant sensation crawl across his skin. "Tell me about the reverend."

The Dancer looked at him blankly. "Whatcha mean?"

"How long has he been the vicar here?"

"I dunno. Couple years, maybe."

"Do you know if he keeps a riding horse?"

The question seemed to puzzle the boy, but he nodded.

Sebastian glanced again at that austere, redbrick church. Could a simple vicar afford to lease houses in other parishes and keep carriage horses he used solely in the pursuit of a sick taste for torture and murder? It seemed unlikely. And yet what did Sebastian really know about the Reverend Leigh Filby other than that he had gone out of his way to befriend the area's street children?

Just then, the tower's bell began to strike the hour, its deep vibrations swelling out across the wet churchyard. Sebastian said, "You can't think of anyone else?"

Once again, Toby's gaze met his. And in that tense, revealing moment, Sebastian caught a glimpse of all the anger and hopeless despair that roiled so deep within this skinny, ragged boy. "There ain't nobody else."

Toby Dancing had bright green eyes the color of a grassy meadow on a warm spring day. His features were regular, his mind sharp and quick. In just a few years he would grow to be a young man who, if he'd been born to even the most basic of opportunities, could have looked forward to a bright future. Instead, he was lucky not to have ended up like the dead boy buried at their feet.

And they both knew it.

☙

Sebastian spent the next half hour searching for the Reverend Leigh Filby.

He found the church of St. James empty except for the bell ringer, who suggested Sebastian try the vicarage. The vicar's aging housekeeper told Sebastian she thought the reverend was visiting a sick parishioner, only she couldn't recall which one. But she did provide Sebastian with two interesting pieces of information: Filby's wife had died some eight years before and he had never remarried. And he enjoyed a comfortable income from what she called a "tidy sum" left to him by a cousin and skillfully invested in the Funds.

Chapter 47

Half an hour later, Sebastian was in Drury Lane's darkened pit, one shoulder propped against the nearest column, his arms crossed at his chest as he watched Hector Kneebone. The actor had stripped down to his shirtsleeves and was helping a carpenter make last-minute alterations to the stage. The season had been under way nearly a week now, but the theater was not yet open every night and they were still working the kinks out of their productions. The actor cast him three or four long, frowning looks. Then Kneebone threw down his hammer and hopped off the stage.

He came to stand in front of Sebastian, legs splayed wide, hands dangling at his sides. "You're doing this to rattle me, aren't you?"

"Is it working? Are you rattled?"

"What do you think? I have someone trying to pin a murder on me. Who wouldn't be rattled?"

"Actually, at this point we're talking about 'murders,' plural."

Kneebone shook his head in a credible display of confusion. "Who else is dead?"

Rather than answer him, Sebastian said, "How familiar are you with the hills above Pentonville?"

"What?"

"Pentonville. It's a village to the west of Islington."

"I barely know where Islington is."

"There's an ancient, half-timbered farmstead there called Morton House, on Penniwinch Lane. Are you familiar with it?"

"No."

"Ever spend much time in Bethnal Green?"

Kneebone shook his head again, a shock of nearly black hair falling forward to gleam in the theater's dim interior. "Bethnal Green? What are you talking about?" His face remained utterly blank except for a faint display of puzzlement. But then, he was an actor; he made his living counterfeiting reactions and emotions.

"I'm talking about a mysterious man named Richard Herbert whom no one seems to have ever met. A brick cottage with some ugly secrets buried in its back garden. A trail of murdered children that stretches back seven years—if not longer. Any of this sound familiar?"

Kneebone's shirtfront rose and fell with the agitation of his breathing. "You've got the wrong man."

"Where were you Saturday night?"

"Where do you think? We had a performance. I was here until at least one. And then I went home. Ask anyone; they'll tell you."

Sebastian studied the actor's handsome, carefully controlled features. All theaters were required to drop their curtains by midnight on orders from the Bishop of London. Even if he'd somehow managed to leave almost immediately, it would have been nearly impossible for Kneebone to make it out to Penniwinch Lane in time to kill Les Jenkins and thoroughly remove anything that might identify him. And Kneebone could never have escaped right after the performance—not this early in the season, when he would be mobbed with well-wishers and admirers.

The inescapable fact was that of the men Sebastian had originally suspected, Hector Kneebone, Sir Francis Rowe, and Viscount Ash-worth all possessed solid alibis for at least one of the nights in question, while Icarus Cantrell had been exonerated by the only boy known to have escaped the killer. Which meant that, except for the recent addi-tion of Reverend Filby, Sebastian's list of suspects now had only one plausible name left on it: Amadeus Colbert, the comte de Brienne.

De Brienne was inspecting samples of wool cloth with his Bond Street tailor when Sebastian finally tracked him down.

"Walk up the street with me for a moment if you would, *monsieur?*" said Sebastian, pausing beside the French nobleman.

The comte glanced up, then deliberately returned his attention to the samples spread out on the table before him. "I fail to see why I should," he said, then addressed the silent tailor at his side. "What is your opinion of this blue Bath?"

"We could of course switch to French," Sebastian continued in an amicable tone. "Except that Monsieur Bondurant here was born and raised in Calais. And I really don't think you want what I'm about to say getting out."

De Brienne seemed to consider this, one cheek poking out as he explored the inside of it with his tongue. Then he said to the tailor, "I shan't be but a moment."

"I thought I'd answered all your questions before," said the comte to Sebastian as they turned to walk down Bond Street.

"Hardly. I asked where you were at certain critical times, and you told me you were playing games. Only you refused to say where or with whom."

"And you find that surprising?"

"As it happens, the killer has struck again."

"When?"

"Saturday night. So where were you? Playing games again?"

De Brienne drew up. "This is preposterous. I don't have time for this."

"You don't have time for a dozen or more dead children and three dead men?"

"You think I should be interested, do you? In the past twenty years, millions of men have left their bones strewn across the battlefields of Europe, while untold hundreds of thousands of women and children have also died. And you expect me to care about a paltry few dead London pickpockets? Seriously?"

Sebastian studied the Frenchman's thin, aristocratic face. "I didn't realize caring is a finite commodity. That deploring the death toll of the war across the Channel means I must remain unmoved by the suffering of street children here in London."

"Oh, please," sneered the comte and started to turn away.

Sebastian put out a hand, stopping him. "Let me explain something to you. I'm looking for a monster who tortures and kills poor children for pleasure. Do you understand what I'm saying? *Children.* I'm going to find out who he is and stop him, even if that means destroying you in the process. So I'll ask you one last time: Where were you Saturday night?"

The Frenchman's dark eyes narrowed, his bony face hardening into angry, arrogant lines. "I don't need to answer that question."

"I really think you do."

"Or you'll—what? Have me hauled before the magistrates down on Bow Street? That will never happen and you know it."

"It wasn't Bow Street I had in mind."

He said it quietly. But his meaning was not lost on de Brienne, who went utterly still. "You can't be serious. You're an Englishman; you even fought Napoléon yourself for six years. If you expose me to Paris now, who knows how many of your compatriots will die unnecessarily as a result? You wouldn't do that."

"So certain?"

De Brienne poked his tongue into his cheek again and looked away, as if carefully considering his options. Then he said, "You did see the news in this morning's papers?"

It had been days since Sebastian had done more than glance at a newspaper. "What news?"

"A boatman found the Honorable Sinclair Pugh floating off the Westminster Steps at dawn this morning. The official story is that he must have slipped on the wet steps in last night's rain and fallen into the river. But you and I both know how improbable that is."

Sebastian had a vision of the stout Member of Parliament for Gough standing in the opulent front room of Number Three, his full face flushed with anticipation as he viewed the two young girls being offered for his selection. "What are you suggesting? That he was murdered?"

"It's possible, I suppose. But I think it far more likely that he simply killed himself."

"Why would Pugh commit suicide?"

"Because he's been quite vocally insistent on the folly of restoring the Bourbons to the throne of France after the eventual defeat of Napoléon. And then he was too stupid to keep from stumbling into the nasty little snare that Jarvis inevitably set for him at a certain nefarious establishment."

Sebastian shook his head. "I know Pugh was a patron of Number Three, Pickering Place. But I can't believe the threat of that getting out would be enough to drive him to kill himself." Very young girls prostituted themselves on the streets of London all the time and no one seemed to give it a second thought, while as for the Bligh sisters' other specialty . . . Such activities might bring embarrassment were they to become known. But would that be enough to drive a man to suicide?

Sebastian doubted it.

De Brienne said, "I don't think you know everything that goes on at Number Three. But Jarvis does; in fact, he orchestrates some of it. If you want to know who's killing London's street children, ask your wife's father."

Chapter 48

*S*ebastian went first to the house in Berkeley Square.

Jarvis was not there. But Lady Jarvis heard Sebastian's voice and sent down a servant to ask him to step up to the drawing room and see her.

He found her seated on a sofa beside the fire, a rug spread across her lap. The change in her appearance was startling, her complexion an unhealthy gray, her eyes sunken and bruised looking. "You'll forgive me if I don't stand up," she said with a smile, holding out one trembling hand. "Hero has walked down to the apothecary's with Cousin Victoria to pick up some vile potion the physicians have prescribed me, so I thought I'd seize the opportunity to tell you something I've long wanted to say to you."

"This sounds ominous," he said with a smile as he took both her hands in his and settled beside her.

He saw a faint, answering gleam of amusement in her cloudy blue eyes. "Not so ominous. I simply want to thank you."

"Thank me?"

"For the joy you have brought my daughter. She never intended to marry, you see."

"I know."

She tilted her head to one side. "Yes, I suppose you do. I used to worry about her a great deal. I never thought she'd find someone who could change her mind. I'm glad I was wrong."

Sebastian smiled. "So am I."

Lady Jarvis squeezed his hands. "Marriage can be a living purgatory. But it can also be something wondrous and deeply enriching. I can't tell you what it means to me, knowing that my daughter has found the latter and not the former." Her head turned as the sound of women's voices drifted up from the entry hall below. "Ah; there they are. Don't give me away to Hero, will you? I've no doubt she'd ring a peal over me if she knew. And now you must stay and meet my delightful young cousin."

Sebastian rose to his feet as Hero entered the room with her typical long-legged stride. "Devlin," she said, her eyebrows rising in puzzlement as her gaze shifted between Sebastian and her mother. "What have you two been plotting?"

"What a thing to say!" exclaimed her mother with a betraying laugh.

Hero bent to kiss her mother's cheek. "I don't hear you denying it."

"I wanted Cousin Victoria to meet Devlin," said Lady Jarvis. "Where is she?"

"Ignobly bringing up the rear, I fear," said Victoria Hart-Davis, her cheeks flushed with a combination of cold and exercise and her eyes a bright, sparkling blue. "You must forgive me, my lord," she said as Lady Jarvis performed the necessary introductions. "But you find me shamefully winded. Cousin Hero sets a shocking pace."

"She always has," said Lady Jarvis, smiling fondly. "She was leaving me in the dust by the time she was ten."

"She's been known to leave me in the dust," said Sebastian, bowing over Cousin Victoria's hand.

"Well, really," said Hero. "The three of you make me sound shockingly rude."

"No," said Sebastian, smiling at her over her diminutive cousin's head. "Just resolute."

"Resolute?"

"Resolute."

❧

"Your cousin is extraordinarily lovely," Sebastian said to Hero a few minutes later when she drew him away to the morning room.

"She is, yes. And I must admit, she has been a ministering angel since Mother's been ill."

"How is Lady Jarvis?"

"Slightly better, I think. We've had half a dozen Harley Street physicians here. They've diagnosed everything from consumption to influenza and hopelessly contradicted each other's prescriptions and treatments. But she is stronger today. "

"Thank God for that." He searched her face. "Shall I stay a while? I can, you know."

"What would be the point?"

"To be here for you."

"I have Cousin Victoria."

"But you don't like her."

Hero gave a soft laugh and pressed her fingers to his lips. "Hush. I'll be fine. Truly. Now, tell me what you've discovered."

He told her the grisly results of the excavations at Bethnal Green, and their puzzling failure to find anything more at the Penniwinch Lane farmstead. But he left it at that.

In the end she said, "Grisham says you originally came to see Father. Why?"

"He has some information I need."

Normally she wouldn't have been content to leave it at that. But she was too distracted by her mother's worrisome health to question him further, and he saw no reason to burden her with his suspicions.

Jarvis was crossing the forecourt of Carlton House when Sebastian fell into step beside him and said, "You didn't tell me of your association with Number Three, Pickering Place."

Jarvis kept walking. "Why should I have?"

"It seems every time I turn over a rock to expose more of the ugliness that lurks beneath the surface of this city, I find your tentacles there too—first entwined with the comte de Brienne and now with Number Three."

Jarvis drew up and swung to face him. "I warned you to leave de Brienne alone."

"So you did." Sebastian glanced toward the tall, former hussar officer who stood waiting beside one of the arches separating the palace forecourt from Pall Mall. "And you use Number Three for—what? Blackmailing your enemies? Driving them to suicide?"

"If you're referring to Sinclair Pugh, the man is responsible for his own death. He should have known better than to meddle where he didn't belong."

"You mean, in the future of Europe? You don't think that should concern him?"

"Only a fool tries to turn the tide of history."

"Are you so certain you know history's direction? What if you're wrong? What if the future belongs to republics and democracies?"

Jarvis snorted. "Don't be preposterous." He started walking again.

Sebastian walked with him. "I find it difficult to believe that the public exposure of a taste for very young whores or even *le vice anglais* would be considered shameful enough to drive a man such as Pugh to suicide. So why was he found floating off the Westminster Steps?"

Jarvis's eyes creased with amusement. "Really, Devlin; use your imagination."

Sebastian shook his head. "Your capacity for nasty machinations is beyond me."

"You yourself suspected at one time that the Bligh sisters were working for Paris."

"So you—what? Tricked Pugh into thinking he'd been compromised at Number Three by French spies?"

"It wasn't particularly difficult. The man wasn't nearly as intelligent as he liked to believe."

"In other words, Pugh committed suicide over a lie."

"I did say he was a fool. My intent was merely to pressure him to shut up. But this outcome works just as well."

Sebastian knew a sudden, wild urge to plant his father-in-law a facer. He took a deep breath and forced the impulse down. "You seem to make it your business to know the dirty secrets of everyone who is anyone. So who do you think is torturing and killing London's street children?"

"Do you seriously believe I've given extensive thought to the matter? The deaths of this city's gutter spawn are of no interest to me."

Sebastian studied the big man's familiar features, the aquiline nose and fierce gray eyes that were so much like Hero's. And it came to Sebastian that the longer he knew Hero, the better he was learning to read her Machiavellian father. "I don't believe you. You know who's doing this. You know, but you're protecting him for some reason. Why?"

Jarvis's chin lifted. "I will admit to certain suspicions. But do I know for certain? No. I've far more pressing matters to deal with at the moment."

"So whom do you suspect?"

"If I am correct and he threatens to become an embarrassment, then he will be eliminated. You need have no fear of that."

Sebastian felt another rush of such pure rage that he was practically shaking with it. "I will find out who's doing this," he said, keeping his voice low with difficulty. "And if it's someone you've been protecting, the blood of each and every one of his victims will be on your hands."

"Oh, please," said Jarvis with an arrogant sneer.

Sebastian reached out to clench his fist on the neatly tailored lapel of Jarvis's coat and jerk him around. "You bloody—"

"Is there a problem, my lord?" said Major Edward Burnside, stepping forward.

Sebastian's gaze shifted from his father-in-law to the former hussar major and back again. He opened his hand, his lips twisting into a smile as he patted Jarvis's crumpled coat and took a step back. "Each and every death," he said.

And then he turned and left, before the urge to punch Hero's father became overwhelming.

Chapter 49

*W*hom would Jarvis protect?

Sebastian asked himself this question over and over as he sent Giles home with the curricle and turned to walk up the Strand toward Bow Street.

Whom?

The most obvious answer was his sources: the Bligh sisters and the comte de Brienne. Except that Jarvis had minions everywhere, which meant the killer could easily be someone Sebastian didn't suspect, didn't even know existed.

Who else? Prominent members of the government, surely. Also prominent clergymen such as the Archbishop of Canterbury and the Bishop of London. But Sebastian could think of no reason for Jarvis to protect a clergyman as insignificant as Leigh Filby, the lowly vicar of St. James's, Clerkenwell.

What about a young, up-and-coming actor such as Hector Kneebone?

Sebastian pondered this possibility as he walked. Could Kneebone be one of Jarvis's sources? Sebastian could certainly see Jarvis paying Kneebone for—or pressuring him into providing—information about the

various wellborn women who passed through his bed, damaging information Jarvis could then use to blackmail and control those women's
husbands.

The problem with that explanation was that Kneebone had an alibi
for the last killing.

So who else?

Sebastian turned to cut up Southampton Street toward Covent
Garden. Would Jarvis feel the need to protect the son and heir of a
wealthy, powerful nobleman such as the Marquis of Lindley? Perhaps.
Anything with the potential to undermine the common people's respect
for the aristocracy was by extension a threat to King, God, and country. The problem with that explanation was that Ashworth, like Kneebone, had a solid alibi—in Ashworth's case, for the deaths of both Benji
and Les Jenkins.

Which left—what?

Sebastian kept walking. *Who else?* More than anything, Jarvis's talents were dedicated to protecting the House of Hanover. And that
translated into carefully shielding the reputations of the royal family
and their closest relatives.

Relatives such as Sir Francis Rowe.

Sebastian turned the name over and over in his mind. He'd largely
abandoned his earlier suspicions of the King's unsavory cousin, both
because the Baronet had a solid alibi for the night Benji was snatched
off the streets of Clerkenwell and because Sebastian's understanding of
the boy's murder had evolved. Once he began to realize he was looking
for a killer who'd spent years torturing and murdering the city's poor,
homeless children, it made little sense to suspect Sir Francis simply
because of a purloined snuffbox. Except . . .

Except just because Sir Francis targeted Benji out of personal malice didn't mean he couldn't also have killed Mick Swallow and Mary
Cartwright and a dozen other children whose names Sebastian would
probably never know.

Thoughtful, he pushed his way across the crowded, raucous market. The problem with that theory was that Sir Francis Rowe had an alibi for the night of Benji's abduction, just as Lord Ashworth had an alibi for the night of Benji's death and Hector Kneebone had an alibi for the time of Les Jenkin's death. But what if . . .

Sebastian drew up abruptly, a sense of possibility coursing through him. He knew he was making a giant leap. But it was a way to make sense of much that had bedeviled and misled him.

"Bloody hell," he said softly. And then he said it again, loud enough this time to catch the attention of a passing matron, who frowned at him sternly. *"Bloody hell."*

❧

"By the time I left, they'd found six more graves in the gardens of the Bethnal Green cottage," said Lovejoy, rubbing his eyes with a splayed thumb and forefinger as he and Sebastian walked along the terrace of Somerset House. The magistrate had spent most of the day out at Bethnal Green watching the bones of the city's forgotten, murdered children slowly emerge from the earth. His eyes were sunken and red, his face slack with exhaustion. Most of London's magistrates were content to exercise their duties from the comfort of their chambers. But there had always been some such as Lovejoy, men who never hesitated to go out into the streets to view crime scenes themselves and actively help catch killers.

"What about the family that's been living there?" asked Sebastian.

"I understand the woman is refusing to return to the house with her children."

"Good," said Sebastian, pausing to stare out over the choppy waters of the Thames, now turning a glorious gold with the sun's descent. He'd always believed that places absorb the emotions, good and bad, experienced by those within their walls. No child should have to grow up in a house that had witnessed such horrors. "What about the Penniwinch Lane house?"

Lovejoy shook his head. "Nothing. After our killer moved on from Bethnal Green, he must have begun burying his victims at the shot factory."

"No word yet on the factory's owners?"

"Ah, yes; I almost forgot." Lovejoy drew a folded paper from his coat. "We received the heirs' names just today." He handed Sebastian the paper. "There are fourteen altogether."

Sebastian ran quickly through the list of men and women. Most were unknown to him. But there, second from the last, was a name that leapt out at him: *Sir Francis Rowe.*

"My God," whispered Sebastian.

Lovejoy looked at him in surprise. "Something interesting?"

Sebastian held out the list. "Sir Francis. He was suggested to me days ago as someone with a grudge against Benji Thatcher. But until recently I'd virtually eliminated him because he had a solid alibi for the night Benji was abducted and because I quickly realized we're looking for a killer with a long-standing practice of targeting street children."

"Rowe." Lovejoy frowned down at the list. "The name sounds familiar."

"He's the Regent's cousin—a grandson of Prince William Augustus, the old Duke of Cumberland, via a natural daughter. In fact, he was with the Regent himself the night Benji was taken."

"Oh, dear," said the magistrate. Bow Street had a well-founded terror of tangling with the palace. "But you say he was with the Prince."

"Not the night Benji was killed."

Lovejoy shook his head. "I don't understand. If he has an alibi for the night of the boy's abduction, he can't be the killer."

"He can if we're dealing with more than one killer."

Lovejoy stared at him. "You can't be serious."

"I wish I weren't. Ironically, I started out thinking we were looking for two killers—a gentleman and a boy. Then I realized the boy digging the grave was probably a servant and the idea of two killers was dismissed. But what if there actually are two killers—*two gentlemen* with the same sick tastes, working together? One could have abducted Benji, while the other killed him."

"*Two* such vicious, depraved killers, drawn from the highest ranks of Society? But . . . surely that's impossible." Lovejoy stared off across the river at the timber yard on the far bank, his features tightening. "Isn't it?"

Sebastian thought about the comfortable armchairs drawn up before the hearth in that soaring, ancient hall, the marble-topped table with its fine brandies and crystal glasses. "I think it's more than possible; it's probable."

"So who is the second killer?"

It was a question Sebastian had been asking himself. Kneebone was one possibility, although Sebastian found it difficult to believe that an arrogant aristocrat as proud of his royal lineage as Sir Francis Rowe would condescend to consort as an equal with a common actor. The same argument applied to both the Bligh sisters and Reverend Filby—unless, of course, Filby was one of Rowe's distant cousins, which was certainly conceivable. De Brienne was a nobleman and must also remain a candidate. But if Sebastian had to put his money on anyone, it would be Ashworth.

Unfortunately, all he had to back that up was his own intense dislike of the bastard and the memories of a white-haired old man with a tragic past.

"I have some ideas," he said vaguely, "but nothing definite yet. As it stands, the only thing we have tying Rowe to the killings is his standing as one of the shot factory's heirs—and there are fourteen of them."

Lovejoy stared at him, hard. "If you're right—if there are two killers—how can we possibly prove it?"

Sebastian watched a wherryman rowing his fare toward the nearby steps. "I don't know. But I will. Somehow."

γ

Sir Francis Rowe lived in the same sprawling, Upper Grosvenor Street residence once occupied by his infamous royal grandfather, the Butcher of Culloden. It was a massive, opulent house filled with exquisite French crystal chandeliers, gleaming polished woods and marbles, priceless furniture, and objets d'art. The cost of a simple doorknob would have fed a good chunk of Clerkenwell's street children for a year.

Dressed in an elegant evening coat with satin knee breeches, silk stockings, and diamond-buckled shoes, the Baronet sat sprawled on a settee in his drawing room drinking a glass of wine when Sebastian was shown up by Rowe's stately butler.

"You're lucky to have caught me," said Rowe with a pointed glance at the ornate French clock on the mantel. "I leave in a few minutes for a dinner engagement. You'll forgive me if I don't offer you any refreshment?"

"That's quite all right," said Sebastian. His host did not invite him to sit, so he went to stand with one arm resting along the room's marble mantel. "This won't take long."

Rowe raised an inquiring eyebrow and took a slow sip of his wine.

Sebastian said, "You didn't tell me you're one of the owners of the Rutherford Shot Factory in Clerkenwell."

"I don't recall your asking, but yes; it comes to me from my father's family. Is that relevant for some reason?"

"That's where Benji Thatcher's body was found."

"Who?"

"Benji Thatcher. The pickpocket who stole your favorite snuffbox on Clerkenwell Green and was later found tortured, raped, and strangled. At your shot factory."

Rowe settled more comfortably against the cushions of his settee and smiled. "And you think my connection to this abandoned factory somehow implicates me, do you?"

"Yes."

"I fail to see why. To be frank, I scarcely give the place any thought. Why should I? It's essentially worthless."

"Except, of course, as a place to bury murder victims."

"There are fourteen heirs altogether. Have you looked into the other thirteen?"

"Not yet."

Rowe scratched his cheek with one curled finger. "You do recall I was with the Prince at the time you say the boy was abducted, don't you?"

"Yes. I also recall that you pointedly refused to say where you were the night he was killed."

"You can't be serious. People are murdered in London all the time. Do you yourself have an alibi for the precise moment of each and every death?"

Sebastian kept his gaze on the man's full, self-satisfied face. "Where were you last Saturday night?"

Sir Francis frowned as if in confusion. "When?"

"Saturday night. At around midnight."

"Ah. As it happens, I dined that evening with the Prince—and Liverpool and Jarvis and half a dozen other such men."

"Again? Convenient."

"Evidently. Why do you ask?"

"You know why," said Sebastian.

The Baronet's eyes narrowed. Then he drew his watch from his pocket and flipped it open. "Shall I ring for a footman to show you out?"

Sebastian pushed away from the mantelpiece. "That's quite all right; I can find my own way. But I'll be back."

Sir Francis Rowe's lips curled into another of his tight smiles. "This is supposed to worry me, is it?"

"'In order to know virtue, we must first acquaint ourselves with vice,'" said Sebastian, quoting de Sade.

"What's that supposed to mean?"

"Think about it," said Sebastian and saw the royal cousin's smile slip.

Chapter 50

"You've been talking again, haven't you?" The gentleman stood with his legs spread wide, his fashionable beaver hat pulled low over his eyes, his deadly, silver-tipped walking stick gripped in one hand. The cold night wind billowed his silk cape out around him.

The boy shook his head, his gaze fixed on the man's pale face, his chest squeezing so tight he could scarcely breathe. "No, sir. No, I haven't. I swear, sir."

"You swear?" The gentleman's lips contorted into a hard sneer. "This is all your fault. All of it. If you'd told me some one-legged soldier had taken to sleeping in the warehouse, none of this would have happened."

"I didn't know!"

"You're supposed to know that sort of thing. Why do you think I keep you?"

The boy hung his head, narrowing his world to the darkness and the gentleman's glossy boots and his own broken-down shoes. The silence filled with the rasp of his own breathing. Then he heard the silken voice that would forever haunt his nightmares say, "There's something you must do."

The boy looked up, a sick dread seizing his stomach. "What, sir?"

The gentleman smiled. "Come with me."

Chapter 51

*H*ow *do you tell your wife that her father is in all probability protecting a vicious child killer?*

The answer, Sebastian decided, is that you don't.

Sleepless and with a glass of brandy at his elbow, he sat at his desk in the darkened library. He wore only a pair of breeches and a dressing gown; the house lay dark and quiet except for the fire that flickered in the nearby hearth. From the distance came a passing watchman's cry, *"Three o'clock on a wet night, and all is well."*

Except all was not well.

Sebastian scrubbed his hands down over his face. He'd sent a carefully worded message to Liverpool, inquiring into the movements of the Prince and his cousin on Saturday evening. Liverpool's response lay open on the desk before him. The Prince had hosted a dinner party that night and Sir Francis had indeed been amongst the guests. But the Baronet had pleaded illness and departed well before midnight.

"Damn," said Sebastian. *Damn, damn, damn.*

He heard a distant door open, a familiar light step on the stairs, and looked up to see Hero standing in the darkened doorway. Her beautiful dark hair was loose about her shoulders, her face pale in the faint, flickering light of the windblown streetlamps.

She said, "You're hiding something from me. What is it?"

He pressed his hands flat against the surface of the desk and leaned back in his chair. "Is it that obvious?"

"It is to me." She came to crouch down beside the cat that lay on the hearth, watching her. "Why did you want to see Jarvis this afternoon?" she asked, her attention seemingly all for the task of petting the cat.

He watched the firelight play over the planes of her face, watched her mouth curl into a soft smile as the cat bumped its head against her hand in a rare show of affection. And he knew he couldn't tell her. Not now, when her emotions were already raw with worry for her mother's health. And so he lied. Sort of. "Sir Francis Rowe claims he was with the Prince and Jarvis the night the caretaker was murdered out at the Penniwinch Lane farm. I wanted to know if he's telling the truth."

She looked up at him. "And is he?"

Sebastian shook his head. "He was with the Prince earlier in the evening. But he left well before midnight."

"You didn't tell me you were back to suspecting Francis."

"He's your cousin," said Sebastian. He was surprised to hear the steps of two men coming up the street and wondered who would be abroad, afoot, at this hour. "I didn't want to say anything when I had so little to go on."

"You have more now?"

"More. But not enough. I'm beginning to think—" Sebastian broke off.

The footsteps had now stopped in front of the house. He heard a whispered word he didn't quite catch and then a soft tread on the front stairs.

"What is it?" asked Hero, watching him.

He put a finger to his lips and rose to his feet just as they heard a sharp cry and a *thump*, followed by the sound of one person running away fast.

Hero pushed up. "What was that?"

Sebastian unlocked the secret drawer in his desk to grab the pistol he kept there primed and ready. "Stay here," he said, coming from behind the desk.

Pistol in hand, he sprinted for the entry hall to shove back the bolts and jerk open the front door.

Cold and damp, the night mist swirled into the house. He could still hear someone running away, down Davies Street now. But crumpled at his feet lay a ragged boy, his chest a dark wet sheet of blood.

It was Toby Dancing.

Chapter 52

*T*oby's chest was jerking, his soft green eyes liquid with unshed tears, his lower lip quivering with pain and fear.

Sebastian crouched down to ease an arm beneath the boy's shoulders and lift his head. He could hear the killer's running footsteps growing fainter and fainter in the distance, but he could not leave the dying boy. "Tell me who did this to you, Toby."

The boy's gaze met Sebastian's and he choked on a broken sob.

"Tell me!" said Sebastian, aware of Hero coming to stand beside him.

But the pain and fear had already faded from the boy's eyes, leaving nothing.

❦

Sebastian rode in the cart carrying Toby Dancing's body across the dark, silent city to Gibson's surgery.

He sat with his elbows resting on his drawn up knees, his body swaying with each jolt and thump as the cart rattled over the cobbled streets. He'd sent Giles on ahead to warn Gibson they were coming. But he somehow couldn't bear to let the boy make this penultimate journey alone.

The night was cold, the fog damp against his face and heavy with the pungent scent of coal smoke and manure. Moisture glistened on the boy's upturned face, the movement of the cart rocking his otherwise still body back and forth.

Sebastian supposed it was possible the killer had lured Toby to Brook Street or somehow hauled the boy across London at knifepoint. But he doubted it. He had heard no hesitation in the footsteps coming toward them down Brook Street. So that meant—what? That Toby had known his killer? Had come willingly to Brook Street in his company? Why?

Sebastian brought his gaze, again, to the pale, still face of the boy who lay dead beside him, honey-colored hair curling softly in the humid air. "Was it you, Toby?" he asked softly. "Were you the lad Rory Inchbald interrupted digging Benji's grave?"

But Toby simply stared unseeingly at the white, starless sky above. And Sebastian reached out a gentle hand to close the boy's eyes.

❧

Sebastian leaned against the rough stone wall of the outbuilding at the base of Gibson's yard. He doubted the surgeon could tell him anything about the boy's death that he didn't already know. But it had seemed somehow negligent not to exhaust every possibility.

After a time, Gibson came to stand in the building's doorway. His haunted gaze met Sebastian's. "Please tell me you know who's doing this."

Sebastian pushed his breath out in a ragged sigh. "I'm becoming more and more convinced it's Sir Francis Rowe and Lord Ashworth, working together. But I don't know for certain and I can't begin to prove it."

"Christ," said Gibson. "Come look at this."

Sebastian suspected he didn't want to see what he was about to see, but he pushed away from the wall and followed his friend into that dank, death-haunted room. What was left of Toby Dancing lay naked on the stone slab.

"He was stabbed in the back," said Gibson. "Probably with the same swordstick that killed Les Jenkins since the blade was long enough for the tip to come out his chest."

"This killer seems to make it a habit of stabbing his confederates in the back."

Gibson nodded. "And look at this—" He broke off to roll the boy to one side, revealing a thin, bony back crisscrossed with old flogging scars.

"My God," whispered Sebastian.

Gibson eased the boy back down. "From the looks of things, I'd say your killer—or I suppose I should say 'killers'—had their hands on this boy maybe a year ago and abused him much the same way they abused Benji. Only for some reason they didn't kill him."

Sebastian shook his head. "It doesn't make any sense."

Gibson stood with his hands braced against the stone table's edge. "It might. When I was in India, I knew a colonel who abused a little Hindu boy something terrible. For the longest time, I could never understand why the boy didn't run off. That boy would do anything the colonel ordered him to do, without hesitation or complaint. I finally realized that the colonel used the boy's fear to control him. The boy was afraid that if he didn't do what the colonel told him or if he tried to run off and got caught, then the colonel would hurt him that way again—only worse."

Sebastian went to stand looking out at the darkened yard. Already the sky was turning a golden pink on the eastern horizon, and he could hear the hungry roar of the lions in the Tower looking for their breakfast. He felt his own exhaustion settle over him like a heavy blanket, weighing him down. After a moment he said, "I knew Toby was afraid. When I talked to him yesterday, any idiot could have seen he was terrified."

"But you didn't know why."

Sebastian shook his head. "I should have."

Gibson scrubbed a hand across his unshaven face. "There is one other thing."

Sebastian turned. "What?"

The surgeon held out a folded sheet of expensive parchment paper. "I found this in his pocket."

Sebastian had to force himself to open the page. The writing was the same carefully disguised block printing as before: bold, black, and mocking.

ANOTHER GIFT FOR YOU, DEVLIN. CHEERS.

$\approx$

Tuesday, 21 September

Sebastian arrived at the Professor's Attic in Clerkenwell in the pale dawn light to find the shutters still up and no smoke rising from the chimney. He banged on the door with his fist and kept banging until Icarus Cantrell stuck his upper body out an upstairs window. He wore a ruffled nightshirt and a nightcap with a pointed tip that dangled in front of his gray-beard-grizzled face as he shouted, "For the love of— Oh; it's you. What are you doing here? I thought your lot didn't even roll out of bed until noon."

"I need to talk to Hamish McCormick."

"He's not here."

"I know. I'll wait while you get him."

$\approx$

Hamish sat on the low stool beside the Professor's kitchen fire, one fist wrapped around the handle of a spoon as he shoveled hot porridge into his mouth. Every once in a while he cast a look toward where Sebastian stood, watching him. But Sebastian waited until the boy was halfway through his second bowl before saying, "You told me you were walking by Charterhouse Square with another lad when the gentleman pulled you into his carriage."

Hamish shoved another spoonful of porridge into his mouth and nodded.

"Why were you there? By the Charterhouse, I mean."

"Paddy said he had somethin' he wanted me t' see."

"Do you know what?"

"No."

"And afterward, when you went looking for Paddy Gantry, you say you couldn't find him?"

Hamish nodded and swallowed. "Never seen him again. Far as I know, nobody ever did."

"Is it possible that Paddy deliberately led you to a place where the gentleman was waiting, and that's why he ran?"

Hamish's spoon clattered against the earthenware bowl as he stopped eating, and his gaze darted to where Icarus Cantrell sat at the trestle table.

"Tell him," said the Professor, leaning forward.

Hamish swiped the back of one hand across his mouth. His gaze dropped to the bowl in his hands.

"Hamish?"

The boy nodded, his face tight and pinched.

Sebastian said, "How long had you known Paddy?"

Hamish rolled one shoulder with the indifference of one to whom the passage of time meant little. "I dunno. Forever."

"Did Paddy ever disappear for a few days?"

Hamish frowned as if with thought. "Once, yeah. He was gone a good week or more and then he come back walkin' kinda stiff. Said he fell and hurt hisself. Why?"

Rather than answer, Sebastian said, "You told me the man who abducted you had red eyes and soft hands and a gentleman's voice. Is there any chance there could have been two gentlemen that night? Not necessarily when you were pulled into the carriage, but later. At the house."

The boy's gaze shifted from Sebastian to the Professor.

"Is it possible?" said Icarus Cantrell, leaning forward.

Hamish set his empty porridge bowl aside and hunched over with his hands thrust between his knees and his gaze on the floor. "I was never sure. There was times I thought I could hear two of 'em talkin' to each other. But then I'd think it was me head playin' tricks on me, dividin' one man into two and then meltin' them back into one again."

"Do you remember anything they said to each other?"

He shook his head.

"What about names? Did you ever hear them address each other by name?"

Hamish looked up, his eyes bleak with an old, old fear. "I thought they was callin' each other 'Duke' and 'Bishop.' But that don't make no sense, does it?"

And then, when Sebastian could only stare at him, the boy said it again. "Does it?"

Chapter 53

*S*ebastian sat before his library fire. The day was wretchedly gloomy, with a light rain pattering against the windowpanes. He was so absorbed by his thoughts that he wasn't aware of Hero coming up behind his chair until her hands settled on his shoulders.

"You need to rest," she said, kneading his tight muscles. "You didn't sleep last night at all. Or the night before."

Sebastian tipped back his head so that he could look up at her. "You think I can rest?"

She gave him a crooked smile. "No. But just because you don't think you can doesn't mean you shouldn't try."

"I keep thinking I should have seen it sooner."

She shook her head. "Seen what?"

"The killers were always careful to abduct street children who had either been orphaned or abandoned—those without a parent or grandparent or other adult relative who might cause an uproar or demand action when they disappeared. That Bethnal Green magistrate—Alexander Robbins—was unusual in that he actually did notice when the area's street children complained of friends or siblings who went missing. But he still didn't do anything about it, did he?"

Hero shifted to massage his sore neck. "So what do you think you should have seen?"

He bent his head forward, exposing more of his neck to her soothing hands. He hadn't realized just how tight and sore his muscles were. "Someone like Sir Francis or Ashworth—or de Brienne or Kneebone—would have no way of knowing which of the tens of thousands of ragged children running the streets of London have parents and which don't. I should have realized that the killers must be using someone to select their targets."

"You mean, someone like Toby?"

He nodded. "I think they used Toby—and Hamish's friend Paddy Gantry before him, and doubtless others before that—first to select their targets and then to lure the victims to places where they could be easily abducted."

"And to bury them," said Hero quietly.

"Yes. God knows how long they've been doing this, moving from one area of the city to the next, selecting and grooming a child in each new location to use as their tool. I suspect they killed Paddy Gantry after Hamish escaped, both because they blamed Paddy for picking the 'wrong' boy and because they were worried that Paddy might identify them. They replaced him with Toby."

"But why would Toby help gentlemen abduct and kill his own friends?"

"It has something to do with being vulnerable—and very afraid. But I'm not convinced I entirely understand it myself."

Her hands stilled. "Whoever these men are, they must be stopped."

He reached up to close his hands over hers and draw her around to face him. "How well do you know Sir Francis?"

"Not all that well. I never liked him, even when we were children. And there's a nearly ten-year difference in our ages. Why?"

"I keep thinking Sir Francis and Ashworth are the most likely combination of killers, except the two men don't run in the same set. Ashworth is a Corinthian, while Sir Francis is not."

"True. But they were at Cambridge together."

"They were? Sir Francis is several years Ashworth's senior, is he not?"

"He is. Francis's mother doted on him quite shamelessly, though, and didn't like him to be away from her for long. He didn't go up to Cambridge until after her death, with the result that he and Ashworth were there at the same time. I remember because he brought Ashworth on a visit to Glenside one summer when I was something like thirteen or fourteen." Glenside Castle was Jarvis's Scottish estate.

"In other words," said Sebastian, "they could have been doing this for ten or twelve years."

"Surely not."

He squeezed her hands and rose to his feet. "I think I need to find someone who knew them at Cambridge."

While Hero went to sit with her convalescing mother, Sebastian spent what was left of the day in discreet conversation with men he knew who had been at Cambridge around the turn of the century. He heard a number of sordid tales, of abuse of innkeepers' daughters and poor girls picked up off the streets and brutalized—all hushed up at the time by the Marquis of Lindley and the old Baronet.

At Cambridge, Ashworth and Rowe had mainly limited themselves to rape and flagellation, although Rowe had also used a knife to cut a few of the girls. Sebastian wondered when they had moved on to murder. At the same time they expanded their victims to include young boys as well as girls? Or before?

More disturbed than ever, he donned evening dress and went in search of his beautiful, troubled young niece.

꙰

Miss Stephanie Wilcox was sipping a glass of lemonade at Lady Mary Jessup's fashionable soirée when Sebastian walked up to her. She wore a high-waisted gown of virginal white, with small puff sleeves and a V-necked bodice laced up the front à la grecque. A white satin ribbon beaded with crystals and tiny pearls threaded her golden curls. She looked both utterly lovely and frighteningly fragile.

"Uncle," she said, flashing him a wide smile that did nothing to dislodge the storm clouds lurking in her pretty blue eyes. "If you're looking for Ashworth, he's spending the evening with the Marquis in a show of filial devotion."

"Actually, I was looking for you."

"Oh? I noticed you skulking about at Lady Farningham's last night. Mother tells me you think my betrothed guilty of a string of horrific murders. Is that true?"

"Yes," he said baldly.

Stephanie threw a telling glance toward where Amanda stood, her back to them, in conversation with one of her cronies. "She's here, you know—Mother, I mean. She's left strict orders with the staff that you are to be turned away, should you venture to show your face in St. James's Square. And I've been instructed to cut you dead if you should chance to speak to me."

"And yet here we are."

"Yes." She smiled in a mischievous way that reminded him of the little girl she'd once been. "But then, as you know, I don't generally make it a habit of doing what I'm told."

"No," he agreed. She had the same disastrous, rebellious defiance that had characterized her grandmother Sophia—along with Sophia's tragic air of vulnerability. And he felt a helpless rush of affection for this vibrant, doomed girl. He said, "How friendly is Ashworth with Sir Francis Rowe? Do you know?"

"Quite friendly, actually. He's asked Rowe to stand with him at our wedding. Why?"

Something about the tight way she said it told him much that he needed to know. "You don't like him, do you?"

"Rowe? No."

"Any particular reason why?"

She tilted her head to one side. "Do you like him?"

"No. Yet Ashworth obviously does."

"Yes."

"Would you happen to know Ashworth's opinion of the Marquis de Sade?"

"Oh, Uncle; and what do you know of the Divine Marquis?"

He'd been hoping she'd say simply, *Who is de Sade?* "More than I'd care to, actually," he said. "I take it Ashworth is familiar with his works?"

"Familiar? You could say that. Although it would be more accurate to say he's obsessed with the man. He has a complete collection of de Sade's work, including one volume magnificently bound in black leather that he claims is so rare only five copies were ever smuggled into England."

It was a troubling thought, that Ashworth had discussed de Sade with his virginal future wife. For a long moment, Sebastian found it difficult to breathe. "You've seen it?"

"No. He only boasted of it to me. I understand Sir Francis gave it to him. They each have a copy." Her eyes narrowed, and he wondered what she had seen in his expression. "Why?"

Sebastian looked into her pretty young face and saw for one stolen moment all the tension and despair she had been keeping so well hidden.

"You don't need to marry him, Stephanie," he said, his voice low and rough with urgency. "A broken betrothal might give the Beau Monde something to tut-tut about for a week or two. But the chatter would die down eventually."

He saw something flare in her eyes, something that looked almost like amusement but was not. "Oh, Uncle," she said with a forced laugh. "A baby born 'early' a scant seven months after the wedding will be bad enough. I don't think I could live with the alternative."

And with that she moved away toward her mother, leaving him hollowed out by consternation and regret and a raw, sharp twist of fear.

꙳

"You're certain Ashworth is the killer?" said the Earl of Hendon, standing before his library fire, his hands clasped behind his back and his broad, familiar face set in grim lines.

Sebastian sat in a nearby leather armchair, a glass of brandy cradled in one hand. "One of them, yes. But can I prove it? No."

Hendon drew his pipe from his pocket and then paused with the bowl cupped in his hand, his gaze on nothing. "And Stephanie is with child by this monster?"

"Yes."

"Dear God. Do you suppose Amanda knows about the child?"

"I doubt it. Would you tell Amanda if you were her daughter?"

Hendon shook his head.

Sebastian watched the Earl open his tobacco pouch and begin to load his pipe with studied care.

"Stephanie can't be allowed to marry him," said Hendon after a moment. "I shall tell Amanda she must move to end the betrothal."

"Amanda won't listen to you. She knows I suspect Ashworth; they both do. Amanda doesn't care and Stephanie is too desperate and afraid to listen to reason."

Hendon let out his breath in a weary sigh. "Amanda reminds me sometimes of my mother. She was a hard woman. Angry and resentful and never satisfied."

"I doubt my grandmother would have married one of her daughters to a killer—even if he were the heir to a marquis."

Hendon tamped the tobacco in the bowl of his pipe and reached for a spill. "The wedding is this Thursday. If you don't think Amanda or Stephanie will listen to reason, then what is to be done?"

"I wish I knew."

The Earl settled in a nearby chair and sucked hard on his pipe. They sat in silence for a time, united by their shared concern for the beautiful, willful, damaged young girl who was so dear to them both.

"The other killer," said Hendon, looking up. "Who is he?"

"Sir Francis Rowe. It looks as if they deliberately switch off. Ashworth abducted Benji Thatcher—and presumably his sister too—on Friday evening when Rowe was with the Prince. Then Rowe killed the boy and tried to bury him on Sunday night when Ashworth was with Amanda and Stephanie. But from what I saw in the farmhouse on Penniwinch Lane, I'd say they both took part in what was done to the poor lad in between. And then Rowe killed the caretaker."

Hendon shook his head, his pipe clenched between his back teeth. "Ashworth is the son of the most powerful marquis in the Kingdom, while Rowe is cousin to the Prince Regent himself. Yet you say you've no proof?"

"Nothing that will convince a jury."

"You must find it. Before it's too late."

Sebastian met the old Earl's gaze. And for one moment out of time, it was as if the estrangement between them and all the anger and hurt that accompanied it had never been. "I know."

❧

The key, Sebastian decided as he left Grosvenor Square, was Number Three, Pickering Place.

He kept coming back to Jane Peters, the young girl who had died there in August. Grace Bligh had given him the names of Lord Ashworth and Hector Kneebone, but she had been steely in her refusal to surrender the identity of Jane Peters's killer. Which told Sebastian she feared the killer—or the killer's protector—more than she feared Sebastian.

But Sebastian was about to change that.

Chapter 54

The soft glow of firelight filled the elegant private withdrawing room of Number Three with long, dancing shadows.

Sebastian sat alone at his ease on one of the room's delicate, silk-covered chairs. After more hours without sleep than he could count, he was tired enough that he had to be careful not to let his eyelids droop. It helped that the very fine Van Dyck on the wall behind him had been hung so low that he kept banging his head against the heavy gilt frame. He'd extinguished the branches of candles that flanked the marble fireplace, but he'd left the crystal oil lamp burning on a table near the room's entrance. He could hear in the distance a man's laugh followed by a woman's anguished cry that he suspected was not feigned. It wasn't the first cry of pain he'd heard, and if he sat here much longer, he thought, he was going to need a good, stiff drink.

He could smell the promise of more rain as a cold wind kicked up, billowing the heavy velvet drapes at the window he'd left open. But he had not long to wait. He heard a soft step in the corridor and rose swiftly and silently to his feet. By the time Grace Bligh entered the room, he was in position. Stepping forward, he gently closed the door

behind her with his foot as he jerked her back into his arms and pressed
the blade of his knife against her bare throat.

She went utterly still. "I take it you're the reason the room is in near
darkness, my lord?"

"How did you know it was me?"

"I know men," she said cryptically, her voice calm and admirably
under control. "How did you get in past Joshua?"

"I know ways," he said and was surprised to hear her huff a soft
laugh.

She said, "What do you want?"

"The name of Jane Peters's killer."

He felt her stiffen in his arms and for the first time sensed a ripple
of fear course through her. "I can't give you that."

"I rather think you can."

She carefully shook her head, wary of his blade.

He said, "I could slit your throat."

"You could. But what would be the purpose in that? I can't tell you
anything if I'm dead."

"True. But I suspect it would inspire Joshua to be a bit more cooper-
ative. Or Hope."

"Leave Hope alone," she said quickly. Too quickly.

He pressed his advantage. "Then tell me what I need to know."

He saw her tongue creep out to wet her lips. He expected her to
try a lie, but she didn't. "Very well; I'll tell you. But it won't do you any
good. Jane Peters was killed by Rowe. Sir Francis Rowe."

"Jarvis hushed it up?"

"What do you think?"

"Yet you didn't ban Rowe from the house?"

"Of course we did. But I wasn't about to tell you that."

"Because of Jarvis?"

"Obviously." The wind gusted up again, shifting the drapes and
drawing her attention to the open window. But all she said was, "You

don't strike me as surprised. I take it you suspect Rowe of killing the street children out at Clerkenwell?"

"Yes."

"Can you prove it?"

"No."

"So why are you here? Do you seriously think to see him hang for the murder of Jane Peters?"

"Something like that."

She laughed out loud. "Jarvis will never allow you or anyone else to bring Rowe to trial. And if by some miracle it should come to pass, I can assure you that neither I nor anyone else in this house will ever testify against him. There is nothing you can threaten us with that begins to compare to what Jarvis would do to us if we went against his wishes."

He couldn't say he blamed her. How many people would behave differently in her position? And yet . . .

"It doesn't bother you?" he asked, taking her with him as he backed toward the windows, the knife still at her throat. "That someone like Rowe can slaughter one of your girls with absolute impunity simply because of his wealth and birth?"

He expected her to shrug it off, to dismiss the girl's death as the cost of doing business. Instead she said, her voice harsh, "Of course it bothers me. Jane Peters was barely fourteen years old. But I learned long ago the futility of railing against the realities of this world we live in."

"If we simply ignore injustice, nothing will ever change."

"Easy enough for you to say." She paused, then added, *"My lord,"* laying heavy, mocking emphasis on his title.

"Perhaps," he agreed, pausing beside the billowing curtains.

"So will you kill me now?"

"No. Why should I?"

"I might scream when you take your knife from my throat."

"You could. But I move rather quickly. I doubt Joshua will arrive in time to do me any damage." He let her go and swung one leg through the open window.

She did not scream. But she did turn to face him, her features pinched with a passion that both took him by surprise and made him like her a little bit better than he had. She said, "Will you kill Rowe?"

He met her gaze and shook his head. "I'm not an executioner."

"Then you'll never stop him."

❧

Feeling the need to do something to keep himself awake, Sebastian sent his town carriage home and turned to walk up St. James's Street. But he was only half-conscious of the boisterous, elegantly dressed masculine crowd and overpriced activity that swirled around him.

Jarvis would never allow the King's cousin to be brought to trial for the murder of either a young Pickering Place prostitute or any number of butchered street children; Sebastian knew that. But Jarvis could conceivably be persuaded to eliminate him. If Jarvis became convinced that the murder of Jane Peters was not an aberration but part of a pattern of brutal, repeated killings, then for the sake of King and country, Jarvis would not hesitate to have the Butcher of Culloden's troublesome grandson killed. Quietly and efficiently.

The problem was, how to convince him?

❧

Sebastian was still pondering that question when he arrived back at Brook Street some fifteen minutes later. "Is Lady Jarvis still in Berkeley Square?" he asked, handing Morey his hat and gloves.

"She is, my lord." Morey hesitated, a worried look pinching his normally wooden features. "Did you—did you by chance send for young Tom?"

"Tom?" Sebastian paused in the act of shrugging off his greatcoat. "No. Why? What the devil has the boy been up to now?"

"It's Giles, my lord. He has something he thinks you ought to know. Shall I send him to you in the library?"

"Yes, please."

Sebastian was pouring himself a brandy when Giles knocked at the door. "Giles. Come in. What's this about Tom?"

The middle-aged groom stood awkwardly just inside the entrance to the room. "It was earlier this evening, m'lord. I was up in the hayloft setting a mousetrap—we've had quite a problem with the little buggers lately, you see—when I hears a gentleman down in the mews hailing the lad."

Sebastian felt a swift tide of sick apprehension wash over him. "By name?"

"Well, calling for 'Lord Devlin's tiger,' he was."

"And?"

"I heard Tom say, 'That's me.' And the gentleman, he tells the lad that your lordship needs him, and he's come to take Tom to you right away."

"My God. And Tom went with this gentleman?"

"He did, m'lord. He's been ever so cast down since you quit taking him with you in the curricle. Fair jumped at the chance, he did."

"When was this?"

"Must've been an hour or more ago, m'lord. I didn't think much of it till the carriage come back to the stables just now, and Coachman John, he says he don't know nothin' about you sendin' for Tom. That's when I started worryin' maybe somethin' weren't right."

"Did you see him? The gentleman Tom went off with, I mean?"

"I did, m'lord. There's a window up there overlooks the mews, and I was curious enough to go have a peek. Driving a bang-up yellow-bodied phaeton, he was, pulled by a lovely dapple gray. Didn't have no groom with him, though, which struck me as a bit queer even before I spoke to Coachman John."

Sebastian could feel his breath coming hard and fast. "And the gentleman himself? Did you get a look at him?"

"Aye, m'lord. Appeared to be somewhere in his thirties, I'd say. On the short side and stocky, with a full face and a right dapper way of dressing."

"Did you hear anything at all to indicate where they might have gone?"

"No, my lord. But I did watch to see which direction they went as they left the mews."

"And?"

"The gentleman turned north, my lord."

Chapter 55

 $\mathcal{S}$ ebastian stood in a pool of soft lamplight at his library desk, methodically loading his double-barreled flintlock pistol and trying to think.

Where had Rowe taken the boy?

Where?

Not to Upper Grosvenor Street, surely. The Baronet's big, elegant town house was overflowing with watching, listening servants. Yet it had been only days since Rowe lost the use of the Penniwinch Lane farmstead. Surely he hadn't had time to secure another such property?

Had he?

Think, Sebastian told himself as he rubbed a thin layer of beeswax around the edges of the pistol's twin pans to keep out the rain he could hear lightly pattering against the library windows. *Where would Rowe take the boy?*

Try as he might, Sebastian could come up with only one answer: the Clerkenwell shot factory.

He tied an oilcloth lock cover over the primed pistol, then slipped it into his pocket. Looking up, he found Morey hovering in the doorway.

"Giles has brought your mare around, my lord," said the major-domo, his face a tight mask of concern.

Sebastian reached for his greatcoat and gloves. "Send one of the footmen to Sir Henry Lovejoy with an explanation of what has happened. Tell him I plan to look for Rowe at the shot factory but I have no real evidence that's where he's gone."

"And if they're not there, my lord?"

Sebastian moved from behind his desk. "I've no idea. Hopefully something will come to me."

※

Sebastian galloped up Oxford Street toward Clerkenwell, heedless of the cold, misty rain that wet his face and glistened on the slippery cobbles. It nagged at him, that he could be wrong, that the shot factory seemed too obvious, that surely Rowe would expect Sebastian to look for Tom there first. But then he reminded himself that Rowe had no way of knowing that his conversation in the mews with Tom had been overheard, no way of knowing that Giles had been there to peer out an upper window and see the Baronet's round, smiling face and elegant phaeton. If Sebastian had returned to Brook Street to find his tiger simply absent from the stables, would anyone have suspected foul play?

No.

It struck Sebastian as the height of irony, that if he had kept Tom at his side as his tiger the boy would not at this moment be in the clutches of a brutal killer. By attempting to protect Tom from harm, Sebastian had succeeded only in leaving him vulnerable.

No point, Sebastian reminded himself; no point in dwelling on the past. He forced himself instead to consider the Baronet's purpose in snatching Tom from the stables. Rowe must be intending to abuse the boy and then kill him, quickly, in order to deposit his body someplace conspicuous—no doubt with another taunting note addressed to Sebastian.

At the thought, his breath caught painfully in his chest.

How long? Sebastian wondered as he galloped the mare through increasingly wet, windswept streets. How long had Tom been in Rowe's hands? An hour? Two? The knowledge of what the boy must already have endured tore at Sebastian. And what if he was wrong? What if Rowe wasn't at the shot tower? Then what?

A jagged streak of lightning split the blue-black clouds roiling overhead and lit up the hills above Clerkenwell in a quick white flash. A mist was billowing up from the Fleet to creep across the lane, so that the lights in the windows of the row of cottages near the crossroads were barely visible. But as he drove the mare relentlessly up the slope toward the old shot factory, Sebastian caught sight of an elegant phaeton drawn up beside the broken stone wall.

He reined in hard.

A swift glance was enough to tell him the phaeton was empty, its dapple gray grazing lazily in the grassy verge. Without a groom, Rowe had simply abandoned his carriage here at the factory's chained gate.

Swiping his sleeve across his wet face, Sebastian narrowed his eyes against the rain and studied the somber bulk of the shot tower soaring dark and silent against the storm-tossed clouds. Through the tower's arch-topped windows he could see the faint, flickering glow of what looked more like a fire than a lantern.

"Easy, girl," whispered Sebastian, patting his mare's neck as she fidgeted beneath him. He was still some distance from the factory, but he slid out of the saddle and left the black tied there to the low branches of a young plane tree, lest the two horses be tempted to nicker at each other and warn the Baronet of Sebastian's approach.

He ran the rest of the way on foot, thick globs of mud exploding from beneath the slapping soles of his boots. When he reached the stone wall, he stripped off his greatcoat and left it there. It was raining harder now, water dripping off his face and trickling down the back of his collar. But the greatcoat's bulk constricted his movements. In a fight, that could be deadly.

Vaulting over the wall, he crossed the rubbish-strewn field at a slower, more cautious trot, the tall, frost-bitten grass bending around him beneath the assault of wind and rain. He could hear his own breathing so loud he wondered it wasn't audible to everyone for miles. And as he neared the tower he caught the sound of Sir Francis's calm, well-modulated voice saying, "True morality consists of taking our darkest passions to their natural and therefore logical conclusions. Does that make sense to you, I wonder?"

Tom—assuming this statement was addressed to Tom—didn't answer. Probably couldn't answer.

Crouching low, Sebastian forced himself to draw up some ten feet from the tower's curving brick base and consider his options. The tower's old wooden door still hung drunkenly on its hinges, the weathered panels cracked from when Sebastian had kicked it in what seemed like ages ago now. But Rowe had pushed the broken door shut against the night, blocking Sebastian's view of the interior. Sebastian looked for a window, except the lowest opening was a good eight feet off the ground, too high for him to see though. That meant there was no way for Sebastian to know what was happening inside the tower; no way to calculate Rowe's or Tom's positions. No way to know the best or worst moment to rush through that door.

A flash of lightning lit up the clouds and set thunder to rumbling in the distance. Then the sky opened up and the rain came down harder, pounding loudly on the old slate roofs of the nearby warehouses.

Sebastian eased his pistol from his pocket and hunched his body over it in an effort to protect the frizzen, flint, and pan from the driving rain as he slipped off the lock cover. The problem was, black powder had a way of drawing moisture from the very air. Even if he managed to keep the priming powder dry, the main charge might still be too damp from that long ride through the stormy night to ignite, resulting in a hangfire, squib, or misfire. He'd seen it happen far too often in the war.

He thumbed back both hammers, the double *snick* of metal sounding painfully loud to his ears despite the noise of the storm. His heart was beating so hard he could feel it pounding in his fingers. He heard Rowe say, "It's only through pain that one can truly appreciate pleasure, boy. I suspect that's a truism beyond one with your simpleminded, brutish instincts, but this . . ." Rowe paused, and Sebastian could hear the smile in the man's voice. "*This* just might awaken some base level of cognizance."

Pushing up, Sebastian hurtled forward to kick open the door and burst into the tower in a rush. In one blazing instant he saw Tom hanging in the shadows beneath the winding wooden staircase, his bound arms stretched high over his head, his bare back crisscrossed with bloody wheals. Sir Francis Rowe crouched beside a small fire he had kindled near the center of the big round room.

As Sebastian crashed into the tower, Rowe's head jerked up, the fire glowing golden on a face slack with shock, his fist tightening around the shaft of an iron bar he had heated in the fire until its tip glowed an ugly red hot. Sebastian saw Tom swing around, his mouth distorted by a tight gag, his eyes going wide.

Hesitating only long enough to be certain he had a clean shot, Sebastian leveled the pistol on Rowe's chest and squeezed the first trigger.

He heard the hammer strike the frizzen and saw a shower of sparks hit the pan. But the barrel's main powder charge had obviously sucked too much moisture from the damp night. The pistol misfired.

Bloody hell. Sebastian was shifting his finger to the second trigger when Rowe scooped up a fistful of hot ashes with one gloved hand and threw them in Sebastian's face.

Instinctively, Sebastian closed his eyes against the stinging hot embers and threw up a protective crooked elbow. This time the pistol fired, exploding in an ear-ringing roar and flash that filled the air with the bitter smell of burned powder. But that sudden jerk had deflected his aim. The shot went wide by at least a foot.

Rowe surged to his feet, the iron bar now held in both hands as he swung it like a cricket bat at Sebastian. Sebastian leapt back, but not fast enough. The glowing tip raked a painful arc of fire across his upper arm, and the air filled with the sizzling stench of burning cloth and charred flesh.

"Hurts, does it?" said Rowe with a smile, his grip shifting on the iron bar.

Sebastian threw the useless pistol at the man's head and reached down to yank the knife from his boot when the man ducked. "I'm still between you and the door," said Sebastian, settling into a practiced street fighter's stance.

Rowe took another swipe at him. But the hot metal was already beginning to cool, and this time Sebastian feinted away easily. "You might as well give up, Rowe," he said. "It's over."

"I think you overestimate your abilities, Devlin."

"Perhaps. But it doesn't really matter. Your life as you know it is finished. You were seen abducting my tiger. The constables are already on their way here."

"I think you're forgetting who I am."

Sebastian shook his head. "Are you imagining Jarvis will save you? He won't, you know. You've become an embarrassment. He'll simply have you eliminated as he has so many others high and low. My guess is you'll be found floating in the Thames one morning. Elegantly dressed fish food."

Rowe gave a ringing laugh of disbelief. He had known nothing but a life of rare privilege and great wealth, protected at every turn from any possible consequences of his actions. He had no reason to expect this latest development to be any different. "You want me, Devlin?" he taunted. "Come and get me."

With the iron bar still clenched in one hand, he turned to rush up the rickety old wooden staircase that spiraled toward that small, arsenic-encrusted room a hundred and fifty feet above.

Sebastian leapt to hack with his blade at the rope binding Tom's wrists. As the last fraying strands gave way, the boy slumped to the floor.

Sebastian paused to rest a gentle hand on Tom's thin, bloody shoulder. "Can you walk?"

Tom looked up and nodded, his eyes watering as he reached back stiffly to fumble with the ties of his gag.

Sebastian cupped one hand under the boy's elbow to lift him to his feet. "Then get out of here, Tom. Now. Run if you can but whatever you do, *don't stop.*"

Without waiting to see if the boy complied with his orders, Sebastian whirled to dash up the stairs behind Rowe.

When he'd climbed these stairs before, he'd gone cautiously, carefully testing each aged, rotting tread. Now he charged up them, ignoring the way the old staircase shuddered and swayed beneath the combination of his weight and Rowe's heavy tread clattering far above.

The Baronet went swiftly at first, the glow from the fire below casting his leaping shadow like a long, distorted live thing across the curving brick walls. But as the two men wound round and round, the light from the distant fire dimmed and the steepness of the climb quickly took its toll. Sebastian could hear the other man stumbling, his breath coming in ragged gasps as he labored to climb higher and higher in a growing darkness lit only by intermittent pulses of lightning.

Sebastian was within five or six feet of closing the gap between them when Rowe whirled, his mouth open in a pained, air-sucking rictus as he came charging back down at Sebastian in a rush, the iron bar held over his head in a two-handed grip.

"A miscalculation, I think, Devlin," he hissed, throwing all his weight behind the bar as he brought it smashing down at Sebastian's head.

Sebastian jerked sideways and heard the bar whistle through the air a scant six inches from his face and chest as his back slammed against the filthy, rough brick wall beside them.

Still grinning, Rowe swung again. Sebastian skittered back two steps—and felt one of the old wooden treads crack and give way beneath his weight.

He pitched forward, crashing down onto his hands and knees and then slipping back as he scrambled to catch his balance. The knife he'd been holding spun away into the yawning void beside him, the clatter of it hitting the ground far below almost drowned out by the wind whistling in through the open windows and the rain thrumming on the roof.

Lightning flashed. Over the gaping hole that had now opened between them, the two men's gazes met. Rowe hesitated, sucking air hard. Then he whirled to take off up the stairs again. Sebastian tore off the thick slab of old stair tread that still dangled at an angle and took it with him as he leapt over the broken stretch to race upward again.

Up and up they spiraled in an ever-tightening coil. Then he heard Rowe's footsteps halt and knew the Baronet had reached the room at the top of the tower. As he swung around the last curve, Sebastian saw Rowe waiting for him on the wooden platform, the iron bar raised in both hands, his plump face blotchy and flushed, his body shuddering as his breath came in wheezing gasps.

"You bloody son of a bitch," swore Sebastian, plowing up the last few steps with the stair tread held before him like a shield.

"So eager to die?" said Rowe with a grim smile as he brought the iron bar down, hard, aiming at Sebastian's face.

Sebastian caught the blow on his makeshift shield, the impact reverberating down his bruised and burned arm in a pulse of raw agony. If Rowe had been able to hit the board face on, the blow might well have shattered the old wood. But Sebastian had been careful to position the tread at an angle so that the iron bar simply bounced off the thick edge.

The shock of the deflected blow sent Rowe staggering. His smile slipping, the Baronet backed away across the room's weathered floorboards as Sebastian advanced on him.

"Who's your partner?" Sebastian demanded.

Rowe swung at him again. "Do you seriously think I'll tell you?"

Again the blow bounced off the thick old stair tread. Wheezing hard, Rowe gritted his teeth and swung once more, wildly this time, laboring to recover his control of the iron bar as it bounced away. He was already winded from the run up the stairs, and the bar was heavy, the effort required to strike and then recover from each deflected blow considerable. The sound of his ragged breathing filled the dusty round room; the air was heavy with the smell of his sweat and the cold damp roiling in through the open door to the parapet.

"At least you don't deny you have a partner," said Sebastian, pressing forward. He was hoping to maneuver the tiring man back over the edge of the open trapdoor in the center of the room. But then Rowe stumbled against the rusting iron tripod and cauldron and staggered sideways, missing the yawning hole by inches.

"Why should I?" said Rowe, swinging at him again as a new flicker of lightning lit up the round room. "I do believe you lied, my lord. There are no constables hurrying to your rescue. The truth is that no one in this city would dare bring charges against me, and you know it."

"Probably not," agreed Sebastian. He was aware of the footsteps and heavy breathing of someone rushing up the stairs behind him and hoped to God it was Tom disobeying orders to run or maybe one of Lovejoy's constables. Anyone but Ashworth.

"Then why persist?" said Rowe, shifting the angle of his swing in an attempt to bring the bar down on Sebastian's hand.

Gritting his teeth against the shooting agony that was his upper arm, Sebastian pivoted to catch the blow in the center of the board again, forcing the Baronet ever backward, aiming now toward the open doorway onto the parapet. "What makes you think I play by the rules?"

"Because you're a fool, and that's what fools do," said Rowe, altering the angle of his swing again.

Sebastian tilted the stair tread to block the new blow. Only this time as the heavy iron bar bounced off the board's side, Sebastian took a swift step forward to slam the heavy stair tread into Rowe's face. He heard the crunch of smashing nose cartilage and bone, felt the hot spurt of the other man's blood as Rowe grunted and dropped the bar. It hit the old wooden floor with a bouncing clatter and rolled away.

"Think so?" said Sebastian. Shifting his grip on the board, he swung the stair tread again, this time clipping the side of the man's head with a blow that spun Rowe around and sent him staggering through the arched doorway to slam his back against the low brick parapet.

Tossing the board aside, Sebastian lunged after him. Bracing his hands against the brick doorframe, Sebastian slammed the heel of his right boot into Rowe's face with enough force to send the bastard toppling backward over the parapet wall.

Arms flailing frantically, uselessly, Rowe gave one long, high-pitched scream that ended far below in a jarring *thump*.

Breathing heavily, with one hand coming up to clutch his burned and bruised arm to his side, Sebastian stepped to the edge of the parapet and stared down at the motionless, broken body sprawled far below.

He was conscious of Tom coming up beside him, the boy's naked torso glowing a pale bluish white in a fitful flash of lightning. For a long moment they simply stood side by side, their gazes on the Baronet's pale, upturned face glistening now with rain. Then Tom said hoarsely, "Is he dead?"

"After falling a hundred and fifty feet?" Sebastian eased his good arm around the boy's trembling shoulders and drew him close. "He's dead."

Chapter 56

*W*ithout waiting for the arrival of Bow Street, Sebastian gently wrapped Tom in his own greatcoat and drove the boy in Rowe's phaeton toward Tower Hill.

Tom sat beside him in silence, shivering slightly as they clattered through the rain-drenched streets with Sebastian's mare trotting behind them. The rain had slackened again, the fog rolling in wet and heavy and smelling of sodden autumn leaves and smoke.

"You all right?" Sebastian asked, glancing over at him. It tore at Sebastian, thinking about what the boy had been through and worrying about how Tom was going to come to terms with it in the days ahead.

Tom nodded, his nostrils flaring on a quickly indrawn breath. "He was gonna do t' me what he done to that other boy, Benji. He kept talkin' about it, describing everything he was gonna do and sayin' how I was gonna enjoy it." Tom stared straight ahead, his face oddly leached of all color. "I ain't never been so scared in me life. It's shameful, how scared I was."

"Anyone would have been scared, Tom. Anyone."

Tom shook his head. "It ain't jist that. He made me feel . . . he made me feel like I were nothin'. Ain't nobody ever made me feel that low before."

Sebastian was aware of the night air cold and damp against his face, and the throbbing ache of his burned, bruised arm. How do you convince a boy born to a deadly combination of poverty and the endless scorn of those labeled his "betters" that his real worth is infinitely above that of the savage, twisted spawn of kings? How do you explain a world that gifts evil men with privilege and wealth and looks the other way while they torment and abuse the weakest members of society?

There must be a way, Sebastian thought, and he vowed that he would try to find it. But for now he contented himself with saying, "He was an evil man. Now he's dead."

Tom kept his gaze fixed on the dapple roan's mane streaming out pale and flowing in the darkness. A muscle bunched along his set jaw. "I wish I'd 'ave been the one to kill him. I ain't never wanted to kill nobody before. But I wish I'd killed him."

The boy subsided into silence again, and Sebastian felt his heart ache for the turmoil he knew roiled within his young friend. There were questions Sebastian needed to ask him, perhaps things that might help identify Ashworth as the second killer. But now was not the time. The boy needed to find a way to recover from what had been done to him, not revisit it.

They'd almost reached Gibson's surgery when Tom said, "Do you believe there's a hell?"

Sebastian glanced down at him. "I honestly don't know. Why?"

An oil lamp set high on the corner house near the Tower sent golden light flaring across the boy's pinched features. "I hope there is. 'Cause if there ain't, then he died too easy."

Sebastian reined in before Gibson's ancient stone house. "If there's a hell, that man is in it."

※

Sebastian left Tom in Gibson's care and, ignoring the surgeon's concern for Sebastian's own wounds, drove next to Berkeley Square.

"*My lord,*" exclaimed Jarvis's butler, eyes widening at the sight of Sebastian's ripped and burned coat, his muck-smeared breeches and grimy, rain-streaked face.

"Grisham," said Sebastian, his gaze going beyond the butler to where Jarvis and a woman Sebastian recognized as Cousin Victoria stood in low-voiced conversation with a plump, middle-aged man exuding the officious air of a Harley Street physician.

His father-in-law's gaze met Sebastian's across the length of the marble-floored entrance hall. Animosity arced between them, potent and dangerous. Then Jarvis said, his voice gruff, "Now is not a good time, Devlin."

Sebastian brought up a crooked elbow to swipe the rain from his face. "I thought you'd like to know there's a body out at the Clerkenwell shot factory that belongs to someone in whom you seem to believe you have an interest. Bow Street has already been notified, which means if you want to control what happens from here on out, you need to hurry."

"I don't know who you are, young man," said the Harley Street physician, puffing out his chest with self-importance. "Nor do I know what this is about. But you must be made aware of the fact that this is a house in mourning. Lady Jarvis has just died."

Sebastian sucked in a quick, startled breath, feeling the shock of the pompous little man's words slam into him. A faint footfall at the top of the stairs drew his gaze to the landing above, where Hero stood with one hand clutching the banister. Her beautiful, beloved face was ashen with shock and tight with a grief that only those who've lost a mother can understand. And Sebastian felt her pain as raw and piercing as if it were his own.

He glanced again at his stony-faced father-in-law. He wanted to scream at the bastard, *How long? How long did you suspect Rowe? How many of those dead children could you have saved?* Instead he merely said curtly, "I beg your pardon; I did not know. My sincere condolences."

And then he climbed the stairs to draw his wife into his arms, his heart filling with the helpless ache of his love for her. He wanted so badly to do something to ease her pain. And yet in truth there was nothing he could do.

Nothing except hold her and love her and whisper over and over as she wept with great, soul-shuddering sobs, "Oh, God, Hero; I am so sorry. So sorry."

*

"I don't understand why you felt the need to warn Jarvis," said Gibson much later when Sebastian returned to Tower Hill at Hero's insistence. He hadn't wanted to leave her, but he knew she was right: His arm was a mess.

He sat now on the table in Gibson's surgery, a single oil lamp casting stark shadows around the room as Gibson finished cleaning the oozing, ugly wound and began to smear an herb-rich salve on a pad of gauze.

Sebastian held the pad in place as Gibson began to wind a length of bandaging around the arm. "Hero thinks I shouldn't have told Jarvis. That I should have let Rowe's name be dragged through the mud for all to know and see."

Gibson looked up from his work. "So why didn't you?"

"If there were any justice in this world, the bastard would have stood trial and been executed in front of a howling, jeering mob of those he considered his worthless inferiors. But the man is dead, and these are dangerous times in which we live. The poor are already starving in the streets, and winter isn't even upon us yet. So while on one hand I feel the people should know—that everyone should know where our damned beatification of wealth and power can lead—I can't help but think, *What would be the result if the people discovered one of their King's cousins had been allowed to prey on their children like some ogre from a fairy tale come to life?* It could easily provoke a disturbance on the scale of the Gordon

Riots—if not worse. And I don't want any more innocent deaths." He paused. "It would be different if Rowe were still alive, but he's not; he's dead. So when it comes down to a choice between making a philosophical point or saving people's lives, I'll err on the side of life."

Gibson tied off his bandage, his lips pursed into a frown. "Maybe. But I must say, if anyone ever deserved to be gibbeted, it's that monster. Tom's right: He died too easy."

"I can't argue with that." Sebastian slid off the table. He was feeling sore and stiff and utterly bone weary. "How is Tom?"

"His back should heal in a couple of weeks."

"It's not his back I'm worried about."

Gibson looked up from gathering together his implements. "You reached him before Rowe had time to do any other damage."

"You're certain?"

"Yes. I'd like to keep him here for a day or two, mainly to make certain he gets the rest he needs. I've put him in the front bedroom, but he's refusing to go to sleep until he sees you."

Sebastian eased on the ragged, stained remnants of his shirt. "I wish to God this had never happened to him."

"Tom's a plucky lad. He'll be all right."

Sebastian found Tom lying facedown in Gibson's bed, his face turned toward the wall. At the sound of Sebastian's footsteps on the old house's stone flagged floor, the boy swung his head to look at him, his gray eyes wide and stark in a pale face.

"Does it hurt much?" asked Sebastian.

"Not so much," Tom lied. "Gibson says I can go back to work in a few days." He paused. "If you'll let me."

Sebastian came to sit on a nearby straight-backed chair, his hat turning round and round in his hands as he searched for the words that were so difficult to say. "When I stopped taking you with me as my tiger, I thought I was keeping you safe from a truly monstrous killer. But all I did was leave you vulnerable to the very danger I was trying to avoid, and for that I will forever be sorry."

Tom swallowed, hard. "I been layin' 'ere, thinkin'. I'll 'ave been yer tiger fer three years come February. I ain't denyin' I was a young 'un when ye took me on. But I ain't so young anymore."

"No. No, you're not. And you're right; it's time I quit treating you as if you were." Children as young as five risked their lives every day going down in the mines, while boys of eight and nine went off to war as cabin boys and drummer boys. Perhaps it was because Sebastian had buried too many of them over the years that he'd found himself so protective of Tom. But Tom would soon be a man grown and he deserved to be treated that way. "Giles tells me you've ambitions of becoming a Bow Street Runner."

"Aye," Tom answered warily, obviously worried about where Sebastian was going with this.

Sebastian rose to his feet. "I'm thinking that with a future Bow Street man as my groom, I should start giving him more responsibility when he's ready to come back to work."

Tom let out his breath in a rush. "Ye mean it?"

Sebastian saw the shadows that still clouded the boy's eyes. He knew it would take time for Tom to work through the ramifications of what had been done to him, and more time still to overcome the feelings of terror and helplessness it had provoked. But Gibson was right; Tom was plucky.

Sebastian rested his hand briefly on the boy's tousled head. "I'll be both proud and honored to have you working at my side again."

❧

Later that night, Hero lay in Devlin's arms, her head resting in the warm, comforting crook of his shoulder as she watched the fire's glow flicker over the darkened bedroom. She felt hollowed out and shattered by the day's events. Her thoughts kept flitting painfully from the loss of her mother to the terror of how close she had come to losing Devlin to the horror of Stephanie's looming wedding to an unimaginably cruel killer.

"It's obvious Rowe could not have kidnapped and killed those children alone," she said suddenly. "There must be some way to prove Ashworth's involvement in all this."

Devlin ran his hand up and down her arm. "If there is, I haven't found it."

She could feel the tension that thrummed within him; Rowe might be dead, but for Devlin this wasn't over. She said, "I can't bear the thought of Stephanie wed to such a man. And yet it's happening."

"I'm not giving up. I will get him. Eventually."

She was quiet for a time, her thoughts returning inevitably to her crushing grief for her mother. After a moment she said quietly, "I thought she was getting better."

He brushed the hair back from her face. "So what happened?"

"Dr. Blackburn says he thinks her heart stopped. But the truth is he doesn't know." She drew in a ragged breath. "I've always considered myself a level-headed, realistic person. And yet somehow a part of me can't quite believe she's gone. I think about going through the days of my life without her—without hearing her laugh or seeing her smile, without having her there to talk to, to *be* with—and it hurts so badly I wonder how I'll bear missing her like this forever." Her voice cracked, and she had to pause for a moment. "I keep thinking about all Simon's growing-up years she's going to miss and all the joy she'd have taken in him. She'll never have the chance to see the man he will become, just as he'll never know the incredible woman his grandmother was. And that grieves me more than anything I've ever known."

She felt his hand shift to wipe the tears that coursed silently down her cheeks. "Simon will know her," said Devlin. "Because he'll know you."

Wednesday, 22 September

They buried Toby Dancing early that morning, along with the bones of Mick Swallow and the unknown children they'd recovered from the grounds of the shot factory and the house in Bethnal Green. The day was cold and damp, with a thick cloud cover that hovered low over those who'd gathered to pay their respects: Sebastian, Constable Gowan, Paul Gibson, Sir Henry Lovejoy, Jem Jones, and Icarus Cantrell. Sebastian watched the Reverend Filby blink back tears as he poured a handful of dirt into the yawning graves, and he knew a measure of quiet guilt for having once suspected this gentle, caring man of murder.

Afterward Sebastian sat with the Professor at his kitchen table as they drank warm cider from heavy pewter tankards that had probably been filched from some local tavern. "I've been thinking about Benji Thatcher's little sister," said Sebastian, his voice casual, his gaze hard on the other man's face.

Icarus Cantrell kept his expression neutral. "Oh?"

"It occurs to me that if Sybil thought she was in danger, she might have come to you. The way Hamish did."

Icarus Cantrell rested his cider on the worn boards between them and sat for a time, regarding it thoughtfully and kneading the muscles at the back of his neck with one hand. Then, seeming to come to some sort of decision, he pressed both palms flat on the table and pushed to his feet.

"Come," he said. "There's something you might be interested to see."

Chapter 57

*I*carus Cantrell led Sebastian up a steep staircase to the upper floor of the old medieval house, where a ragged little girl of seven or eight hunkered down on her heels at play with pieces of brickbat she'd lined up like soldiers in formation. She was humming softly to herself, and so involved was she with her game that it was a moment before she looked up, her pale blond hair falling away from a sharp little face. Her resemblance to Benji was unmistakable, her soft blue eyes flaring in alarm as she looked from Cantrell to Sebastian and back again.

"Don't worry; everything's all right," said the Professor. "The gentleman here just wanted to know that you're safe."

She stared at them a moment, puzzled, then went back to her game.

Sebastian waited until they were downstairs again before saying, "Why tell me about her now and not before?"

"Because I realized it would grieve you, continuing to think she's dead."

"It's been grieving me for the past ten days now."

"Yes. But I didn't know that for certain, did I? You are married to Jarvis's daughter."

"What the bloody hell is that supposed to mean?"

"I think you know."

Sebastian swallowed another angry retort. "So what changed your mind?"

"You killed Sir Francis."

It had been given out that the King's cousin had died in a tragic fall while inspecting the abandoned shot factory. Why he would choose to do so at night in the midst of a foul storm had never been adequately explained. "How the blazes did you know that?"

The Professor simply smiled and took a deep swallow of his cider.

Sebastian went to stand beside the old leaded casement window that overlooked the rain-soaked yard. "I take it Sybil saw her brother pulled into the carriage that night?"

"She did, yes."

"Could she identify him? The man in the carriage, I mean?"

Cantrell shook his head. "She saw a gentleman's grand clothes and his half-obscured profile, but nothing more."

"The man she saw in that carriage was in all probability Lord Ashworth. Yet you sent me after Sir Francis Rowe. You suspected him from the very beginning—and it wasn't simply because of the theft of his snuffbox, was it?"

Cantrell drained his ale and went to throw more coal on the fire. "Believe me, I didn't know anything for certain. But I knew children had been regularly disappearing from around here. I knew what had happened to Hamish, and I knew the boy's suspicions about the part his missing friend had played in his abduction. So when I chanced to see the Dancer talking to Sir Francis Rowe a few weeks ago, it struck me as . . . odd. Odd enough that I didn't forget it."

"But not so odd that you felt moved to tell me precisely what you suspected—or why."

The old man crouched before the fire and reached for his poker. "I didn't tell you my suspicions about Toby for the same reason I hid Sybil:

Sir Francis Rowe is—was—related to the King, and you are Jarvis's son-in-law. I had to be careful of both what I told you and how I told you."

Sebastian pushed away from the window. "If you were a younger man, I swear I'd plant you a facer for that."

The Professor kept his attention on the fire. "You fault me for being careful? With Sybil's life in my hands?"

Sebastian shook his head. "And Ashworth? You knew he was working with Rowe?"

"No. I'd no idea there were two of them. But I knew what had happened to Anne Leary's daughter, Bridget, so I thought I'd pass that along as well. Believe me, I wish I had either known for certain or had the courage to act on my suspicions. If I had, Toby Dancing would still be alive today."

"What will become of the girl now?"

"Sybil? I'll keep her here with me. Without Benji she'd never survive on the streets alone. She's too young. Too . . . vulnerable."

"Please tell me you don't intend to raise her as a thief."

Cantrell set aside his poker with a clatter. "You think she'd be better off as a whore, do you?"

"She wouldn't hang for being a whore."

"True. She'd simply die of the pox—if she weren't murdered first by one of her uglier customers."

"Why should you care?"

"Why?" Cantrell pushed awkwardly to his feet, an old man whose life—and the choices he'd made—had led him to a very different place from where he'd begun. "I've never been a religious man. But when I worked in the sugarcane fields of Georgia there was an old Irish priest who used to talk to me a lot about sin and atonement."

"I'd have thought seven years under the lash in the Colonies would be more than enough atonement for anything a man had done."

"You think so, my lord? I'd have said we're alike, you and I, in this respect if in few others."

The two men's gazes met and held. And the silence filled with the distant patter of rain and the whispers of old, insistent memories that would never be laid to rest.

🙢

Later that evening Sebastian sat beside the library fire in Hendon House in Grosvenor Square, a glass of brandy at his elbow, his left arm in a sling.

"How's your latest wound?" asked Hendon, filling his pipe's bowl with tobacco.

"Better," said Sebastian, when the truth was it throbbed like the devil.

Hendon grunted. "You could have been killed. You need to be more careful."

"Don't start."

"You've a wife and child to worry about these days."

Sebastian reached for his brandy and tried to swallow his irritation along with a good, long drink. "At least you now have the heir you've always wanted—just in case."

The two men's gazes met. Hendon's broad chest lifted with the intensity of his breathing, and he surprised Sebastian by saying quietly, "You are my last surviving son." His hand came up when Sebastian started to speak. "No; let me finish. When you were born, I thought I'd hate you. You were a living, breathing, squalling testament to your mother's infidelity and to my own failings as a husband. I wanted to hate you, but . . ." He shook his head. "I couldn't. You were such a delight. So bright and quick, so full of joyous curiosity about every-thing around you; you were a wonder to me. As you grew I found I could forget for long stretches of time that you weren't actually my son. I took a father's pride in the child you became—in your incredible marksmanship, in your horsemanship and your quick mind and your fierce, determined sense of right and wrong. But then I'd remember you weren't mine, and it would cut at something deep inside me."

He paused to draw a shaky breath, his aged features pinched with pain. "For thirty years, Sebastian, you have baffled me and enraged me and filled me with great pride. But I stopped thinking of you as anything other than my son long ago. Because in every way but one, you are."

For a long moment, Sebastian said nothing because his throat was so closed up he could not speak. He wanted to say, *You never told me.* Except he suspected that at several points in the pain-filled months since he'd learned the truth, Hendon had said at least some of these things, although not all.

He let his gaze rove over the Earl's familiar face, with its blobby nose and wide forehead and the incredibly blue eyes that were so tellingly different from Sebastian's own yellow ones. And he felt a welling of emotion that he didn't want but that was no less real for being unsought.

Hendon said, "It is my hope that someday you will find a way to forgive me for the things I felt I had to do. But I won't apologize for allowing you and Kat to continue to think yourselves brother and sister. Such a marriage would have ruined you—ruined you both. I fought your entire life to keep you from knowing the truth. Why would I then betray myself simply so you could do something I believed a mistake?"

"Why?" Sebastian somehow managed to say. "Why didn't you want me to know the truth?"

A faint line of color appeared to ride high on the Earl's cheeks. "I suppose because I always wished you really were my son. I was so proud of you . . . I wanted you to think I was your father. I wanted you to love me as a father, because I love you as my son."

"I—" Sebastian began. But his voice threatened to crack and he had to start over, his gaze fixed firmly on the fire on the hearth before them. "Lately I've found myself looking at Simon and thinking, *How would I feel, were I to discover he is not my son?* And I've realized . . . it wouldn't make any difference. Oh, I'd be shaken and hurt and angry. But my love for the boy would remain unchanged." Sebastian paused, and the silence filled with the crackle of the fire and the tick of the clock on the mantel. "I still think of you as my father. I've spent the past fourteen months reminding myself that you're not, but . . ." He glanced up to find Hendon watching him intently. "Maybe it's time I stopped trying."

He saw the leap of hope in the old man's blue St. Cyr eyes before Hendon blinked rapidly and turned away to fiddle with his pipe. "How about a game of chess?" said the Earl gruffly. "It's been a long time since I suffered my usual humiliation at your hands."

"Too long," said Sebastian with a low, shaky laugh, and went to help him set up the board.

Thursday, 23 September

The wedding of Anthony Ledger, son and heir of the Marquis of Lindley, to Miss Stephanie Wilcox, daughter of the late Lord Wilcox, was held at St. George's, Hanover Square. A startling number of those members of the Upper Crust then in London managed to roll out of bed for the occasion—quite a feat, given Society's habits and the fact that, unless under special license, weddings were required by law to be held before noon.

If Amanda had been content with a small family wedding, Hero would have been able to attend. But a woman in deep mourning for the recent death of her mother could not appear at so public a celebration. And so Sebastian stood alone beside the Earl of Hendon, a black riband tied about his arm. The bride's mother, the Dowager Lady Wilcox, stood triumphant at the Earl's other side. Sister and brother did not converse.

The Marquis of Lindley himself was in attendance, a rail-thin, frail, elderly man with a pleasant, gentle smile and sad eyes. Sebastian found himself looking at the old man and thinking, *Do you know? Do you know what a monster your son is?* And then he remembered what Hendon had suggested, that the Marquis was the driving force behind his son's marriage. And he decided Lindley probably knew a great deal about his son—although surely not all.

The bride's father being deceased, Miss Wilcox was given away by her brother, Bayard, Lord Wilcox, now returned from his sojourn in Scotland. There were no bridal attendants, and the recent tragic death of the groom's dear friend Sir Francis Rowe meant that Ashworth stood alone at the altar.

For one telling moment Ashworth's gaze met Sebastian's, and the groom's eyes narrowed with what looked like amusement. Sebastian felt his hands curl into fists at his sides and he forced himself to open and close them several times.

The bride was undeniably lovely in an elegant gown of white gauze over a silk slip of the palest pink embroidered at the hem with a garland of ivy and snowdrops. A wreath of white and pink flowers crowned her glorious golden hair. But her cheeks were pale, her lips pressed into a determined line. Those who noticed doubtless attributed it to maidenly modesty.

Sebastian knew better.

At the wedding breakfast that followed, while others rushed to congratulate the bride, Sebastian found occasion to pause beside his niece's new husband and say in a low voice, "I know the part you played in Rowe's ugly little hobby. Just because I can't prove it—yet—doesn't mean I won't. Make no mistake: This isn't over yet. I will be watching you. Even when you don't think I am."

Ashworth stood at his ease, his brows arching in mock dismay as he looked out over the crowd of wedding guests. "That's supposed to frighten me, is it?"

"It should. If you think your marriage to my niece will protect you, you're wrong. It's my ambition to see Stephanie a widow before the year is out."

"Well. That should make for some interesting family gatherings," said Ashworth, a faint, provocative smile on his handsome face as he moved to take his place beside his bride.

Author's Note

$\mathcal{S}$treet children have been a part of cities since at least Roman times and doubtless long before. According to British philanthropist Lord Ashley, thirty thousand runaway, orphaned, or abandoned children were scrambling to stay alive and keep warm on the streets of London by the middle of the nineteenth century. The problem is still with us: UNICEF puts the current number of street children worldwide in the tens of millions, with some estimating the number much higher.

For Britain's disturbing practice of transporting the mothers of small children, see *The Women of Botany Bay: A Reinterpretation of the Role of Women in the Origins of Australian Society*, by Portia Robinson.

The ancient monastic area of London known as Clerkenwell takes its name from the famous Clerks' Well ("clerk" being the Middle English term for a clergyman), which can still be seen there in Farringdon Lane. Victorian urban planning and twentieth-century bombs have destroyed much of what was in the seventeenth century a fashionable place of residence (Oliver Cromwell once owned a house in Clerkenwell Close). But both the Charterhouse and St. John's Gate, a relic of the vast monastic complex that once served as the English headquarters for the Knights Hospitallers of St. John of Jerusalem, are still preserved. Parts of the order's chapel also survive, as do St. James's Church and churchyard. The former Middlesex Sessions House still stands on Clerkenwell Green, made famous in Victorian times by Charles Dickens as the site where Fagin teaches Oliver Twist to pick pockets. Clerkenwell has maintained a long association with radicalism, from the earlier Lollards and Chartists to Vladimir Lenin and friends in the twentieth century.

Holywell Street was farther south, not far from the Thames. Named after a long-vanished sacred well of clean, sweet water, Holywell forked off from the Strand before then turning to run parallel to it. The street disappeared completely early in the twentieth century when the Strand was widened. Once occupied by silk merchants, Jewish tailors, and shops that supplied costumes and fancy attire to theaters and masquerade-goers, by the early nineteenth century Holywell was becoming dominated by booksellers and the kind of radical publishers who—inspired by the French Revolution—operated secret presses in hidden cellars. It also became increasingly devoted to what were known as "licentious books," "libertine novels," or "bawdy stuff." England in 1813 did not have censorship laws, but booksellers and printers could be—and were—imprisoned for "disturbing the King's peace."

It is from the name of Donatien Alphonse François, the Marquis de Sade, that we derive the word "sadism." Born in 1740, he was very much a child of the Enlightenment, albeit a twisted one, and was imprisoned at various times for many years under the monarchy, the republic, and the empire. Although he was most likely a victim of bipolar disorder and perhaps suffered paranoid delusions (given the extent of his persecution, his paranoia may be understandable), he was imprisoned not so much because of his mental health as for the nature of his writings. His numerous letters from prison to his wife and his valet show an unexpectedly brilliant, humorous man and are worth reading. He died in an insane asylum in 1814, in the midst of organizing his fellow inmates to perform one of his plays.

De Sade did indeed write a work called *Les 120 journées de Sodome, ou l'école du libertinage,* composed on small scraps of paper while he was in the Bastille. He kept it as a forty-foot roll of glued-together paper hidden in the wall of his cell and thought it lost when the Bastille was stormed and destroyed in the early days of the French Revolution. But someone actually did find it, save it, and smuggle it out of France. It was not, however, published during Sebastian's time. A nauseating tale of sexual abuse and torture, its first known publication was in 1904, in Berlin. It is now in the Musée des Lettres et Manuscrits in Paris.

The wealthy fifteenth-century nobleman and knight Gilles de Rais was one of the first convicted serial killers. The bodies of some forty of his young victims were discovered in 1437, although he is thought to have killed many more, both male and female. Some believe de Rais the innocent victim of an ecclesiastical plot, but the surviving transcripts of testimony from both his confederates and his victims' parents conform well with modern understanding of killers of his type.

It is important to note that more than ninety percent of child molesters consider themselves heterosexual, and that while a majority of those target only girls, about one-fifth prey on both boys and girls. I would like to thank Dr. Samantha Brown, a psychiatrist with the U.S. Air Force, for many hours of discussion on serial killers and sexual predators. Any errors I have made in interpretation are my own.

To my knowledge, no one in the early nineteenth century performed Body Farm–type studies of the effect of the passage of time and burial on flesh and bone. But there is no reason Gibson could not have done something similar. He was, after all, a very curious surgeon.

The rather distinctive type of house where Sebastian finds Les Jenkins is what is now known as a Wealden house (unfortunately, since the term wasn't applied until the twentieth century, Sebastian can't use it).

Although most typically seen in the wealds of Kent, examples can also be found in other parts of southern England. Built in the fourteenth and fifteenth centuries of timber framing infilled with wattle and daub, these houses were originally the homes of yeoman farmers.

Prince William Augustus, the Duke of Cumberland, known as the Butcher of Culloden, was the third and youngest son of George II. He appears to have had at least one illegitimate daughter, but he never married and suffered a stroke at the age of thirty-nine. He died without legitimate issue.